PRAISE FOR
In a Silent Way

"*In a Silent Way* offers a moving portrayal of a committed, young teacher-activist, Jeanna, who is determined to effect change in her urban school and community. Jeanna's culturally relevant and inclusive pedagogy, and her determination to never give up on her students, ultimately wins their respect and admiration. All the while, Hetzel makes sure to shine a much-needed light on undemocratic practices and unequal gendered power dynamics in social and racial justice movements."

—Jonathan Kozol, education activist and award-winning author of *Death at an Early Age and Savage Inequalities: Children in American Schools*

"*In a Silent Way* is a deeply personal historical novel of importance, because it reveals what happens when the convergence of race, gender, and class struggles intersect inside people's lives and communities. Mary Jo Hetzel has written an unconventional coming-of-age story of a young white woman swept up into the political whirlwind of urban America in the late sixties. A must-read for those who want to know the roots of today's #BlackLivesMatter Movement, as well as the contemporary offshoots of the Occupy Wall Street Movement."

—Sam E. Anderson, co-editor of *The Black Activist Journal*, writer, and education activist

"*In a Silent Way* captures the racial, class, and leadership issues of the 1960s that continue today as they play out in an alternative school and multiracial movement group. The main character of the teacher is well developed, and her students' quandaries, anger, fear, despair, then hope and action ring true. Leading by listening, in the classroom and within the movement, emerges as an essential touchstone. In the novel, as I've learned in my own work, students can and do lead, often seeing more clearly and less encumbered by ego than adults."

—Monty Neill, executive director of FairTest

"Much as her main character does with her students, author Mary Jo Hetzel grabs hold of your heart and mind in this compelling, beautifully written, and breathtakingly honest story of an idealistic young teacher's struggle to connect and work for a better world. *In a Silent Way* will resonate powerfully with teachers, students, parents, and anyone involved or interested in today's struggles for educational, social, and racial justice."

—Lisa Guisbond, executive director of Citizens for Public Education

"As I read *In a Silent Way*, I was filled with hope and empathy for the main character, a young teacher named Jeanna. Self-empowerment is learned, not taught, and once learned it is the greatest gift of all. I wish we could assign this book to all teachers in urban communities, so that the conversations that need to take place toward quality education can happen with clearer understanding. This will be our parent group's first read."

—Malikka Williams, black parent and organizer in Dorchester, MA

"Teacher Jeanna's willingness and courage to confront the social, racial, and political realities of urban life, and to give her students the powerful literacy tools needed to achieve social, economic, and educational justice, is nothing less than astounding. On the other hand, her tortuous coming-of-age journey through a world riddled with traps and snares, and her suffocating silence, evoke the reader's empathy and rage. *In a Silent Way* is a must-read for all educators of urban students."

—Junia Yearwood, BPS English teacher of 32 years and literacy empowerment facilitator

"*In a Silent Way* is a riveting debut novel that starts with what appears to be a familiar trope—the idealistic, young, white teacher who takes on a classroom of inner-city kids—and turns it on its head. However, this gripping, nuanced portrait set in 1969 also reflects a difficult reality for women in progressive movements, one that is often glossed over."

—Lisa Borders, author of *The Fifty-First State* and *Cloud Cuckoo Land*

"At its core, *In a Silent Way* is about a young teacher unleashing the brilliance and unique talents of her students, while seeking to remain true to herself within a fractured grassroots social justice group. By sharing Jeanna's educational practice, Mary Jo Hetzel offers compelling guidance to all those interested in creating an urban educational system that promotes the aspirations of youth, teachers, parents, and community.

—Ellen Hewett, director of the National College Transition Network at World Education

"This riveting, engaging journey of a young, white, activist educator in the late 60s unfolds unlike any other story previously told. This young woman chooses to join in the struggle for Civil Rights, while allowing her students to utilize their passions to change the course of their lives in an urban alternative high school. The reader is drawn in as the story unfolds, and taken along unanticipated pathways where the incidents and learnings that occur are completely applicable to this day. Since learning from our history may prevent future missteps, this powerful novel is a must-read."

—Karla Nicholson, executive director, Haymarket People's Fund

"A fascinating and compelling story showing how the choices we make shape the world in which we live."

—Chuck Turner, Boston community organizer/activist

"Mary Jo Hetzel is an activist and humanist of the first order. Her weaving of students' projects into exciting presentations shows how students can soar when a teacher believes in them. I hope this novel will help people see the need for change in our 'change' organizations and our schools."

—Sandra McIntosh, chair of The Coalition for Equal, Quality Education and former parent coordinator at English High School

In a Silent Way

mjindigo66@gmail.com

In a Silent Way

A Novel

by

Mary Jo Hetzel

SHE WRITES PRESS

Published 2016
Printed in the United States of America
ISBN: 978-1-63152-135-5 pbk
ISBN: 978-1-63152-136-2 ebk
Library of Congress Control Number: 2016939979

For information, address:
She Writes Press
1563 Solano Ave #546
Berkeley, CA 94707

Book design by Stacey Aaronson

She Writes Press is a division of SparkPoint Studio, LLC.

This novel is dedicated to Beverly Anne Sypek —

and to all my beloved students

CHAPTER ONE

Yeah, But It Still Be School

"YOU CAN *DO* THIS," JEANNA MUTTERED UNDER HER breath as she approached the vast, bleak North Side. Charcoal black and blood red graffiti covered every inch of wall space. She could barely decipher their messages but saw them as an assertion of self against the odds—I'm here, I'm alive, and you will, goddammit, pay attention to me.

Large oval craters began to replace potholes as she drove the last few blocks to the long-abandoned school building. Broken glass flashed amber and green across an infinity of empty lots. Dirt-encrusted newspapers and Styrofoam debris crowded the ground next to the high chain-link fence, from which bags fluttered like ghosts. The school looked like the only sign of hope in block after block of what could have been Vietnam bomb scenes from the nightly news.

Jeanna thought back to the crazy, yet intriguing, hiring process in June. Twenty-five teaching candidates, winnowed down from over a thousand applicants, had been thrown into a gym and told to decide, themselves, who should be selected for the six positions for West Side Alternative High, while the hiring committee sat on the bleachers and watched them. She'd been overwhelmed by the display of talent, experience, and intense desire to finally be in a truly progressive program that emerged—and taken aback by all the jockeying for position. She'd been one of the last to speak, and when she had, she'd made it clear that at only twenty years of age, she thought others with greater experience and accomplishments would and should get the six spots. She had written off the job until she'd gotten the call from the new principal, Matt Jensen. She kept asking, "But why me?" He offered some reasons, such as his desire to steal part of her cover letter for the school's mission statement, but she was too overwhelmed to take in his other points. He finally gave up, laughed and said, "You got the job, Jeanna, be happy, okay?" And she was; she had overflowed with happiness all summer. But now, when it mattered, she was drop-dead terrified.

She pulled sharply into the one remaining staff parking spot, her wrist aching, alarmed that she was the last to arrive. She looked at her watch, reassuring herself that she was early. It wouldn't do to be late on the first day of her first real job, doing the thing she most wanted to do in the world. She willed herself to look older, to look the part of a seasoned, capable teacher, as she hurried up the path to the stairs, joining the waves of students who were talking, laughing, and shouting. She looked up and saw a banner stretched high above the doorway: WEST SIDE ALTERNATIVE HIGH, 1969.

By the time she found her classroom, most of her students were already there. They lined the wall to her right, staring at her as she came in.

"Whatchu think, she the teach or one a us?" someone muttered.

"Hmm. Believe she be the teach, but she sure green as hell," his buddy muttered back.

Jeanna swallowed the dryness in her throat, angry that the room wasn't set up, that she was somehow late, that she'd already been nailed as green.

"Hey, everybody. Could I get some help setting up these tables and chairs here?" Without waiting or looking at anyone, she stepped up to a table and reached for an end. A solid young man sprang forward to catch hold of the other end. Together, they moved it a few yards from the wall, pulled out the legs, and righted it. She looked at him and forced a smile.

"Tommie Lee Johnson," he said, smiling back with an ease she envied, his eyebrows dark against his bronze skin.

A towering young man with polished ebony skin and surprising neon-blue eyes stepped forward and grabbed an end of a table with two fingers while a wiry little redhead with pale matchstick arms grabbed the other end with two tight fists. They righted the table awkwardly.

"What the fuck we got here, Baby Nelson and King Kong hisself?" whispered the guy who'd nailed Jeanna as green.

The wiry kid's face blazed crimson. The towering youth turned the full force of his stare on the wiseass, who was soft, round, and half his size. The wiseass raised his hands in pre-emptive surrender.

"It's cool, man."

The tall boy's glare got harder.

"You cool. He cool. We all cool," the wiseass jabbered.

"Then cool it, brotha," the tall fellow said with a hint of a smile.

Everyone laughed, including Jeanna.

"I'm Earl Jones by the way, better known as Big Blue, or Blue, to you," he said, nodding at Jeanna.

"Ho," the wiseass said. "I'm King Oliver, better known as Olly." He was a short, brown, roly-poly kid with annoying chipmunk cheeks. He peered up at his adversary. "By the way, where'd you get them blue eyes?"

"From my ancestors a'course," Big Blue said, scowling.

"More like your motha got it on with some down-South cracka," Olly sneered in a singsong voice.

Jeanna wondered if this kid had a death wish; she sweated at the thought of having to defend him against a virtual giant.

"Hey, take a seat why don't you?" Tommie Lee had already begun effortlessly handing down the stacked chairs, and he swung one Olly's way.

"Don't mind if I do," Olly said, grabbing it. He sailed it up to a table and plopped down.

Jeanna breathed a sigh of relief.

"Thanks, everyone," she said when the room was set up and everyone had taken a seat. She fished in her bag, pulled out name tags and markers, and handed them out. "Please write your name, or what you want to be called, on these tags so we can get to know each other better." She wrote hers, JEANNA KENDALL, in large blue script and smoothed it onto her beige jacket. Diving into her bag again, she brought out the icebreaker questions she had prepared for the first day and passed the simple forms around the room.

Jeanna glanced down at the attendance sheet and up again at the various name tags, trying to get a feel for these ninth and tenth graders in the room, to bring the blur of faces into focus. A slight sandy-haired boy sat immediately to her left, painfully rigid, staring at a knot in the table. He had not even looked at the questions or pulled out a pencil. Jeanna saw ALLEY written in a childish scrawl on his name tag.

The elegant young woman to Alley's left had filled out the first page already and was taking a break to buff her silver-toned nails. Her straightened hair was pulled back in a long black stream, her eyes focused in exquisite concentration on her task. A budding model? With a brief glimpse, Jeanna could make out two responses to her questions: Favorite color? *Silver*. Future occupation or future dreams? *Civil rights lawyer, Supreme Court Justice*. Whew. On the far left a row of hostile, brooding eyes gazed steadily at her from young men on chairs uniformly tipped back against the wall. She moved on, not wanting to get into a war of nerves. She had already worked with plenty of tough-looking kids who'd turned out not so tough after all.

Jeanna was relieved to see Big Blue studiously bent over his task across from her, filling out the form. The little redhead, meanwhile, shifted constantly in his seat, scribbling on his paper in quick rushes and stealing glances at the brooding four. He seemed fascinated by them. In his eyes, Jeanna guessed, they must be all muscle and fierceness; to her, they were packages not yet opened.

To the redhead's right was a small, chubby, blond girl—conventional in every way. Next to her sat Jeanna's original rescuer, Tommie

Lee, a dark bronze Adonis reflecting on what he'd just written; it was hard to take her eyes off him. She noticed she wasn't the only female stealing glances his way, and moved on quickly.

To Tommie Lee's right was Olly, refusing to write anything, and then a heavy-set girl in a matronly housedress, her arms folded protectively across her plush bosom, hiding her name tag. She wore a thoughtful look on her pale, moon-shaped face. A large black girl with a close-cropped Afro and sharp nose—VALLE, her name tag said—sat to her right. She looked like an eagle surveying the scene before her, unusually self-possessed. Jeanna couldn't see the names of two students who looked like a hippie couple, both with long hair, beads, and sandals, or that of a lanky kid with tanned skin, brown hair that fell across one eye, and a harmonica sticking out of his shirt pocket. Next to him was a small, skinny kid wearing a tattered gray T-shirt who was fidgeting all over the place.

On Jeanna's immediate right was Karima, wearing patched jeans and a shaggy Afro. Her arms were rounded, firm, and dark brown against the cropped sleeves of her white sweatshirt. She reminded Jeanna of the local athletes she had coached the last few years. An intensity radiated from her. Jeanna glanced discreetly at Karima's paper. Future dreams? *Varsity basketball, then the People's Revolution.* She already loved this kid.

The bell rang with such ferocity that Jeanna felt electrocuted on the spot. The students didn't bat an eye, all of them staring at her, their shiny name tags glinting in the sunlight that poured through the windows.

"Why we gotta be here anyways? I wanted Mr. Jensen," Olly said. "I thought this was an al*tern*ative school," he added in a nasal whine, slumping back in his chair.

Jeanna felt her face redden as she tried to remember how she'd planned to begin.

"Yeah, I was hopin' for Coach Jakim, if it okay to switch, Miss," Big Blue drawled.

"Me too—me too!" The little redhead was bouncing up and down in slow motion, a surreal jack-in-the-box.

A rumble of curses and groans began to crest, and Jeanna felt the class flying apart.

"Hey, wait a minute here guys." The chubby blond girl cut through the whirlpool. "Miss Kendall ain't even had a chance to say one good hello and we're all climbing down her throat like there was no tomorra."

Jeanna took her measure anew. If this kid could take on the multitudes with a little shrug of her shoulders, why couldn't she?

"I'm with Abby. Let's find out what this place is all about." Tommie Lee.

The rumble quieted and everyone turned their attention back to Jeanna.

She took a breath. "I want to begin by welcoming each of you—"

"Puh-leeze!" Olly snarled.

"Maybe that was too formal, but I'm glad to see all of you here—"

"You don' even know us," someone growled.

Jeanna looked over at the one of the brooding four who had spoken. His name tag read Cassius. He gazed at her from under hooded eyelids. He wore a sleeveless black sweatshirt that showed off his muscles; his hair was a cascading waterfall of gelled Afro curls, and his lips were set in a sneer.

"That's true. I don't know you yet. That's what this Group Inquiry and Basic Skills class is about: getting to know each other, finding out what each person is most interested in—"

"What d'you mean, 'basic skills'?" interrupted another of the brooding four. "We're sick to death of those basic skills classes for us so-called re*me*dials."

That's exactly what she'd said in the only faculty planning meeting they'd had at the end of August. She scanned the room and saw nearly full agreement again.

"I know what you mean. I didn't like the name they gave the class either." The students looked surprised at this admission. Encouraged,

Jeanna said, "I wanted to call it 'Learn What You're Into,' but they wouldn't go for it."

"Whatchu mean 'learn what you're into'?"

Olly.

Jeanna was hot with frustration, her mind racing to think of ways to connect with this group.

"Study what you're *in*to, man, what you like," the redhead said. He glanced at Cassius, who was drumming his hands on the front of his seat. "What beats your drum."

"Ooooh, that could be interesting," Tommie Lee said, "a lot different from regular school."

Jeanna felt her whole body lift up.

"I don' care *how* ya dress it up, it still be school." With that, Cassius brought his chair down with a thud, got up, and walked out.

Jeanna looked after him helplessly, wanting to reach out and draw him back.

Students were shifting in their seats in the echoing silence. Then the muttering began again, like mice scratching in her head. Jeanna was paralyzed with fear that the whole class might get up and leave—she could see the principal, Matt Jensen, shaking his head sadly as he asked her to resign so they could fill the job with someone who could handle it—but she was also furious that the kids hadn't given the class, or her, a chance.

"Don't mind him, that's just the way he is," Tommie Lee said, pulling his chair closer to the table and looking straight at her.

"He just thinking it old school here too, Miss," Valle said, still in eagle pose, her powerful arms crossed across her chest.

Jeanna's mind had gone utterly blank. It had never occurred to her that anyone would just walk out. She tried to speak, but no words came. Then, out of nowhere, they gushed forth:

"Look guys, here's how it is. There's a law that says you have to go to school. We both know the regular schools stink. You came here either because you didn't want them or they didn't want you. I came here because I didn't want to teach in a traditional school. I don't like the way students get treated there, and I don't like the way they treat teachers either."

She paused, amazed that she finally had their full attention.

"This is my first year teaching, but I've worked in youth programs and community centers since I was a kid. I don't believe in the way traditional schools do things, but I do believe that we can make this school what we want it to be. A place where we can help each other learn what we really want to know, where we can become who we really want to become—whether that's an athlete, lawyer, musician—"

"What if you don't wanna learn nothin'?" challenged Olly, puffing out his cheeks.

"Then *nothin's* exactly what you'll learn," Jeanna shot back to a few grunts of approval.

"What about those basic skill things? We've had enough of that BS," one of the brooding four said, looking like a young W.E.B. DuBois with his straggly goatee and serious manner. Jeanna strained to see his name tag. Wesley.

"Good question. At this school we believe that people learn best when they're involved in things that really matter to them, whether it's music or sports, community organizing, the law—whatever. In the process, you'll pick up all kinds of skills, like communication and teamwork, writing, research, and problem solving. You might even learn how to change the world." She was beginning to hit her stride.

"Change the world?" Wesley interrupted in a husky whisper, not looking at her.

"Yeah, meaning *what*?" Karima bit out from her right.

"We need to learn how to change all kinds of things. Like not having enough money to live on while others live in luxury right outside the city. Like being put down because of your race, sex, or age."

Wesley looked down at the table and shook his head. All Jeanna could see was his well-manicured Afro. Then he slowly looked up, frowning. "Don't go there."

Jeanna was stymied. If she couldn't go there, she had nowhere to go. She just looked at him. Their eyes met in a stalemate.

Jeanna could feel Karima's eyes piercing her from the right.

"Hey there," Olly waved at Jeanna as if she were far away. "You must be livin' on some other planet, cause you outa *touch.* They ain't gonna let us study what we want; you crazy if ya think so."

"Shut it, Ol," Valle said without raising her voice or moving a muscle. A mountain next his round ball of baby fat.

"Who's gonna make me?" Olly half rose out of his seat, but Valle ignored him.

"Olly's got a mouth on him, always did back at the Mason," Karima said, "but he's telling the truth." She turned to face Jeanna squarely. "Don't be messin' with us, lady. If you ain't for real, don't be telling no fancy white lies, or we're out of here."

Jeanna turned and looked right into Karima's eyes. "If they won't let us learn what we really want to, I'll walk out that door with you."

Karima held her gaze, her face impassive, but Jeanna could feel the war going on inside her.

"Yeah," Wesley said, "that's cool, but you got somewhere to go and we don't."

Jeanna looked at him and nodded slightly, her lips tight. "Okay, how about we hang in then and do the best we can?"

He shrugged. She could tell he hadn't believed a word she said, and couldn't afford to; it mattered way too much. At least to him. And Karima.

"Hey," it was Olly again. "You all forget about us livin' out here in the real world?"

Everyone laughed; even Wesley smiled.

"Okay, let's put it to the test," Big Blue spoke. "Some'a us ain't interested in nothin' but no basketball, so you tell me how we gonna work *that* into this here class." He ended with a look of challenge that shifted to vain hope and then to pleading. It was like watching a camera lens focus, refocus, and focus again.

"C'mon man," Olly retorted, "this here school not no gymnasium, ya dumb square-ball."

Big Blue narrowed his eyes at Olly. Looking at the huge physical difference between them, Olly was definitely riding for a fall.

"Actually," Jeanna said, "Blue probably *can* focus on basketball for his class project, and if a few other students want to join him, you can do a project on it together."

"What kind of project?" Olly and the redheaded boy asked at the same time.

"Well, you'll have to ask Blue what he's interested in, not me," Jeanna said. All faces shifted to Big Blue.

"What makes for a winning team; that's what I'm interested in. Simple as that."

Every face swung back toward Jeanna, breath held, lips slightly parted, eyes fixed on her.

"That's perfect," Jeanna replied.

"Whatchu mean, perfect!" Olly exploded in utter confusion.

"Well, count me in," Tommie Lee said, ignoring Olly. "Basketball's my game."

"Yeah, I done heard about you," Big Blue said with a big smile.

"I want in too!" cried the redhead.

"Well, I guess I'm in too then," Olly said, "leastways until big fat Matt blows up all our big-time plans." He looked pointedly at Jeanna.

The bell shrieked, making Jeanna jump. "Time for assembly on the second floor," Jeanna said. "We'll finish this on Wednesday."

The students got up to leave, some chatting comfortably, the rest looking skeptical, confused, or even angry. She wished she'd done a better job of explaining the school and igniting sparks, like she'd always been able to do in her youth programs. But there she'd been a natural ally; here she was their enemy. She prayed she had what it took to turn that around.

As she followed the group out of the classroom, she noticed Karima hanging back in the hall, a dark scowl on her face.

"Can I ask you something?" Karima asked as Jeanna drew closer.

"Of course." Jeanna looked down at the floor to show she was listening without directly confronting her.

"I like basketball and all—I mean, I love it for real—but it's not... I mean, what I want to know is, can I study the fight for black rights?" she ended in a rush.

Jeanna looked up and saw Karima's scowl deepening, her dark eyes burning through Jeanna, the wall, the century.

"Absolutely. I hope you will, Karima," Jeanna said, looking at her directly.

"Hmm," the girl grunted low, with involuntary force. "But I gotta, like, find others to do it too, right?"

"Right."

"Oh, okay then." Karima offered a hint of a smile, which she tried to hide by turning her face away as she walked off.

Jeanna felt an intense surge of satisfaction, even as she knew she had light years to go—with Karima, the class, and herself most of all.

Jeanna hurried downstairs to the bathroom. By the time she made it up to the assembly, the auditorium was full.

Matt Jensen was motioning for her to join the rest of the teachers up on the stage with him. She hated this sort of thing. She knew they were all supposed to say something after Matt had highlighted some of their accomplishments, but she had not prepared more than a few words and could not even remember them. She felt an aching heaviness in her stomach.

The first faculty member Matt called up to the mic had a master's degree and two award-winning history books to her credit on the labor and women's movements, and had been best teacher of the year um-ti-ump times. She spoke in a frank, compelling way to strong applause.

Jeanna was sweating.

The next teacher, Jakim, was a Mathematician's Mathematician, whatever the hell that was—Jeanna herself had failed algebra—not to mention Chair of the Black Teachers' Association, a lay minister in his

Islamic Mosque, and the only basketball coach in the state to have made it to the playoffs in eight of the last eleven years. He was a black belt in karate and had three children to boot, all brown belts. There he stood, all sculpted and perfect in his mysterious sunglasses, getting a very respectable hand.

Up next was the literature, arts, and humanities teacher— also the leader of the world-renowned Shanna Breem dance troupe. She was tall and willowy in her simple lime dress with black wave design as she stepped up to the mic. She spoke about esteem and the African heritage, about self-expression and pride in who you are. She got a standing ovation.

Jesus Christ. Jeanna was about to try and sneak off the stage unnoticed, but it only got worse.

Their science, health, and media arts teacher was on now. A man clearly ahead of his time, standing free and easy in a white tunic and faded jeans. An Afro-urban environmentalist; the guy who blew the whistle on lead paint in town and ignited a statewide movement. A Tibetan Buddhist and filmmaker to boot.

Jeanna was about to be seriously ill. She heard the applause for Roy through a dense fog.

Matt called her name. She hated him and the grievous error he'd made in having her go last. She'd never felt more disheveled and foolish in her life. She stepped to the mic and began speaking before Matt could say anything. He took a long, graceful step back.

"Hi. I'm Jeanna. What can I say? I have no master's degrees, no books, no dance troupes, and no teaching experience, much less any awards for it. I don't own a single belt of any color, and to be honest with you, I've never heard of Tibetan Buddhism, though I'm definitely going to find out about it as soon as I get home. I truly don't know why the heck they hired me, but you know what?"—she spoke with soft intensity—"This job, and all of you, are the most important thing that's ever happened to me." Her voice broke and she stopped, turned awkwardly away, and took her seat in the deadly silence.

She didn't blame them. She wouldn't have clapped either. She was having trouble seeing through eyes that had suddenly become very blurry. Then applause erupted like a mini-volcano. A half smile crept over her face; she was uncertain what all the noise was about. Whatever the cause, it came to an abrupt halt as Matt stepped back to the mic, and Jeanna didn't really hear the rest of what he said. Something about how could someone so young have done all she'd done, about her youth group successfully fighting racism in their school, and that was what this school was about, and she realized he was saying all this important stuff and she was missing most of it, which upset her, and she heard nothing after that.

Matt had stopped speaking and everyone was getting up to go. It must be over. He sent the few remaining students on their way, then came over and sat next to her.

"Hey, how're you doing? How'd it go today?"

"Oh, fine."

"Really? The first day can be tough for all of us."

"Yeah, it really went fine."

Jeanna had absolutely no idea how to tell Matt about the intense roller coaster that had been her day. She wanted to go home, find a way to stop reeling, and gather a modicum of poise for the next day, when at 8:30 am she would meet with a whole new set of students, and a whole new blizzard of challenges.

~

Arriving home, Jeanna was wound so tight she couldn't see straight. Her head was filled with a strange static that would not go away. She went to her old oak table and rifled through her bag of school materials, not finding what she needed, realizing with exasperation she didn't know what she was looking for. She walked over to her tiny bedroom, jumped onto her bed, slid her back against the wall, and pulled her grandmother's quilt up around her to try to calm down.

She looked through the entrance of her bedroom and saw nothing but chaos: unopened boxes everywhere, a mess of pots and pans and dishware on the kitchen counter. She had just moved into her new apartment on the previous day by herself. There had been no one to help. Her mother had just reopened her new horticulture business, Greta-Jean's Greens, and this was a big weekend for sales. Her Dad was in DC now, and soon off to Ghana to explore setting up a Peace Corps site there. Not that he'd help her anyway. She hadn't seen him in years—not since he left her mother and his civil rights legal practice for the glitzy Peace Corps woman he was still with. Her brother was with him in DC and would soon go back to Yale Law. Her few friends from college had scattered around the country or gone abroad.

She couldn't waste time putting her stuff away; she needed to focus on tomorrow's new Basic Literacy and Current Issues class and her afternoon US History class, and she'd like to get a head start on the following day's Group Inquiry class while it was still fresh in her mind, too. But her head was still overflowing with static anxiety.

Her eyes wandered across the grimy bedroom wall and up to the top of the closet where she had stuffed her flute case. *That* would help if nothing else could. It always had. It always would. But she didn't take it down. She got up and walked into the next room instead. She knew that once her music took hold, she'd lose all track of time for sure—something she could not afford to do, at least not this week.

She picked her way around piles of junk until she found the file of ideas and teaching materials she was looking for, then grabbed her notebook and pen and settled back in bed with them. She pulled out some hot topics for the students to compare: two contrasting articles on police brutality, and two on school attendance policy. They could take their pick. She jotted down some questions to guide their reading and writing and help them connect the materials with their lives. She looked at her roster from that morning's class and fixed names to faces.

By the time Jeanna looked up, it was completely dark outside. She was hungry and chilled, but at least her head was clearer.

That night she dreamt that she went from one end of the old school building to the other, opening up countless classroom doors, each time to a blur of frozen faces, but, full of dread, she could not find the class she was supposed to teach. She finally gave up, only to arrive at the end-of-term Parents' Day, where all her lost students and their parents lined the dark corridors and judged, taunted, and condemned her for her negligence.

CHAPTER TWO

It Way Too Late for Me, Miss J

THE BELL RANG AS JEANNA WALKED INTO HER GROUP Inquiry class. Everyone was there except Cassius.

"Yo," Olly said loudly, "the bell rang." He stared at Jeanna.

Ignoring him, Jeanna began, "Today, we need to, together, establish some ground rules, or guidelines, for how we treat one another here at West Side—"

"You never did tell us what to call you yesterday," Olly interrupted. "So far I've heard you called Jeanna, Miss Kendall, Miss Jeanna, and Miss J, so hey, 'Yo' is what it's gonna be till you clue us in."

"You're right. I like to be called Jeanna." She pointed to her name-tag. "So feel free to call me that. Most teachers here prefer their first names."

"Mr. Jakim Al Kaleem doesn't," the redhead said. Jeanna could see his name today—Pepper.

"Well, I said most, not all," Jeanna said. "One thing I like about this program is that we're not all forced into one mold. We're allowed to be ourselves here. Now, what I mean by guidelines—"

"You mean just the same old tired rules," Olly said, his tone sullen.

"No, actually, I don't, but I don't blame you for assuming that. What I'm talking about is different from the kind of rules that come from the top and get laid on everybody, like 'no talking, no running, no laughing…' What's different is that *we* make them together so that we can shape our school and this class in a way that feels right to us, not to some boss upstairs."

"So, like, we can say 'F-you' to the teacher?" Olly stared at her, clearly wanting a fight.

"Does that feel right to the rest of you?" Jeanna asked, looking around the table. A few shook their heads no, and some "of course nots" and "that's stupids" could be heard.

Olly was looking less smug.

"Why don't we begin with the issue that Olly has placed on the table," Jeanna said.

He looked up in surprise.

"The issue of respect," she clarified. "Now in most schools, how do you hear this term being used?"

"Ya gotta respect the teacher! The principal, adults!" a number of students called out.

"Exactly," Jeanna said. "You always hear about students needing to respect teachers and other adults, but you rarely hear about them needing to respect students. So respect has gotten a bad name. But here's my question: Is respect important? Do people need respect?"

"Yeah, people need it." Will fingered his harmonica as he spoke, a shock of brown hair falling across his eye. "Everybody needs respect."

Jeanna nodded at him.

"But don't you have to earn it?" Felice, the elegant future Supreme Court justice asked.

"Why?" Karima challenged.

"Yeah, why can't people be respected just 'cause they're human?" Abby, the fearless, chubby blonde asked.

"Because it doesn't happen that way," Wesley said. "I'm sure Mr. Jakim Al Ka*leem* doesn't call his students Mr. this and Miss that."

"Yes he do," Big Blue said. "He call me Mr. Earl Jones every time he sees me."

Wesley stared at him in disbelief.

"Yeah, he calls me Mr. Arnold Wolpert, and I hate it," Pepper whined.

Everyone laughed.

"So what kind of respect do you call it when it's two-way, with *both* teachers and students respecting each other?" Valle asked.

Everyone looked at Jeanna.

"Mutual. Mutual respect."

"Mutural..." Olly scrunched up his nose. "I never hearda that."

"Mutual," Karima said. "It's like two people acting like they're on the same level and treating each other good and equal, back and forth." She moved her cupped hand from her chest toward him and back again.

"Yeah, but there's always one up and the other down," Big Blue said.

"Yeah, usually the man," Abby said and laughed.

"You mean the *white* man," Karima bit out.

Abby raised her eyebrows at her tone.

"Yeah, white people gets lots more respect than black," Olly ventured.

Jeanna saw Alley, the quietest youngster in the room, looking back and forth in alarm as if something had gotten way out of control.

"What you thinkin,' lil' squeak?" Big Blue bent down and asked.

Alley's face ignited bright pink.

"That ain' respect, man! That's punk-jive, white or no," Karima said.

"You right," Big Blue said. "I'm sorry, little man."

Alley's face was now aflame in full scarlet.

"Just dig it in a little deeper why don't you," Felice said.

Big Blue threw up his hands. "I can't say nothin' right today. I thought I was, but maybe I ain't cut out for this respect thing."

"Oh shoo," Felice said, laughing. "Your mouth just got in your way. It needs a rest."

Big Blue sank back into his chair, eyeing her with a touch of admiration.

"Going back to what Olly said," Tommie Lee said, "white people get more respect than black people do. I know that's true most places, but how bout here in this class so far?

A long silence.

"You know, Tommie Lee's got a point," Karima finally said. "I think it's been pretty equal so far. Don't get me wrong"—her eyes flickered in Jeanna's direction—"I don't expect it to last, but so far it's been pretty equal. Maybe even more than equal—Olly here's been going at it pretty strong. Fact is, more black kids been speaking than white."

"Yeah, why some-a you so quiet?" Valle asked.

"I'm not quiet," Pepper said.

"You don't count," Big Blue said with a laugh.

Everyone in the room turned to stare Blue down.

"Honey, you is *one lost cause*," Valle said in a slow, sultry tone.

"You right, you right." Big Blue slid down in his chair, hiding his face with his hands.

"Wait a minute." Felice pointed to Meta, the matronly looking girl. "How 'bout you? You haven't said more than two words in two days."

Meta drew herself up and looked straight at Felice. "I know. I haf been asking myself thee same thing. My answer is that vee don't speak in our family."

Felice looked at her questioningly.

"I mean vee children don't speak. And . . . vee vimin don't speak."

Pepper looked at Jeanna. "What did she say—'vee vimin'?" he asked.

"Women," Karima said harshly.

"Wow, that's heavy," Pepper said. "Where're you from anyway?"

"I was born right outside thee city in thee country?" Meta's voice was singsong melodic. "My father is Cherman?"

Pepper giggled. "Cool."

"Thank you, Meta," Jeanna said, "for telling us about your family. I hope you'll join in when you feel comfortable." She turned to the others. "I think your whole discussion about respect was right on. Everyone who spoke made really good sense. And Karima gave a good explanation of what mutual respect means—where we all try to treat each other as equally worthy of being listened to." She paused. "So my question to you is, do you want mutual respect to be one of our guidelines for how we relate to each other, or do you want the same old up/down stuff that goes on out there?" She waved toward the window.

"Definitely mutual," Tommie Lee said to a chorus of "yeahs," "yeses," and "of courses." Even shy Alley was nodding up and down.

"I want it too," Big Blue said, "in spite of all my mess-ups—but what if we do slip up?"

"We'll have you for dinner." Felice chomped down with her teeth and laughed.

"C'mon guys, nobody's perfect," Abby said. "We'll just have to clue each other in, that's all."

Jeanna was about to move on when Olly said, "Haven't we beaten this respect thing to death?"

"Okay," Jeanna said, "let's take a ten-minute break and come back and brainstorm issues to form group projects around."

Everyone got up in a rush of chatter. Jeanna noticed Olly eyeing her as he made his way toward her to the door. She gave him an almost imperceptible wink. As he passed her, he leaned toward her and muttered, "Don't you fucking wink at me, bitch," hatred in his eyes, and walked out.

Jeanna gasped, but turned it into a cough so none of her other students would notice. Why had her class clown gone so suddenly evil on her? She hurried outside, taking in a deep breath of air, and looked right into the weathered, creased face of an old man sitting on the step, calmly smoking his pipe. He started to speak, but Jeanna turned away, angry that there was nowhere to be alone and regroup, and went back inside without a word, glad she hadn't challenged Olly or reacted. She knew from all her youth work that it just created a big push-pull, never-ending power game. They had plenty of time to deal with whatever was causing his rage. Even so, it hurt.

Back in the classroom, still feeling Olly's anger like scalding water, Jeanna kept everyone in the large group at the start. She reminded them of the basketball group with Big Blue, Tommie Lee, Pepper, and Olly, and asked what issues the rest of them were most interested in that might lead into inquiry projects or study groups. She warned them against judging or correcting anyone's ideas.

She looked first at Karima, who called out on cue, "The fight for black freedom, past and present," loud and clear. Jeanna wrote it on the board as she heard Felice say, "The *legal* struggle for equal rights."

Karima and Felice eyed each other warily.

"Yeah, I'd like to look at that too," Abby said.

Karima and Felice both swung in her direction, eyes narrowed.

"How would you put your interest?" Jeanna asked.

"I don't know." Abby scrunched up her face. "The fight for human rights or freedom?"

Karima frowned and shifted uneasily, while Felice gave Abby a long, disdainful stare. Abby blushed. Jeanna knew from all the cross-race youth work she'd done that white kids always wanted to erase race, to act as if everyone was on an equal plane. She saw Karima tightening her jaw and had a feeling this issue would get dealt with in fairly short order.

"Next?"

"I'd like to be part of that group, too," Wesley said quietly.

Abby smiled at him.

"Okay, how would you state your issue?" Jeanna asked.

"I don't know," he said in a low tone. "The way they already did is fine."

"UFOs! Stars! Astronomy! Aliens from outer space!" other kids shouted out to a chorus of "yeahs," clapping, and laughter.

Meta drew her body up as if summoning the courage to speak. Jeanna called on her.

"Finding a cure for breast cancer," Meta said with extreme clarity. "Finding thee causes, understanding thee treatments. Finding a vay to prewent it."

"Wow," another student said. "Let me add sickle cell to that. I want *her* group if it's gonna be about anything medical."

Meta's face brightened.

"Music," the hippie girl called out.

"Music and the freedom movement," her friend added.

"Like?" Karima asked.

"Anti-war, anti–Jim Crow…"

"Jim what?" Olly asked.

Karima and Felice started speaking at once.

"After you, madame," Karima said, gesturing gallantly with her hand.

Felice bowed slightly from the waist and said, "They were statutes whites passed to keep blacks in their place in the South after the Civil War."

"That's it, like she said." Karima nodded, scowling, which seemed to be what she did when she was trying to cover up some real feeling. Jeanna guessed she was intimidated by Felice.

"Statues?" Olly glared back and forth between the two budding activists. "I don't understand what the bejesus you're talking about…"

"Statutes, laws, rules, regulations," Karima exploded, throwing her arms up in the air. "Will you give it up and let us finish the brainstorm, for Christ's sake?"

Whew, she had a temper. Jeanna hoped it never landed on her.

"Okay, okay!" Olly turned to his neighbor, Will, and said just loud enough to hear, "She a *scary* sister."

Everyone laughed but Karima.

Will leaned toward Olly, his brown hair falling over one eye, and said softly, "Yeah, but her balls is prettier, *way* bigger, and a *damn* sight smarter than yours."

Olly was speechless; his mouth hung open.

The silence was deafening—then a "Yeow!" erupted from Big Blue, followed by foot stomping and laughter all across the room. They laughed until they cried. Even Meta's plump body was shaking and tears were streaming out of the corners of her eyes. Everyone was wiping away tears with shirtsleeves, Kleenex, the ends of scarves.

"Excuse the language, Jeanna," Will said. "Getting back to the brainstorm, I want to throw the blues up on the board."

"As in music?" Jeanna asked.

"The same," he responded.

"Gospelllll!" Valle sang out, the tail end of the note quivering forever in the air.

Jeanna looked down at her roster again to get Valle's full name: *Valledonia Stallworthy*. Great name; unforgettable voice.

"Amen!" Will sang out, beaming at Valle.

"All right, gospel it is," Jeanna said, writing it on the board. "I feel a music group coming on." She glanced at the clock. "Okay, time for a break. Take a few minutes to look over these ideas; add any new ones you come up with, then put your initials up next to what you're interested in."

She was pleased to see the students milling about, signing their initials, and convincing each other what to sign up for. She gave them fifteen minutes, then reconvened the class.

"It looks like we have a basketball group, a racial justice group, one on UFOs, one on music and the freedom movement, and a medical group," she said, reading off the board. "Before we break off into groups, I see that a few people haven't signed up for anything yet." She looked at Lonnie, one of the brooding four who had been dozing in and out of the morning's discussion.

"Lonnie, do any of the groups interest you?"

He paused for a long time, the silence in the room deepening. Finally he spoke in a hoarse voice, "Tommie Lee and them all—they a cut above us… *way* above. *Me*, I mean." He lowered his voice, "I can't touch 'em… I'm just tryin to get from one day to the next, you know, like sur*vive*…" he trailed off, shaking his head, looking at no one. His clothing was soiled and his coal black skin was ashy and scabbed in places, like he'd been through the wars. The room was stone quiet.

Jeanna felt his meaning in her core. "I hear you, Lonnie, but please keep with it; you might come up with something better than you think." She looked at the fidgety boy next to him. "How 'bout you?" She couldn't see his name tag. "What's your name, please?"

He looked up abruptly, as if caught by surprise, looked around the room as if seeing it for the first time, then flung his stick-thin arm out toward Lonnie. "Like he said." He paused, his eyes darting around the room again. "Name Cat."

"Okay, Cat… for now, anyway. Alley?"

"Same," Alley said in a voice barely above a whisper, his body tense as a coiled spring, a rosy dot blooming on each soft cheek.

"I know you guys have some real interests," Jeanna said. "Maybe it's just too soon to decide. Chuck?"

He was one sloppy mess—heavyset, the only white youngster lined up on the far end of the brooding four, his chair tipped back against the wall.

"It's *Chef*man. I'm with Lon." He gave her an odd stare—belligerent yet humorous, like this was one big game, his belly protruding over his belt, legs hanging apart.

"Okay." She wrote *Survive and Thrive* up on the board and wrote Lonnie, Cat, Alley, and Chefman's names next to it.

"Miss?" Lonnie said.

"Yes?"

"Just survive."

"Why not thrive?"

"Don't have no idea what it mean."

Jeanna blushed.

"It means doin' great, going to the top of the heap, everything fine and dandy," Chefman said.

Jeanna looked back to Lonnie. He shook his head. "That don't make no sense."

"Okay," she said, and erased "thrive," feeling uneasy as she did. "For now. Thanks for clarifying that." She looked at her watch. "We still have twenty-five minutes to go, so let's get into groups and explain to each other why you chose that group, why it matters to you. And please pick a note taker so I can have a sense of how the groups are coming together."

All the groups were going great guns before group Sur*vive* back in the lounge area had said a word to each other. Cat had darted out of the room; Alley was staring a hole in the floor; Lonnie was dozing in and out, waking up with a jerk every minute or so; and Chefman, off to the side, had stuffed his mouth so full of food it was unclear how he would ever get it down. Cat reappeared and alighted on the edge of a chair, his feet pedaling the floor. Jeanna walked over to see if she could help them get to first base. She sat down next to Cat and he froze.

"Cat, would you like to be the note taker?"

He looked at her like she was crazy and shook his head no.

She leaned a little closer to him and asked quietly, "Why not?"

He tried to look everywhere but at her, as if in doing so he could somehow escape the whole situation.

"Why not? It's okay, just tell me," she said even more quietly.

"I cain't," he said in a strangled whisper, looking down, showing Jeanna a patchy scalp and frizzled hair that made him look like a man fifty years older. In fact, she realized as she took in his gaunt frame, bent over in a perpetual crouch as if to spring away at any moment, he looked like a brittle, wizened old man. Cat began patting his thighs a mile a minute with both hands.

"Why?" Jeanna pressed.

"I cain't read. Cain't write neither," he whispered.

Jeanna was shocked, though she knew she shouldn't be. She'd seen grown boys in her teen programs who couldn't read or write worth a dime. She put a hand on Cat's arm to reassure him and he jumped away, startling her.

"That's okay, I'll help you learn," she said, taking her hand away, feeling awkward.

"It way too late for me, Miss J." He looked off into the distance, his eyes dull as old nickels. "I ain't never gonna learn." He hesitated. "An Lon, he cain't read neither."

"Really!" she exclaimed, making Cat jerk back and waking Lonnie up.

Lonnie gave Jeanna a big smile. "Scuze me, Miss J. I musta fell asleep. What we doin'?"

"Why're you so tired?" She noticed that his lower lip was fat and split down the middle, oozing a pinkish-red substance.

"I gets up at three-thirty every morning to go get the papers ready for my boys for their five-thirty routes. North Side. *Daily Inquirer*."

"Jesus, that's early!"

Lonnie smiled again, causing more oozing. Jeanna touched her own lip, letting her eyes ask the question.

He touched his lip with scraped knuckles and said, "I hadda protec one a my boys workin' Oxford turf this morning. Worked my boy over pretty good. New gang leader over that way. But when he come to, I promised his little brother a route. We cool now."

Jeanna reached into her pocket for a tissue and very gently touched his lip with it and held it there a second. "There," she said, smiling. "Sounds like you've had a full morning." She paused. "With all that responsibility on your shoulders, would it help if you learned to read and write better?"

He nodded his head vigorously. "Shore would. My main man, Chef, here," he motioned with his chin, "was always going to teach me, but our work schedules conflic. Ain't it crazy, me sellin' papers all over town an' I can't even read the headlines?"

Jeanna nodded, wondering what the hell had happened in his previous schools.

As if reading her mind, he asked, "Miss J. How comes you act like you like me? All my other teachers hated me."

"Hated you!"

"Yeah, they just look at me and saw a baaaad dude, which I ain't. Guess it mighta had something to do with me almost burnin' down my last school."

Chefman snorted, his mouth still full.

"Excuse me?" Jeanna said.

"All I did was set fire to the closet where they kep dozens of pink slips on me—all of 'em uncalled for, but the fire got a little outta hand."

"I remember reading something about that fire... at the Madison, last May?" Jeanna asked.

"Yeah," he said, squinting at her.

Jeanna smiled slightly at him, thinking it served the bastards right.

Chefman snort-laughed again, glancing sideways at them from time to time, as he chowed down. Jeanna was surprised that these two were buddies since, according to the student list, they were from racial communities totally at odds with each other.

She looked to her left at Alley, who seemed desperately to want to disappear. Remembering his inability to fill out the forms the first day, she said, "Alley, is it possible that you might need a little help with reading and writing too?"

He nodded, a wave of mauve overtaking his face.

Jeanna looked at all three of them—Lonnie, Cat and Alley. "What d'you three say we meet after school a couple times a week and get into this reading/writing thing? Lonnie, do you have any time after school?"

"Yeah, I have till four-fifteen."

"Cat and Alley, do you have anything you have to do right after school?"

They shook their heads no, slowly in unison, as if agreeing to their own execution.

Jeanna rubbed her hands together and said, "Great, let's begin tomorrow! Two forty-five here, okay?"

"Like I said, Miss J, it way too late for me," Cat said.

"But the group won't be nearly as good with*out* you, Cat."

"Without *me*!" With a look of utter consternation, he flew out of the room again.

The bell rang then, and without another word, Lonnie and Alley got up and left.

Chefman remained seated, eyeing Jeanna, and said, "Good luck with all that, but next time can we have our Group In-Quy-Ree meeting to ourselves?" and gave her that crazy-belligerent look again.

Jeanna laughed. "Yes, next time I'll steer clear of group Sur*vive,* and let you guys have at it."

"And the time after that?"

"We'll see."

"Yeah, we will." He walked off, a cocky look on his face.

Jeanna hurried to the doorway to take notes from students as they were leaving.

"Great class," Tommie Lee said, smiling at her, as he gave her his basketball group's notes.

"I like this group thing," Valle said, handing her the music group's notes. "It gets you to thinking."

"This place not so bad as I thought it would be," Karima said as she flicked her racial justice group notes on top of the rest and followed the others out.

Jeanna turned away, exhausted yet happy, when she noticed a new student she had not seen before seated in the shadows at the far end of the table. He was big. He was not moving a muscle, not looking around. Formidable.

She walked over to him.

"Hi. You must've just come in when I was in the back."

He looked at her.

"I'm Jeanna Kendall... and your name?"

"Jam."

"Okay, Jam. Your last name?"

He shrugged. But after a pause—"Jones." He gave another shrug.

Jeanna looked down at her list. He was not on her roster, but she felt he was there for a reason. So she explained what they had been doing and gave him the sheets she had made up for those who were not yet ready to join a group. He looked right through her, then down at the questions. She had no idea what to do with him, but she knew enough not to push him.

CHAPTER THREE

Chefman's Blessing

The next afternoon, Lonnie and Chefman sauntered into Jeanna's classroom after school and pulled four chairs into a tight circle by the window. Chefman leaned up against the window ledge and began chatting with Lonnie. Alley stood apart and quiet, as usual. Jeanna rigged up an easel with newsprint, and Alley and Lonnie took their seats in the circle. Chefman remained standing, leaning back against the window ledge near Lonnie's seat.

Then Cat appeared out of nowhere and perched on the edge of a chair, not speaking or looking at anyone.

"Cat, I'm so glad you made it!" Jeanna said.

"Hey, Cat," Lonnie said softly. "Hey, Alley."

Both Cat and Alley seemed paralyzed with shyness. They merely blinked their response. The tension in the room crackled as Jeanna pulled out big markers and placed them on the edge of the easel.

Chefman snorted loudly, "Whatta we got here, a coupla salt-an-pepper Looney Tunes for a reading group?"

Jeanna blanched as she saw Alley shrink back into himself. Lonnie laughed, but reached up and put his hand over Chefman's mouth.

"Shut yer mouth, Chef."

Cat darted a look at Chefman. "I ain't no Looney Tune, goon," he said with a grimace of a smile that came and went so fast Jeanna wondered if she'd imagined it.

Chefman chuckled. "No, guess you're not, not with that quick lip."

Everyone laughed with him, the tension broken.

"You go on now an cook up some poison for them rich folk downtown," Lonnie said. "We's about serious business here."

"I know. Actually, I come here to bless ya's."

They all laughed at the ludicrousness of it: Chefman's stomach rolled out over the opening at his belt, which was unhooked and hanging loose. His face was pasty white and pockmarked, his hair greasy and unkempt, his T-shirt spattered with what Jeanna guessed were many nights of cooking—even the laces on his high top sneakers were untied and drooping on the floor. This was not a priestly look.

"It just warms my heart to see ya's beat back the system," he continued.

Jeanna was suddenly on alert.

"Them ole schools tried their damnedest to keep ya's as dumb an ignorant as they could, and now you're gonna show 'em how smart you really are"—his voice had gotten real quiet and intense—"with the help of your fine leader here, Jyeena." He smiled, and his tone turned jocular again. "More power to ya's. An now I'll be on my way."

Lonnie and Chefman slapped hands smoothly, and Chefman shambled off. Jeanna let the power of his words sink in as they all watched him shuffle away, shoelaces flopping. Then she launched in: "Okay, here's how we can start. Instead of using some boring old kids' workbooks, we're going to come up with our own words, words *you* want to be able to read and write. Each of you will call out a word that you want to be able to read and write, and then we'll do some rhyming to see if we can find words that look and sound like your word so it will be easier to remember them. We'll go in a circle. Short words for now."

The boys nodded.

"I'll start," she said. "Book." She wrote it down, then gestured at Lonnie.

"Gang," he said.

Alley was next. He waited a long moment. "Man," he finally said, and blushed.

Cat was quiet for a few seconds, then said, "Hit."

They did another round—gun, run, bum.

"Great words," Jeanna said. "Let's stop here and see if we can do some rhyming. Sometimes words that rhyme also are spelled the same, but not always. Let's take my first word, 'book.' See how it's spelled? Is everyone familiar with the letters themselves?"

They all nodded.

"Okay, try to think of a word that rhymes with book—like what Chefman does, for instance."

"Cook!" Lonnie exclaimed.

The other boys clapped excitedly. Jeanna wrote it down.

"Shook," Cat said with a quiver in his bony shoulders.

Alley couldn't think of one.

"Hey!" Lonnie called out and pointed out the tall windows to a plane rising over the rooftops.

"Look!" Alley called out.

They cheered him as the late-afternoon sun lit up their faces.

And so it went. Jeanna had them write their words and read aloud each other's writing.

After over an hour of this, she turned to them. "What did you each just do?"

"Read?" Lonnie whispered.

"Yes! What else?"

"Write!" This time all three boys yelled it.

Lonnie looked up at the clock and yelped. It read 4:30. "Shesus, I gots to go, but this was fun! I could keep doing this all night."

"Yeah," Cat said in an amazed tone.

Alley just sat there beaming.

"I had fun too," Jeanna said. "You guys are naturals."

The boys filed out of the room, smiling shyly. Jeanna gathered up her class-planning material and walked out to her car. Hers was the second-to-last one in the lot. Matt's was still there; he was always the last to go.

As she turned out of the parking lot, she saw Cat in the distance, his jacketless figure bent against the chill wind as he made his deft way across a lot strewn with broken glass. She would have to ask Matt about ways to make sure that the kids had enough to eat and coats to wear. If it couldn't be done at the school right away, she'd noticed that the Panthers were running a free breakfast program at a church not far from the school. She vowed to stop by someday after work and get more information. They might not take kindly to her, but she could give it a try.

~

After Jeanna got home, her mother called.

"Hi sweetheart. How's your new job going? Grandma stopped in today and was asking about you. I've been meaning to call you all week, but by the time I get home it's so late I'm too exhausted to remember my own name."

Jeanna didn't say anything. Of course it had been at her grandma's urging that she'd called.

"You there, Jeanna?"

"Yes, the job is scary, amazing, awful, wonderful. The kids are fabulous. I love every single one of them already, but—"

"I'm so glad, dear. Honey, customers are beginning to come in, I have to get off, but I'm glad you're doing so well."

Jeanna went into a slow burn.

"I'll be with you in just a moment," Jeanna heard her say.

"One more quick thing—I know Grandma would really appreciate a visit from you. She had a setback early in the week."

Jeanna gripped the phone. "What kind of setback?"

"She had a series of minor strokes Sunday evening and had to be hospitalized for a few days, but she bounced back—"

"Strokes! And you didn't *call me*?"

"I *told* her you'd feel this way, but she wouldn't let us, darling. She didn't want to interfere in your first big job. She said you'd have too much to deal with as it was."

Jeanna was silent. She couldn't imagine how she would have juggled the crazed confusion of her first week teaching along with her grandmother's crisis. "I'm sorry, Mom. I hate to admit it, but she was probably right. I'll make sure to visit her Sunday."

"Thanks, sweetheart." Her mom hung up.

Her grandmother; her lifeline. Jeanna felt the excitement of her own new beginnings fade as she pictured her grandmother being forced to deal with life's endings. All evening she felt subdued as she worked, sensing something that she couldn't quite grasp, and couldn't let go.

First thing Saturday morning, Jeanna called her grandmother. She asked about her health, but her grandmother passed over that, wanting to know about her first week of teaching.

"Well, on the very first day of class a student walked out while I was in mid-sentence—"

"Walked out! How demoralizing."

"Yeah, really. Cassius, a pretty tough kid."

"But isn't that your specialty?"

"It used to be, but working in a school is a lot different from after-school youth work; the kids are so turned off. It's like I'm guilty until proven innocent." She laughed, and her grandma laughed with her.

"Don't worry; he'll probably come back. But if not, certainly don't see it as your fault. The kids these days have so many problems to contend with."

"That's the truth. Actually, I was wondering if you'd be up for a visit Sunday?"

"Oh, thank you so much, darling, but Loretta's on her way over and we're driving out to the country for a few days. I can really use that peaceful country feeling, if you know what I mean."

Jeanna was relieved. As much as she loved her grandmother, she had too much to do—unpacking, class prep, a paper already due for her evening master's program.

"Let's get together when you can catch your breath from your new job, okay?" her grandma rushed along, not giving her time to answer. "I know what it's like, especially in the beginning. You need to take care of you right now."

"Thanks, Grandma. I'll be in touch when I have it a little more together."

"I'll look forward to it, sweetheart. And don't you worry about those kids; they'll come around sooner than you think. They're lucky to have you."

Jeanna never believed things like that, but it made her feel good to hear it.

"Have fun with Loretta, Grandma; give her my best."

"I certainly will."

Jeanna felt buoyed up after talking with her grandmother. She put on some jazz and started putting her apartment in order. She set up shelves, opened boxes, and put things away to the breezy sound of Lester Young, another special someone in her life who made even the most difficult things seem easy. She'd get a start on her paper. Maybe she'd even have time to play her flute before she fell asleep tonight. That would make it a perfect Saturday.

CHAPTER FOUR

It Was the *People*, Not No Lawyers

In Monday's Group Inquiry class, Jeanna found that the racial justice group had commissioned its own private consultant: Felice's grandmother. Mrs. Jeffries sat in the wing-back easy chair that Felice normally claimed as her own, a cane by her side, grey hair pulled back in a bun, her full attention on the debate raging between her granddaughter and Karima. Felice was sitting on the cushioned footstool by her grandmother's side. Across from Felice, Karima sat on one end of the couch, while Abby sat on the shag rug, leaning against the other end, her arms wrapped around her knees. Wesley was sitting not far from Mrs. Jeffries on a folding chair, listening intently.

Felice, dressed in a brown suede vest and tapered jeans, her hair swept up, announced, "It was the *law*, the work of the NAACP Legal Defense team that did it . . ."

Karima, in a plain black T-shirt and loose jeans patched at the knee, her Afro big and wild, retorted, "What you mean NAACP lawyers? They didn't want nothing to do with no street marches and boycotts, sit-ins and a whole messa stuff. It was the *people*, workers like my daddy, and maids like his mama, and school kids—not no *lawyers*—who got the whole thing going."

Felice grabbed her vest in both hands and looked to her grandmother for help against this tirade from the street.

"See what I mean, Nana?"

"Baby, this little girl's got the beginnings right. She sure does, and I'll tell you a story just so you can see what she means."

Jeanna moved to sit at the round resource table so she could hear without actually joining the group. She pretended to be looking through her files as she thought about when she and her grandmother had taken the bus to the 1963 March on Washington six years earlier—the long, snaking line of yellow buses as far as the eye could see, the rolling cadence of Dr. King's voice, the singing that had made every nerve vibrate, that had brought the crowd to a kind of intimacy of spirit...

"It was in the mid-fifties," Mrs. Jeffries began. "I'd gone back down south to Cleveland, Mississippi, to help my brother take care of my ma, who was very sick. He owned an auto repair shop and had a wife and five kids, so he couldn't keep up with all that and Ma too." She clasped her hands over her lap. "One of my brother's best friends was a man named Amzie Moore. He was a man to contend with. President of the NAACP down there, and had been for as long as I could remember. That's when the NAACP stood for something. That was the summer we began organizing for voting rights in a big way. He'd been working on it for a long time, but twasn't till the young people started getting involved that things really began to shake up."

At that, the group leaned in.

"Now back then most folks in the Negro community, what we now call the black community, could not vote. If they tried, and a few did from time to time, they were killed—shot in the head, or the back, like as not. In the early years, they were just plain lynched, hung from the trees. So as you can imagine, most of us did not vote."

"Didn't the police do anything?" Abby asked.

"Oh, they were part of the lynching parties," Mrs. Jeffries said. "They brought the beer and hot dogs."

Abby's rosy face turned pale. She tightened her arms around her legs and dug her chin into her knees, never taking her eyes off Mrs. Jeffries.

"Well Amzie'd come over to my brother's place when I first came down in '55, and we'd set on the porch and talk all evening about the goings on in Montgomery. We had a sister living in Montgomery at the time. She was very active in a women's political action group, and she wrote me every week. It *was* the everyday black women, mind you—the maids, the washerwomen, the nannies, you name it—who stopped taking those buses. They were the spark plug. Just like the young lady here says." She nodded toward Karima.

"The Negro women's political group had a leaflet drive right after Mrs. Parks refused to give up her seat on the bus. They laid paper all over that city in a matter of hours and not a black soul boarded those buses. Matter of fact, it was these everyday Negro women who pushed Dr. King into signing on to the boycott. He was new in town, young, you understand, had just got his first church. He had a reputation to keep up, and was more than a little shy about this direct action kind of thing. Let's just say that the washerwomen helped him *overcome* his shyness. They pushed him into the leadership role in spite of himself." She smiled broadly.

The kids laughed.

"We were proud, Amzie, my brother, and I, when we heard about it. It gave us considerable hope that maybe we could bring down the voting wall. One night, Ma and I were sitting on the porch and Amzie brought a young fellow by from up north in Harlem, just a few years older than yourselves, asking if we could put him up. A handsome, well put together young man by the name of Moses, Bob Moses, a teacher-type. Had a scholarly look—quiet, like this one here." She gestured toward Wesley. "That youngster meant business. He said he'd come to help with voter registration. Amzie'd been taking young Moses round town to meet folk, stir up support.

"Well, down in the town of Liberty, Moses took some locals in to register, but on the way up to city hall, some good ol' white boys knocked that northern boy down, kicked him in the head and bloodied him up pretty bad. But he did not give up. He surely didn't. He went back again the next day, and kept going back, taking folk in to register to vote.

"Young kids around town saw what was happening and joined the voting rights fight right quick. The parents got involved after a while, too. We began meeting in the churches. A few of the ministers stood with us; many didn't, of course, but enough did so we had a place to hold meetings, pray-ins, sing-ins and such to get our strength up. The young folk began going door to door, marching, and starting freedom schools—that's the part they asked me to help with, and I was mighty proud to do it. It was literacy we were teaching, so people could pass the voting tests. And we got into a lot of other issues as well; anything that was holding people down, we talked it through, hatched plans, took on the powers that be." Mrs. Jeffries paused to take a sip of water.

"Mrs. Jeffries?" Karima said. "Who do you see as the hero of the black struggle?"

"The hero?"

"Yeah, the real leader. We always be havin' these fights. I say Malcolm X without a doubt. But everybody else says Martin Luther King."

"Well, you already said yourself it was the everyday people, and it *was*," Mrs. Jeffries said. "Beyond that, if I personally were to pick, which I frankly don't see the sense in doing, I wouldn't choose either Martin or Malcolm . . . I'd say Ella Baker."

"Who?" the entire group asked.

"Ella Baker, an older black woman. You see, King was a great speaker, a smart sort and a man of principle, but he was out of *touch*. Ella reached out to people in every nook and cranny of nearly every community in the South throughout the sixties and decades earlier, starting back in the forties—the poorer, the blacker, the more oppressed, the better. She laid the groundwork for King, for the movement in the South. Without Ella, there would've been no King, no one for him to speak to, no masses ready to move."

"What was she like?" Abby asked.

"Ella? Ella's still going strong. Works up in Harlem on school and police issues, and down South too. She's *very* down to earth, never puts on any airs. She never put much stock in big-time leaders like King, Walter White, or Roy Wilkins, or their organizations either. It was too top-down for her. She's always felt people should be their own leaders, fight for themselves—and she's helped them do that, young and old. She's always had a special feeling for the young radicals, black and white. She nurtured them from the start, insisted they make their own decisions, helped them build SNCC, which I know you know about from what Felice has told me."

"A black woman did all that?" Karima asked in a hushed tone. "Did you—I mean, *do* you know her, personally?"

"Oh child, just about everyone knows her personally—or more to the point, she knows *them* personally. That's what organizing is. Building those personal relationships. But to answer your question, it was always my great pleasure to put her up whenever she came to town. Down in Mississippi, I'd send her off early in the morning after a hot cup of coffee and breakfast bun, and bring her home late at night, exhausted, with a hot cup of tea—and a drop of rum." She laughed. "Oh, would we ever talk, and *laugh,* about all the craziness of trying to do the impossible. Ella's as human as you and me."

A noisy argument from the group nearest them threatened to drown Mrs. Jeffries out. She paused. Felice shot the basketball boys a look of pure venom. Jeanna wanted to hear the rest of the story too—she'd never heard of Ella Baker—but stepped quickly toward the offending group, and the volume automatically went down a few notches.

Big Blue was speaking in his long, drawn-out baritone drawl. "We gots... to deal... with the stars, man... the high scorers... they's the ones that wins the games."

"No sir!" Pepper, waving his bony arm to halt Blue, drilled out in staccato soprano, "We-gotta-deal-with-the-whole-team-man-its-the-team-that-wins-not-just-superstars-no-way!"

"That's true," Tommie Lee agreed. "One man doesn't make the team."

"No Pep, that ain't right. Ain't Blue right, Jeanna?" Olly cut in.

Jeanna raised her palms to the ceiling and said, "I know you all will find a way to work it out—without my interference, heaven forbid." Jeanna couldn't resist this dig at Olly, who had objected to her intervention in the last class. Before he could respond she walked on, satisfied that at least two opposing views were emerging in the basketball group. That would help set the stage for their research, analysis, and debates.

"I don't get the teachers in this school," Olly said in his usual pissed-off tone as Jeanna walked away. "They always hangin' round when you don't need 'em and gone off somewhere when you do."

"Funny, Ol, I see it just the opposite," Tommie Lee said.

Jeanna made her way to the music group, which had broken up so each person could do their own thing. Will had headphones on, and his eyes were closed, a blissful look on his face. His chair was tipped back, his hands in mock guitar position, his ragged sneakers keeping time on the metal chair in front of him. Occasionally he would leave off his invisible guitar strumming and write furiously in his notebook.

She stopped by Jam's chair in the shadows. He'd been sitting there, silent, all morning with the chaos going on around him. She wondered what went through his mind day after day, never saying anything to anyone.

"You okay, Jam?"

He just looked at her.

"You have any interest in any of these groups yet?"

He shook his head almost imperceptibly.

"Anything else interest you?"

He just looked through her as if she hadn't spoken. She pressed her lips together, not wanting to push against a blank wall. She turned away. Maybe someday he'd come around, but it sure as hell wasn't going to be anytime soon.

Jeanna looked in on Group Survive. They had taken over the back of the classroom, where bean bags, some low-slung easy chairs, and a fuzzy rug created a cozy atmosphere. They were listening to rhyming words that were rolling off Chefman's tongue—"cool, fool, drool, pool." Between laughs, Lonnie wrote them, painstakingly, up on the easel, and Cat and Alley copied them into their notebooks. Apparently, they had decided that increasing their literacy was a prime survival skill. Jeanna was thrilled. A couple afternoons a week of tutoring was not going to make up for ten years of lost schooling.

Loud enough to get everyone's attention, she said, "Next Friday we're going to begin our 'Report and Support' process, so you all have exactly two more sessions and all your free time in between to really accomplish something, so that each group will have something of substance to report to the whole class. That should include any library research you've done so far, books or articles you've begun reading, interviews you've had, and journal entries about issues that have come up in your group, both positive and not so positive. Literacy and survival skills you've been working on, and anything you need help with, okay?"

They responded with a chorus of reluctant "yeahs."

Jeanna shook Mrs. Jeffries's hand as the students filed out and thanked her for coming in. As she watched the elderly woman lock arms with Felice and walk out the door, she thought of her own grandmother—the only person whose opinion she trusted without question. She needed to visit her.

CHAPTER FIVE

What the Hell He Done Now

A FEW WEEKS LATER, JEANNA SET ASIDE A TUESDAY night to call her students' parents. She knew it was a good thing to do, but found it nerve-racking. She was especially worried about Jam; she looked for his parents' number, but none was listed. No address either.

Her first call was to Tommie Lee's mother, Lillian, who was amazingly supportive.

"Tommie Lee told me how he'd always wanted school to be different, but he couldn't explain how until he found your class—he just loves it," she said, leaving Jeanna feeling incredibly affirmed.

She tried Cassius's number.

"Yeah?"

"Is this Cassius's mother?" All the *s's* in "Cassius's" sounded strange and awkward to her own ears.

"Who the hell wants to know?"

"I'm his teacher, Jeanna Kendall." Jeanna could hear how young, white, and insubstantial she sounded.

"So what the hell he done now?"

"Nothing, I just—"

"Well, what you expect? He a nothing no account boy of a nothing no 'count man. Be happy all he do is nothing. Why you call?"

"I haven't seen Cassius since the first day of school, and it's almost October."

"Well I ain't seen 'im lately neither an' don't know when I will, little lady." The woman gave a croaking laugh and hung up.

Jeanna felt like she'd been kicked in the stomach. But she had an image of Cassius's mother—a bone-tired, strung-out woman being kicked in the teeth, the side of the face, the head, stomach, chest, thighs, and butt, in and out of the house, up and down the street.

Where the hell did that *come from?* She ran her hands over her own body and shook herself, trying to climb out of the phone call, but couldn't.

She hung up her clothes. Put the dishes away. She went to bed and lay in the dark for hours, the woman's dead voice inside her.

In the next day's Group Inquiry class, Jeanna was pleased to see all the groups in full swing. She was touching base with each one to check on any issues they were having.

A gust of chilly autumn wind swept the room as the door opened and in waltzed Cassius.

"Hi Cassius, good to see you!" Jeanna called out, caught off guard. As every face in the room turned toward him, Jeanna realized that she had sounded *too* glad to see him, and that she had put him on stage to boot.

"Hey, what's happenin'?" Cassius muttered to no one in particular as he strutted across the room. He leaned up against a pillar and examined his nails. The room fell unnaturally silent.

Knowing she was being overeager, but not knowing what else to do, Jeanna walked over to him. "Everybody's working on those projects we talked about the first day of class, remember?" Jeanna realized too late that she was putting him on the defensive by pointing out that he'd missed every day since the first day of school.

"Yeah, I ramember," he growled.

Jeanna stubbornly pushed through all her inner storm warnings. "Why don't you come to my office and I'll fill you in on what people are doing, and maybe you can get started on something . . . or join an ongoing group."

An uneasy shuffling of feet and coughing around the room greeted her last remark.

Cassius leaned toward her until he was practically in her face. Anger sparked from his eyes and a tinge of burgundy welled up his throat. She could see each and every heavily lacquered Afro-curl that framed his face and tumbled nearly to his shoulders. The smell of his hair gel nearly knocked her out.

"Lady," he spat out, "I just now got here. I don't want nobody jumpin' on my case just like that, see?" Without a backward glance, he sauntered over to a round table littered with colorful magazines and paperbacks. Drumsticks stuck out of the back pocket of his jeans. He picked up a *Down Beat,* sat down, tipped his chair back, and seemed to become engrossed in his reading.

Jeanna saw her own hand still ludicrously held up in midair as if to make some point. Feeling every eye in the room on her, she brought it quickly down to her side. She was aware that most teachers would see Cassius as insolent and not tolerate it. She was more concerned with her own stupidity, knowing she'd blown it. She braced herself against ridicule from the class. None came. After a moment, chairs scraped, conversations resumed, and the groups got back to the business at hand.

Jeanna breathed again—she had been holding her breath ever since Cassius brought her up short—and went into her office to regroup. She was still regrouping, uncertain what to do, when Cassius appeared in the open doorway.

"So what's happenin'?" It was a real question this time.

Jeanna explained about the projects different groups were working on, lingering over the Music and Freedom group, especially Will's focus on the Delta Blues, and when that didn't take, on Valle's Roots of Gospel, hoping he might see a drumming connection in it.

His looked at her, his eyes completely impassive.

Jeanna finally stopped explaining. "Do any of these ideas sound good to you, or is there anything else you'd like to work on?" She tried to hide the futility she felt.

"No," he shot back, flat and clipped.

She felt herself blush even though this was the exact response she had anticipated. "Well, I know you have interests, right?" she floundered on.

"Yeah, I got interests." A smile that verged on contempt crossed his face.

She was willing to fall into the trap to keep the conversation going. "And what are those interests?"

He looked her straight in the eye. "Makin' love to my baby and beatin' a drum; they's my interests."

Jeanna held his gaze and smiled slightly. "Well, maybe you could do a project of some kind on drumming."

"I just wanta drum," he flashed back, "not talk about it or do no kinda school project on it, and that's it."

Stymied, Jeanna could see no way of immediately involving him in the class. Not wanting to give up, she plowed ahead anyway. "Do you have a set of drums? How do you practice?"

"'Course I ain't got no drums. I ain't rich, now am I?" He whipped the sticks out of his back pocket and played a hot rhythmic pattern on the back of the chair in front of him. "That's how I practice." He stuck the drumsticks back in his pocket and turned to go. "Oh, yeah, one more thing," he added over his shoulder. "Ya got no call callin' my house. If I come, I come, if I don't, I don't. Callin' my house ain't gonna make no difference." With that, he walked out the door.

CHAPTER SIX

Does This Look Like Madison Square Garden?

JEANNA HAD SLEPT BADLY FOR THE PAST FEW NIGHTS. She had always had a tendency to feel inadequate, but lately her anxiety had become overwhelming. Now she was running late for her Group Inquiry class.

She parked in the school lot, hoping she would beat the bell. As she got out of the car, she noticed three boys pinning a girl over the hood of a car and laughing. One boy had grabbed the girl's breast and she was batting his hand away, another had his hand on her thigh under her skirt and she was kicking at him. She was laughing too; but she *had* to, Jeanna realized, or it could turn uglier. She'd been seeing a lot of this—boys pushing girls up against lockers, cars, walls, a whole lot of laughing going on and a lot of feeling up.

"Hey, you guys are going to be late to class," she called to them. The boys looked up, startled, and the one youngster who hadn't been grabbing at the girl said, "Yeah, let her go. Jakim'll make me do fifty push-ups if I'm late."

The boys took off at a run to class. The girl looked embarrassed and defiant as she slid off the car. Jeanna went over to her. "You okay?"

"Yeah, they just jokin' around. I gotta go." She brushed by Jeanna without looking up.

Jeanna hurried to her own class and made it through the door just as the bell rang. She wished she could have talked to the girl longer. She had brought the issue up in staff meeting a week ago, but Matt had been called away and her colleagues had dismissed her concerns with comments like, "You can't make over nature."

An hour into class, Jeanna looked over at Meta, who was sitting alone in a study cubicle she had rigged up for herself. A hefty pile of library books was stacked up in front of her. Note cards were organized into little piles with rubber bands around them.

Meta had told Jeanna several weeks ago that her mother had been given a radical mastectomy of both breasts and had fallen into a deep depression. For days on end Meta had been buried in her research, seeking greater insight into her mother's situation and wondering if such radical surgery had really been necessary. But today she hadn't opened a book or made a single notation. Jeanna walked over and was alarmed to see silent tears running down Meta's plum-red cheeks, making dark splotches on the well-worn desk.

She pulled up a chair and reached out and placed her hand over Meta's.

"Is it your mother, Meta?"

The girl nodded. "Father put her in the mental hospital today because she couldn't take care of the children, or even herself. She hasn't gotten out of bed for days, but I vas helping with the kids, and taking care of her . . ."

"That's an awful heavy load."

"She didn't want to go. She was crying the whole way. He said it was for her own good. He said I had to be the mother for the little ones now, which is vat I've been doing, but it's harder now that Mother isn't even in the house." Meta used the sleeve of her blouse to wipe her cheeks.

"How terribly, terribly difficult, Meta. I just can't imagine anything harder to deal with." She put an arm around Meta's shoulders and held her tight. "Is there anyone you can talk to about all this? An aunt, or a grandparent?"

Meta shrugged. "No . . ." She hesitated. "Just you, Miss Kendall."

"Please call me whenever you need to." Jeanna scribbled her home number on one of Meta's cards. "You have way too much to carry alone."

"Miss Kendall? I haven't been able to sleep, and I just can't concentrate on my project."

"Of course you can't. Come with me. There's a very comfortable couch in the A/V room down the hall." Jeanna scanned the classroom to see if she could leave. All the groups were intent on their work, showing no signs of trouble.

"Let's make a break for it," she whispered to Meta, putting an arm around her waist. They scuttled out of the room with Meta giggling in spite of herself.

Jeanna settled Meta on the couch and pulled down the one window shade. She saw a radio on the shelf and turned the dial looking for some peaceful classical music—*Ah, Chopin. Perfect.* She found a soft, plaid blanket tossed on top of some boxes in the closet and placed it over Meta, then brushed the girl's hair back from her forehead.

"I'll come get you after lunch so you won't be late for your afternoon class."

A look of contentment covered Meta's face at Jeanna's touch. "Thank you so mush," she slurred, already slipping under.

Jeanna hurried back to class. She opened the door and saw Tommie Lee, of all people, and Big Blue squared off and circling each other warily. *What the hell?* The entire class surrounded them, waiting to see who would throw the first punch.

Jeanna felt a surge of anger go through her. How was it that all the mutual trust she had worked so hard to build in the class had evaporated the moment she left? She closed the door behind her abruptly, breaking the tense silence. In slow motion, every face but the two in the center of the ring turned in her direction.

Jeanna forced herself to walk unhurriedly to the edge of the circle. From her years of youth work, she could tell that neither boy wanted to do battle, but had felt compelled to face off for some reason.

"Does this look like Madison Square Garden?" she asked.

"No'm," the two answered in unison, still eyeing each other warily but no longer circling.

Turning to the onlookers, she asked, sharply, "Did you all pay admission? Why aren't you in your groups?"

Muttering and shuffling, they drifted away, disappointed at the missed drama.

"Each project group needs to be ready with a progress report in twenty minutes, to be delivered to the larger group before we break for lunch," she said sharply. "You two"—she pointed at Tommie Lee and Blue—"I want to see over here."

Jeanna pulled three chairs together and gestured for the boys to sit down. "What was this about?"

"Well," Big Blue began, "I been listening to Pep make fun a the way I speak and talk about me and my 'Staaar Syndrome' for weeks, and this morning he call me a ball hog and a limelight shooter and say that's why our team be losing, 'cause I'm stealin' the show."

Weeks ago Jeanna had spoken to Pepper about imitating Blue's southern accent.

"And for that you had to backhand Pep across the room?" Tommie Lee countered.

Jeanna scanned the room for Pepper and saw him on the floor with his back against the wall, looking stunned. He had a huge red splotch on one cheek. Abby was leaning over him, touching his shoulder, and Olly was crouched down on his other side. With their help, Pepper got up and moved closer to Jeanna and the two boys. Even Olly was subdued.

She was relieved to see that Pepper was moving without difficulty. He slid up onto the desk closest to Jeanna and Olly followed suit. Abby gave Jeanna a helpless look and went to join her own group.

"You okay, Pepper?" Jeanna asked.

He nodded and shrugged at the same time.

"You're in one piece, but you're not really okay?" she translated.

He nodded. She could see his legs trembling uncontrollably.

"Well, I ain't proud of it 'cause he so little, but he started making fun a the way I talk an' play ball an' I had enough of his shit."

"Well you do take a lot of shots, don't you, like Pep says," Tommie Lee said.

"I do exactly what Coach tells me to do, man," Big Blue spat out, "so you-all can talk to him about it. Maybe I'm not so wild about it my own self, but Coach say put it up, you bet I'ma gonna put it up. An' I didn't have no bone to pick with Tommie Lee here, who be a star in my book anyhow—only with Pep."

Pepper had been hanging on every word; he scowled when the business about the coach came out.

"Why can't you talk with Coach?" Pep asked in a trembling voice.

"That's not the way it works, Pep," Tommie Lee cut in. "What the coach says goes, no questions, no nothing."

"Yeah," Big Blue said, "it ain't no democracy like this here class. Coach Jakim was assistant to Coach Robinson in the Marines, and that man was a player's nightmare. But they never lost them a game, an' now Coach Jakim got the best winning record in the Northeast—but it his way or the highway."

Blue had gotten Pepper's attention.

"It sounds like you know what you're talking about," Jeanna said.

"Maybe, but I was wrong to be mishanlin' Pep, here, even with his lip." Big Blue started to rise from his seat, but Pepper slid down from the desk and walked over to him. Blue settled back into his chair as Pepper extended his small hand, saying, "Yeah, and I feel like a real idiot."

Blue reached for his hand and enveloped it without hesitation. "An' I shouldna been using you for no basketball. I lost my head. If it hadna' been for your bro here," he pointed to Tommie Lee, "we mighta lost our best stat an' strat man."

Pepper beamed at the compliment.

Jeanna wiped the clamminess from her palms on her blazer. Another crisis overcome, and pretty much by the kids themselves, as usual. But she had one more thing she needed to do.

"Hey, everyone, come on over here."

Everyone congregated around them.

"I have a question for all of you, but I don't want anyone to answer it right now. I just want you to think about it and write in your journals about it in case anything like this comes up again. Here's the question." She looked around the circle of faces. "Why did all of you just stand here and allow this fight to continue?"

"Well—" someone began.

"Just think it through, that's all I'm asking you to do," Jeanna said.

The students turned away in the silence, gathered their things, and left without their usual banter.

That night, Jeanna wondered how she could find a way to deal with the lousy conditions her students had to live with. She needed to figure out what was going on in the city—what change groups were active, and if she could fit into them in some way. Otherwise her work at the school was destined to be only one very skinny finger in the dike. She had been keeping her eyes open and reading the local papers faithfully. A community leader named Landon Waters came up frequently, but the papers never clarified what organization he was with.

She'd gone to a few meetings of this or that group claiming to want liberation or community uplift, but every one she'd tried had been either too conventional, not into real change at all, or too damn crazy. She wondered if she'd ever find an activist group that felt right. She missed the work she'd done on campus with her friend Cam—fighting against the war and for affirmative action in admissions and teacher hiring. Cam might have been a sleaze with women, but he'd known how to work the left-wing political scene, and together they'd made quite a team. She missed him. And here she thought she had gotten him out of her system.

CHAPTER SEVEN

I'd Rather Be Killed Here Than Die in a Straitjacket

GROUP INQUIRY WAS OVER, AND MOST OF THE STUDENTS had gone on to their next class. Jeanna was in her office when she heard someone growl, "I need that money, man."

She got up from her desk to take a look and saw Jam with his back to her, towering over Olly's short, chubby frame.

"How'm I gonna buy my lunch, you take my money?" Olly sounded three years old.

Jam turned slightly, lifted his heavy boot, and stomped down piston-like on Olly's foot, grinding it with his heel. Olly fell back against the wall, and began to slide down. Jeanna was out of her office and moving fast when Jam turned and saw her. His face went hard.

"Don't you ever touch another student in this school or you'll be thrown out of here so fast you won't know what hit you, do you understand that?" Adrenaline rushed through her; thinking Jam might lash out at her too, she steeled herself for the blow. But he looked through her and left the room.

Olly had taken his shoe and sock off and was gingerly holding his foot, tears running down his face.

Jeanna knelt beside him. "That must really kill. Is anything broken?"

“I don’t know. It hurts so bad I can’t tell.”

“Olly, I’m so sorry. This never should never have happened.”

“I should’ve given him the damn money in the first place. Here I’m thinking how I’m gonna last ‘til dinner with no lunch, like some baby, and coulda got myself killed.”

“Wait a minute; this isn’t your fault—”

Tommie Lee ducked into the room. “Jeanna, can I leave my backpack in your office?”

He looked from Jeanna, to Olly’s tear-stained face.

“What happened?”

“Jam wanted my lunch money; I wouldn’t give it to him and he stomped my foot to death with that two-ton boot of his.”

Tommie Lee dropped his bag on the floor and crouched down to look. Olly’s foot was swelling and turning a deep purplish-black.

He shook his head. “Man, that’s not pretty.” He squeezed Olly’s shoulder. “Hang in Ol,” he said and stood up. “Can I use your phone?”

Jeanna nodded. “Sure.”

He went into her office and came out a minute later. “My mother will be right over. She’ll take Ol and me to the North Side Community Health Center. She’s only a few minutes away.”

“Great, thank you,” Jeanna said weakly. She hadn’t even thought that far yet.

Tommie Lee bent over Olly. “You hangin’ in, Ol?”

Olly nodded, his eyes wet. “I don’t think I can get the shoe back on, though.”

“Just let it be. Here, I’ll take it.” Tommie Lee slipped the shoe into his backpack. He looked at Jeanna. “Can I talk to you a minute?”

“Of course.” They got up and went into her office.

“You throwing Jam out, telling Matt?”

“I’m not sure. Everything’s happened so fast.”

“Could you give it a few hours? Mom could call you tonight. She’ll know what to do.”

“Okay, I’ll hold off until I hear from her.” She wrote down her number for him, relieved not to have to make an immediate decision. He slipped it into his jeans pocket, then returned to Olly, who he half-carried out of the room and out to the front steps. Jeanna followed closely.

In a few seconds a dusty brown Chevy drew up to the curb. Tommie Lee helped Olly down the steps and settled him into the backseat so he could stretch his leg out.

Jeanna went around to the driver's side.

"Thank you so much for coming, Mrs. Johnson."

"It's no problem—I work nearby at Roosevelt Elementary, where my two little ones go. They said they could manage without me. I know Olly's mother; I'll drive him home afterwards. I thought you'd have another class to teach."

"My god, I do!" Jeanna had completely forgotten where she was supposed to be.

"You must be really shaken up."

"I am. Tommie Lee said that you might call me this evening to let me know how Olly is?"

"I will." Lillian turned to Olly. "Here, take these aspirin and put this next to your foot. It might numb the pain a little." She handed him an ice-cold can of soda.

"Thanks. Mrs. Johnson, please don't tell my mother. She'll yank me out of school and put me in Raleigh Academy or Catholic school. I'd die there."

"Let's see what the doctor says first, and then we'll figure out the next step." Lillian turned to Jeanna. "Let's talk it out tonight after we know how bad it is."

"I'd really appreciate that," Jeanna said, and Lillian drove off.

Telling Matt what had happened would be tantamount to throwing Jam out, since West Side High had a serious no-violence policy. Maybe Jam should be thrown out. Lord knew he'd done absolutely nothing productive so far, and now this. But she felt Jam was there for a reason . . . always had. She hurried to her next class, her head full of static.

Lillian Johnson called that evening to report that Olly's foot was only badly bruised.

"Thank god nothing's broken. How's he doing otherwise?"

"Oh that boy, all he talks about is don't tell my mother, don't tell Matt, don't tell this person, that person. He definitely wants to stay at West Side."

"Does Olly want Jam out of the class?"

"No, partly because that would blow his cover and he'd end up in a private school. But he's right. It wouldn't exactly be a perfect fit."

"Too strict? Traditional?" Jeanna asked.

"Exactly. He must be quite a handful in class."

"Let's just say we have our days . . . every day," Jeanna said. They both laughed. "But to be honest, I'm really worried about this. I've been going back and forth in my mind. Should I tell Matt, knowing Jam will be thrown out, or not? If I do nothing, am I jeopardizing the kids, Matt, the program, and the parents, not keeping their trust? But every time I toss it back and forth, it comes down to the fact that I just don't want to see Jam thrown out."

"I gather he's not your normal student," Lillian said.

"No, he's not." Jeanna didn't want to admit he hadn't done any work the whole time he'd been there.

"Tommie Lee feels he'd be in danger out on the streets."

"I've thought the same thing," Jeanna said. Why else would a rock-like mountain of a young man seek refuge in her classroom the better part of each day with nothing to do, interacting with no one, least of all her?

"Do you think he would lash out again? How often has he done this?"

"To my knowledge, he's never done anything like it at our school," Jeanna said. "Frankly, I was surprised. I've always suspected that his life is very harsh, even brutal in some way, outside of school, but inside it's seemed like he's decided to leave well enough alone. I can't guarantee he won't do it again, but I'll keep a closer eye on him."

"Well, Tommie Lee and I been talking. He suggested that he and Olly speak to Jam themselves and get his word not to cause any more damage. Tommie Lee thinks he's hungry, has no steady money, which is why he pounced on Olly. I could speak with Jazzmine Guffrey, we know each other through her old Uncle Guff. She's really good people; she might give him a free lunch every day. Carl and I and some of the other parents could cover the cost."

"I'd be happy to chip in too," Jeanna said.

"Well, I think it's better for the parents to take it on, but thanks. Also, I'm pretty sure Olly's right that his mother would pull him out of the school if she got wind of this. I hate not telling her the whole story—I mean, I'd be furious if one of my kids got hurt and I wasn't told—but Tommie Lee's convinced he wouldn't make it a day in a private school. Said he has a stubborn streak that would get him kicked out."

"Then we'd have two kids on the street in even worse trouble, all because I followed the proper protocol," Jeanna said. "Not that anybody's told me what that is!" She laughed weakly, realizing how unprofessional she sounded.

"Sometimes you just have to do what you have to do and beg forgiveness later. It's tough being a teacher these days. Olly told us you already laid it on the line with that boy—said he'd be thrown out if he did one more thing. He was impressed that you marched right up and confronted him, really gave him a piece of your mind. I think you won yourself a convert."

"I wish." Jeanna barely remembered she'd done that.

"I think that if this big fella pulls anything else, you should go straight to Matt and the parents involved, and have him kicked out. But for now I think Tommie Lee and Olly stand the best chance of dealing with it—if you feel the same."

"I do. I can't thank you enough, Mrs. Johnson. It's a tremendous weight off my shoulders to be able to talk this out together."

"It's Lillian. Listen, good luck tomorrow."

"Thanks."

Jeanna hung up smiling, feeling she'd finally met a kindred spirit and actual source of support at the school.

~

Olly was the first to come in the next morning, favoring his leg, but walking under his own steam. He sat on the edge of the chair next to Jeanna's desk.

"How're you going to feel, Olly, if Jam and you are still in the same class?"

He shrugged. "So long as he don't do anything else. To tell the truth, I'd rather get killed here than die in a straitjacket at Raleigh or St. Anne's. But anyway, Tommie Lee don't think Jam'll try anything more."

"Why not?"

"Well, he never done it before, an' I . . ." he stopped.

"You what?"

"I did get in his face. I don't know why. I knew when I was doing it, it was stupid as hell."

"What'd you do?" Jeanna felt a coldness come over her.

"I waited till after class and went over and asked him why he never says nothing. I, I said, 'What're you, a spook or something?'—you know, to get his goat, get a response or some damn thing like I always do? Well, I got a response alright."

At the word spook, Jeanna felt an urge to slap him herself. "I guess you did. It wasn't right what he did; nothing excuses it. But when you egg people on, it does make them angry."

"Yeah, I know. I'm a pain, not a fool."

"Are you nervous about speaking with him today?"

"Yeah. But Tommie Lee's gonna carry the ball. I'm-a be there though. That's the hard part. Standing there."

"I admire that—the way you and Tommie Lee are handling it. I'll be right here as back-up."

He snorted. "Scuze me Miss J, but we dealing with a six foot two hard-ass here. We all three screwed he decide to go off."

She laughed. "I hear you. I guess we just have to keep the faith on this one."

"That's exactly what Tommie Lee's mom said. You women-folk all think alike."

"I'll take that as a compliment."

Tommie Lee appeared at the door to the office. Jeanna saw that Jam had taken his seat in the shadows at the far end of the table without a word.

"You still up for this, Olly?"

He nodded.

"You okay with this, Miss J?"

"Absolutely."

"Okay, let's go." Tommie Lee gave Olly's upper arm a squeeze, then led the way to Jam's corner. Jam stood up as they approached, his hands loose by his sides, his face impassive. Tommie Lee began to talk, but too softly for Jeanna to hear. Jam looked a little surprised, then he nodded. Tommie Lee extended his hand and held it there until Jam took it. Olly put out his hand too. Jam didn't shake his but put a green bill into it instead. Olly slipped it into his back jeans pocket. He and Tommie Lee left the classroom. Jam settled back in his seat.

Jeanna took a deep breath and went over to him. "I want you to know I meant what I said yesterday. I can't put these kids in any more danger."

He nodded.

She walked to her office, emotionally exhausted but knowing that she needed to be normal for the rest of the students, for the rest of the day.

CHAPTER EIGHT

Land? He Ain't Going Nowhere

JEANNA AWOKE FEELING RESTED. IT WAS PROFESSIONAL Development Day at the university for teachers in the city's schools, and she was looking forward to the workshops she had signed up for. As she walked across campus, she drank in the fresh autumn air and reached out for leaves that drifted down like pieces of gold, twisting and tumbling just beyond her grasp. She looked up and saw a small crowd gathering not far from the library on the edge of campus where there was a large field. A TV van was there, its silver waffle of bright lights shining up high. She walked over to see what was happening, and made her way to the edge of a huge construction pit.

Four black men were chained to bright yellow bulldozers. It was eerily quiet. Little puffs of mist were rising from the dark earth. The TV crew was silently shooting away. It looked like a movie set.

She asked a young man with long hair and bell-bottoms standing nearby, "Do you know what's going on? Is it a movie?"

"No, it's for real. It's a demonstration against university expansion into the community."

Jeanna looked around her. There were about thirty demonstrators. Off a ways a number of pickup trucks, vans, and cars were parked in the field. Men in jeans and yellow work boots were sitting with the doors open, staring at the demonstrators, drinking from thermoses, smoking, and talking.

"Hey Jeanna! I didn't expect to see you here!"

She turned and saw Matt hustling toward her, bursting with his usual energy. Her spirits lifted.

"Hi Matt! I got here early to get a film at the library before my workshops, and noticed something going on. Do you know who they are?" She pointed to the chained men in the pit.

"They're part of our political action group. The one on the far end, in khakis and black sweater, that's Landon Waters." He pointed him out. "He's the leader."

"So that's him. I've read about him in the papers," Jeanna said. "I've wondered about him."

"Land's about the best there is as a community leader, by a long shot. I've worked with him for over twenty-five years now."

"Wow. I didn't realize you were so involved. So you and Landon Waters are pretty close then."

"Oh, definitely. Land's close to everybody—that is, everybody who cares about change. He's been involved in just about everything worth doing in the community."

They both had their eyes on Land down in the pit. He was looking far beyond the crowd, as if at some vision only he could see. Jeanna took a deep breath. She wondered how someone could be close to everyone and involved in everything. But one thing was clear: here was someone willing to put his life on the line for what he believed. And the group he and Matt were involved in—maybe this was what she'd been looking for.

"I'm glad I ran into you. I've been looking for a way to get involved politically, but nothing's clicked. What's the group's name again?"

"It's just called the Group. Land's kind of an understated guy. It's about the community, organizing, it's a real grassroots thing."

"Sounds good," Jeanna said. She'd never liked all the showy talk that never went anywhere—at least until Cam came along. He'd had a way of doing the impossible. "What have you worked on?"

"Racism in jobs and housing, police brutality, the schools, youth issues; lately we've been getting into local elections."

"That's a lot. Who are the other men?" Jeanna pointed down at the chained men.

"The one to the right of Land, in the white T-shirt and blue jeans, that's Carl Johnson—Tommie Lee's stepdad?"

He was strongly built, his face dead serious. He was standing quite still and centered.

"Good man," Matt said. "Works down at the steel mill."

"Do you know who Tommie Lee's biological father is?" Jeanna asked.

"Not really. Lillian's never said. It's all so long ago. But Carl's done really well by Tommie Lee. He actually adopted him a few years back."

"Lillian's great. She's my favorite parent call," Jeanna said.

"Don't come any better," Matt said.

"Who's that next to Lillian's husband?" She pointed down into the pit at a smaller man who seemed agitated, constantly shifting position, wiping the sweat off his face, waving flies away, making the chains rattle each time.

"That's Abe Barnett. He's head of the Black Construction Workers Union. They've had a rough go of it."

"In what way?"

"They just can't seem to make any headway getting access to construction jobs, which is one key reason we're here demonstrating. Now to Abe's right is his older brother, Gideon Barnett. The big guy with the beard. He's director of the West Side Community Center, where the Group meets. It's kind of a hub of a lot of community stuff. Gideon's probably Land's best friend."

To Jeanna, Gideon was the spitting image of Frederick Douglass, maybe even more majestic. She would have thought that Land would look more like that instead of this rather subdued guy he'd turned out to be—but she liked that she was wrong.

"Are there other members of the group here?"

"They should be, unless they had to work. I'm supposed to be at the city-wide principals' meeting myself, but I can't tolerate those things, and given my views on education, they think I'm from another planet."

"Hopefully, since their planet's a disaster. I'm glad I live on yours," Jeanna said.

"Likewise." He smiled broadly at Jeanna and then he shaded his eyes from the sun to peer across the pit. "See on the other side, the older woman seated at the leaflet table? That's Ma Carrington. She's the co-chair—well, really the chair of the group, when it comes right down to it."

Jeanna saw a woman who could be well into her seventies.

"I thought Land was head of it; isn't she kind of old?"

"Yeah, she's up in years, but Ma's sharp as a tack," Matt said. "Nothing gets by her. Land's kind of the ex-officio leader, but Ma's a real chair, not just a figurehead. Land's more like the core of the core group if you know what I mean. But he doesn't go off and make decisions by himself. For the most part. He's a real 'of, by, and for the people' kind of guy. And he definitely collaborates closely with the rest of the core group, like Ma, Helene, Gideon, Cam—"

"Cam!" Jeanna blurted out.

"Uh-oh. You've met I see," Matt said, raising his eyebrows and giving her a knowing smile.

"Cam and I worked closely together at the U. All that change stuff on my resume? Half of that was Cam's fault."

They laughed.

"So you two weren't . . .? Not that it's any of my business."

"Say no more. No, no, no. I watched him go through an entire legion of women for the cause and decided to save myself the trouble of a broken heart." Jeanna laughed, but back then it had been no laughing matter. Even now his name caused some unwanted sparks.

"Wise girl," Matt said.

Jeanna saw a tall, handsome man in a dark suit, striding their way.

"Ah, here comes Frederick." Matt lowered his voice. "Watch the men around here. They eat the fair gender alive, convinced they're doing them the favor of a lifetime."

Jeanna laughed, loving the way he put it. "That's okay, Matt. The movement is what I care about. The men-thing will have to wait." But she'd surely love a friend or two, maybe even a community of them. Especially if they were connected with the struggle. She was in no way ready for a relationship, especially with the likes of Cam—or this Frederick guy. She wanted a relationship that meant something.

"Well then, you've come to the right place," Matt said in his hearty voice.

Frederick stopped to greet Matt, and as he did he gave Jeanna a full-body scan. Matt attempted to introduce her, but Frederick hurried on while Matt was mid-sentence. Jeanna felt like she'd been undressed and discarded by the guy.

He turned around after he'd gone a ways. "Hey Matt, where's Helene?" he shouted.

"It looks like she and Cam are meeting with reporters," Matt yelled back, pointing to a bunch of trees where Cam and a tall, slender woman with long black hair were talking to several men, all scribbling away on notepads.

Jeanna was still recovering from Fred's brash once-over; now the sight of Cam caused an unwanted surge of all-too-familiar feelings. She let the feelings go right through her and out into the air, as she'd learned to do when they were constantly together back at the U. "I guess I failed that test," she said, gesturing at Frederick's retreating back.

"I wouldn't be so sure," Matt said, holding back a smile. "But one thing I am certain of."

"What?"

"He surely failed yours."

They were having a good laugh when Lillian appeared, handing out leaflets. "Hi Matt!" They hugged. "I see you've brought one of your fine teachers." Lillian smiled at Jeanna.

Jeanna smiled back. "Hi Lillian. It's good to see you, especially here." She couldn't believe that Lillian and her husband were involved in all this. Matt and Cam too. And the man she'd been reading about in the papers ever since she moved to town. Could her dream of finding a movement group to join actually be coming true?

Lillian looked down at Carl in the pit, standing as still and centered as he had a half hour ago. "Ma gave me these leaflets to keep me busy and my mind off Carl, but I can't help thinking something's going to happen. Matt, you know how they do black men, especially the strong ones."

"I do, Lil." Matt put his hand on her shoulder.

Jeanna heard a rumble from the crowd, and looked up, surprised at how much it had grown in the last half hour, from thirty to close to one hundred and fifty people, most from the black community. Jeanna saw police gathering not far from the crowd. Now Cam and the tall woman he'd been talking to reporters with were handing out signs and people were holding them aloft. SAVE OUR HOMES! STOP UNIVERSITY EXPANSION! JOBS & HOUSING, YES! SAVE OUR CULTURAL ARTS CENTER!

Police in riot gear began moving the black demonstrators back from the edge of the pit, prodding at them with their batons like they were cattle.

Matt turned to Jeanna. "I need to go, but I think we're bringing new people into the Group next month. I'll let you know, if you want to go?"

"Definitely. I'd love to," Jeanna said.

"Great. See you Monday." He bustled off toward the leaflet table.

"This is campus security," a man's voice boomed through a bullhorn. "You are trespassing on university property. You are obstructing campus construction and causing a public disturbance, disrupting the education of students who attend this university."

The students nearby jeered.

"You're breaking the law. If you do not free yourselves of your chains and leave in fifteen minutes, you will be arrested and taken to jail. Anyone who interferes with our attempts to arrest and jail these men will be arrested and jailed as well. Do you have a spokesperson? I repeat: Do . . . you . . . have . . . a spokesperson?"

No one said a word. No one moved.

Jeanna was struck by the discipline and solidarity of this silence in the face of power.

After a few minutes, two uniformed policemen, not in riot gear, began to escort a gangly young man in white overalls, carrying a metal toolbox, to the edge of the pit. He stopped at the top. His face was drained of all color except for a spray of freckles, dabs of brown paint against a ghost-white canvas. A murmuring arose from the crowd.

"He just a boy," members of the crowd spoke. "Lookit there, they haven a child do the man's job."

One of the officers helped the boy down the steep incline. He slipped on some loose earth and dropped his toolbox. The students near Jeanna whooped and hollered, but the wiry officer scooped the box up in one hand and gripped the boy above the elbow to keep him upright. Jeanna saw him smile reassuringly at the boy. She was annoyed at the college kids. This wasn't a comedy show.

The boy bent down on one knee. He looked up at the massive man in front of him, the Frederick Douglass look-alike. Gideon, that was it. The boy chose a slender rod. He raised it toward Gideon, but he would not extend his hands to be released. The boy held up the rod, waiting. His hands began to tremble noticeably.

A stone whistled by Jeanna through the air, hitting the boy in the back of the neck. She gasped with the rest of the crowd as he went slack, slumping forward on his knees. The cop was by his side in an instant, putting his head down next to the boy's. A bunch of other officers had already grabbed the stone thrower, dragging him along the ground away from the crowd. Other cops jumped in to block his friends from going after him. Cops surrounded the kid, but Jeanna could see through one of their legs. One cop gave him a vicious kick to the lower back and the boy arched backwards. Another rammed him in the stomach with his baton full force, and he snapped forward, his long black hair flopping as he gripped his midsection, gasping. A third cop raised his baton and walloped him behind the ear with a terrible thud. Jeanna's whole body jumped with each blow. The boy sprawled on his stomach, limp.

The cops grabbed him up, handcuffed him, and roughly shoved him face-down into the backseat of a patrol car, spinning dirt as they raced away. Jeanna was worried the kid would be brutalized further once out of public view, but was angry at him for throwing the stone. It discredited what the community was trying to do.

Jeanna looked down into the pit. A gauze bandage had been taped to the back of the young locksmith's neck, but blood was already oozing through. The men chained to the bulldozers looked dismayed by this turn of events. The two officers helped the injured young locksmith climb to the top of the pit, taking most of his weight between them.

A new voice came through the bullhorn. Jeanna recognized it from previous protests; she turned and saw that it was the assistant chief of police. Campus security had been replaced. "If anyone else does anything illegal, we will clear the area."

The place became a tomb. Jeanna caught the shadow of movement and turned to see a van with WILLIAMS LOCKSMITH: SAFE & SECURE written on the side drive around to the far side of the pit, where no one was standing. The driver parked and got out. He was an older black man, wearing old-fashioned denim overalls, his big pockets filled with tools. Round, steel-rimmed glasses gave him a scholarly look. A ripple of surprise went through the crowd.

The same two officers who had helped the other locksmith walked around the circumference of the pit, but as they approached the old man he shook his head and said something, and they stood back. The crowd, already subdued, turned preternaturally silent as he made his surefooted way down the incline. He stood in front of the younger Barnett brother, Abe, who gave him a slight nod, looking relieved. The locksmith bent to his task. In seconds Abe was freed.

The two officers quickly scrambled down the hill and joined him on his left and right. He walked forward stiffly, as if still shackled. As he tried to make it up the incline, his legs buckled. Jeanna realized he must be scared shitless. The wiry officer caught his upper arm and held him up until he regained his footing. In a few steps they made to the top, escorted him into the backseat of a police cruiser, locked him in, and returned to the pit.

The locksmith repeated the process with Carl. When his chains fell to the ground, Carl turned to face Gideon, clearly not going anywhere until he was also freed. Gideon scowled and pulled his hands toward his body, but the locksmith said something and Gideon reluctantly extended his arms to be freed. The newly freed men, flanked by the officers, looked at Land, who nodded. They moved up the hill.

The elder locksmith made his way toward Land, the last man left in the pit. The two men held each other's gaze for a few long moments. Land shook his head slightly. The locksmith let his tools slide out of his hands into a large pocket in his overalls. Before the police could react, he was up the hill and in his van, driving away.

There was no sound from the crowd, no applause, just a soft murmuring.

"He a good man, Mr. Williams."

"That's right, he done the right thing."

"Yes he did, he sure did."

"Will you look at our Land down there?"

"Land? He ain't going *no*where."

"'Course not, he'll stand his ground."

"Yes he will."

The cops began clearing the area. Jeanna saw Lillian being hustled off by Cam and the tall woman into Cam's car, probably on their way to the jail. Matt was helping Ma Carrington walk toward the parking lot.

Jeanna took a last glimpse at Land, who was looking off into the distance where the sun was piercing the clouds with a brilliant gold.

An officer waved his baton at her to move out. Jeanna walked to her car and drove home, the image of Landon Waters, alone at the bottom of the pit, looking off into the distance, still in her mind.

CHAPTER NINE

Promise Me Something

As Jeanna opened the door to her apartment, her mind still whirling from the demonstration, the phone was ringing. She hurried to pick it up.

"Sweetheart, I'm so glad you're home. I've been trying to reach you."

Her mother's tone was sober and quiet.

"Mom? Are you okay?"

"It's your grandmother. She's taken a turn for the worse."

"Oh my god." Jeanna sat down hard, her legs trembling. "How bad is it? I thought she was okay."

"So did we, sweetheart, but she had a heart attack last night. Fortunately Loretta was visiting when it happened and called the ambulance. She's a little better now, she's able to talk, but she's quite weak. We've been at the hospital all last night and all day and just got home. We tried to call you at your job, but the secretary said everyone was off at some staff development session."

"Yes, I was at the U all day. Will she be okay?" Jeanna had gone from hot alarm to cold dread.

"She's holding her own now. Early this morning was the worst. We just didn't know if she was going to pull through . . ." Her mother's voice broke. "But she rallied. As we were leaving, she asked to see you tomorrow."

"Of course, I'll go over right now, if you think I should."

"No, the nurse said she needs to rest. But if you come by here tomorrow morning, we could go over together. Say about nine-thirty?"

"Absolutely, Mom. I'll pick you and Garner up and we can go over in my car."

"Thank you, Jeanna. I know she really wants to see you."

"I just can't believe it . . . she was always the one we . . ." Jeanna couldn't finish. She had somehow gotten it into her head that her grandmother was the one sure thing in life that would always be there, never change, never go away.

"I know, sweetheart." Her mother's voice cracked again.

"Try to get some sleep, Mom, you sound exhausted."

"I'll try, and you too, honey."

Jeanna sat on the edge of her bed, bent over, her hands covering her face, remembering the time her grandmother took her to an outdoor concert, fireflies sparkling in the dark, candle flames flickering behind glass domes, her skin shivering with the vibrations of Jean Pierre Rampal playing "Prelude to the Afternoon of a Fawn." Jeanna had snuggled up to her grandmother afterwards and whispered in her ear, "Do you think I could learn to play the flute like that, Grandma?"

"I sure do," her grandmother had whispered back, hugging her close.

For Jeanna's tenth birthday, her grandmother had given her a fine silver flute, the best birthday present she'd ever received. She'd played it ever since, off and on. More than once it had kept her afloat when she was close to drowning—from her father's leaving, her mother's zombie-like state afterwards, her own lost loneliness.

The next morning, Jeanna picked up her mother and Garner and drove them to the hospital. Garner was such an anchor for her mother, compared to her own father. Jeanna had trusted him from the start, and he had supported her mother's shift from cashier to assistant manager, and now owner, of the nursery. And unlike her father, he didn't need to be the center of attention. He loved her mother, and, by extension, everyone connected to her. Jeanna admired the fact that after years of mourning, her mother had slowly, day by day, week by week, month by month, rebuilt her psyche, her home, her work, her life.

At the hospital, Garner let them walk ahead of him down the hall. Jeanna took her mother's hand. It was icy.

"You okay, Mom?"

"I'm fine!" her mother snapped, a deep groove between her eyebrows, her lips tight.

Jeanna let go of her hand, suddenly feeling as helpless as she had as a teenager when her father left.

Her mother gently squeezed her arm. "I'm sorry sweetheart, I'm just so scared."

"I'm scared too. Do you want me to go in with you?"

"Why don't you let me go in first, then I'll come get you."

Jeanna nodded, relieved. She needed more time to prepare herself.

Her mother reached for Garner, who gave her his arm, and they stepped into the private room.

Jeanna sat on a cold metal chair across from the room. A big clock ticked above her head and a draft of frigid air blew over her body. What if this was it, and her grandmother didn't recover? She crossed her arms and moved her hands up and down her upper arms, trying to keep her fear at bay. In a few minutes, the door opened and her mother and Garner came out. Her mother's face was more relaxed.

"She's doing much better, darling."

Jeanna sprang out of her seat and hugged her mother, a feeling of relief coursing through her.

"Go ahead, sweetheart."

Jeanna walked slowly into the sunny room and saw her grandmother propped up, her face gaunt and pale, almost lost in the plush pillows, but smiling at her. She kissed her grandmother's cheek.

"Well, Jeanna, it looks like I escaped again."

"You better!" Jeanna forced out in a hoarse whisper. "We were so worried."

"Thank you, dear. Now sit here," she patted the bed, "and tell me about you. How's the teaching going?"

"Oh Grandma, I'm here for you, not me," Jeanna said as she sat down.

"Nonsense, my heart skipped a few more beats than usual. I'm better now and I want to hear about my favorite granddaughter."

"*Only* granddaughter," Jeanna said, and they laughed together. "The teaching is wonderful, tough, crazy, scary. Half the time I have no idea what I'm doing and the other half it works like magic."

"I'm so glad they had the good sense to hire you." She patted Jeanna's hand. "You're just what these young kids need."

"I don't know. They're up against so much."

"That's why you're perfect for them, Jeanna. You know something about their real lives."

"Maybe."

"Don't worry, it'll get easier. Is there anything else going on?" She paused. "A new friend, perhaps?"

"Oh no, nothing like that, but I did go to a demonstration yesterday, against university expansion into the community. It was amazing. The leader, Landon Waters, and some other men were chained to the bulldozers, and in the midst of it all I ran into my principal and he invited me to join the group that was leading the protest. It's just what I've been looking for."

Her grandmother smiled at her. "I love to see that passion in you, Jeanna. And that name, Landon Waters, sounds familiar. From the newspapers, maybe. Now how about your music, sweetheart?"

"My music?" Jeanna said blankly. "I barely have time to go to eat, much less play music."

"Oh?"

A nurse came bustling in with medication and left. Her grandmother gathered herself up higher in the bed. "Now Jeanna, there's something I want to tell you. And I need you to promise me something."

"What's that, Grandma?"

"That you won't forget your music."

"But—"

Her grandmother held up her hand. "I know now is not the time. You're busy teaching, and I suspect you'll get involved in this community group. You never were a superficial girl, Jeanna. But you have real talent, real potential, as a musician. So, I've set aside a sum of money for you for music school."

"Grandma!"

Her grandmother put her hand up again. "It's enough to pay full tuition and living expenses so that you can pursue your music if you decide that's what you want to do at some point down the road. You should choose for yourself, but I'm partial to Cardienne, they're much more liberated in their approach than most music schools."

Jeanna was struck by the sound of that, but knew she had let her formal pursuit of music go for far too long. She couldn't imagine going the music route at this point.

"But I'm not nearly as good as you think—"

"Jeanna, you have a gift. It's real. Don't lose it."

They looked at each other for a long moment.

"Should you decide that you don't want to pursue your music, you may use the money for whatever else you wish. So long as you use it strictly for you. But my hope is that you will pursue your music."

"I don't know what to say. You've already been so generous."

"Just promise me, Jeanna, promise me you won't lose yourself."

"I'm not sure what you mean, Grandma." Jeanna was confused. She loved to play the flute, and in some dim way she knew her grandmother had it right, but she couldn't see putting her love for music before all the other things that she'd begun at such a tender age—the struggle against racism, for the right of kids to live and grow and not be thrown onto the scrap heap. Not only that, when she had tried to pursue her music, there had been no place for her . . .

"I know. It's all right. You will someday. Just remember, your dreams are just as important as everyone else's." She reached out to hug Jeanna, who bent toward her and gently embraced her fragile frame. "Thank you for hearing me out. Now I think I'll just close my eyes."

Jeanna saw that she was exhausted, a dry leaf on the pillow.

"Thank you so much, Grandma," she whispered, but her grandmother was already asleep.

CHAPTER TEN

We Were Both Out of Line

AT THE END OF CLASS A COUPLE OF DAYS LATER, Jeanna noticed that Karima was still sitting in her chair, glowering down at her notebook, in no rush to leave. She realized this was an invitation and walked over.

"Everything all right, Karima?" She'd learned that if she phrased a question Karima could disagree with, she was more likely to respond.

"No. Not all right."

"Really."

"Yeah, I wanted to help out with the Panthers breakfast program, but my father won't let me. Said it isn't for girls."

That pissed Jeanna off. What *was* for girls? Still, she found Karima's response unusual. The more radical kids didn't expect their parents to agree with such things, and they went ahead and did what they wanted to anyway.

Karima was looking at her, waiting for a response.

"I probably shouldn't say this, but does he really need to know?"

She saw Karima's eyes fill with fury and regretted her words immediately.

"Who the fuck are you to say?" Karima yelled at her. "I'll fucking do what my goddamn father tells me to do." She lurched up, knocking her chair over backwards.

Tears came to Jeanna's eyes. "Okay, I was out of line," she said, trying to make eye contact.

But Karima ducked her head, muttering, "Fuckin' lily-white, nicey-nice bitch," and walked out.

Ouch. Jeanna knew Karima saw her as sheltered, maybe a bit of a Pollyanna, but . . . Her eyes smarted. She *had* been out of line. Karima was right. She looked up and saw Tommie Lee, still there in the far corner of the room. He turned his head, slipped his notebook under his arm and left.

The rest of the day, Jeanna made her student apprenticeship calls, including to Legal Aid, where Tommie Lee and Felice interned, and the university's music department, where Will was assisting an oral history of the blues. At the end of the day, still demoralized about Karima, she walked into her studio, dead tired, climbed into bed, and slept.

Jeanna had arrived early to the last three Group Inquiry classes, hoping that she'd get a chance to talk with Karima alone, but Karima hadn't shown up. But finally, on the third morning, the door opened, and it was Karima. *Thank god.* Jeanna looked at her as she approached.

"I've been afraid to come in," Karima said, looking vaguely in Jeanna's direction.

"Me too." Jeanna smiled slightly.

"Guess we were both out of line, especially me," Karima said in a rush. "When I lose it, I have a mouth."

"You got my attention. I used really poor judgment in what I said to you. Let's move on, what d'you say?" Jeanna looked directly at her.

"Yeah, let's." Karima looked back at her for a brief second, then took her seat, pulled out a beat-up Nat Turner paperback, and buried herself in it.

Jeanna was just glad Karima was back. The past few days she'd been thinking about what her whiteness and middle-class status might mean to Karima and her other students. She thought about how the regular schools always made it seem like the kids themselves were to blame if they didn't do well.

But Jeanna was acting like everything was possible for them too. She could literally see them ten years hence—Lonnie a licensed electrician, Blue a coach, Felice a civil rights lawyer, Karima a community organizer, Chefman a big-time chef, Cassius a professional drummer, Meta a medical researcher, Valle a great Gospel singer—all their dreams coming true, even when everything, absolutely everything, was stacked against them. What was in the back of her mind was all that needed to change to make their dreams possible, and the ways she needed to help make that happen.

Funny thing was, it was their present they were faced with every grinding day. Lonnie was black and poor, and black men were not allowed into the electricians' union. If he worked under the table, would he earn enough to keep body and soul together? Maybe the struggle to open up these unions to black men would be won by the Group by the time Lonnie was ready. Maybe this was the way to go.

As for Big Blue, you could count the number of black high school coaches in the country on one hand, and they were invariably assistant coaches. Except for the all-black colleges, she knew of no black coaches at the college level. Felice should be a shoo-in for a scholarship into a pre-law program, then law school, but she could expect to be the only black woman law student almost anywhere she went, and maybe she wouldn't get a scholarship after all.

Karima was capable of becoming a great community organizer, but who would ultimately pay her to rabble rouse? Chefman could certainly be a high-class cook. He was well on his way. But could he count on getting a position with decent money? Especially with the mouth on him? Because that was not going to change.

Cassius could certainly learn to play the drums, he had the passion and the balls, but if he needed training, mentoring and actual gigs, would enough someones in the jazz world come through? Would Meta ever make it beyond her family's demands and father's tyranny to go to nursing school, much less fulfill her dream of becoming a medical researcher to help find a cure for cancer? Valle was already one hell of a gospel singer, but who would pay her to sing? Would she keep to her nursing plan, and would that be enough to fill her expansive soul?

Was Jeanna leading her students astray in a white, middle-class way? Is that how they saw her—as a fluffy-headed, "nicey-nice" do-gooder who ignored their reality?

But that was why she had to work to change things, why even as a small child she had known this. She hoped Matt's group would be the answer to at least some of these barriers.

The bell rang and the kids were out the door. Only Karima hadn't left yet. She was fooling with some books on the floor beside the couch where she sat. Jeanna walked over. She sat on the padded arm at the other end of the couch.

"How's it going?" Jeanna asked.

"Not bad. Just finished Nat Turner and the one on John Brown. Nat I got. But ol' man Brown, him I didn't get."

"Why not?" Jeanna asked, knowing exactly what she meant.

"Well. I don't know." She twisted in her seat uncomfortably. "He's white. Why'd a white guy get so hot and bothered about the slave thing?"

"I can't see how a human being couldn't get outraged by it, but as for him, I don't know for sure. I haven't read it. What do you think?"

"Damned if I know. Would you?"

"Would I what?" Jeanna smiled slightly, knowing full well what she was asking.

"You wouldn't put your life on the line like that spook job, would you?"

Jeanna thought back to the student demonstration against racism at the U that had ended with a police riot. Her wrist had been broken and Cam's head had been bashed in. Her wrist still ached something fierce in bad weather or when she was afraid.

"You never know," Jeanna said, massaging her left wrist with her right hand.

"That all you got to say?" Karima looked straight at her, her lips jutting out.

"At the moment," Jeanna said. "Say, how's your dad?"

Karima brightened. "Real good. He's all hepped up. Haven't seen him this happy since . . ." She paused, clearly not sure she wanted to say more. "Since before Ma left."

Jeanna looked at her. This was new. "It's been hard," she said.

"Yeah." Karima looked down. "He don't say it, but he blames himself."

Jeanna waited.

"He's hard to live with."

"How so?"

"He got these set ideas about men and women, right and wrong, and everything else. He and Ma were Muslims. I was raised Muslim. Ma loved it. But after awhile she got sick of it. Right around the time my dad was finally totally into it. He was on the rise. People looked up to him. He was angry she dropped out."

And Karima talked on, telling Jeanna the story of her life: her parents' revolutionary book store, their involvement with the Black Muslims, her mother's free spirit and father's rigidity, her brother's death in Vietnam and her parents' separation, her choice to stay to support her dad while her mother flew off to Berkeley to live. A decision no fifteen-year-old should have to make.

CHAPTER ELEVEN

You Ain't Acting Like We Know You to Be, Tommie Lee

At Check-In the next week, Jeanna asked if anyone had anything to bring up.

"My dad lost his job yesterday," Tommie Lee said.

Jeanna was surprised. Tommie Lee had always supported others during Check-In, but had never said anything about himself.

"That's terrible, what happened?" Karima asked.

"They closed down the whole steel mill. Everyone lost their jobs. And he'd finally just got the promotion he's been fighting for forever." He spoke in an oddly remote voice.

Jeanna had never seen Tommie Lee so out of it. Usually he was so willing and able to handle anything that came up.

"Wasn't there any warning?" Valle asked. "I mean, they must have prepared the workers for what was to come, right?"

"Yeah, right. He was working one day and laid off the next."

Valle narrowed her eyes, probably at his tone.

"But they're going to help them find new jobs, right?" Abby asked.

"Are you kidding? In steel? In this state? Don't you read? Not hardly."

Jeanna knew he was referring to the plant closings that had happened over the past several years. Still, it wasn't like Tommie Lee to respond in such a biting manner to anyone, Abby least of all. Jeanna studied his face. He seemed lost, smoldering beyond anyone's reach. She wondered if something else had also happened that he wasn't telling them.

Abby was clearly hurt; her lips quivered and she tightened them together, looking helplessly through moist eyes at Tommie Lee.

"It must have come as quite a blow to your whole family," Jeanna said.

He shrugged, so far inside himself he didn't seem likely to return any time soon. Jeanna was completely baffled. No matter how awful the job loss was, this was not Tommie Lee.

"What else happened?" Valle asked. "Did sompin' else bad happen in your family with all this goin' on? You ain't acting like we know you to be, Tommie Lee." Her tone was intense and low, and other students nodded, all the feeling in the room infusing every word.

Tommie Lee's head jerked up and whipped around. He looked at Valle for a long, savage moment then sank back into himself again.

Jeanna was beyond her depth and knew it.

"Let's give him some space to regroup from everything that's happened," Jeanna said. "Let us know, Tommie Lee, if we can do anything—job networking, say, with other parents, or help with food, or anything, okay?"

He made no sign of having even having heard her.

"Let's take a short break," Jeanna said, "then get into groups."

During the break, Jeanna went to find Matt, worried about Tommie Lee and not sure what to do. But he was involved in a stand-off between two students. When she came back, she peeked into her own room, looking for Tommie Lee. He was gone, and only half the class had gotten into their groups. She looked outside. The rest of the students were standing in small clusters near one another, obviously worried about Tommie Lee. A hush descended as Jeanna came out on the top step. Without a word, they filed past her and back into the class, filtering into their groups, slowly finding their rhythm again.

CHAPTER TWELVE

Report and Support

JEANNA STEPPED OUT OF HER OFFICE AND LOOKED with satisfaction out over the room. Some groups were brimming over with energy, having impassioned arguments at full volume. Others were more subdued as they scribbled on newsprint. Several individuals had broken off from their group to write in their logs and journals. Even Cassius had dropped back in. Why, she had no idea, and would not be asking. She had given them a half hour to get their act together.

"Okay everyone," she called out, "it's Report and Support time. Let's pull into a circle."

Some students dragged chairs into the circle; others sat on the desk, the couch, the sturdy end tables, the shag rug. Except for Tommie Lee, everyone was there, Jeanna noted with a touch of pride. Still, she had to find out what was happening with Tommie Lee.

"The basketball group went last two weeks ago, so why don't you start," Jeanna said once everyone was settled.

Olly began from his seat on top of the desk, "We did our interviews last week. We met with Ray Hunter, the assistant coach at the U, in the cafeteria. He answered all our questions, and introduced us to the players. We got them talking about our questions and they started having the very same fights we been havin'!" Laughter around the room. "Tommie Lee spoke for us at the start, but after a while we all got into it. It was really cool. We totally hit it off with them. They couldn't get over that we was doin' this for school. They invited us to their games and give them feedback."

Pepper took over from his cross-legged perch on the wide arm of the couch, his hair aflame against the white wall. "The questions we asked were like, 'What do you see as your greatest strengths and weaknesses as a player and a team? Is it more important to have a big star or a blend of good players? Should a coach be a dictator, or a leader who listens to everyone?'"

"Geez, great questions," someone from the UFO group said, and everyone nodded.

Big Blue spoke from the couch. "We got some interesting answers, too. Like our star/team fight, Coach say that sure, star players are very important. If you can get a player who shoots thirty-forty points a game, can pull in over ten rebounds, you got you a diamond mine. But he say you need your craftsmen to round out the jewel,"—this phrasing elicited some "oohs" around the room—"guys who can do a lotta other stuff, too, like be a playmaker, pass to the open man, guard good an tight, steal the ball with three seconds to go an the score tied, you name it."

The boys took turns talking for the next few minutes, sharing what they'd learned from the coach and players, their faces lit up with excitement. When they'd finished updating everyone, Jeanna asked, "And what obstacles have you run into in the past two weeks?"

"Our biggest problem was with Tommie Lee out sick," Olly said. "We called his house but his mom wouldn't let him come to the phone. It sucks after last week being such a high. Now we're fighting with each other."

"What about?" asked Karima.

"We all did all this reading, but we argue like we read totally different books 'stead of the same book. So we just been goin' around in circles." Olly rolled his eyes to laughter.

"Yeah," Pepper said, "so we talked today about taking notes with real page numbers so when we have a difference about what the book says we can take a look at it together."

Jeanna sighed, having suggested this more than once.

"We're also havin' a problem with our follow-through. And we fight all the time. Without Tommie Lee we're like a boat without a rudder."

"Nice job guys," Jeanna said. "Support and feedback?"

"So you-all going to wait till Tommie Lee comes back to get your act together?" Will asked.

"Yeah," Abby said, "can't you figure out what Tommie Lee does that works so well, then some of you do it?"

"Yeah, but it's not that easy," Pepper said.

"It's partly a respect thing," Big Blue said. "Tommie Lee special. We don't want to step into his shoes, realizin' we can't really fill 'em, and then somebody call us out on it, like who do you think you are?"

"Wow, that is what we're doing!" Olly said. "Waiting for the one and only Tommie Lee to lead us lil' chil'ren to the promised land."

"Well, will you listen to me sometimes like you do him?" Pepper asked.

Big Blue laughed.

Pepper's face got red. "See? Just 'cause I'm small, you don't think I can do anything." Pepper was on the verge of tears.

"Yeah," Olly said, staring at Big Blue, "how big you gotta be to be a leader, anyway?"

Big Blue shook his head. "I don't know why I keep doin' that."

"Anyway," Olly continued, "I'm so used to playing the clown, ain't nobody take me serious even when I am."

Jeanna stood up. "Thanks guys. You've done a really great job. You're a lot clearer about what you need to work on. Okay, how about the racial justice group next?"

Karima spoke from the floor, where she was leaning up against the couch. "You guys ain't the only ones fighting. We been goin' at it too.

Abby helped us see it didn't have to be just one way, but when Abby was out sick, we was back at it like cats and dogs. Felice's into the law and all the proper-correct ways of going about things, but I'm pulled into all the liberation movements everywhere. I'm reading Fanon, Malcolm, everything I can get my hands on.

"I say Felice is too technical-like, everything by the book, but she says I'm too all over the place, which I am, but I have to be." Her voice had become a hoarse whisper. "It's life or death for the race. I question everything now. I'm mad all the time."

"What's the matter with being mad?" Will asked. "Seems to me you got plenty of reason to be mad. I get mad just hearing you talk about it."

"Yeah, maybe mad is good," Cassius said.

Abby spoke from atop the end table near Karima. "I think Will and Cassius are right. I get angry too, and sick, reading about all the racial brutality that just keeps going on and on. And I do think Felice's law stuff and Karima's radical action in the streets are both important. I've been reading everything they turn me on to.

"But Felice asked me a question last week that brought me up short. She asked what my part is in all this. Am I just an innocent bystander or is it my struggle too? I said I want to be involved and make a difference, but Karima said it's none of my affair, it's a struggle for black people."

Some nods around the room by both black and white students.

"But it's a question I've been thinking about ever since. Why am I in this group? Why do I hang on every word they say? Is it really none of my affair?"

"Vat did you come up with?" Meta asked.

"I'm still thinking."

Karima gave an angry half-snort, and Cassius followed suit.

"C'mon guys," Olly said. "Giv'er a break."

Jeanna smiled inside. Olly was finally growing up.

"But so far," Abby continued, "this is what I've come up with: I do care. I'm not faking it. It just seems to me if white people are the ones keeping black people from their rights, white people should do something about it."

"Like what?" Wesley asked quietly.

"I'm still thinking."

Karima laughed again, short and edgy, but she was scowling like she did when she was wrestling with something.

"I think you cut to the heart of the issue, Abby," Jeanna said. "Let us know where you all get with this next time." She turned to Wesley. "Wesley, you part of this report?"

"They covered it pretty well."

Jeanna remained silent, waiting to see if anyone would draw him out. No one did. "Okay for today, but everyone is supposed to be part of the report, and I seem to recall you didn't have much to add last time either. Don't forget, everyone needs to present on Project Day." Jeanna knew he'd actually never contributed at Report and Support, but didn't want to humiliate him.

Wesley shrugged, his brow furrowed, body tense. "What if you don't want to present?"

"Yeah," Lonnie said, looking at Jeanna, "what if we not ready to present on parents' project day?"

"Thanks everyone," Jeanna said. "I see real deep work going on in your group. Anyone who's uncomfortable presenting on Project Day should see me on Monday. In the meantime, try thinking of ways to present that will be comfortable for you. And I want to leave you all with two questions to explore in your journals. First, we all have a sense of what leadership means out there in the world, like being the big man in charge, but what do you think real leadership is or should be, and who can and can't be leaders in your view?" She looked around the room into their faces. "The second question has to do with the value of anger. We're often told not to be angry, but what is anger good for? How can it be helpful instead of harmful? Oh, actually, I have one more for you: Whose responsibility is it to overcome racism—those who seem to benefit from it, or those who are most hurt by it?"

She was satisfied to see all of the students scribbling down the questions in their journals.

Later that day, Jeanna stuck her head in Matt's office. It was late, going on five, but she knew he was just getting started on all the administrative work he had to do.

"Matt, do you have a minute?" She felt awkward. She'd never sought support before and worried it might make her seem incompetent.

"Sure Jeanna, come on in." He cleared a space for her to sit.

"It's about Wesley Brooks. He's one of the most promising students in my group class, but I don't know if he's done a stitch of work since school started."

"Tough nut to crack," Matt said, nodding. "Have there been any conflicts or incidents with him in the class?"

"No, he's just very quiet. I've felt since the first day that he's in sync with the school, but I can't get him to do anything. I wonder if he needs a black man for his group project teacher, say Jakim or Roy."

"Yet you've done wonders with Olly, who's impossible from what I've heard . . . and who's that kid with the perpetual split lip? Lonnie?"

She nodded.

"And that jumpy kid, what's his name?"

"Cat." Jeanna had no idea Matt had even noticed all this. "Thanks," she said, "but Wes has me buffaloed. You don't think he might be better off in another class?"

"No. I would hold off on that."

"Do you mind my asking why?"

"It's instinct, mainly, but Wesley's attending much more than he did in his previous school. He may not be on fire, but my guess is he's absorbing more than you think. Your analysis has merit, though. I know his family, and he does need black men in his life. These issues are central for him, so you're right on the mark."

"But?"

"But he has access to Roy in his science class now, and Jakim for college math next term. I'd rather place him with Roy for Group Inquiry next year so it will be seen as a normal transition, not a special move that will draw attention to his alleged dysfunctionality."

"But what if he is dysfunctional? Or I am? I feel like a failure with him."

"He's not dysfunctional, and you're not a failure. He's finding his way in the program and so are you. I think you are actually the best group teacher for him his first year with us precisely because he needs someone who won't hammer away at him from without, but will let the pressure within him build until he can't stand himself." He smiled. "Let me assure you, he has plenty of strong folks hammering away at him to live up to their extremely high expectations."

"So you think his family's expectations are too high?"

"No, but I do think you're a good balance for where he is in his development right now."

She got up to go, feeling twenty pounds lighter. "Thanks, Matt."

"Any time, Jeanna."

"Could I ask you about one more thing?"

"Sure," he said, but was looking down at a file.

"It's Tommie Lee."

Matt jerked his head up again.

"He seemed really out of it at Check-In a week ago. Kind of mad? We're all worried about him. He said his dad lost his job, but it seemed like something else too. And he missed class all this week."

Matt looked troubled. "I'll definitely follow up with his parents, thanks for telling me; I'll get back to you on it."

"Thanks a lot." She got up to go.

"By the way," Matt said, "do you still want to connect with the political action group? The next meeting is this Wednesday at the West Side Center."

"Absolutely."

"Good. It starts at seven. I'll meet you ten minutes early at the front door."

"Thanks, Matt!" She sailed out of his office, excited about his invitation.

CHAPTER THIRTEEN

He's Always Been a Real Fine Boy

WEDNESDAY EVENING JEANNA WAS WAITING FOR Matt in front of the West Side Community Center, excited about going to her first meeting of the group that had instigated the big demo at the U. She was nervous, though, at the prospect of seeing Cam after all this time, and even more intimidated by the possibility of meeting Landon Waters. She was glad Matt would be with her.

She saw him coming toward her, a smile on his face. He led her down the cracked sidewalk, and leaned against the heavy door. Metal scraped along the concrete floor as it swung open. The rich aroma of freshly brewed coffee greeted them. They walked past a darkened office—MR. GIDEON BARNETT, DIRECTOR was the nameplate on the door—and rounded the corner to a long table laden with refreshments. A stick-thin elderly woman was busy behind the table. Her beige hands fluttered birdlike across the table as she laid out paper napkins, plastic forks, and cups. Her grey hair was pulled back into a bun, and steel-rimmed glasses were perched forward on her nose. She disappeared back into the kitchen as Matt and Jeanna walked over and helped themselves to cake and coffee. Jeanna thought she looked familiar and asked Matt if she was the one who chaired the group.

"That's right, Ma Carrington. She always takes care of the food, and a million other things. I'll introduce you when she comes out."

A wide doorway opened into the next room, where a number of people were already sitting, many chatting while they waited for the meeting to start. Matt pointed to the far side of the room.

"There's Lillian and Carl."

"Oh, great, I'm glad they're here." Ever since connecting with Lillian around the foot-crushing episode with Olly and Jam, and at the demonstration at the university construction site, Jeanna had been wanting to get to know her better. She noticed that the Johnsons were completely quiet, almost stoic, as they sat there. There was a dignity about them as a couple—and a somberness.

"That's Land over in the corner in the black sweater."

Jeanna barely recognized him. It was hard to match this quiet, slender figure with the legendary status he had acquired in her mind after seeing him chained to the bulldozer in the pit. She thought about Matt saying that Land knew everyone and was into everything in the city that had to do with change. She wondered how he did all that.

"Does Land have a family?"

"Well, yes and no," Matt said. "His wife, Pearl, is rarely around. She has a mental illness of some kind and stays in a rehab center out of state most of the time. They have a daughter, but I believe another family member is taking care of her on the West Coast."

A very familiar man was talking to Land, but Jeanna could only see his back. His powerfully rounded shoulders brought up a visceral recognition just as Matt said, "And that's Cam, Land's right-hand man. But you know him."

"Oh, yeah," she said, and they exchanged a knowing smile. "Whatever else he is, he's a heck of a political strategist."

"He is that," Matt said.

Cam shifted in his seat, and Jeanna felt the familiar surge of electricity swirl inside her, then evaporate. She was the only woman she knew who had known Cameron Vandencamp and not slept with him.

She had wanted to in the worst way, but he had never come anywhere near stating any real feelings for her, so she'd always backed off—which, happily, had strengthened their political bond, and his respect for her.

Matt nudged her out of her reverie. "See the man coming in?"

"Wasn't he one of the men chained to a bulldozer? Gideon?"

"Good memory. He's director of the center here."

Gideon lifted a hand of greeting to Land in the far corner, and took a slice of cake from the table.

Matt stuck out his hand, saying, "Hey Gideon." Gideon took it mechanically and said, "Matt." Matt put his hand on Jeanna's arm to introduce her, but Gideon glanced at her, turned away, and walked toward Land. Jeanna withdrew her hand, embarrassed.

A few boys were shooting pool not far from the entrance. Before he took a seat next to Land, Gideon looked their way and flicked his fingers. Within seconds they had vanished out the door. Jeanna was impressed, and repelled, by the arrogance of it.

Ma Carrington reappeared from the kitchen.

"Ma, I want you to meet Jeanna Kendall," Matt said. "She teaches with us over at West Side. Jeanna, Ma Carrington."

"Nice to meet you," Jeanna said.

"Likewise," Ma said. She set down a platter of cheese and crackers and looked right into Jeanna's eyes as if appraising her.

Jeanna felt like she'd already transgressed in some way. Odd.

Matt took her arm. "It looks like they're ready to start, let's find some seats."

As Jeanna and Matt walked to their seats, she noticed out of the corner of her eye that Land was looking at her. Cam was gesturing toward her and talking animatedly to Land. Jeanna wondered what he was saying. He'd always made way more of her than she was, but she liked that. It gave her something to shoot for.

Ma Carrington had already taken a seat behind a small table facing the group.

Matt touched Jeanna's shoulder. "See the woman in back with the notebook? Long black hair?

"Yes?" Jeanna was struck by the woman's beauty: tall and willowy, chiseled features, tan skin, long silver earrings.

"That's Land's right hand, Helene Bouve."

"I thought Cam was," Jeanna whispered.

"Well, actually they both are. Two peas in a pod. Very sharp."

"Well folks, glad to see you all here tonight on such a cold, damp evening," a man bellowed into the low buzz of the room. Between thirty and forty people were there—mostly black, a few white.

"That's Reverend Barrows," Matt whispered.

"I especially want to thank Ma here for her spread, which is mighty delicious, as usual." Reverend Barrows beamed at her, and a number of people clapped.

Ma stirred uncomfortably. "I'm quite sure people want to get down to business, Tom," she said crisply.

"Quite right, that's just what we'll do," Reverend Barrows said. "But first I want to welcome the newcomers. Matt, could you introduce the lovely young lady?"

Matt stood. Jeanna felt her face get hot. "I'd like to introduce Jeanna Kendall, a teacher at West Side Alternative High. Jeanna's been a real godsend to the program, and I think she'll have a lot to offer the Group."

Jeanna blushed with surprise at Matt's words.

"We have two committee reports tonight. Mary, you ready?" the reverend bellowed.

Jeanna was annoyed with his need to yell.

"Well I'm happy to report that after two years we finally have our Teen Health Center up and running at Jefferson High, where I'm the school nurse. I will be manning it every Tuesday and Thursday from three to four, and one Wednesday evening a month we'll have a teen health workshop. We also have a public health intern facilitating a weekly peer counseling group."

A hand went up.

"Yes?"

"What's the topic for the first workshop?" a young woman asked.

"Sex and pregnancy prevention."

A few "oohs" rippled around the room. Land was smiling.

"Well, these are the things on the kids' minds, and I'm just glad they were honest about their concerns," Mary said. "I want to thank everyone here who's helped out: Helene, Jody, Land, Lillian, Matt"—she paused—"and Frederick." She sat down to a loud round of applause.

A tall, slender, well-dressed man got up to speak without seeking acknowledgement from the chair.

"I just want to say how pleased we are with the health center and Mary's dedication. I know, because we've worked with her every step of the way."

"Remember him?" Matt whispered.

Jeanna was puzzled, then it came to her. The guy at the demo who'd given her the once-over. She nodded, making a face. He grinned, whispering, "Actually, he didn't do a thing." Jeanna nodded, thinking of all the guys she'd met in different groups who were all talk and no action. Cam was the exception; if anything, he took on too much.

Reverend Barrows was explaining at full volume, "For those of you who don't know, Frederick Holmes is the principal over at Jefferson. Thank you, Frederick, very much indeed."

Ma Carrington looked annoyed. She moved her head in Gideon's direction while another patter of applause was heard.

"Mr. Gideon Barnett will give the next report," the reverend boomed.

"This'll be short," Gideon said, rising. "The police chief has refused our request to meet with him around establishing a police community review board. So we've lined up some youth and men who have been brutalized and have appointments to meet with several state reps and city counselors next week. We want them to call for a hearing on police brutality that will result in a proposal for the review board."

Lonnie had just told Jeanna yesterday in their reading and writing group about how the cops made quite a sport out of picking up guys like him and dropping them off on other gangs' turf, where they were beaten within an inch of their lives.

"Any other committee reports?" Reverend Barrows cast a look all around the room.

"None of the other committees are functioning, Tom," Ma Carrington cut in testily, "you know that." She tapped her pencil on the next item on the agenda.

"Well now," he said, "we do greatly appreciate Mr. Gideon Barnett's efforts on behalf of those folks who have been so sorely mistreated."

Ma Carrington whispered something to Reverend Barrows, who said, "Yes, yes of course," and looked directly over at the Johnsons, who had remained silent so far.

"The Johnsons, Carl and Lillian"—he smiled and gestured in their direction—"would like to share something with us this evening, and I think we all need to listen real close to what they have to say."

Carl tightened his grip on his wife's upper arm and let go. She stood up.

"Carl and I couldn't stay quiet any longer," Lillian said in a soft but intense tone. "I guess we're just at a loss as to what to do. Some of you know our Tommie Lee . . ." Her voice broke.

Jeanna was immediately alarmed. Tommie Lee had been out of class, but she had been told that he was sick.

Lillian took a breath and smoothed her hands on her dress. "He's our oldest, and he's always been a real fine boy."

"That's the Lord's truth," a heavyset woman with a frizzle of grey hair intoned from the front row.

"We hate to speak aloud about it, but Tommie Lee's been arrested."

There was a sharp intake of breath around the room, and a loud, involuntary "No!" erupted from nearly everyone there, Jeanna included.

Jeanna was shocked to the core. She couldn't believe it. Not Tommie Lee.

"He's in jail now," Lillian continued through the gasps and outbursts of denial. "They won't let him out and he won't speak to Carl because of his shame."

Her husband stared straight ahead.

"It seems like all the trouble started when Carl got laid off at the steel mill and couldn't find work anywhere." She hesitated and looked down at her husband. He nodded slightly. "And there were other issues, too, but since he lost his job, Carl got a part-time job at the A & P bagging groceries and doing maintenance after hours. Money's been slim, and our two other little boys been getting into fights at school since they started standing in the poor kids' lunch line.

"I guess Tommie Lee decided to take matters into his own hands. He was picked up for crossing state lines in a car with drugs and guns in it. He had no idea about what was in the trunk of that car. Some older men said they'd pay him good money to drive the car to such and such a place and he agreed. His lawyer says it's a shame, but he'll go to Chisolm's Farm no matter what." Lillian broke down, tears streaming down her face. She sat back down.

Carl stood up. "We don't want you to think we want special favors for Tommie Lee. If he has to do his time, we'll stand by him every day until he gets out and hope he's still our boy when he does. But we want help from the Group to see how we can cut this cycle. A lot of families are in the same trouble. Thanks for hearing us out." He sat down and put his arm around Lillian's shoulders.

Jeanna looked at them and then at Land, whose face seemed strangely bleached out. His legs were stretched out in front of him, crossed at the ankle, and he was staring at the floor. There was a long silence as everyone in the room took it in. She wondered why Land seemed so removed.

A hand went up.

"Abraham?"

"Carl, if you come by the labor hall Monday morning at six-thirty they may be putting more construction workers on at the U."

"Much obliged," Carl said, nodding to him.

Another youngster with a wild Afro had his hand up.

"Young man!" the reverend bellowed.

The young man gave him a hard, slow look. "How comes Tommie Lee goin' up to Chisolm's so quick? Ain't this his first offense? He a do-good dude, not like us." His two friends laughed proudly, their Afros sticking out a full six inches.

A confusion of murmuring filled the room.

Lillian stood up again. The room fell silent.

"You right that Tommie Lee's been a good boy, not that he ever put hisself above anyone else. But he did have some other offenses."

A surprised buzz riffled across the room.

"These was for him sticking up for other youngsters getting beat," Lillian continued through the noise. "Once by other boys and once by the police. And once for protecting a girl at a demonstration. He caught the cop's stick 'fore it hit her head, and they beat him bad and arrested him."

The group erupted. "That's our Tommie Lee!" "He's no trouble maker. Trouble gotta come find him!" "He deserve a medal, not no detention center."

"So he wasn't doing wrong, but officially, he does have a record," Lillian finished.

The boy nodded at her respectfully as she sat down.

"That's why we need our review board." Gideon's voice cut through the seething resentment.

Cam put his hand up.

"Cameron?" the reverend acknowledged him.

"I want to go back to what Carl said about the plant closings. This is a long-term strategy, I know, but out in Seattle the workers took over a lumber mill that they were going to close down, and they're running it themselves as a co-op. Maybe we could explore something like that here."

Jeanna saw Land sit up straighter at that.

"A co-op what?" Abe asked, looking irritated.

"It's when the workers get together to run a business themselves and share in the profits," Cam said. "It's a lot of work, but it's doable. There's a whole region in Spain that runs on this model—everything, industry, banks, schools, hospitals . . ."

Jeanna remembered studying that with Cam as her TA in her political economy class at the U, but would never have had the wherewithal to suggest it in this situation.

"Whoa there, boy, you always got these big ideas outta a book, but I ain't never seen none a that," Abe said.

"I have, Abe. My brother has been developing co-ops in Ghana going on ten years." Land's quiet, husky voice had caught everyone's attention. "Maybe we should set up a group to explore it here."

Abe still looked confused, but shut up.

Ma started a clipboard going around. It came to Matt and Jeanna first. She saw three different committees listed to choose from: a Youth Detention Diversion Committee, a Job Networking Committee, and a Business Co-op Development Committee. Ma sure was quick: Jeanna signed up for the Youth Committee, no contest.

"I surely do want to thank Lillian and Carl for sharing that with us." Reverend Barrows had returned to his hearty style. "We know it wasn't easy. And I'd like to get my hands on the men who manipulated that boy. I've never met a finer young man."

Jeanna was beginning to like Reverend Bellows, as she'd begun to think of him.

Everyone clapped long and hard in Lillian and Carl's direction. Tears began streaming down Lillian's face again. Carl's remained impassive. This time she saw Land looking at them, his lips tight, jaw set hard.

After that, announcement after announcement was made about virtually everything under the sun, the most important being the need for volunteers to help design the new Community Cultural Arts Center, one of the victories from the bulldozer demonstration.

After the announcements, Ma Carrington took over the chair role from Reverend Barrows. She looked at the names on the clipboard, then peered over it at the group.

"Thank you. It looks like just about everyone here has signed up for something." She looked out at the young man in the back who had spoken up about Tommie Lee. "I'd like to suggest that Jody Terrell and Lillian Johnson convene the Youth Detention Diversion Committee. Is that satisfactory to everyone?"

Lillian and Jody nodded, and everyone clapped.

"And Abraham, I would like to suggest that you and Carl co-convene the Jobs Networking group?"

Abraham looked up at her and smiled angelically. "Ma, you know I would do just about anything you want."

Ma looked over her glasses at him. "Thank you, Abraham. Carl?"

Carl nodded. "I appreciate having something to do."

Ma looked down at the clipboard. Jeanna could see some of it from where she sat. There were three stars next to Gideon's name. "I gather you're interested in the Co-op initiative, Gideon?" Ma said.

He nodded.

"Well then, let me suggest that you and Cam co-convene the Co-op Committee with Land as ex-officio."

They all nodded.

"Co-conveners should meet and call everyone on their lists and set up a first meeting to plan specific goals and begin to make some progress on them to report at our next meeting." She peered over her glasses at the room. "Alright, then, a very productive meeting. And I would like to extend my gratitude to Lillian and Carl as well."

There was one last round of applause.

"We are adjourned," Ma said in a crisp, satisfied tone.

Jeanna was impressed with the whole night. She had finally found her political niche. If they'd have her.

She went over to Lillian and offered her a hug, one of many she was receiving, and was surprised at how strongly Lillian hugged her back. Carl was shaking hands and saying, "We appreciate it," over and over. Jeanna extended her hand. He gripped it firmly and looked her right in her eyes.

Matt appeared at her side. "You okay getting home, Jeanna?"

"I'm fine, Matt. Thanks so much for inviting me. It seems like a great group."

"I thought it'd be a good fit," he said.

"I'm shocked about Tommie Lee, though," she said.

"Yeah, we all are. It's a damn shame. We need to find a way to get him out." He glanced at his watch. "I've gotta run. See you tomorrow!"

He hurried out. Jeanna looked over at Cam, and was relieved to see that he was busy talking with Gideon and Land, probably about the co-op thing. She wasn't ready to deal with him yet, or to meet the great Landon Waters. She strode out of the meeting and out into the cool night air.

Saturday morning the phone rang loudly, waking Jeanna out of a dream she'd wanted to stay in. She tried to catch the fleeting images, but they were gone. She looked at the clock. Who would call her at seven on a Saturday morning? She picked up.

"Hey," uttered a familiar male voice.

No name was given—an arrogance of Cam's that used to repel yet attract her. She didn't speak.

"Jeanna?"

"Yes?"

"It was really good to see you at the meeting."

For Cam, such minor niceties as stating one's own name, or the other person's, or thanking someone, was completely superfluous.

Jeanna's annoyance mixed with a perverse pleasure. Her communications with Cam were always laced with a potentially costly seductive tinge. The upside was that around Cam she always felt about ten times more capable than she normally felt.

"Hi Cam. Good to hear from you. That was some meeting."

"Yeah, that's partly why I'm calling . . ."

Jeanna's pleasure point dipped. This wasn't personal, then. He was in his inimitable organizing mode.

"If you want flyers about the Group to share with parents at your school, you can pick them up at the office before noon today."

"The office?"

"Yes. The Group has a storefront at 402 Pine Street. Helene should be there."

"Helene?" She wanted to hear him describe her. Knowing Cam, he was probably sleeping with her.

"Helene holds down the fort, pretty much. She's good. Takes care of business."

High praise coming from Cam, the all-time know-how-to-take-care-of-business guy. She wanted to meet this Helene, but it made her nervous as hell.

"Thanks, maybe I will drop by."

"Great. Let's hook up soon, okay?"

"Sure, let's." Jeanna said. His words were deliberately ambiguous. It was impossible not to feel attracted to the man. He was handsome, committed, courageous, and effective. But such a jerk.

After breakfast, she drove down to the office, curious and apprehensive. If Helene was Land's and the group's "right hand," then she would have a big say in whether or not there would be a place for Jeanna in the group.

The office was in a modest-sized, two-story building in a low-income area, mainly black.

She knocked softly on the store front door, not wanting to barge in. Getting no response, she knocked again, louder this time.

"It's open!"

Jeanna stepped inside. The blue-and-white linoleum floor gleamed, a row of tall black file cabinets stood at attention, the windows were washed, and the sun shone on the clean white walls. Labeled boxes of literature were neatly stacked in corners. Long tables, completely free of clutter, had chairs tucked in around them.

Helene sat behind a large metal desk. Her black hair was swept into a loose French twist, accentuating her high cheekbones; turquoise and silver rings decorated her slender fingers. She looked up from her typewriter. "Can I help you?"

"I got a call from Cameron Vandencamp this morning saying I could pick up some flyers here for the parents over at West Side Alternative High. I came to the meeting last Wednesday."

"Oh, of course. You must be Jeanna. Cam told me you might drop by." Helene smiled, a flash of white teeth, then walked to a file cabinet, reached in and pulled out a large yellow envelope. As she handed it to Jeanna, she said, "If you're not doing anything tonight, would you like to meet Cam and me over at Jason's Pub near the U? We're going to talk over future directions for the group and we'd love to have you join us."

Jeanna was surprised and flattered, excited that Helene and Cam were including her in their inner circle so quickly. *But why are they meeting in private about the group's future?*

"I'd like that," Jeanna said, "though I'm not sure what I can offer, being so new to the whole thing."

"Cam told me you took the U by storm a couple years back." Helene flashed her smile again.

"Oh." Jeanna laughed, looking away. "I don't know. We did a few things."

Helene had returned to her seat at the typewriter.

"Thanks for the flyers. See you at Jason's around eight?"

"That's fine. Look for us way in the back."

CHAPTER FOURTEEN

It Just Slipped Out

After a long Saturday correcting papers and calling parents, Jeanna drove over toward the U. Jason's Pub was crowded and noisy. Puerto Ricans and Blacks, Irish and Italians, Asians and East Indians bobbed and wove, argued, laughed, and burst into occasional song. Jeanna loved it. She threaded her way through the first room into the next, where she found Cam and Helene in intense conversation in the far corner booth. Cam waved at her without interrupting his thought. She squeezed in next to him.

"I see you found us through this hellish crowd," Helene said with a smile.

Cam said, "Hey, Jeanna," and kept talking.

Thirty minutes later, they were still going at it. They were definitely calling the group's shots, Jeanna realized, with Land as a kind of anchor or touchstone. A pattern of arrogance emerged from under all of the complicated give and take. Jeanna's fingers curled tightly around the wooden lip of her seat to keep from being blown out of the booth by it. Arrogant power games rubbed against her grain more than anything else.

"She just isn't capable of handling that piece. It's too big. It'll blow up in her face, in our face, and she won't even know what happened," Helene said.

"So what did you tell her?" Cam had to yell over the rising din.

"Nothing, but I was talking to Land a few hours later, and he said he'd ask Gideon to handle it at the next meeting. That should take care of it." She turned to Jeanna. "So, what brings you to the big city, to teach in the toughest neighborhood in town, and to come to radical political meetings?"

That was a mouthful, and implied a degree of courage on Jeanna's part. She liked this Helene.

"You should have seen Jeanna at the U," Cam said. "The administration didn't know what hit them."

Helene looked intrigued. "You started to tell me about that the other day; tell me more."

"The radical faculty went out on strike," Cam said, "for a great African-American studies teacher who'd been axed by the administration. Then the TAs, and the teacher's students, with Jeanna in the lead, went out in support. But the faculty caved in and never told Jeanna. She stood her ground and the TAs stood with her. Then nearly all the students in the social science department went out too, and they shamed the faculty. The administration reinstated the teacher a week later. It was a real moment of glory." Cam was beaming at her.

Jeanna remembered that "moment of glory" as one long migraine of contradictions and betrayals. And while it was true that her personal relationships with TAs and student leaders had helped to turn the tide, the aftertaste had been more bitter than sweet. Her closest faculty mentors had turned their backs on her, and she'd had to leave the Politics and Sociology department to find another school entirely—the Ed School.

"Well, I'm impressed," Helene said.

"Tell me more about the Group," Jeanna said. "I'm still not clear what I can offer or where I might fit in."

Cam waved away her words. "Nonsense."

But her self-doubt was genuine. She yearned for an ounce of Cam and Helene's self-confidence—without the arrogance. The two of them were literally rubbing their hands together with relish at sharing their plans for the group, their plans for her.

"We've got maybe a third of the city organized, a big piece of the North Side and some of the Southwest," Cam said. "Forget the Northeast—that's too white, backwards, and corrupt—but we do want to make more inroads on the West Side, and the Northwest Side where you teach."

"Doing what?"

"We want to start with the schools and parents. We think a number of spots on the School Committee will open up in the next election, and several on City Council, which could tip both well left of center. If Land decides to run for Mayor a few years after winning a city-wide council seat, we could push a progressive agenda across the board. It could change the face of the city. Five other cities are likely to go that way over the next few years as well: Oakland and Detroit are already on their way, and Chicago, Milwaukee and Atlanta look good, which leaves us in the Northeast."

Jeanna was shocked at their scope. She had forgotten how grandiose Cam could get. Was he serious?

"I don't know what to say. I thought this was a fairly small grassroots community group."

"Cam gets carried away." Helene said. "That's a long-range vision, and right now a bit of a pipe dream. You're absolutely right, we are relatively small, but the potential for a lot more is there—we sense it every day with everyone we talk to. Land is the key. He's managed to make contact, personally, with half the people who live in the city, and they trust him and respect what he's—we've—tried to do all these years. It feels like we're on the verge of something major, and we're looking for people like you with the savvy and energy to move it to the next level."

This was a much taller order than Jeanna had imagined. Organizing with peers and neighbors was one thing; taking over the Eastern seaboard, or even the city, another. She felt honored that they thought she could make a difference. But she was bothered by the way they seemed to own the Group's future.

"We don't want you to think you have to take on the world here," Helene said, as if reading her thoughts. "It's more the grassroots organizing and base-building through the schools, the parents and the teachers, that matters to us. As a teacher who works with kids and their parents, you're well situated to reach out and help create a progressive network that could move our agenda forward."

"But what's the *group's* agenda?" Jeanna blushed. It had just slipped out, but she wasn't going to take it back.

Helene's and Cam's eyebrows shot up, and they exchanged a split-second look. Jeanna pretended not to notice. She hadn't meant to be so blunt, but she hated it when people thought they were above the process. Her face felt prickly hot in the silence.

"It's essentially what we've been saying, Jeanna," Cam tried to smooth things over. "We've had a series of strategy sessions that virtually everyone in the Group has participated in, and what has come out of that year-long process is pretty much what we've been telling you about tonight, though cast in shorter-run terms. You're not going to find a more democratic group anywhere—it's been the key principle with us from the start."

"Great," Jeanna said, smiling. She was still a bit uneasy, though. And she could sense Helene taking her measure anew, but couldn't tell if the other woman liked or disliked what she saw.

Cam was getting ready to leave. It was already 10 p.m. He squeezed her shoulder and said, "Jeanna, I don't know anyone who can handle this education piece better than you."

"This is real important to Land too," Helene added. "He'll want to meet with your committee periodically, and you won't be alone out there. We'll all be backing you up. Lillian Johnson and Matt Jensen are involved, and a few others you haven't met yet."

That did it. Jeanna hadn't expected Land to be that involved, and she loved the idea of working with Lillian and Matt.

"Well, count me in," she said. "I just hope I can handle half of what you seem to think I can."

Jeanna and Helene ordered another round of beer after Cam left, and their conversation became much more intimate. Helene seemed to have decided Jeanna was someone she could be open with—she told her all about how, when she was just finishing high school, her father, a Red, had been killed on the waterfront in Seattle by an opposing union faction, and her mother, drunk with sorrow, had crashed into a telephone pole a year later and died instantly.

"The longshore union guys gave me a college fund—enough to get me through all four years—so I put thousands of miles between me and my past, moved here, and majored in Urban Planning and Community Development at the U. I met Land there, got involved in the Group, and the rest is history."

Jeanna raised her beer mug. "That's a hell of a story." They clinked their glass mugs together.

The lights brightened and waiters began stacking chairs on top of the tables. Most people had already left. Jeanna looked at her watch.

"I can't believe it. It's 1 a.m.!" Jeanna exclaimed.

"I hope I haven't talked you to death."

"Not at all, I was hanging on every word. You've had a tough ride."

Out in the parking lot Jeanna gave Helene a hug before parting ways to go to their cars. "Let me know how I can help out down at the storefront, okay?"

"I will. Thanks, Jeanna."

Jeanna settled behind the wheel, one of only six cars in a lot that had held hundreds just hours ago. She couldn't believe that she and Helene seemed already on their way to becoming friends. So many wonderful things were happening, finally, in her life.

CHAPTER FIFTEEN

Jam

JAM WAS AS REMOTE AS EVER. AFTER CLASS ONE Monday, everyone had gone on to their next class but him. He sat in the shadows at the far end of the table, more fixture than student.

Jeanna walked over, a now-or-never feeling in her gut. "I'd like to talk with you," she said, "but not here. It's nothing bad."

Jam looked at her, his face a granite wall.

"How 'bout my car? Just to talk."

He moved his huge shoulders a fraction of an inch.

"Great." She turned to go, wondering if he would follow her.

She heard his chair scrape, and felt his presence behind her. He walked lightly for a big man in those heavy boots.

She walked with purpose down the hall. He followed at a distance. No one was in the parking lot, thank god. Jeanna got into the driver's seat of her blue Falcon, and stretched across the seat to open his door. He scrunched his powerful frame into the passenger seat and looked straight ahead.

She gripped the cold steering wheel. "Jam, I know this school isn't meeting your needs. I can tell none of it's really helping you. So what do you want?"

Stone silence. She held her breath.

"Isn't there anything you want to learn?"

He was all hard gray rock. Jeanna forced herself to remain quiet for what felt like an eon. The tension rose and surrounded them like a thick mist.

"Work on cars," Jam said.

She breathed again, thrilled. "Auto mechanics?"

He nodded.

"That's good to know. Anything else?"

He shook his head.

"Do you mind my asking where your home is?"

"Don't have none."

"Where do you live then, sleep at night, eat?" Her voice was almost a whisper.

"Pool hall." He gestured up the street. "Sleep on a bench. Man own it give me some pizza for cleaning up after he close down."

That explained his ashy gray skin, the color of a deathly tired, old black man.

"Want to live somewhere else? DYS? Foster Care?"

"Too old."

"Okay. Thanks Jam. I'll let you know if I can set something up."

He unfolded carefully and eased out of the car. She watched him walk slowly across the lot, knowing that he could turn on a dime and kill any fool who meant him harm.

After work Jeanna decided not to waste any time. She looked in the Yellow Pages for auto mechanics in the neighborhood near the school and came up empty. She knew there was at least one that she saw on her way to work. She could start there. She desperately needed the exercise; she decided to walk. It was cold out, but thankfully not windy.

At the first place she tried, Charles Brown, the owner turned her down, saying, "Can't do it, got too much to handle as it is. Don't have time to mold a kid like that. Wouldn't take anyway." He waved her away.

"Sorry to bother you," Jeanna said and walked away, demoralized but not about to give up. She walked quite a ways with no luck, and the few people she asked said they didn't drive and didn't know any auto mechanics. She kept on.

A large vehicle slowed down and moved alongside her, making her hands clammy. She looked straight ahead and kept walking.

"You looking for something, miss?"

She looked up. It was a black pickup with an old man at the wheel. "I'm looking for a service station."

"You break down?"

"No, I just thought I'd walk." The truck and driver were familiar. He was the guy who smoked the pipe out on the step. She broke out into a smile. "Aren't you the one who helps out with Jazzmine's lunches over at West Side High?"

"Sure enough am. Name's Guff. Why you searchin' out a service station?"

"I'm looking to set up an apprenticeship in auto mechanics for one of my students, who's, uh, kind of a tough kid. I just got turned down at Charles Brown's."

"Not surprised. How often these apprenticeships meet?"

"Usually one afternoon a week on Fridays but I was hoping to get him three days a week or more, one to five."

"He don't go to other classes?"

"No, just mine." She didn't want to say any more.

"There's only one other service station around here. It's about six blocks up to your left, off Main and Harris. Mr. Nate Smith's. You might have better luck there. You want a ride?"

"No, that's okay, I need the walk. But thanks, I'll try it." She smiled up at him.

"Nothin' to it," he said, and drove off.

She quickened her step, feeling more hopeful. When she got to

Nate Smith's, she waited for him to finish talking with a customer, then stepped up to the counter.

"What can I do for you?" he said.

She explained what she was looking for.

"I think I could take on a young man to help out around here and train. Three times a week, afternoons."

"Really?" Jeanna was exhilarated and didn't try to hide it.

He chuckled. "You love them kids, or what?"

"Yeah, I do. Especially this one." Though she didn't know why this one in particular.

"He expect any pay?"

"He doesn't know what to expect, but he needs it more than any other kid at the school."

"Well, I'll give him enough for a decent meal to start with, and if he shows promise and can handle some real work, I'll give him more down the road."

They shook hands.

"I can't tell you how much I appreciate this," Jeanna said.

"We'll see how it works out. Send him over Friday."

"I will," Jeanna said. "He'll be thrilled." *But he won't show it.*

Jeanna floated back toward the school, puzzling over Mr. Smith's quick yes and his offer of three afternoons a week. How did he know? Then it came to her—old man Guff must have paved the way before she got there. Maybe they were friends. She needed to thank Guff, and she couldn't wait to tell Jam about his new training gig.

CHAPTER SIXTEEN

I Just Do What He Say

JEANNA GOT TO HER NEXT GROUP CLASS EARLY AND found Jam at his place at the table and Valle about to take her seat. Jeanna moved her head slightly to indicate she wanted some time alone with Jam, and Valle headed back toward the lounge area.

Jeanna sat a comfortable distance from Jam. He looked at her, then down at the table.

"I found a car mechanics apprenticeship for you yesterday."

His head jerked up and he looked right at her.

"Where?"

"Mr. Nate Smith's Auto Repair at Main and Harris, about six blocks from here. He said he'd take you on three days a week right after your lunch here, Monday, Wednesday, and Friday. He said to go over today."

"Okay," he said. Jeanna thought she saw a quick streak of fear in his eyes, something she'd never seen before. Maybe because this was something he wanted. That always made people afraid. It did her, anyway.

~

It was pretty quiet at Check-In. She'd been worried that it might be getting too personal and touchy-feely, as Cassius would say—on those rare occasions he chose to show up. Maybe she should back off it for a while.

"Hey, Will," Olly said, interrupting Jeanna's thoughts.

"Yeah?"

"How comes you ain't ever got anything to say at Check-In? You one a them little burbies got no problems? We don't know nothing about you 'cept you love the blues an play the mouth harp."

"Speak for yourself," Valle said. "And how'd you like it if the burbies, which Will ain't, called you a slummie?"

He laughed. "That's stupid."

"Precisely," Felice said.

"What exactly would you like to know?" Will said.

"Well, you got a mother?"

"I do."

"She a stay-at-home mom?"

"She's a fifth-grade teacher over at St. Ann's. She works from seven to four-thirty at the school, then works most of the evening on her classes."

"Your dad?"

"My dad's a paralegal at Legal Aid, but I don't see him that much." Will shifted uncomfortably in his seat.

"Why not?"

"Well, not that it's any of your business, but he got involved with a client and they're together now. Ditched my mom." He looked away.

"Wow. Ain't that kind of low down and dirty. I mean, hittin' on the one you're supposed to be helping an' all, an' dropping your moms to boot."

"That's what I thought," Will said, looking down at his hands, his fingers tightly interlaced in his lap. "Here she—the client, I mean—was in a . . . I don't know the right word for it. She was weak, all beat up over and over by her husband."

"Vulnerable?" Abby interjected, looking at Will.

"Yeah, that's it," Will said.

"Whatchu mean 'vunerable'?" Olly asked. "Never heard of it."

"Lot you never heard of," Karima said harshly. "Do you want to hear Will out or not?"

"Hey, now you gonna make me vunerable," Olly said in a sissyish tone.

Jeanna saw Will's jaw tighten. Sometimes she'd like to wring Olly's neck.

"See, you do understand it, but have to act stupid," Karima said. "But that's just for actors on TV, showing that vulnerable stuff. We can't be that way."

"You're right," Will said, turning to her. "But why is that?"

"Oh, we have to be cool," Karima said.

Nods all around the room.

"I mean, what would happen if we let our guard down and cried? When's the last time you saw a kid in high school break down and cry?"

No one said a word.

"You're right, you're always right on, sis," Valle said, "but it's not the regular schools no more, it's here, and if you right, that means we can't be our real selves like Jeanna's always telling us to be. I mean, don't get me wrong, you feeling good and tough on a certain day, fine, but you feeling low when your world done fall apart, then I say cry, baby, cry. Ma says a few tears water the soul, or you just dry up and blow away."

"Uhm," Will grunted in appreciation. Everyone was nodding.

"Yeah, she one deep chick, ain't she?" Olly said to Will, real admiration in his voice.

"She's deep alright, but does she look like a chick to you?" Will responded.

"Hey, that was a compliment!" Olly cried.

"Yeah," Karima responded, "one side a the hand's a compliment, the other's a fresh-ass backslap."

"Whoa." Olly put up his hands. "Why all the broads in this room always ganging up on me?"

"Will you shut your motherfuckin' mouth, motherfucker?" Karima yelled in a strangled whisper.

"But—" Olly started to speak.

"No, she's right," Will said. "She just doesn't say it pretty and nice like you like to hear it."

"Well in my house," Olly said defiantly, "my moms rules the roost. She tells everybody what to do, when to do it, and how to do it. My father, my two brothers, my sister, and I, and anyone else steps foot in the house, do what she say do."

"What she rule outside the house?" Karima asked softly.

Olly fell silent. "Nothin'," he said finally, looking down at the table. Jeanna knew that his mother was an all-night cleaner in a downtown office building, and hell to talk to on the phone, like every conversation with someone from a school had to be a battle.

"I'll be honest," Valle said. "I was with Karima at the start—you know, be cool, strong, hold it all in—but now I see that's not always the way to go."

The girls in the room were nodding.

"But a man can't cry, or show his real feelings," Big Blue said. "I don't care what Valle says, it ain't realistic."

"Is a man human?" Valle asked.

"Yeah."

"Can he talk with his man-friend, his homeboy, about stuff he really cares about?"

"Uh no, almost never. But, uh, we talk with Tommie Lee." Big Blue squinted in confusion.

"Does that make him less a man?" she asked.

"Makes him twice a man," Will said, and Blue nodded, along with everyone in the room.

"But yet he don't talk about his shit," Big Blue said softly, looking at Tommie Lee's empty seat, where everyone was looking.

There was a long pause. "Maybe he just ain't there yet," Lonnie said.

The whole group let that one be. Jeanna was thinking she wasn't there yet either, never had been. No one in her family had. Maybe everyone was thinking something like that.

Valle turned to Jam and opened her mouth. Jeanna held her breath. No one had ever directly spoken to him in class.

"I don't mean to put you on the spot, Jam, but what do you think of all this, men and feelings and stuff?"

Jam looked at her for a long moment.

"I don't have no feelings. I don't know what they are. But if I did, I'd be dead in a day."

A deafening silence followed his words.

"I think I got it, thanks," Valle said evenly back to him.

"I think that was one of the best Check-Ins we've had," Jeanna said, "because it went deep, as Olly said, into things we all struggle with." She looked at Will. "I hope we didn't stray too far from your issue, Will."

"No." He shook his head. "It was right on."

"Okay, so let's break into groups and try to identify things that have been holding you up, stopping your progress. See what you can do to break through."

Jeanna laughed to herself, feeling amazed at what Check-In had just brought out, just when she'd been about to dump it for the day. But it had little to do with her. Valle was usually the one who managed to bring out the best in everyone, and, with Tommie Lee, handle the worst. She wanted to acknowledge Valle somehow.

A few days later, Jeanna stopped Valle in the hall on the way out of school. "You have a minute, Valle?"

"I got two," she said, smiling, but Jeanna knew she meant it; two was it, or she'd be late for work at the nursing home.

"I've been wanting to thank you for what you say at Check-In. You have a lot of wisdom that seems to roll out at all the right times." She felt a little embarrassed, being the teacher after all.

"Thank you for sayin' that, Miss J." Valle was glowing. "I just do what He say."

"He?" Jeanna was puzzled.

"God."

Jesus Christ. Here she'd wanted to acknowledge how wise and empowered Valle was, and she had to put it off on that.

"Why you lookin at me that way, Miss J? Don't you believe in God?"

"I don't know. An old man up in the sky? Probably not."

"I don't know what to say, Miss J. It ain't about just that. It about faith. The holy ghost moving through you."

The holy ghost. Right.

"I guess the God thing—I mean, God—hasn't been a big part of my life," Jeanna said. Growing up in the Unitarian church, good works had been the thing. And social justice, that's what she cared about. Jeanna could see that Valle's estimation of her had fallen, but she wasn't going to lie.

"Oh, Miss J." Valle shook her head.

Jeanna hated the breach that had opened up between them. Maybe it was just inevitable cultural differences, or education. Maybe Valle and her family needed religion more to get by. That felt kind of noblesse oblige, but she just wasn't the religious type.

"So you don't believe in our savior, Jesus Christ, either?"

Oh, Christ. Our "savior." "No, not really. I see him as a teacher, I guess, more than a savior."

"Teachers a dime a dozen. He a lot more than that."

Jeanna blushed, wiped out by the comment, whether Valle meant her or not.

A cloud passed over Valle's face.

"Rather than having a 'savior,'" Jeanna put it in quotes with her fingers, "I think we need to save ourselves."

"Well, good luck with that, Miss J. I guess I'll be going. I'm not the prozletizin' type. But all that don't jive with what I seen in you since day one here at the school."

Jeanna watched Valle walk away, her head down. Where before she had felt a little shallow around Valle, now she felt empty.

Jeanna felt awkward as she entered her classroom at the next group class and saw Valle already there, doing some homework. This was going to be a problem now. She wished they could go back before the God talk, when she'd felt such ease with Valle.

Valle looked up. "Oh, Miss J, I been rollin' all we talked about over in my mind, it bothered me so."

Oh boy, it was starting already.

"I spoke about it with my mom."

Here we go.

"She say people grow up different, have different beliefs. Well, I suppose I knew that, but I never met someone who don't believe."

Jeanna began to feel heat rising through her body; she was getting mad now. Why couldn't Valle just leave it alone? She tried to shove her feelings back in.

Valle put up her hand. "Hold on, Miss J. What Ma said was that so long as a person good, try to do good, that's what matters. Not do they believe this or that. She right. See, I knowed you was good, and in my mind that meant you was godly. I finally got my mind around the notion that a person can be good and not believe. I felt I was off base, then, puttin' you down for how you was raised or whatever."

"I—" Jeanna began, but Valle put her hand up again.

"Just one more thing and I'll be done and you won' have to worry about me goin' off on you again about the 'God thing.'" She smiled and put quotes with her fingers in the air. "I like to die last night when I thought a what I said about teachers bein' a dime a dozen. You ain't no dime a dozen, Miss J. I didn't mean that by a long shot, but I saw you took it that way. I prayed on it all night."

Jeanna was flabbergasted at this outpouring. Relieved. Rejoicing. She reached for Valle and gave her a furious hug.

"Wow, Miss J, you strong." Valle smiled, and they both had tears in their eyes.

People began to trickle in for Check-In. Jeanna went into her office to grab her roster and notebook. She wiped her eyes with her sleeve. She returned and took her seat at the end of the table.

CHAPTER SEVENTEEN

He Deserve Better

On Sunday, Jeanna met Matt at school to drive out to Chisolm's Farm to visit Tommie Lee. She had been sending him schoolwork from various teachers—and, at her students' suggestion, info on what they were doing on their group projects for his comments and thoughts—but she had yet to visit him.

They headed out of town in Matt's ancient green station wagon. When they hit the interstate, dense evergreen forests sprang up on either side of the road. Jeanna breathed in the fresh forest scent. She was glad to be with Matt one-on-one, but a little nervous, too. She was hoping he would give her some feedback on her teaching, but she was also hoping he wouldn't.

When they got to Chisolm's, Matt swerved the car into a large gravel drive and parking lot. "Looks like this is it," he said.

Jeanna looked up at high cement walls, three feet thick, with jagged glass and coils of barbed wire strung along the top. It looked like a maximum-security prison, not a juvenile detention center. She half expected a tobacco-chewing Louisiana guard on horseback to come riding toward them, rifle raised, but there were no signs of life anywhere. They parked and went through the Visitors' Entrance. Jeanna's heart was racing, and she noticed beads of sweat on Matt's forehead, something she'd never seen before.

Behind a smeary window, a young guard with an acned complexion sat with his feet up on a chair, reading a girlie magazine, chewing a huge wad of gum. Jeanna stood there for a moment, sharing his view of an upended rump, the rosy pink entryway glistening with oil, and she felt a rush of rage go through her. She stepped aside to make room for Matt. When he stepped up to the counter, the guard looked up.

"Yeah?"

"We're here to see Tommie Lee Johnson. We were told to be here at 1 p.m. today."

"Yeah?" The guard chewed his gum, staring blankly at them, snuffling. He seemed to have a sinus problem.

Jeanna glanced down at the girlie magazine again and saw another woman's upended rump with a cattle prod stuck inside. The title read, "Ride 'em, Cowboy!" A bitter taste rose up her throat. She was afraid she might vomit.

"Yes, I'm Matt Jensen and this is Jeanna Kendall."

An older man Jeanna had not noticed before spoke sharply from the other side of the office.

"Take 'em down to Visitors' Screening. They ain't been here before."

"Oh." The young guard got up, slow as molasses, and grabbed a large ring of keys off a hook. He made a show of attaching a nightstick to his belt and clipped on a can of mace beside it before leading the way down the dimly lit hall to a heavy door with an iron bar across it. He lifted the bar and let it fall with a loud clang, went through, turned around, and locked it with a huge key. The only sound came from his snuffling, which grated on Jeanna even more than the medieval décor.

They followed him down another long hall, through two more heavy metal doors that had to be unlocked and relocked, before he finally opened a door to a room full of what looked like large voting booths with curtains. He motioned to one and said, "The girl in there. You in here," looking at Matt.

Jeanna's heart stopped.

"Excuse me? What exactly is the procedure to see an inmate?" Matt asked.

"They juvenile detainees, not inmates."

"Okay, but what's going on?" Matt pressed.

"You'll see." He smiled and walked out.

A large woman came in, her skin a little darker than her light brown uniform dress. She motioned Jeanna into one of the voting booths. "In there."

Jeanna looked at Matt.

"This a search for knives, drugs, an' such," the woman guard explained.

Jeanna moved toward the booth, not understanding why they couldn't perform the search in the open. Out of the corner of her eye she saw the male guard reach inside the bag she had brought for Tommie Lee, filled with assignments from school.

When the two of them were inside, uncomfortably close in the cramped quarters, the guard patted her down briskly, reached under her skirt, pulled down her underpants, and did a quick probe between her legs that jolted Jeanna ramrod straight. Her head buzzed and static overloaded her system. She stood rigid and erect looking at the woman, who reached under her blouse, snaked a finger under her bra, and felt left and right. They were now eye to eye.

The woman peeled off clear plastic gloves that Jeanna had not noticed before, while giving her a slow smile that revealed several gold teeth. "You done, honey." The guard left the booth and walked away.

Jeanna pulled up her underpants, smoothed down her skirt with shaking hands, and adjusted her bra. She stepped out of the booth trembling.

Matt loomed up in front of her. "I'm sorry Jeanna, I had no idea they did this at Chisolm's or I would have warned you. I don't even think it's legal."

She was unable to speak.

"Oh, Jeanna." Matt's eyes were stricken. "Come on, we'll leave right now."

That brought her to. “No!” she cried. Then, in a whisper, “I came to see Tommie Lee, and I won’t leave until I do.”

The girlie magazine guard came through the door. “This way.”

Matt tucked Jeanna’s arm under his as they walked down the long hall. Her body was still trembling.

They entered a large room with an immensely high ceiling. There were ten long tables with benches on either side made of corrugated steel, everything bolted to everything else and to the floor. She saw Tommie Lee sitting on a bench near the wall. Except for a guard, they were the only ones in the barren room.

They walked over to him. He stood up. Jeanna leaned forward to give him a hug, but he held out his hand instead.

“They don’t allow hugs in here, don’t even allow touching.” He dropped her hand. “They’re watching us through that.” He nodded toward a darkly tinted window that took up the whole side of the room.

Matt clapped him on the shoulder. “Good to see you, old man,” he said, and began to sit down next to him.

“You’re supposed to sit on that side and I’m supposed to sit on this side,” Tommie Lee said.

They took their seats across from each other.

“Thanks for coming,” Tommie Lee said. “I know it isn’t pleasant.”

“We’re not here for pleasant, we’re here for you,” Jeanna said.

Tommie Lee gave her a weak smile.

“How are you holding up in here?” Matt asked.

“I’ve been holdin’. I don’t feel good about what I did. It was stupid.”

“We all know that wasn’t the real you,” Matt said.

“Well if it’s not the real me, then who’s been sitting in this cage?” His lip curled as he spoke.

“The guy who made one mistake under a whole lot of pressure and pain,” Jeanna said.

“You always put such a nice rosy spin on things.” Tommie Lee gave a harsh laugh, his eyes moist, red at the edges.

Jeanna hadn’t meant to sound Pollyanna-ish. She bit her lip.

"I mean the way you turn, you know, our worst into our best. It's just that it doesn't work in here. Nothing does. I'm getting what the hell I deserve."

"No one deserves this," Jeanna and Matt said in unison.

Tommie Lee cracked a smile and they managed a laugh. Jeanna was finally glad she had come. She reached into her bag and began pulling his assignments out.

"You have no idea how much I look forward to what you send, Jeanna. The stuff on Karima and Felice goin' at it, Will and Valle, the whole music group, and my guys and all their click and clatter, god, are they great. And Lonnie and Chef's stuff! It's what keeps me sane."

"I've got more for you." Jeanna was still pulling out books, big yellow envelopes, and manila folders from her bag.

"What do they have you doing in here?" Matt asked.

"Oh, they pretend at school. We have a kind of zombie who teaches in the morning. There's definitely something the matter with him. It's all two and two equals four stuff. That's in the morning. Then in the afternoon they have us digging this ditch that just goes on to eternity. We have no idea what it's for, maybe pipe or irrigation or something."

Matt broke the no touching rule again by grabbing Tommie Lee's biceps. "Looks like you're building up that muscle, old man."

Tommie Lee smiled. "That's for sure." Then he pointed to his head. "It's this muscle that's going to waste."

"Not to hear your project guys tell it," Jeanna said.

"Yeah?" He brightened.

"They're so psyched when they get your responses to their work and your suggestions they can hardly contain themselves."

He had a real smile on his face now.

"So tell me what you brought."

By the time Jeanna had finished explaining the various assignments, and Matt had managed another joke or two with him, a guard was stepping in and saying, "Time's up."

They stood.

"Thanks for coming," Tommie Lee said, swallowing hard.

Jeanna reached out a hand and squeezed his.

Matt clapped him on the shoulder, and said, "Everybody sends their love, man, and I mean everybody."

"Thanks, Matt." He stood looking at them until they left through the door.

This time, as they walked down the long hallway, Jeanna put her arm through Matt's. "Thanks for bringing me. I'm really glad we came."

"Me, too," he said, and tightened his grip on her arm. "You got guts, kid."

A little warmth merged with the coldness she felt as they left Tommie Lee locked behind the thick grey cement walls.

When they got into the car, Matt began rooting around in the glove compartment for his eyeglass cleaner. Just then Jeanna saw an old dusty Chevy drive in, and then Lillian getting out, looking at her watch.

Jeanna got out and walked over to Lillian, who was looking at her in bewilderment.

"Hi, Lillian. Matt and I just visited Tommie Lee."

"It's so nice of you to come all the way out here." The look on Lillian's face was a mixture of intense shame and appreciation.

Jeanna tried to imagine what it was like to have a son in what was essentially a prison at the age of sixteen. At any age. "I just need to tell you how special Tommie Lee is to us," she said. "All the kids look up to him, and he speaks so highly of you when most kids complain . . ."

"Tommie Lee deserve better." Lillian spoke with such grave conviction that Jeanna was taken aback.

"But—"

"A lot better. I got to go. I'm late." She turned to go, stumbling in her heels over the stones. She said over her shoulder, "I'm sorry. You so very kind to come. Tell Matt thank you."

"I will," Jeanna said, completely mystified by what had just happened.

Matt walked up. "Wasn't that Lillian?"

"Yes, it was. I wanted to wish her well, but she was in a hurry to make visiting hours. She said to thank you for coming."

"Is she okay?"

"I don't think so, no."

"Well, what parent would be?"

"Right."

CHAPTER EIGHTEEN

Project Day

JEANNA FINISHED HELPING SET UP THE COFFEE AND donuts out in the hall and went into the auditorium. Many of her students were already there, with their parents in tow. Most of the parents she greeted seemed quite skeptical of her—due to her age, no doubt, and possibly her race. This she expected, but it heightened her anxiety.

She spied Lillian and was surprised she'd come. She was looking around awkwardly.

Jeanna went over to her and extended a hand. "I'm so glad you came, Lillian."

"I had to or Tommie Lee'd have my hide. His friend Olly called last night to insist I come. So here I am." She gave a self-effacing shrug, avoiding Jeanna's eyes.

"It means a lot that you're here," Jeanna said. "It's kind of test-time for us as a school, and you've always been so supportive . . ." She stumbled, hoping she wasn't assuming support that had actually been politeness.

"Oh, I am!" Lillian glanced at Jeanna, then quickly away. "This school been a godsend. I don't know any other school that would have kept in such close touch with Tommie Lee . . . where he is." She turned away and found a seat, occupying herself with taking off her coat and arranging her bag on the floor in front of her.

Jeanna felt someone touch her arm and turned to see Pepper standing there, his red hair dripping, waiting to introduce his parents to her. She turned and greeted them. She saw Cassius slip in alone, a makeshift drum under his arm, out of the corner of her eye. He snuck a look at her, and she smiled and gave him a discreet thumbs-up. He smiled down at the floor and hefted his drum up onto the stage. Matt, who had been setting up a microphone, reached down and gave him a hand up.

Felice came in, stunning in a silver-grey sheath dress and matching heels. Her hair was piled high on her head. Jeanna recognized her grandmother from the first month of class, but not the smart-looking black woman in her fifties standing next to her.

Jeanna went over to them. "Good morning, Mrs. Jeffries, I'm so glad you came."

"Child, we wouldn't miss this for the world." She turned to her friend. "This is Felice's teacher, Jeanna Kendall; Ms. Kendall, this is my good friend, Elaine Browning, Wesley Brooks's aunt and a longtime educator herself."

Jeanna felt a shot of anxiety rush through her. She had heard of Elaine Browning, knew she was a powerful parent activist and community leader. Of course Wesley, her one recalcitrant student, would be her nephew.

She took Elaine's outstretched hand and said, "Very nice to meet you." Then she slipped away to avoid any questions about Wesley's progress.

Matt was motioning for her to come backstage, where her students were clustered behind the curtain. The crowd was noisy, and parents were still coming in and milling about, drinking coffee, and examining some of the student exhibits along the walls.

She moved quickly down the aisle and went behind the stage. She heard Felice snarling at Karima, "I am not overdressed. You, as usual, are totally underdressed."

"You are both perfectly dressed," Jeanna cut in, "because you're dressed like you want to be, which is exactly what we agreed to, remember?"

They nodded at her.

"We're all just crazy nervous," Abby said.

"Of course you are. You wouldn't be human if you weren't. But you can do this, each and every one of you. Just be yourself and you'll be great. I'll be sitting with the faculty in the third row. Blue, Olly, Pep, you're on first."

Matt stuck his head behind the curtain. "Jeanna, is your first group about ready?"

"Yes, they are," she said with total conviction in her voice. She turned to go and over her shoulder said, "Just be yourselves."

She walked back to her seat with the packed room tipping this way and that. Who was she kidding? She was ten times as scared as her students.

Olly stepped out from behind the curtain, dressed in a black suit with blue pinstripes, a blue shirt, and a black tie, joined by the rest of his group, who were equally well-dressed. They half-sat, half-leaned against a sturdy table set up on the low stage.

"Good evening—I mean, good *morning*, everyone," Olly said, to laughter around the room. "My name is Olly Howell. This little guy to my right"—he gestured to his six foot six companion—"is Earl Jones, Big Blue to us; and that big fella on my left is our new leader, Arnold Wolpert, known to us as Pepper." He cleared his throat. "We're dedicating our presentation to Tommie Lee Johnson, who couldn't be here today. He's our heart."

A strong ripple of applause arose from the students seated in the audience.

Touched, Jeanna looked at Lillian, who was sitting nearby. Her eyes were moist and focused on Olly, who gave a slight bow in her direction.

"Our project was born on the very first day of school when we were testing out our new teacher here, Miss Jeanna Kendall. She was telling us some nonsense about our being able to study what we really wanted to study, something everyone knows is totally impossible in school, and you know what? She called our bluff. So what we've been studying is . . ."

He looked at Pepper, who said, "What makes for a winning basketball team. That was our central question, and from that we developed a whole series of other questions to guide our research." Pepper spoke without looking at a single note. "The methods we used to get our information included interviewing and consulting with Assistant Coach Ray Hunter at the U, and his players, observing their team both in practice and in games, taking notes and analyzing the patterns we saw, and consulting with sports radio man Chet Ackerman and the *Tribune*'s oldest sports reporter, Guy Harris. With our own Coach Jakim's help, who's also the math teacher here, we did a statistical analysis to show how many wins could be due to star performance versus good all-around team play." Pepper stepped back.

Jeanna was proud of his poised presence.

"Our bi-biggest lesson was that it wasn't an ei-either/or thing, b-but both star performance and good all-around team play," Big Blue said. "The stats show that a star could get him thirty-forty points a game, but if his other players wasn't coming through in their own ways, they often lost the game." Blue looked down at his notes, his hands shaking slightly. "We learned that good play on the court involve a lot more than putting a bunch of talented players on the floor. That a lot of it emotional and mental, like how the players feel about each other and themself. What kind of person their coach is—a dictator type or someone open to learning from everyone around him, big and little." He smiled broadly.

Olly slid off the table, now standing more comfortably, and said, "Some of the most important things we learned had to do with us as a group working together. When Tommie Lee, our natural leader, had to leave for a while, we almost fell apart. Our classmates put it to us to figure out what it was that Tommie Lee did and try to do it ourselves. We found out that we were leaders, too, in our own way. Pepper here really stepped up to the plate and helped us to plan ahead and stay on track, and with some academic skill stuff. I dropped my clown act and took some real follow-through responsibility. Like doin' what I said I was gonna do." He grinned and laughed with the audience. "Big Blue here stepped up instead of layin' back, and everything just started to fall into place again. It was a real good feeling. We still miss Tommie Lee, though, there's no making up for that."

"In case there's anyone in the room who thinks that studying basketball is a poor excuse for real school learning, we have a check list right here of all the skills we developed while working on this project," Pepper said, "and on the other side you can see that we listed the books and articles we read. It's in your packet there. Next term we're co-writing an article that Coach Hunter is helping us with, to submit to *Phys Ed Quarterly*. Valle here's saying we've run outta time so I won't go into the whole list of skills, which you can read anyway.

"I want to end with one last lesson we learned the hard way. It's about language and what it means to people. When you put down someone's accent or the way they use words that comes from their family or region where they grew up, it's like you're cutting them down even if you didn't mean it that way. You're saying that they're no good, that they don't have the right to speak, and you're making yourself better than them, which you're not. We came close to fists on that one, but we came out of it real good in the long run. So thanks everybody."

The three of them clenched hands up in the air to thunderous applause. Their parents and family members were beaming and clapping to shake the rafters, as was Lillian.

Matt said, "The next group is the 'The Struggle for Racial Justice.' The group has asked me to explain that some of the language is rather graphic, and they don't want to offend anyone, but they do want to keep it real. Group?"

Felice, willowy in her silver sheath dress, and Karima, built for power in her jeans, strode out and squared off. Felice went first, speaking with her natural air of supreme authority: "It was the courts, the lawyers, the legal team that made the real difference in school desegregation in 1954, and later in the early sixties, in winning the right to vote, and to eat and sleep wherever we wanted!"

"No way!" Karima's tone was three times as intense. "It was the people taking matters into their own hands, taking to the street, marching, singing, sitting in, laying their bodies on the line for their rights. The law don't mean shit," she ended in a fierce whisper. The room went stone silent.

"How can you say that! The law was and is our best weapon for freedom. Without the law, we'd have nothing to stand on. Just mob rule and who's the strongest."

"You fool! It was the law that lynched us! The constitution that whipped and maimed us! Tore the flesh off our bones by dogs sent by the fugitive slave law. Take off a white robe and you'll find the white pillars of society underneath: the sheriff, the deacon of the church, the justice of the goddamn peace! It was the Jim Crow law that kept slaves in bondage after they were declared free, by a white man who could care less if we lived or died so long as he kept his precious union intact. The law," she sneered.

"But don't you see? You use the law against the law. You use the system's tools to reclaim it for the people. For every lawyer with a KKK robe on there were three for justice. Why, hundreds of lawyers, white and black, in the deep South signed a petition to pressure the federal government to protect black voting rights."

"Ain't that nice. Hundreds of maids and laundresses and laborers, sharecroppers and poor black high school students were being beaten bloody, killed, or thrown out of their jobs and homes, having their surplus food cut off, and dyin' a hunger, and a bunch of fancy dans signed a lily white piece a paper." Karima signed in midair with a flourish. "See, the law, even when you win, is just a worthless piece of paper, lessen it's enforced. And there's only one way to enforce it—through the power of the people saying you have to or you will have mayhem, disorder, and destruction throughout the land until you do!"

"And mayhem and destruction, not justice, is exactly what you'll get," Felice said, "unless you get the lawyers, the professionals, to carve out a piece of justice here and a piece of justice there, like the Voting Rights Act, like the President's order to integrate the armed services."

"So we can go kill off all the other brown, black, red, and yellow people on the face of the earth," Karima interrupted, "and snatch up all the worlds' resources for our pleasure? I don't want no piece of no white man's army, and I don't want no little itsy-bitsy piece of justice here and there. I want it everywhere, and I want it now! We've been waitin' hundreds of years, beggin' an' scratchin' an' doin' our duty, deferring to our betters and pleading our case through all the 'proper' channels. I say no more pleading—it's time for an uprising. And I'm not alone. Half of Africa, Latin America, and Asia are on the move. You need to back up and step off; you're in the way, lawyer-lady."

"Who are you kidding, girl?" Felice fired back. "Last time I looked around this was not Africa or Latin America, and not Asia either. This is white America, and like it or not, you and I are in the minority. Either we play by their game and beat them at it, or we rise up and they strike us down in two seconds flat. It's a matter of simple mathematics. They've got the numbers, they've got the armies, and we've got the jails and the graves if you go that route."

"Not if you get your nose outta that case law book," Karima said. "This isn't a national fight. It's worldwide. We are in the majority, and we have the power to win our freedom."

"Now you're talking crazy. You can't even organize your block and you're talking about taking over the world. While you sniff at my piece-by-piece legal strategy, you know what you'll accomplish with your grandiose, worldwide dreams? Absolutely nothing, that's what!"

"Wait a minute, wait a minute." Abby came walking in from the wings. "Why can't you both be right? Don't you see? You need each other. Just like Martin Luther King needed Ella Baker, who organized all the everyday people—the maids and farm laborers, the factory workers and barbers, the grandmothers and the junior high school kids. Without a sharecropper like Fannie Lou Hamer and the Mississippi Freedom Democracy Party, we might not be having such a strong black showing this year in the southern elections and in the North. But without lawyers who won equal rights in voting and education, we might not all be sitting here today, black and white, in the same school, learning from each other."

"That's all well and good, but how 'bout you, white girl?" challenged Karima. "It's easy enough for you to preach to us about our roles, but how 'bout yours?"

"It takes me, too, and every other white American who can see what's as plain as the nose on my face, that racism isn't a black problem, it's a white problem. It's not about changing black people and making them better, it's about changing white people and the whole system they created to raise themselves up and put everyone else down. From the first day Christopher Columbus came over here and began chopping off Indians' hands, right up to when we brought in slaves and the day we raided Mexico, we've been on a white power trip."

"So what're you going to do, go around feeling guilty and setting up your little 'let's hold hands' workshops? Frankly, I can do without your help," Karima retorted.

"No, I'm setting up a project for next term to develop a curriculum for kids in the regular schools to teach the truth about our history of racism, as well as current issues, and what people, black and white, have tried to do about it. And Wesley Brooks here will be my partner in the project. And we'd like your help too."

"Oh." That shut Karima up for the moment. Jeanna suspected that this was the first Karima and Felice had even heard of Abby's plan. It was news to her as well, although she had encouraged all the groups to begin taking stock of what they'd accomplished and where they wanted to go next term.

Jeanna was doubly surprised to see Wesley step forward, "Hi. I'm Wesley Brooks. Abby's going to do the history and politics of the curriculum, and I'm going to do the cultural piece—the poetry especially, but also music, drama, film, fiction, and art." He pointed backstage and music began to pulse behind him, and Nina Simone blasted out, "Mississippi Goddamn!" The room fell stone silent again. He allowed a few stanzas to play, and then it dimmed and Wesley read the Langston Hughes poem of the same name as beautifully as Jeanna had ever heard it.

Then he said, "The next poem is one I wrote myself. I'm dedicating it to our teacher, Jeanna. It's entitled, "Just Be Yourself."

"I was the nowhere boy
among powerful women and men.
Everyone had an answer for me:
be this, do that, take the lead, make amends
for all the years and years of oppression
that left us without real men.
But I was the nowhere boy
always sure to disappoint
I had such talent, such potential
they were all so quick to point out.
Here, Karima's the rebel, Felice the lawyer-queen.
Abby's the mediator, the one who never needs to be seen.
At home, my mother is the Tigress of the Nile,
and my aunt everything anyone could ever want to be.
My sister knew her one true aim and did not tire—
I, on the other hand, sat in the dark and waited, idle . . .
lost all sense of pride
Where was their brave and sturdy one?
The son they were supposed to have,
their child leader, their Moses man?
He's here, finally, he's come
It's me, O Lord, being myself, the Poet's son."

Jeanna was dumbfounded. She had assumed that Wesley would sit silently throughout the entire proceedings, and had been sure he viewed her as something of a nonentity. The whole audience, Jeanna included, stood and clapped thunderously for over a minute as he stepped back, his aunt among them.

Lonnie spoke next, his sidekicks sitting near him. "This here hard to talk out loud about. When us four came to West Side, we couldn't read or write, 'cept for Chef here. We felt like dirt compared to the groups you already heard from. But Chef let us know it wasn't just us to blame, that the schools gave up on us way back from the beginning, like we were no good, and we come to feel that way too. But just sittin' and listenin' to Karima's race group, we began to see things different, a whole new way. We thought it too late for us, but Miss J wouldn't hear it. She got us to spellin' our own words from our own life and give us books that connect with us, like *The Outsiders* and *Manchild in the Promised Land*, and let Chef here be our main man to lead the way. We lookin' into our futures, like me becomin' a electrician, Chef a real chef, and whatnot.

"Lately we got to thinking there be others like us here at the school, so we starting something new for next term. A student council–like thing for the whole school, to deal with problems kids have, like no pencils and paper, no school clothes, not enough food, need escorts to get to school through gang turf, settling fights with other kids and teachers, get us some more tutors an stuff. We going to ask Miss J to be our group leader, and we taking it to Matt our principal next week. That's our plan. That's it for us."

Lonnie finished to a standing ovation. Hearing the noise, Cat and Alley slowly looked up at the crowd and began smiling. Chefman was slapping Lonnie on the back. Matt was smiling from ear to ear.

The rest of the groups moved quickly through their paces and did beautifully, going only ten minutes over. Cassius offered a drum roll at the beginning and end of each presentation, and he and Will and the rest of the music and freedom group said they were in negotiations with the university to host a monthly four-hour music program. Valle ended by singing "Amazing Grace," with the entire audience joining in.

"Powerful. Powerful," Matt kept saying and shaking his head. "One last hand for the Group Inquiry class taught by Jeanna Kendall," he called from the stage.

It was the highest point of Jeanna's life up to now. All those Sunday nights and Monday mornings of agonized anxiety floated away like so much smoke.

CHAPTER NINETEEN

But Shouldn't the Community Be Involved in This?

WITH HER PROJECT STUDENTS ON FIRE AT SCHOOL, and the rest of her classes humming along, Jeanna turned her attention to the Group. She attended meeting after meeting, quietly absorbing everything she could, and helping out however she could. She began to notice that while Land didn't say a whole lot and never threw his weight around, he was central to everything that happened. She loved his quiet leadership, and hated when others dominated the airspace.

It was the women who really took the initiative in the Group, and often at Land's suggestion. Even if most of the men weren't at all respectful to women, Land was. He provided affirmation that the women soaked up like they'd been living in a desert all their lives. When the nitty-gritty work needed to be done, it was mostly the women who did it, and when they did they exuded a sense of empowerment and competence.

Jeanna still wasn't sure what her role was, but she was as happy as she'd ever been just to be part of it all. She observed the dynamics of the group—what made it tick, who had the power and who didn't, and why. The thing that surprised her was how childish so many members were—grown men, egotistical and insecure at the same time, always wanting Land's seal of approval. It was embarrassing to see men act like that. Jeanna wanted his approval too, of course, but she handled it differently. She never pushed herself forward. She and Land had barely spoken to each other. Yet they always seemed to be on the same wavelength.

Jeanna was the third person to arrive at the meeting. It was a freezing January day, and the radiator was clanging as usual. Helene was absorbed in typing something, fast, on the far side of the room. Frederick Holmes was the other early arriver. As usual, he was dressed to impress, his tightly-cropped Afro immaculate. He ignored Jeanna as she took a seat across the circle from him. Gideon walked in next, his burly body radiating angry energy, and took his seat without acknowledging either one of them.

Cam came in and walked fast, straight for Helene, lifting a hand as he passed them, saying, "Hey." Jeanna waved, but he didn't notice.

Lillian and Carl Johnson came in, greeting everyone in a friendly manner. At five minutes to seven, Land showed up. He nodded to Jeanna as if he'd known her for ages rather than a little over four months. She smiled slightly, and to her surprise, he brightened and gave her a real smile just before four people converged on him, seeking his approval of this, that, or the other.

Reverend Barrows bellowed his greetings, and Land turned his full attention to the meeting. Jeanna planned to sit tight, stay quiet, and take everything in, just as she had in the five previous meetings.

Ma Carrington was chairing. "Okay everyone, this meeting has been called to decide whether we should move ahead on the campaigns for City Council and School Committee, or do more groundwork first in the community. The floor is open for discussion. Let's keep it civil," she ended crisply.

"I don't know what there is to talk about," Frederick said, jumping in right away. "If we don't move on the elections soon, we'll lose people's attention. They'll start to focus on other candidates. You get in late and you're lost."

"You mean *you're* lost, Fred," Phil said. Phil was business manager of the teachers' union and loved to snipe at people.

"Jesus." Fred threw his papers on the floor.

Stupid, Jeanna thought. *If he wants to win people's support, why throw a tantrum?*

"Civil," Ma Carrington reminded them.

"I didn't realize we'd endorsed anyone yet," Gideon said. "I thought we had some process for that. Have we gone through it or has Fred here anointed himself?"

Fred opened his mouth to answer, but Cam cut in with, "Gideon's right. Of course we have a process, and we'll do the process, but everyone knows that Fred's been planning to run for some time now, and as far as I can tell no one has ever objected . . ."

Was Cam behind Frederick's assumption that the Group's endorsement was his? Side-stepping the Group's decision-making process once again?

"No one's had a chance to object or not because the process hasn't happened yet," Gideon said. Jeanna and others nodded in agreement.

Lillian raised her hand to speak, but before anyone could acknowledge her, Phil said, "What the hell process you talking about?"

Everyone looked at Cam and Helene, sitting side by side in front of the office desk. Helene swiveled around to pick up a file folder. She opened it as she swung back to face the group. "In our by-laws it says that candidates are nominated by Steering Committee secret ballot. However, it strongly recommends that other members of the community, such as allied groups and organizations, be invited to join the process of platform development prior to Steering Committee nominations—to be followed by a final secret ballot vote by the entire group membership."

Fred scowled. "Oh, for Christ's sake, let's invite everyone and their grandmother in for what we already know we want to do."

"Excuse me?" Ma Carrington said icily. Titters erupted around the room. At seventy-four, Ma was the oldest member of the group by far.

"We," Gideon said. "Who is *we*? We don't know what we want to do until we decide."

"Okay, wait a minute," Cam interjected, "Helene just described the process. It calls for secret ballot nominations by the Steering Committee. So does anyone have anyone else to nominate, or are we wasting our time over formalities?" He looked at Gideon.

Jeanna was confused. Was Cam taking over?

"If it's a secret ballot nomination, then why are you asking me to state out loud if I have someone else to nominate?" Gideon said. "That goes directly against the process you, yourself, just described." He shook his head. "Am I the only one in the room who wants to follow the process the way we set it up?"

Jeanna raised her hand hesitantly. "I do," she said.

Gideon gave her a look of annoyance and shrugged his burly shoulders. "Well, if no one here cares about the process that's been established," Gideon said, "then I will leave and you all can decide to do what Fred and Cam have already decided—and we didn't really need this meeting after all." His chair scraped the floor as he moved to rise.

Jeanna's face burned as she looked down at the blue-and-white floor tiles. If she was no one, maybe she didn't belong here.

"Wait a sec, Gideon," Helene said. "Let's see who, besides Jeanna, wants to pursue the process we've already developed." She raised her hand.

Every hand in the room went up except for Fred's and Phil's.

"Opposed?" Ma Carrington had taken back the Chair role with a nod from Helene. No one lifted a hand.

"Abstentions?" No hands again.

"Let it be noted that there are two abstentions," Ma said, looking at Fred and Phil. "Okay, now . . ." She seemed to be feeling her way. "Shall we proceed to secret ballot nominations?"

Still smarting from Gideon's dismissal, Jeanna surprised herself by speaking up. "Before we move to the formal nomination process, what about the broader community inclusion piece? Shouldn't the community be involved in this?"

"What're you, crazy?" Fred exploded. "First you want to expand the nominations process, despite the fact that no one here has spoken up for months about anyone else running; then you want to bring the whole world into it!"

"Yes, do we really have time for this?" Phil demanded.

"But isn't that the process Helene just read off to us?" Mary Ranier said in an even tone.

"I don't know, is it?" Phil rejoined.

"We're right back where we started," Ma said. "Let's focus here, folks. So far we know that most of the members of the group would like to follow the secret ballot nomination process we set up for ourselves. Congratulations. What we don't know is, do we want to bring more folks in, build more of a groundwork in the community prior to finalizing our own nominations and final endorsements?"

"No, we don't. It's too much work and there isn't enough time," Fred said.

"I think we're familiar with your views, Frederick, but what about others here?" Ma asked.

There was a long pause.

Jeanna knew she was probably slitting her throat by speaking again, but said, "What about the All-City Congress idea? It is a lot of work, and it does take time, but it would help us come up with positions on issues the community thinks is important, which could be part of the criteria we use for endorsement—"

"What did she just say?" Abe interrupted. It seemed to Jeanna that he was trying to dismiss her as he'd seen his brother just do.

"You must be hard of hearing, Abraham," Ma said. "The proposal is that we have an All-City Congress or big meeting prior to our own nominations and endorsements to bring out wider community input into issue positions, which we will then shape into criteria for endorsement."

"Whatever!" Abe threw up his hands.

"Any further comments?"

"I think Jeanna is right," Land said. "If we can come together to pull it off, organizing an All-City Congress will give us a much better basis to run a slate of candidates."

Jeanna was elated.

"I agree," Cam said. "I think it's the best way to go."

"I like Jeanna's suggestion, too," Lillian said, finally able to complete a sentence now that Land and Cam had given their endorsement.

Helene was nodding vigorously, as were Mary Ranier, Matt, and Carl.

Fred slumped down in his chair, clearly angry but unwilling to challenge Land.

"Hands for the All-City Congress proposal?" Ma said.

All hands went up, except Fred's.

"All opposed, who prefer to go immediately to the nomination process?" she asked.

No hands went up.

"Abstentions?"

No hands.

"Let the record show that there is one abstention," she said, looking at Fred again. "Alright, we're just about done here." Ma raised her voice over the noise of the group getting ready to break up for the evening. "Can I have a show of hands for those here willing to serve on an Education Planning Committee to work toward the All-City Congress and the School Committee elections thereafter?"

Hands went up.

"Let the minutes show that Phil Snyder, Lillian Johnson, Frederick Holmes, Jeanna Kendall, and Mary Ranier will serve as the core organizing committee. I'd like to suggest that Frederick and Jeanna co-chair, unless there are other suggestions? All in favor?"

Most hands went up. Jeanna was floored to be named co-chair. She looked over at Fred. His forehead was scrunched up in anger, and he avoided her gaze. How could she ever work with a guy like him, and why had Ma named her, of all people?

The meeting came to an end soon after, and a group formed immediately around Land, each person impatiently seeking his attention. On the other side of the room, Jeanna noticed that Fred had latched onto Helene, no doubt still trying to plead his case.

Helene looked past him at Jeanna and mouthed, "I'll call you."

Jeanna nodded and smiled back.

Cam slipped past her, squeezed her arm, and said, "Nice going, Jeanna." As she turned to close the door behind her, she saw Land looking at her. She pretended not to see him, and practically floated out into the cool night air.

CHAPTER TWENTY

The Last Word

JEANNA HAD GOTTEN INTO THE HABIT OF STOPPING by the storefront after school to help Helene with typing, filing, mailing, and calling—the million and one tasks that kept the group going. This time Helene had set her up in the office Land used when he was around, and gave her a large pile of handwritten papers.

"This grant is due day after tomorrow," she said. "Let me know if you can't read my hieroglyphics."

Several hours later, Jeanna was done, and anxious to get home. She placed the papers on Helene's desk.

Helene looked up. "Thanks, Jeanna. With all this other stuff I still have to do, you saved me an all-nighter. Say, would you drop this proposal off with Gideon on your way home? Don't you live near the West Side Center?"

Jeanna didn't want to have to do one more thing before she went home to dive into her prep for the next day's classes, and she definitely didn't want to deal with "Mount" Gideon.

"Sure, I drive right by," she said, trying to sound upbeat. Helene wouldn't understand her discomfort. She was the Group's queen bee, and Gideon treated her with respect.

As she handed Jeanna the packet, Helene smiled and said, "Would you like to do dinner sometime? How about Friday, my place?"

Excitement almost wiped out Jeanna's trepidation. "Friday's perfect."

They hugged, and off Jeanna went. She couldn't remember the last time someone had actually invited her over for dinner, and no one like Helene ever had.

Jeanna got out of the car and hurried down the sidewalk, past the Center's glass-enclosed pool. The late-afternoon sunlight dappled the blue water. Jeanna entered the Center, and as she headed down the long hall toward the director's office, she noticed a woman in an elegant dress walking toward her. An iridescent gold mesh shawl was wrapped loosely around her shoulders, and she wore her Afro high, like a crown, and spike heels on her slender feet. Her eyes were remote, intent upon something within. She looked at Jeanna without seeming to see her. As the woman passed her, the mesh shawl brushed Jeanna's arm and she felt a sharp tingle of electricity. She turned to look at the woman as she walked away, her body in sparkling motion like flowing champagne.

Jeanna turned back and hesitated at Gideon's office door, hearing voices.

"I told Pearl there was no need to come by here, that I'd be home soon," Land said, irritation verging on anger in his voice.

Pearl must be his wife. Jeanna remembered Matt telling her that she had a mental illness of some kind.

"Well, what can you do?" Gideon said.

"Nothing. Not a damn thing."

Jeanna knocked lightly on the door.

"Yes?" Gideon's tone was impatient.

"It's Jeanna. Helene asked me to drop off a grant proposal for you to review."

Gideon opened the door and put out his hand, a look of annoyance on his face. Behind him, Land was in a chair by Gideon's desk, framed by a window overlooking the Center's swimming pool. He lifted his hand in greeting and gave her a distracted smile. Gideon snatched the packet, muttered "Thanks," and shut the door in her face.

Jeanna turned to go, unsettled by his curtness. She'd interrupted them. Apparently, Pearl had too. As she left the Center, she saw Pearl through the glass, moving quickly down the side of the pool. Her golden brown skin, shawl, and hair shimmered in the evening light. Jeanna stopped breathing as Pearl stepped up onto the diving board, arms wide, her shawl and dress billowing. At the end of the board she stopped for a moment; then raising her arms straight up, palms together, and stepped off the board. The water swallowed her.

Jeanna felt like she was caught in a dream in which Pearl's mad behavior made perfect sense. Pearl was thrashing underwater, entangled in the swirling web of her dress and shawl, unable to swim to the surface. Jeanna started to run to help when she saw Land coming fast through the open door to the pool, kicking off his loafers, his face grim. Before he could go in, Gideon passed him and plunged in headfirst. He swam up behind Pearl, grabbed her by the waist, and heaved her above the water. Land, who had entered the water a half-second after Gideon, reached them and pulled her slack body on top of his, leaned back, and swam toward the shallow end of the pool. Pearl's cheek rested on his chest and water escaped from the side of her mouth. Her chest was rising and falling, but her eyes were dull and lifeless. There was nothing on Land's face but resignation.

Jeanna hurried to her car and took off. She was frightened and chilled to the bone. It seemed like neither Land nor Gideon wanted to deal with Pearl, like she was just too much trouble. But how did that jive with Land, a man who cared deeply about so many people and was always there for them? One thing was certain: Land had wanted to avoid Pearl, but she'd surely had the last word.

~

That Friday, Jeanna went over to Helene's for dinner. She enjoyed everything immensely—the food, the wine, and all the artistic touches in her apartment—but most of all she enjoyed their gossip about different members of the Group and how crazy they could be. Frederick with his oversized ego and refusal to do any work, Abe and his childishness, and "Mount" Gideon's high-handedness. What was odd, though, was Helene's reaction when Jeanna brought up Pearl stepping off the diving board that evening, and how it had puzzled and frightened her.

"What's puzzling about it?" Helene asked. "She's mentally ill."

If anything, her response troubled Jeanna even more. Didn't she care about this woman? Did Land?

CHAPTER TWENTY-ONE

You Were Awfully Quiet Tonight

IT WAS 9 A.M. SATURDAY WHEN JEANNA WALKED INTO the office to help with a massive mailing Cam had called her about. She was to meet Cam and others there to work on the mailing, then they were going to take stock of her organizing work with West Side parents.

"Lilly, if you could coordinate whoever else shows up for the mailing, then I can finish up the newsletter calls and finalize the articles, okay?" Helene called across the room as Jeanna entered.

"Sure thing, Helene," Lillian said, but a cloud crossed her face.

Hadn't the newsletter been Lillian's idea in the first place?

As the door clicked shut behind Jeanna, Lillian looked up, her face brightening. "Hi Jeanna, how are you? I'm so glad you came."

While Helene was on the phone at the other end of the room, Jeanna leaned across the table toward Lillian.

"What happened with the newsletter, Lil?"

Lillian looked embarrassed. "Well, I'm afraid I just made too many mistakes. You know, with the grammar and all. And there were these things I had in the first issue that, well, Helene and Cam didn't think were all that important."

"Like what?"

"Oh, I suppose low-budget recipes, information on used clothes and furniture shops, free legal aid, babysitting swaps, and such. I mean, we covered all the political stuff too, upcoming events and whatnot, profiles of people making a difference. But I guess we needed to do more of that."

"Come on, people need that other stuff!"

"Well, you know, Jeanna, Helene can do it so much better. I had to let it go."

"But you were so excited about it."

"Yes, but I couldn't make the deadlines."

Jeanna was about to say something more—why couldn't Helene have collaborated with Lillian, rather than cutting her out?—but just then the door clicked shut again and Mary Ranier came in. "Mary!" Jeanna smiled. "What brings you here?"

"Well, you know Cam. He'd have me digging in the mines if he could. I came to help with the mailing. He said he was coming too. Where is he?"

"I guess he just decided to send us instead," Jeanna said coolly. The three of them burst out laughing.

Helene waved a long, imperious arm in their direction from the far end of the room. "SHUSHH! I'm doing a phone interview."

Mary rolled her eyes. Lillian frowned and bent back over the mailing.

Helene's insensitivity to Lillian—her arrogance in general—bothered Jeanna. But she knew she had a lot to do to keep their ship afloat. Who was she, the new kid on the block, to judge?

A few days later, Jeanna's attempt to chair the education committee meeting turned into a mini-nightmare. Every time she or Lillian tried to speak—at least ten times, she lost count—they were cut off by Frederick or Phil, who had decided to run the show. This after Frederick, Jeanna's supposed co-chair, waltzed in late and spent over half of the meeting in the next room on the phone.

When Fred finally did join the meeting, he and Phil took over dividing up the organizations from Jeanna's list to be contacted, leaving themselves with two each, Lillian five, Mary Ranier four, and Jeanna seven. The grand climax came when Fred pulled out the statement Jeanna had written to be used as the basic script when contacting the organizations and pretended he had written it himself, to kudos all around. Neither Jeanna nor Lillian were able to get a word in the entire night, not even to correct Fred's sleaziness.

"Jeanna, you were awfully quiet tonight," Fred said as he was leaving. "If you're going to co-chair you might want to speak up a little more. If you're not comfortable, I'll handle it all myself." Then he directed her to get the minutes out to everyone and send reminders about the next meeting.

Jeanna wanted to slap him, and then point out each and every insensitive thing he'd done that evening. But surely Ma and Land wouldn't want them fighting it out instead of taking care of business.

She looked through him and said, "I'll do what I was asked to do."

"Suit yourself," he said, shrugging, and took off.

As she and Lillian closed up the office, Lillian said to her, "Don't pay Fred and Phil no mind."

"I just wish I could've let you get a word in, Lil!"

"You sweet," she said, "but don't lose no sleep over it. I'm used to it—that's just the way they are."

But on her way home, Jeanna couldn't shake it off. The way they were didn't sit right with her. In the meantime, though, she had bigger fish to fry—namely, getting people to support the All-City Congress.

CHAPTER TWENTY-TWO

It Was Land, the Way He Does Things

THE WEEKS FLEW BY. JEANNA WAS IN THE THICK OF the political whirlwind, playing off Helene's cues in all manner of settings and situations. They were like finely tuned instruments, picking up where the other left off, stepping in, stepping back. Meetings lost their nightmarish quality as she and Helene traded subtle looks at every moment of significance. Stopping by the storefront became a pleasure, as Helene always welcomed her with a smile and gave her something of substance to do. Their phone calls clicked. Before Helene's words were out, Jeanna knew what to do.

Before long, she realized that interim community-based planning meetings with various organizations across town were needed. A range of constituencies could then come to the All-City Congress already prepared with their own issues and goals. She spoke with Helene about it, and Helene said she would ask Land about bringing it up at the next meeting of the Group.

The night of the meeting, Jeanna got there early. She took her seat in the circle, pulled out her class prep book, and made notes about what to focus on in each class—skills that specific students needed, resources to bring in—and quickly became lost in all the intricacies.

A shadow covered her paper. She looked up. "Karima!" she exclaimed with a big smile.

"You're the last person I expected to see here," Karima said, giving her a dark look.

Jeanna blushed. *Thanks a lot.*

"How long you been involved?"

"Since November." It was February now.

"Whyn't you never say anything about what you be doin', like in Check-In?"

"I figure that's the students' time, not mine."

Karima shrugged. "I guess."

Karima seemed disappointed she was there, like it made the group less radical or exciting for her; or maybe she was just surprised and didn't understand why Jeanna had never mentioned it.

"How did you happen to come tonight?" Jeanna asked.

"Land told me about it at a youth meeting last week. How 'bout you?"

"I ran into Matt at a demonstration and he invited me."

"Matt's involved too?"

"For decades."

"Hum," Karima nodded, scowling, her forehead creased in confusion.

Jeanna knew that Karima was convinced that all white people couldn't care less about racial justice—that they'd never done anything and never would.

The room filled up and the meeting was ready to begin. Helene came over to Jeanna and whispered, "Land said to go for it."

Jeanna put out her idea of building more specific community planning processes into the congress and got the typical response: Fred nearly had a stroke, Phil panned it, Abe said he didn't understand, and Ma restated it with great clarity. Gideon maintained a stony silence, which meant he supported the idea but was unwilling to say so. Lillian said she thought it made tremendously good sense. Carl and Matt backed it too. Cam said of course, it went without saying. Finally, Land gave his full support and Jeanna a lot of kudos, after which all previous dissenters nodded their assent. Ma offered herself and Helene as office coordinators for all such engagements, so the left hand would know what the right was doing. Thrilled with Land's support, Jeanna walked out of the room.

At the next Group Inquiry class, Karima came in earlier than usual.

"Hey Miss J."

"Hi Karima. It was great seeing you at the meeting the other night."

"Yeah, I can't get over it."

"What's that?"

"You know, Land inviting me to the steering committee and all that. Here at school, Tommie Lee's the one everyone looks up to, and Valle, of course, and I'm like the mad, crazy one all up in arms about everything . . . but at that youth meeting the other night, Land said he really liked what I was saying and was glad that I could see the bigger picture, when you know how Felice's always putting me down for that like I'm all grandiose or something, and I'm just spouting radical rhetoric and stuff, but that's not it"—she stopped to gasp for air—"but Land, he acted like that was really good, you know? My dad always gets gruff with me, like don't get too big for your britches, girl. But Land, he got this light in his eye and a smile on his face when I spoke, and it made me feel so different, like I'm okay the way I am."

"Yeah, I know. He really gets you doesn't he?" Jeanna said, aware that she had been affirming Karima ever since day one but it had taken Land to lift her up and make her feel good about herself.

"Yeah, he does." Karima sat there shining and brimming over with a whole new kind of energy.

Over the next month, Jeanna had three or four organizing gigs a week, at the end of the work day and some evenings, and most of the group did at least one every week. Karima got involved in the outreach, and a few times Jeanna and Karima went out door-to-door together. They had gotten into a nice rhythm, and Jeanna could feel some real trust building between them.

One evening, when Jeanna was commenting on her students' papers, she got a call from a Jacqueline O'Keane, the facilitator for the key youth group in town, the City's Finest. She had been referred by Land to help organize for the All-City Congress. They met the next day after work at Jeanna's office and talked for hours. Jackie had dozens of youth group connections. Jeanna suggested that Jackie go down to the storefront and get info on the congress from Helene to take to her youth groups.

They got together for dinner that Saturday evening at the West Side Café and really hit it off. Jeanna asked Jackie what made her decide to get involved in the education struggle.

"It was Land, the way he does things. I had brought together three youth groups from three different schools who were caught in the middle of all this gang violence and one of the youth leaders invited Land to come to one of our meetings. Land sat there most of the night and never said a word. He was just listening to what these kids were saying about how bad it was, how impossible. So finally the guy who invited Land asked him what he thought they could do to deal with it, and Land turned to the whole group and said, 'No, you're the ones facing this every day, what do you think would help?'"

"Sounds like Land." Jeanna smiled.

"You wouldn't believe all the ideas that came rolling out of these kids. It was like a dam had burst. I was scribbling down everything they said. Finally Land looks at me and asks if I can summarize what they said, and I do, and he says, 'You-all have a real leader here, because she knows how to listen,' and everyone looked at me different after that, like I was worth something. Then to top it off he comes over to me after the meeting and tells me about the Group and says if I'm interested, to call you. He said he thought I'd be a real asset on the Ed Committee. I was floored. I'm not exactly used to anyone noticing that I'm doing something worthwhile. Like my parents keep saying, they hope I'm going to get a real job after I graduate!"

They laughed.

"Yeah," Jeanna said, "Land really has a way of making people feel good about what they have to offer."

CHAPTER TWENTY-THREE

Helene Told Me Not to Bother

ON THE FOLLOWING SATURDAY, SNOW FLAKES DRIFTED down outside Jeanna's window and melted on the sidewalk as she worked away at her table. She'd been digging herself out from under a huge mound of student papers all afternoon, and her energy was flagging. The phone rang.

"Hi, Jeanna. It's Jackie. I'm sorry to bother you, but do you have a minute to talk?" Jackie's voice broke.

"Sure. What's the matter? Where are you?" Jeanna had never heard her sound this down.

"Actually, I'm just a few blocks away, at Gil's Market." Her voice caught again.

"Come on over," Jeanna said. "I'll put on some coffee."

"Thanks."

Jackie arrived at the door just as the coffee was ready. Jeanna gave her a hug and moved her papers aside to make room.

Jackie sat at the table and took the mug of coffee gratefully, clutching it in both hands.

Jeanna poured a mug for herself and sat kitty-corner to her. "What's going on?"

"You know how you encouraged me to go down to the storefront to get info about the All-City Congress to give to my youth network?"

"Yes?"

"Well, I went down to the storefront this morning to get literature from Helene to take to my groups, and she said not to bother, that those bases were already covered. But I knew they hadn't been because I had just called these groups and they knew nothing about the Congress."

"Not to bother!" Jeanna exclaimed, mystified.

"When I asked if there was any other way I could help, she said 'No, but I'll call if anything comes up.'" Jackie's eyes were filling. "When I left, Cam was on the sidewalk, and I tried to explain to him what had just happened but he brushed me off."

"I don't understand. Why would Helene want to discourage you from helping out when we need all the help we can get?"

"I don't think Helene trusts me." Jackie's voice cracked again, and Jeanna wanted to put her arms around her, but thought better of it. Let her get her anger out first.

"What's not to trust?" Jeanna asked.

"I've tried to figure it out. Maybe I'm too young, too inexperienced, too white."

"I'm all those things!" Jeanna's frustration was mounting. Who did Helene think she was?

"Helene has one thing right. My family is and always has been racist to the bone. We go way back in city politics. My uncle was a big-time Antonelli supporter, and was made head of probation after that fascist bigot became chief of police. My other uncle is vice president of the carpenter's union and refused to let any black workers in. My dad was a building contractor until he got too drunk to function, and he never hired a single black worker. My brother's a cop, and he's so racist he scares the hell out of me. But I went against all that."

"But that's them and you're you."

"Well silly, stupid me, that's what I thought too," Jackie bit out, her voice rising. "I've stood up to those jerks my whole fucking life. I've made an enemy of all of them, including my father, because every time he turned around, some relative would complain about me. He said he'd had it when they started calling me a 'cock-sucking nigger-lover' to his face."

"How lovely."

Jackie was beyond tears now. Her eyebrows were knit together, her shoulders hunched tight, her knuckles white against the burnished russet of the coffee mug.

"Jesus, talk about being between a rock and a hard place," Jeanna said. "Here you've got the guts to fight your family tooth and nail. Then you try to join the Group in the face of all that and get dismissed. That's totally fucked."

That made Jackie smile, her face opening up a little like her old self. "It's not like you to cuss, Jeanna."

"It's not like you to cry," Jeanna said. "But now that I see why, I want to take Helene and Cam and shake them."

"I guess they're trying to do what they think is best for Land and the Group, but—"

"By rejecting the best people?"

"Jeanna, you are so naive."

Jeanna bristled at that, but Jackie was probably right.

"Besides, I'll bet you get your share of shit in the Group."

Jeanna was quiet for a minute. "I do get some shit, but I think it's warranted in a way. Why should men like Gideon trust me? Even though we agree on virtually everything, from what I can tell. I mean, I wouldn't trust me either if I were him. It does wear thin, but it's not at all a mystery to me."

"Well, there you have it."

"Have what?"

"They don't trust me either, and I understand it too. Lord knows, anyone coming from my family could hardly be seen as trustworthy. But I still don't know what the hell to do. I'd love to talk with Helene about it, but she won't listen, I know she won't."

Jackie's tears were falling freely now. Jeanna leaned over and put her arms around her, resolving to help her new friend find a way around Helene and into the Group. And she was sure that Land would want the same thing. Hadn't he sent her to the Group in the first place?

A week later, Jeanna came early to the storefront to prepare for the Ed Committee meeting. She was glad to see that no one was in the big front room. She'd be able to use the typewriter to type up the minutes and agenda. She'd just sat at the desk, her fingers poised over the keys, when she heard a gravelly voice coming from Land's office in the back.

"Listen here. Last time I'm gonna say it. You got you a coupla gatekeepers, white as right an' fulla themselves, gonna keep out a lotta good folk. I'm not meanin' me. Don't want in anyways, so get that outta your head. But if'n you can't see what's right in front of your nose—"

"I heard you the first time, Guff, and I'll tell you what I told you before—"

"Save it. I ain't wasting no more breath on you. It's just I hate to see a halfway good thing go bad."

Jeanna had never heard anyone speak to Land that way.

"Thank you, Guff," Land said, his voice dripping with a sarcasm Jeanna had never heard from him before. "Thanks for everything."

She heard a chair scrape and she quickly began typing with a fast mechanical clatter before either of them could come through the door.

"Evenin'," Guff said, not skipping a beat as he passed her on his way out.

"Hi," she said. He went out without looking back.

She continued typing. In a few minutes Land came out with his coat on.

"Hey, Jeanna. I didn't know you were here." He shifted his eyes uneasily across the room. He hunched up his shoulders as if against the cold.

"I just got here," she said. "I have to type up the minutes and agenda before the Ed meeting."

"You go ahead then. I have to head out." His face was drawn. He stopped a few feet from her and ran a hand through his hair.

"You look tired. Anything I can do?" she asked.

He looked at her and smiled. "No, but thanks. You've been doing a lot as it is."

She hadn't known he'd noticed. "A lot to be done."

"You got that right." He gave a rueful half-smile, his face engraved with lines of weariness that somehow drew Jeanna to him. "Don't work too hard, Jeanna." He smiled again, but she could see he was hanging by a thread.

"Don't you, either," she said, returning the smile.

After the door closed, she sank back in her chair, feeling Land's bone-tiredness, wishing she could somehow make it easier on him. She thought about what Guff had said about Cam and Helene and smiled. He'd surely nailed those two power-hungry peas in a pod, whether Land could see it or not.

CHAPTER TWENTY-FOUR

That's Old As Time

JEANNA HAD FINALLY MADE A DATE TO VISIT HER grandmother Saturday afternoon and was looking forward to it. After a full and successful morning of organizing with Matt, Lillian, and Carl, she stopped off at a local gift shop, where she picked out her grandmother's favorite box of soap, Carnation, and a sepia photograph of a woman playing the piano with obvious feeling and grace. She missed her grandmother's piano playing almost as much as she missed her grandmother.

She stopped at the florist and bought one large, luscious yellow rose, swaddled in ferns, a tradition that had begun when she was preparing for her first flute recital at age eleven. Seeing how scared and inadequate Jeanna was feeling, her grandmother had given her a stunning yellow rose. "This is you," she said, "full of beauty and power and ability, perfect just as you are. Whenever you feel down, or scared, or less-than, remember the yellow rose."

Jeanna had played her simple piece beautifully at the recital, without a trace of self-consciousness, surprising herself and everyone around her.

She arrived a few minutes after one, and her grandmother came out to greet her with a big smile, wearing a Julia Child apron over comfortable dove-grey slacks and a plum-colored turtleneck, her lined face framed with a spray of white hair, the forward curve to her shoulders more pronounced than before. They hugged for a long minute, close and tight. She was thinner, bonier, than Jeanna remembered.

Her grandmother gathered in her gifts. "Roger and Gallet Carnation! I haven't had any of that for the longest time, how thoughtful." She peered into the wrapped flowers. "Such a gorgeous yellow rose. I'm so glad you've kept up our tradition, sweetheart." She added another kiss on Jeanna's forehead. "Come on in. Soup's on. I made us a butternut squash soup with pear, and those little tea sandwiches, I hope you still like them. And some brownies you used to like too."

"Used to!" Jeanna laughed. It felt so good to be with her grandmother. Why didn't she make time to come more often? "You really made tea sandwiches?"

"I did. Egg salad, ham salad, and cream cheese, olive, and nut. Loretta gave me *Gourmet* magazine for Christmas, that's where I got the soup recipe. You want tea or cocoa? I made both."

"Cocoa, please. You're totally spoiling me."

"I certainly hope so." Her grandmother placed the rose and greens into a simple glass vase on the table, the card resting against it. They settled into their old familiar seats at the kitchen table, sitting kitty-corner to each other so they could both see out the window and talk comfortably. Jeanna kicked off her shoes and hooked her feet over the wooden pedestal. She felt a sense of comfort she hadn't realized she'd been missing.

"How is Loretta?" A former high school social studies teacher turned journalist, Loretta was her grandmother's best friend. They had fought together for women's right to vote, against lynching in the South, and even today they actively opposed the war in Vietnam. She had always admired their friendship and their courage.

"She's good as ever." Her grandmother winked. "Notwithstanding a bad case of asthma, and rheumatoid arthritis so bad she can't bend her left knee or hold a cup of coffee steady in her right hand."

"That sounds pretty rough," Jeanna said as her grandmother

poured some warm milk from the old pottery pitcher into her tea, her hand trembling slightly. That was new too.

Jeanna put her hand over her grandmother's where it now rested on the faded tablecloth. "How about you? I've been worried." She looked straight into her grandmother's blue-grey eyes.

"Don't be, dear, I'm fine as a daisy, just like Loretta." Her grandmother smiled, a little wistful. "They don't tell you about getting old. I don't recommend it until it's absolutely necessary." She laughed. "It's like anything else; you get through it, all the little ups and downs."

"And the not so little ones." Jeanna gave her frail hand a light squeeze and took it away to sip her cocoa.

"Those too. Now tell me everything, Jeanna. How's your teaching?"

"Fabulous. I mean, the kids are incredible. I love them to death. They're all geniuses. They each have their own gift. It's just so amazing to see it come rolling out—along, of course, with a lot of drivel and absolute stupidity."

"Well you can't have genius without its cloak of perversity," her grandmother said, chuckling. "Look at Einstein. He couldn't make simple change and shambled around like a bum. Good for you, Jeanna, that you have the skill to bring out their best. How do you do it?"

"You taught school. You know how. In fact, you used to tell me how smart all your coal miner kids were back in West Virginia."

"Perhaps, but I want to know how you do it."

"Hmm." Jeanna thought. "I try to create an atmosphere where they can discover their own passion, then stay out of their way. Give them the space to be who they are, let them find their own rhythm. I mean, I do help them with all sorts of skills, but it's in response to what they need as they go along."

"Oh, I like that very, very much." Her grandmother nodded and kept nodding. "Now, what about your music? You're keeping up with your flute, I hope."

"I wish." Jeanna gave a helpless shrug of her shoulders. "I mean, I play by myself, when I need to, but not in any group, nothing serious."

"You wish? Meaning, you bring out everyone's music but your own?" She gave Jeanna a long penetrating look.

This was a refrain she'd heard from her grandmother before: that women should do their own thing and not just help others do theirs. But that's if they had a thing, which she didn't, really, although she knew her grandmother was under the illusion that she did. Regardless, she didn't have a scrap of time to even entertain the thought.

"You know how it is, Grandma. When you're teaching, what time and energy do you have for anything else? I'm still finishing my master's two nights a week. Plus, I'm part of that political group I told you about way back when you were in the hospital."

"Yes, I remember. I know I was in a bit of a fog—it's led by a Landon Watson or something like that?"

"Landon Waters."

"Yes, that's it. I've followed him some in the papers. He's like the Race Men we had back when. I always admired them for standing up. And I know just what you mean. I remember how exhausted I got as I ended each day of teaching. Just frazzled to death. Though I did love them, every single one. I was lucky, though—I had a husband who was ahead of his time. He supported me and we worked together on all kinds of political things."

"Like what?" Jeanna asked.

"I've told you all this."

"Tell me again." Jeanna loved to hear her grandmother's stories. She always got a new twist or a whole new piece would be added she'd never heard before.

"Well, in his pharmacy he'd talk about the issues of the day to anybody'd who'd listen: during the Second World War, the Japanese internment camps—oh, he could get going on that. Way before then it was the vote for women, and later, enforcing it for Blacks. And temperance, that was very big with him. He'd stand up to drunks who were beating their wives. I loved him for that. A child would come running for him, and he'd go pull the husband off his wife and drag him to the room we had back of the store, lock him in, and keep him there until he sobered up. We made a lot of use of that room, in fact—the whole community did. I mean the radicals. Our cell back in the thirties would meet in that same back room."

"The cell . . . that was communist, right?" Jeanna asked, knowing the answer. "He was a member of the CP?"

"We both were for a while. They were the only people we knew who were really organizing in the mines and factories. But over time neither of us could stand their anti-democratic way of doing things. They called it 'democratic centralism,' which meant that Party leaders dictated 'the line.' Oh, you should've heard John go on about 'the line.' He was a free thinker; he didn't like to be hemmed in, and neither did I."

"I hear that. The group I'm working with—"

"Yes, yes, I want to hear more about that."

"When you were talking about certain types taking over, I couldn't help thinking about a couple of sort of self-appointed leaders who are very close to Land. I admire them, I really do. I used to have a crush on Cam, I know him from the U. We did a lot of campus organizing together."

"I remember you telling me about him." Her grandmother smiled.

"Right, and Helene Bouve is the other. They've both become friends of mine, but I can't stand the way they handle things sometimes."

"How so?"

"Like when Land's not around, they like to call all the shots, rule the roost, you know? They cut people out that they don't want around, and deal people in that they do."

"That's always the case. There are always those who throw their weight around, have to be in control, and that becomes more important than the cause itself."

"Exactly." Jeanna shook her head. Her grandmother was the only human being she knew who understood these things.

"You say you're friends with them?"

"Well, yes and no. I'm like the junior partner." Jeanna laughed. "I'm not on their level, and I'm not sure I want to be."

Her grandmother looked at her for a long moment. "You never were a superficial girl, Jeanna. You keep doing what you think is right."

"I'll try."

"It's all you can do."

Her grandmother got up and took the copper pot off the stove. She ladled soup into the blue pottery bowls on the table, her hand shaking even more noticeably, and peeled back the foil from the plate of tea sandwiches.

"So how about your colleagues at your school? Do you like them, or are they more or less traditionalists? That was the problem I had as a young teacher, with my radical bent."

"Traditionalists at West Side? No, not really. It's a real alternative school. Maybe one guy, but he's a Muslim, and I'm beginning to get that he's not a straight-out conservative—it's more that he's demanding the best from the kids. It's a Black Muslim high standards thing, you might say. But he can really rip into them sometimes." Jeanna gulped the soup. "This is delicious." She reached for the sandwiches and took one of each kind.

"How about the others?"

"You know, they're amazingly skilled and gifted as teachers, but we have nothing much to do with each other. It's every man for himself. I do struggle with one thing." She was embarrassed to bring it up, feeling it was too petty.

"What's that?"

"Well, every time I bring something up in a staff meeting, it gets passed over like I didn't say a word—like I'm invisible."

"That's old as time. Women, young women especially, are almost never listened to."

Jeanna let that sink in, appreciating the confirmation but angry at the inevitability of it.

"You had the same experience?"

"Of course."

She knew her mom had too, even as a mature adult. You didn't have to be a rocket scientist to understand who did the talking and who did the listening in their family.

"But I thought you were always so . . ."

"What? Sure of myself? What do they call it now—'empowered'? Not by a long shot. In the Party the women worked hard but were always in the shadows, except for maybe one or two who'd been anointed by the male leaders. It takes time for a woman. You have to prove yourself ten times over, and when you try to prove yourself, you undo whatever good you would've done had you simply done the best you could and let the rest go."

Jeanna was getting a little lost but thought she got the gist. It was pretty much the way she tried to operate. "You don't fight them just to be heard," she said, testing the waters.

"Well, mostly you don't, I suppose, but sometimes you do, depending on what's at stake." Her grandmother shrugged. "And of course sometimes you simply don't have the power and you'd be hitting your head against a brick wall."

Jeanna nodded, thinking more about the Group than her teaching colleagues. "Any chance I could get you to play some Chopin before I go?" she asked.

"I'd love to, Jeanna, but my hands gave out on me; I had to stop playing. I've given the piano to Cardienne for one of their recital halls."

Devastated, Jeanna looked at her grandmother. Her eyes were wet, but shining with what seemed more like joy than sadness.

"I'm so sorry. You always enjoyed it so much and played so beautifully." She reached out and covered her grandmother's hand with her own again.

"Yes, true, but not like you."

"I don't know why you always go back to that," Jeanna said, frustrated, wanting the focus to be on her grandmother. "I just don't get it. You loved the piano and didn't pursue it either."

Her grandmother went still and looked out the window, her face impassive. Had Jeanna hurt her? Disappointed her?

"No, I didn't pursue it. I wanted to, but too much got in the way. And I had nowhere near the talent you've had from the very start."

"But—"

"No." Her grandmother raised her hand. "Hear me out just this once and I will stay silent about it forever more. Remember that first flute recital you gave as a child?"

"Funny, I was just thinking of it as I drove over here."

She nodded. "Well, after all the fears and tears were brushed away, you got up there and played as heartfelt a piece of music as I've ever heard. I know it was a simple song, and you were all of eleven, with only one year of flute under your belt, but you held that room in the palm of your hand. Every year your music became more and more powerful because of the feeling you were able to convey. And you were improvising from the start, like it was built into you. It was most unusual, but you didn't realize how special it was because it came so naturally to you—"

"But you seem to be the only one who's ever seen it that way," Jeanna said. "I wasn't first or even second flute in the high school band. I was last, if you'll recall."

"Oh, please, that band leader would have sent Marian Anderson packing for having too deep and resonant a voice. He wanted you to play like a robot, and you couldn't do that."

They laughed, and Jeanna was happy her grandmother wasn't still angry with her. She knew she was right. She had hated band—the leader and all his rules, the mechanical parts she was forced to play, and the musical choices he made that were foreign to her nature. But it hadn't stopped there.

"How about the jazz group I was part of in college? They couldn't get rid of me fast enough. When politics and movement stuff took me over and I stopped going, they didn't even call to find out what happened to me. And even when I was there I felt like I was just thin air."

"Yes, but weren't they all young men?"

"Yes."

"And full of themselves?"

"Yeah."

"Well, there you have it. They were so full of themselves they didn't even know what they were losing. Or perhaps they were a bit envious. And my dear, you never were one to push yourself forward."

"Is that what I should do? Push myself forward? My students have been telling me the same thing."

Her grandmother stopped and held her gaze for a long moment. "Like everything else you do, I think your music will speak for itself someday. As for now, I like—I love—the understated you. You'll never make a big splash, but in your own silent way, you'll cut to the core."

"Oh, Grandma." Jeanna reached over and hugged her tight.

Her grandmother hugged her back fiercely.

The late-afternoon sun was turning the cedars, willows, and birches outside a melancholy rose and gold.

"I guess I should be going. I still have a paper to write tonight."

"Thank you so much for coming, dear, and for the gifts." She touched the rose's petals lightly, wrapped the brownies in foil, and put them in Jeanna's hand. "This will give you the energy to do that paper . . . Oh, wait! I forgot I had a gift for you too, dear." She took a package from the counter and tucked it under Jeanna's arm. "Take a look when you get home, sweetheart."

"Thanks!" Jeanna reached out and gave her grandmother another hug, silently vowing to come more often.

As she walked out, the sun—now an impossibly large sphere of transparent mauve—rested on the horizon, about to slip under.

When Jeanna got home she couldn't wait to unwrap the package. It was a new album by Miles Davis, *In a Silent Way.* She played it all night, letting it soar and shimmer and finally seep into her bloodstream as she fell asleep.

CHAPTER TWENTY-FIVE

This Couldn't Be a Personal Invitation

IT WAS A FRIDAY EVENING IN MARCH, AND A LIGHT RAIN was falling outside the half-open window. Jeanna was ensconced at her grandmother's ancient oak table reviewing her students' critical incidents papers, a towering mound that threatened to fall onto her plate of grilled cheese and tomato.

Lonnie's paper was loosely printed in bold red pencil, the lines sagging on the page like a ruby necklace:

> A turn point for me was when I was bout 8, me an my 2 yonger brothers an sister was waylin arguin an cryin we was jus so hungry an cold. My Ma swep in to the room an pick me up like a fly in her rite arm an the other to lil boys like to fethers in her lef an throwed us up agest the wall, it hurt bad my head an shoulder hit like I can still feel it today. All the noese stop, It was dead quite. I look in Ma's eyes, They was wild bloody an bline. That second I unnerstood. She was be side her self wif no money for food, rent an heat. The lights was just turned off. I sed I unnerstan Ma. She sunk her teeth in her arm an walk out the room. I held the kids close an no one

made no more noese that nite. But my stomik had a big long hole that kep yellin insted. What worse my hart hurt for Ma.

My happy turn point happen nex year when I lyed an sed I was ten to get my paper rout. It was scare, craze in the begin. But by end of to week I had my firs pay chek $15 doller. I come home an give her (Ma) an envope with 3 bills. She hug me so tite I like to bust. It the happyest day of my life.

Those my two incents. Lonnie (I got more)

Jeanna was still lost in the sprawling red strands of Lonnie's story when the phone rang.

"Hello?"

"Hello, Jeanna?"

She recognized his voice immediately. Everything—time, breath, the rain, her heart—stopped for a moment.

"This is Land."

"I thought I recognized your voice."

"Listen, Jeanna, I was wondering if you could come over to my place this Sunday for brunch. There're some things I wanted to talk over."

Surprised to be invited to a special meeting at his home, she managed to say, "Why sure, about what time?" Her excitement at being invited into his closest inner circle rose with each tick of the watch on her wrist, her uneven breathing, and the sudden cascading rain outside.

"About eleven. Will that work?"

"Sure, of course. Can I bring anything?" she asked, as if going to Landon Waters's home were the most natural thing in the world.

"No, just yourself. I'm glad you're free." He laughed. Nervously, Jeanna thought. Was that possible?

"I'm glad too," she heard herself say, then caught herself, not sure what she was glad about, not sure why she was being invited, and certain she would not be asking.

In a haze, she heard Land giving her the directions to his home before she placed the phone receiver gently on its cradle.

She wandered through her small apartment, picking up a stray shirt and sock off her bedroom floor, a dirty towel from over the side of the tub, and discarding them in the corner of her bathroom. As she removed her dinner dishes from the table, the pile of students' papers teetered and slipped down to the floor in a cascade of colored folders, but she scarcely noticed. She walked through the kitchen door to her bed and lay down.

This couldn't be a personal invitation. She was way too young, and Land was beyond her in every imaginable way. He was married, wasn't he? Even if his wife was rarely around, he wouldn't be going behind her back. He had always appeared to be the epitome of integrity, although he certainly had dozens of women coming on to him. He wasn't the kind of man who wouldn't be committed to his wife.

No, this had to be some get-together of his close political confidants, and she was being included on a kind of protégé basis. He must have been noticing all her work these many months. This is what she'd always wanted, to be a genuine part of a real change effort with people she fully respected. To be part of Land's inner circle of friends and allies. She couldn't believe it was happening. She couldn't remember ever having felt this way, flowing with such intense energy, lifted beyond her normal self. She tried to get a grip on reality. *It's just a meeting*, she told herself. She'd sit tight and listen, try to find her way.

On Sunday morning, Jeanna put on her favorite chocolate brown slacks and teal blue sweater, liking the way it set off the peach color of her skin, and took a brush to her unruly auburn hair. When she applied her Adobe Sunrise lipstick, she was pleased to see that she immediately looked several years older.

The day was overcast and grey, with the threat of a storm in the air, as she left her apartment. Land's house was the last on a rutted, dead-end road—a beige stucco with a front door of burnished wood.

The window trim and shutters were sienna red, peeling in places. The grasses and weeds out front were tall, waving back and forth in the chill breeze. Towering evergreens rose up on the left, shadowing the misty yard, and tangled willows blew about in the wind on the far side of the house. A wooded area separated his property on the right from a modest industrial park, and there were two other homes on the lane, but they were unpainted and looked barely inhabited. Weeds overgrew their front yards.

Except for Land's beaten-up VW wagon, there wasn't another car in sight. Had the others parked somewhere else? Maybe she was early. She took a deep breath of damp air and rapped hesitantly on the door.

"Door's open, come on in!" Land called out.

She gingerly pushed the door open and was immediately engulfed by aromas of brewing coffee and bacon, potatoes, and onions frying. Land walked around the counter through the open living area, wiping his hands with a dishtowel. He smiled, took her hand, and gave her a quick kiss on the cheek. Soft strains of jazz were coming from somewhere.

"It smells wonderful in here!" she exclaimed.

"Well, I decided to cook a good old-fashioned breakfast for us. How do you like your eggs?"

"All ways, every way," she managed to say, still feeling his lips on her cheek, wondering if that's how he greeted the rest of the world in his home.

"Good. I'll make an 'everything' scramble, then. Just give me a few minutes and make yourself at home there on the couch."

"Okay." She sank gratefully into the well-worn cushions. From there she could see him as he moved around the kitchen behind the counter, whipping up eggs, pouring juice, setting out a platter of bacon. Five minutes went by, then ten. No one else appeared. This was not looking like a meeting of his trusted inner circle. She felt a flash of disappointment, and then nervous confusion. What was going on?

"Do you take milk or cream with your coffee?"

"Milk is fine. Can I do anything to help?" She felt very strange sitting there.

"Not really, thanks. It's almost ready."

She could hear some Miles coming from a room down the hall, "My Funny Valentine." That had been one of the first albums she'd ever bought; now she had a full collection of Miles, Coltrane, Billie, and Lester Young, half of which her grandmother had given her. Another record came on with a really nice beat. Jeanna moved slightly with the music and she felt that old tug of desire to try to play it on her flute. She hadn't felt that in a while—she'd been too busy.

She caught Land looking at her with a half-smile on his face, one hand holding the fry pan a few inches off the fire, the other holding the dishtowel over his shoulder. He brightened as she looked at him.

"You're really into music, aren't you?" he asked.

"I am—or at least, I used to be," she said. "I played the flute in the high school band and then in college for a few years. We had a jazz group until . . ."

"Until?"

"Until the political bug bit me. There was a meeting every other night and a protest or conference or something every other weekend. It's a wonder I made it through school."

"Yeah." He chuckled. "Politics has a way of doing that."

"And you . . . are there things you've given up?" she asked.

He didn't skip a beat. "Oh, grassroots politics, the movement, whatever you want to call it, is my life. It's what I do." He pulled the pan off the stove and brought it to the snug booth on the other side of the kitchen next to the window. Melted cheese crisscrossed the eggs and potatoes in the pan.

"Come have a seat." He motioned toward the booth.

Jeanna slid onto the bench. The window rattled from the blasts of wind and the rain now coming down in streams. The willows lashed about and lit up gold when sudden flashes of lightning split open the nickel-gray sky. Coltrane's "A Love Supreme" filled the nook.

As Land slipped into the booth across from her, he said, "Don't you love it when it storms outside and you can just huddle up all warm and cozy and listen to Miles and Coltrane?"

"You read my mind," Jeanna said, wondering if they were flirting or just innocently chatting.

As she reached for her napkin, Land put his long, supple hand over hers. "I'm glad you came."

Silent and still as stone, Jeanna looked up at him. He gazed steadily into her eyes, and she felt waves of desire flow through her, filling empty places she hadn't known existed. This was not a business meeting. She was not going to be given a special task. She could not utter a sound, move a fraction of an inch, smile, or frown. She felt a desperate urge to run wild and free, throw herself on the ground, and feel the moist dirt next to her face.

He continued to smile at her. She wondered if she looked as crazed as she felt, and if he was used to such reactions. He finally rubbed his hands together and said, "Let's eat!"

He served her a sizable helping of his "everything" eggs, two thick slices of bacon, and offered her a small basket of plump biscuits. She reached for one and felt its warmth in her icy hand.

"So tell me about your life, your teaching, what your days are like," Land said. "We see each other on the fly at meetings, but I don't know nearly enough about the real you."

Jeanna felt relieved. Teaching, the kids, and the school—that was something she could talk about. She told story after story about her students: Lonnie's dangerous work, Chefman's blessing and Group Survive, Cat's skittishness. Valle's wisdom, Cassius's cockiness, Karima's radicalism. When she spoke of Tommie Lee protecting Pepper against Big Blue's assault and helping Olly with Jam, he broke in, "Tommie Lee Johnson, Lillian's son?"

"Yes, he's a great kid. I'm still sick about him being sentenced to the detention center."

"Yeah, it's a travesty. I'm trying to get his time reduced. I've known Lillian since we were kids. Her family didn't have two nickels to rub together, and I used to stick up for her." He shook his head. "That was a long time ago. I try to make sure things go okay for him."

"Really! Well then he's got a great mentor," Jeanna said. "I'm sure you make a big difference in his—"

"I haven't done much for him, really."

She was confused by Land's curtness.

His expression softened and he added, "He was always special. Lillian and Carl have done a great job with him."

"He's the most mature young man I've ever come across. When crazy stuff happens, he steps into the breach in a way the kids can relate to, when they might just flare up at a teacher."

"Do they flare up a lot at you?"

"Not really."

"I didn't think so," he said, touching her hand again. "It's obvious how committed you are, and that's rare in the schools."

"Oh, I don't know." Jeanna's hand was hot where he had touched it.

"I know. It's rare. People like you are rare, Jeanna."

He was making her feel better about herself than she'd ever felt.

"I suppose when it comes down to it, I have more respect for those kids than I do most adults, present company excepted." She smiled at him.

"Well, thank God for that!" He laughed aloud and she touched his arm playfully, tentatively, surprising herself.

"Just listen to Billie," he said, and they sat listening to the sassy lyrics of "Them There Eyes."

Land leaned toward her. "Jeanna, I can't remember when I've felt so comfortable with someone. What I've wanted to ask you is, do you think it's possible that we could get closer? I mean personally, you know, closer." He seemed at a loss for words. He looked at her, and for the first time she could feel his vulnerability instead of her own.

"I don't see why not. Isn't that what we've been doing?" she said. Part of her still desperately wanted a movement friend and mentor. The other part was amazed that he clearly meant much more.

He smiled. "I need to tell you a little more. First, I'm married. It's not a normal marriage, to be sure, but it is a fact, and one that isn't going to change."

"That's what I thought. That's why I never—" She was slipping around on this strange ground.

"Pearl and I got involved in high school, and we got married right after I finished college and got my first job at the West Side Center. We probably should have waited, but there was a lot of pressure on both of us." He paused. "I love Pearl. But she's mentally ill, severely so. She's able to function somewhat normally only one month or so out of the year, and even then she's extremely fragile. The rest of the time it's a nightmare. Most of the time she stays at a rehab center in the Adirondacks, what they call a therapeutic arts community. It's a very caring place. That's where most of my resources go." His expression had darkened.

"How awful for you both." Jeanna wished she could ease the pain in his face. "When did her problems begin?"

A shadow passed over Land's eyes. "There were small signs when we were still teenagers, and then in college, but it hit hard in her twenties, after she gave birth to our daughter, Justine. We struggled on for a number of years, but eventually Pearl became totally unstable and suicidal. It was damaging Justine."

"What did you do?"

"My sister, who lives out in Seattle, finally insisted that she and her husband take Justine. We hoped that we could take her back as Pearl's condition improved, but it never did, at least not enough for her to be a mother to Justine. For another few years I struggled to deal with Pearl's condition and do my work in the community, but it was tough—impossible, really. A family counselor who understood Pearl's passion for art finally suggested the center."

"Did it help?"

"Somewhat. It's helped us cope. She has a chemical imbalance of some kind they've never been able to get on top of. The way we're living, it's as if we're not married . . . but if I was to seek a divorce, which I'd never do, it could break her completely."

Jeanna sighed. "God, you've been through hell."

"I don't know if it's right or wrong, but I know I can't keep on this way. I need a real relationship in my life. I really like you, Jeanna. I like the way you handle yourself. You seem wise beyond your years. Strong, clear. Committed. I know I can trust you, trust your judgment." He smiled. "And I find you very attractive."

She was floored by that. Flowing champagne she was not. "I've seen Pearl, and I find that hard to believe." She flushed, embarrassed.

"No, really. Pearl is beautiful, of course. But you"—he reached out to touch her hair—"you have your own beauty."

No one had ever said such things to her. She wasn't sure what to make of all of it. How could he be committed to his wife and be coming on to her? But if his wife was never really there, then what else could he do, short of giving up a personal life altogether? The most she'd hoped for was to become part of his inner circle of movement friends and allies, but now her head was filled with wild dissonance and her heartbeat was speeding up and slowing down like a syncopated jazz rhythm.

"The real question is what could you see in me," he said. "I'm married, and in this crazy situation. I'm older. I'm up to my eyeballs in work commitments."

"Well, we have the same commitments," she said. "The other guys I've dated weren't interested in what I cared about. They didn't get my social justice thing."

"So they didn't get you."

"Exactly." She didn't mention the one man she had been obsessed with, Cam, who had understood her activism and fed it, but had also been totally unreliable as a partner to her or any woman. She had a momentary flash of being rammed in bed by a near-stranger; that faded as she looked at Land, who was of a totally different order. She felt so young and unsure next to him, hardly a woman at all.

"I'm afraid I have very little experience. I feel so new to all this." She stopped, embarrassed by all she didn't know and hadn't experienced. "I guess the most I'd hoped for was to be a real part of the

Group—at best, a friend." Deep down that was still what she wanted most: a real friendship with Land. Especially to start with, and for a long time to come, so she could be surer of herself with him if they went deeper.

"I know it will take time, and I don't want to rush anything. In fact, my better self would advise against it." Land let out a self-deprecating laugh. "As far as friendships and political confidants go, I have plenty of them in my life. Too many. I guess I just want something closer, someone in my corner for support. Real support is scarce out there."

She felt a rush of bitterness at his "plenty of friends and confidants" statement, but then a haunted look came over his face—one she realized she had seen other times as well, when he was being very still in meetings, or just coming in the door—and it made her want to reach out and touch his face. She found herself reaching out and putting her hand over his instead.

He lifted her hand to his lips, kissed it, and let it go. He ran his fingers through his hair.

She felt something wholly new click deep inside her.

"How 'bout we give it a week and you come over again next Sunday and let me know how you're feeling?" he said. "I know it's out of the blue and you need to think it through. You've been on my mind for months, but I want what's best for you, and I'm not at all sure this is. I've gone back and forth. Maybe I'm just weak in wanting you."

She had never heard words like these, and never had anyone near Land's caliber be the slightest bit interested in her. He had been thinking about her for months? How could that be? He had seemed so untouchable, so unattainable, that she had not even considered the prospect of a relationship beyond friendship. But clearly a friendship was not an option, and at that she felt another bitter flash of disappointment—a flash that was quickly overtaken by excitement, desire, and fear.

"One last thing," he said. "I guess you know . . . we'd have to be discreet."

"Of course," she responded, now wondering what there was to think about. She was hardly going to reject the most compelling man she'd ever met. The image of him chained to a bulldozer in the early-morning mist came to mind, as did the lines of men and women trying to get a word with him before and after each meeting, and his hand on hers at the breakfast table. No, terrified as she was, she knew her answer.

"All I ask is that you think about it," Land said.

She got up to go. "Okay, but I'm pretty sure I know." She smiled, surprised at her own confidence. She felt then that it was love speaking—her first real reckoning with love.

"Before you go, listen to this song with me. No one sings it like Lady Day."

He stood up and held her close to "Body and Soul." Her body trembled against his. He brushed his lips against hers until they softened, then gave her the longest, deepest kiss of her life.

Jeanna drove home in a state of bewildered rapture. She felt like she'd been lifted from the mundane to the sublime in a single afternoon and didn't know why.

When she got home, she tried to calm down in a hot bubble bath. She sank into the tub and settled back, breathing slowly and deeply. She was aware of thousands of bubbles covering her breasts like weightless snowflakes, vibrating in rose and silver, gold and green, rising and falling with her breath. As the water cooled and the bubbles broke, she returned to her central question: Why her?

Why not one of the extraordinary women in and around the Group, or any of the gorgeous, capable, confident women Land was always connecting with across the city, all of whom lit up in his presence, laughed with him, strategized with him in closed, hushed sessions, and then an hour later flirted with him shamelessly? Why not stunning, capable Helene? Or the assistant principal at Jefferson High, with all her salt and sparkle? Next to these women, Jeanna felt paltry. Young, green, scared. A nonentity.

What had he said? He felt a kinship with her, trusted her judgment, thought she was wise beyond her years and strong, was comfortable with her, found her attractive, and needed support—yes, she could do that. She felt that way toward her students, the Group, lots of people. Maybe that's where she differed from Helene and others. Helene was definitely on the cool side, and many of the other women she was thinking of were coolly intimidating as well. No one could say that about her. *When he realizes how insecure I am, he'll drop me for someone more polished and mature—someone more his match.*

She thought of their twenty-something-year difference in age. His blackness, her whiteness. His experience, her inexperience. Sooner or later, all that would matter. Sooner or later, she would disappoint him. But for now she wanted to soak up all the greatness he exuded. And she wanted to ease the pain she'd seen in him. Amid this haze of exhilaration, that was the one clear thing she could see.

CHAPTER TWENTY-SIX

I'll Never Do Anything You Don't Want

ALL WEEK, JEANNA THOUGHT OF HER UPCOMING Sunday meeting with Land. She thought of how difficult his life had been with Pearl, with her gone most of the time and her illness undermining their marriage even when she was there. And how different Land was from Cam, who'd never said a single caring word to her but used to make a move on her when her guard was down. Land, in contrast, had seemed so vulnerable, and had given her time to think things over instead of just taking advantage.

Jeanna worried about her lack of sexual experience—that she wouldn't know what to do, wouldn't be what he needed. The sexual revolution had pretty much passed her by, and she'd never seemed to fit any of the boxes the boys in high school and college wanted to put her in. To them, her music had been just another distraction, and her activism had intimidated the hell out of them—that is, until she met Cam.

Prior to Cam, she'd had a few minor sexual forays with two nice but conventional guys in college. Both had been in such a hurry, so nervous, they'd left her virginity technically intact. And then Cam set her up on a blind date with an NBA star who had just been let go due to a chronic knee injury—a guy who, Jeanna quickly realized upon meeting him, was in a downright ugly mood about seeing his NBA career go up in smoke.

She remembered him picking her up in his brand-new blue sports car. She wasn't used to that kind of brash display and felt out of place in the low-slung, plush leather seats. They had gone to dinner at a steakhouse—his choice—where he had scoffed at her civil rights efforts as "pussywork." She'd never met anyone so cynical. She couldn't wait to go home.

He had insisted upon using her bathroom when he dropped her off at her place. She had wanted to say no because he made her so uneasy, but felt she couldn't be rude. When he flung her on the bed with a quick flick of his wrist, his huge body above hers, wired to explode at the slightest provocation, her inner instinct told her to go along. In as long as it took to tear her underpants off and undo his trousers, he was inside her. She remembered how surprised he was, and then the little smile that came over his face that terrified her, as he broke through her vaginal membrane. Her initial cries of pain had seemed especially gratifying to him. So she'd shut up, taking the rest of his piston-like ramming in terrified silence, praying for it to be over. Finally it was. He used the bloodied sheet to wipe himself off, tossed it over her, dressed, and left without a word.

She lay there, dazed, for hours, then made her way gingerly to the bathtub and filled it with warm water. She eased herself in, her vagina stinging, and sat, letting the water soak away the blood, the ugly, gamey smell, and her helpless humiliation and rage, certain that she would have been beaten senseless, perhaps killed, had she resisted. She knew, also, that since she had had the good sense not to resist, she would not stand a chance in a court of law, nor in the court of everyday opinion, if she tried to tell anyone what had happened.

Cam never asked how things had gone on the date, and she hadn't filled him in. She couldn't talk about it—especially with Cam, the only man she had ever really wanted to sleep with.

Ever since that, for the past two years, she had stayed clamped shut, disinterested in any and all come-ons, wondering if she'd ever be able to find a man she could truly respect and love. And now wham, like a bolt out of the mystical blue, here had come Land, who surpassed everything and everyone she'd ever known. She was terrified. All week she left the coffee pot on when she left for work and almost burned down the house. She turned on the faucet and forgot to turn it off. She couldn't remember how to put the key in the ignition or roll the car window up or down.

The only time she could focus was when she was at school. In fact, her greatest gift that week had been Cassius. She still had trouble grasping what had happened, except that he had needed her. He'd appeared in her office doorway early that week, worried to death about his girlfriend, the one thing in life he cared about. She was pregnant, and Cassius begged Jeanna to help him find a job to support her; then the very next day he fell into Jeanna's arms, broken and crying his heart out. Apparently his girlfriend had another lover—a pimp, it seemed—and she didn't know who the father was, and couldn't see him anymore for fear that either she or Cassius would be brutalized by the guy, or even killed.

Jeanna had made Cassius promise to come to school every day and stay in her classroom for safety. He had, and by the second day had gotten drawn into the music group by Valle and Will. She could barely believe that this brash young tough who had walked out of her class the first day of school had ended up falling into her arms as the one and only place he had to go. She was humbled by his trust.

The week stretched on for an eternity—then Sunday came with the abruptness of an earthquake. Jeanna was a jumble of nerves, a chaotic mess. She ran a hot bath to relax, but it reminded her of the rape. She was terrified at the prospect of having sex with Land. Everything seemed to be happening at breakneck speed. She remembered the smile on Hudson's face as he rammed into her, even as she knew that Land was made of wholly different, almost sacred cloth. She felt like a lamb going to slaughter one second, and the next she desired it with every fiber of her being.

Dripping, she got out of the tub, and with a hand still foaming with bath bubbles, she dialed Land's number.

He answered.

"Hi Land. It's Jeanna."

"Hi Jeanna. I hope you're not canceling on me. I just heated up some cinnamon rolls."

"Oh, no, no, I'm coming." She paused, searching for a way to say whatever it was that had driven her out of the tub to dial his number.

"Are you okay?"

"I . . . I just need to tell you something before we get together."

"Okay," he said gently.

"I don't know why I need to tell you, but I guess I do. A couple of years ago . . . I went out with this guy, an NBA player—big, you know."

"Yes."

"Well, I'd dated some, but hadn't really you know, gone all the w—"

"I understand."

"Well, anyway, he was angry about something. He raped me. It was pretty bad. I haven't had any, you know, relationships since. Actually I've never told anyone but you, just now."

"Oh, I'm so sorry," Land said softly. "That should never, ever have happened to you. The bastard."

In those few words, filled with sadness, empathy, and anger, Jeanna felt the acknowledgement and compassion she hadn't known she needed.

"Thank you so much for telling me that," Land said. "I want you to know I will never, ever, do anything you don't want. I really want you to know that."

"I know. I'm sorry to bring it up. I guess I just need for you to be patient with me, wait until I can catch up. You know?"

"I do. I'm glad you told me. You come over. We'll just have our breakfast, listen to some music, talk, and catch up on our week, okay?"

"Sounds good. I'll see you soon." Jeanna hung up, feeling foolish yet glad she had called. The heavy weight inside her was gone, and an expansive, jittery hope had taken its place.

When Jeanna got to Land's, they sat on his couch a few feet apart, eating the nutty rolls he'd made and sipping hot coffee, listening to jazz and talking. He asked her about her teaching, and they laughed over the kids' antics. They talked about the possibility of Tommie Lee's early release, and about the Group, and when some of Jeanna's doubts about her effectiveness and acceptance poked through, he said, "Don't you know how powerful you are, Jeanna? You're a very powerful woman."

She knew in that moment that she would never forget those words, though she doubted she would ever truly believe them.

She told him about her encounter with Cassius, ending her story with, "That made up for all the agony that kid has put me through."

He kissed her then, and said, "You're something else, you know that? I'm gonna make up for all that agony, too."

She knew he was referring to what she had said on the phone. He kissed her lips, face, forehead, eyes, and throat softly, slowly. He caressed her breasts and kissed her deep and full on the lips. She never wanted him to stop, even as she knew she wasn't at all ready to go where this was headed.

He stopped, his face full of desire, and whispered, "I don't want to rush you."

She said nothing, but knew that if he didn't go any farther she'd be fine—in Nirvana, in fact. She also knew how unlikely that was. He gathered her up in his arms and led her into his bedroom. Her heart hammered in her chest, and she felt awkward, angry, and scared—and exhilarated.

Land laid her down gently on his expansive bed and lay down beside her, continuing to caress her until she thought she would go mad, despite feeling little sparks of resentment that he had disregarded their phone conversation earlier that morning.

She knew there was no going back now; like it or not, she was in the big leagues, and she would simply have to find a way to skip over the decades of experience that separated them and be what he needed her to be, or he would be gone, on to his next, more mature sexual partner. Waiting was clearly not an option.

He undressed her and himself and lay on top of her, his arms and knees taking much of his weight. Continuing to caress her, he whispered into her ear, "I won't do anything you don't want. We don't have to do this, babe."

Of course they did. Otherwise they'd be doing something different. He'd be holding her on the couch, kissing her cheek, running his hand through her hair, asking her things, telling her things, deepening their connection, not pushing anything, waiting for that divine mutual moment to arrive, letting the initiative come from her too.

She couldn't say no now, not after she'd gone along with it this far. She was suddenly alarmed at how large he was, but he entered her ever so slowly, delicately, as if she were made of hand-blown glass. She melted around him, loving his sensitivity. But as he filled her completely, at the very end point, it hurt. It felt strange and invasive, foreign and ungainly, yet thrilling.

He remained completely still, holding her close, until she moved a little. They rocked slow and long. It didn't feel good—it was painful, really—but she knew she was supposed to think it felt good, and maybe it would soon, or someday. Maybe she just needed to relax more, go with it. What was that word the books were always using for the woman? They "surrendered."

Yes, she could try that, but something in her resisted. She could say "No, I don't want to do this yet"—but hadn't she already said that in a sense on the phone? And now look what they were doing.

She tried going with it and it felt a little better—still very strange, but the feel of her arms around his lean, muscled body, the curved, smooth line of his back, the tightness of his buttocks, the mouth and lips that had become hard somehow against hers, his slippery bigness inside her, was powerful and overwhelming. Her ears were rumbling with a loud dissonance like some jazz drummer on a wild roll; she was still feeling the pain at the end of every long thrust, yet closing her eyes, she was transported into a pulsating galaxy of bright lights against a dark red sky.

Finally, he shuddered and was still. They drifted, entwined, in and out of consciousness—she, lost inside a strange landscape of body, breath, and inner chaos, and he spent, content, separate. Two strangers, interwoven.

They awoke to a crazily repeated refrain from "It Might As Well Be Spring."

Land laughed. "King Pleasure's stuck!" He slid away, wrapped the soft down comforter up around her shoulders, and got out of bed to fix it.

Jeanna admired his long, lithe body, the slender muscles of his hips and legs rippling smoothly as he walked, wishing for a greater leanness of her own. He came back wearing a pair of white terrycloth slacks that contrasted beautifully with his deep bronze skin. The music swelled behind him. Gerry Mulligan again—for her, she knew—playing an up-tempo "I Thought About You."

"Hey, I thought about you . . ." she sang off key. "All week, in fact."

He laughed. "You know more about jazz than you let on. And I thought about you, too."

But I bet you didn't almost burn the house down, she mused. "Do you mind if I take a shower?"

"Go right ahead. Grab one of my shirts on the shelf if you like. I'm starving. I'll fix us something to eat."

She returned from her shower wearing a soft, cream-colored shirt with russet stripes, feeling like she was suddenly living in an entirely new world. Land whistled in appreciation, and they nestled into the same side of the nook and ate, with Moody's "Mood for Love" on—a song with great flute that Jeanna knew once again he was playing for her.

"Nothing like Moody's 'Mood,'" she said.

Land nodded vigorously, his mouth full. They ate in a comfortable silence, their legs touching.

"I forgot to ask you about Cassius," Jeanna said.

"Shoot."

"He loves to drum, and I'd like to find him a set of drums at a discount somewhere, but I'm not sure where."

"You came to the right place . . . Maybe." He laughed. "My brother, Truth, was a drummer before he took up the sax, and just the other day I was hanging with him in his basement studio and I saw a plastic tarp over his old set of drums. He was talking about getting rid of them so he'd have more room, but I think he plans to sell them."

"Oh, I'll pay. I just may need a month-by-month payment plan. God, could Cassius ever use someone like your brother to talk with about jazz and, I don't know, life."

"You're too much you know that? Monthly payment plan." He kissed her, sending her tingling up to the ceiling.

The phone rang. He slipped out of the booth to take it by the kitchen counter.

"He clubbed little Mac? Christ. Yes, yes, no, I'll be there as soon as I can get there. Where are you?"

She was in the bedroom getting dressed by the time he got off the phone.

"I'm sorry. A cop just clubbed a young retarded boy, a big overgrown kid, because he kept laughing at him when he was told to move out of the street, and a crowd has formed. Looks like a riot in the making. Cop cars are coming from everywhere. The ambulance can't get through and he's losing blood fast."

"Please, go!" Jeanna said, reeling from all the drama and already understanding what a relationship with Land would be like.

He changed and was out the door in a matter of seconds, saying over his shoulder that he'd call her.

She did the dishes, smoothed out the comforter on the bed, thought about writing him a love note, thought better of it, remembered she had a chocolate bar in her purse, and put it on his pillow. She gathered her stuff and left, glad to have some time to savor everything that had just happened alone before she went in to teach the next day.

CHAPTER TWENTY-SEVEN

Living in Land's World

FOR DAYS, WEEKS, AFTER THEY FIRST MADE LOVE, Jeanna lived entirely in the world of Land. He worked his way under her skin for good, and settled into her bloodstream. He danced shaman-like in her dreams at night and floated across the periphery of her vision by day. Even when he was not there, she held him close in the solid warmth of her bed and in the gauzy curtains of her mind. When she spoke to her students, he was the affirming glance in their eyes. When she commented on their work, he was in the ink that rolled out on the page. He was the unbidden ache in her womb, the dark thrill in her veins.

She felt like a seagull on the mainmast going out to sea. Because she was so often out beyond her depths, the ride could be quite rough and often was. But she felt a sureness of heart about him that carried her through the frightening absurdities and whirlpools. Land was her inner protection, her 23rd Psalm.

Before there was Land and Jeanna, there were meetings. After there was Land and Jeanna, there were more meetings, with people shouting themselves hoarse, cutting each other off, rearing up on their egos to dominate the scene. But Jeanna and Land wove in and out of each other within the group, silent as water. Land rose and fell with the waves, rising when needed and falling back into the cavern when not. Jeanna watched and listened and moved lightly behind the scenes.

As the days wore on, she couldn't believe how much he seemed to respect her ideas, how he'd consult her on everything, more or less thinking out loud. It was like they were playing a duet, with her in the minor key.

Tonight the question was what to do with the ministers of various churches who were threatening to step in and grab away the grant money that Land had been expecting. The Group had been working on this project ever since Tommie Lee's incarceration: detention diversion, community involvement, and youth leadership. Now the ministers wanted a piece of the action, despite having been totally ineffective in actually engaging young people up to this point.

"They don't see youth as real leaders in their own right. That's the problem," Jeanna said. "The ministers act like they're above them, like they know everything."

"That's it exactly," Land agreed, "but they have the clout to get the money regardless. I got a strong feel from the foundation reps that they liked the ministers' proposal better and they're going to fund it, not ours."

They were talking in bed, under the quilt, their bodies touching comfortably.

"Could you ask the foundation to meet directly with the churches' youth, and then the kids we've been working with? That way the kids could speak for themselves, which could be really powerful, and the foundation could decide which proposal has more real promise."

He laughed. "Babe, you are a genius."

"Well, I mean, it is a youth leadership project."

"I mean," he said, "how else could you do it?" He hugged her. "But you know"—he stopped, his body hovering above hers—"the ministers will prep their kids, if they can find any, within an inch of their lives."

"Let 'em. It'll all sound canned. Nobody needs to prep Tommie Lee at Chisolm's, or his detention diversion group on the outside."

"That's the truth," he said. He rolled away from her onto his back, flung an arm over his forehead, and lay still.

He'd gone somewhere else. She didn't know where, and didn't dare ask. It seemed too quiet and private a place. She kissed his arm and slid out of bed. "I'm taking a bath. If you get hungry, there's a plate in the oven you can heat up."

"Thanks," he said, absently squeezing her thigh. He always seemed so pensive—removed, somehow—when Tommie Lee's name came up.

"He's tough to mentor, isn't he?" she said.

He looked at her sharply; then he softened his gaze with a half-smile. "Damn near impossible."

A few days later, Jeanna was lying with Land as he dozed in and out, trying to get a better handle on the exact meaning of "discreet." She wanted in the worst way to confide in Helene about Land, but something told her not to. But except for her ultra-new friendship with Jackie, she had no other friends in the city. She needed, desperately, to talk with someone about Land, but she worried that he wouldn't like it, and Helene might not either.

Who was she, Jeanna, to steal the star of the show, the center of their universe? And if it got out, couldn't this jeopardize all they were working for?

Maybe she was over-dramatizing, being paranoid. Helene was always taking her to task for being too earnest in matters of the heart. Maybe she would take the news in stride and be glad for her. Maybe Land would say, be discreet, but no need to freak out.

She decided she would ask him when he woke up.

He stirred, reached for her, and pulled her close. Anxiety welled within her as she tried to phrase the question.

"We've been making love so much, I barely know what your out-of-bed life is like," Land said.

"It's good," Jeanna said. "I still love each and every student to death, with one or two exceptions. I seem to survive the daily catastrophes at school somehow. And I think I'm finding my way in the Group pretty well." Her tone was more hesitant.

"I'd say so, without a doubt. Hey, you came in outta the blue and took me and the group by storm, girl." He smiled at her.

"Hardly," she said, loving the comment. Maybe now was the time. "Land, I've wanted to ask you something for weeks."

"Well, ask." His tone was easy enough, but his eyes turned wary.

"When we first had brunch together, you said we'd have to be discreet."

"Mm-hm. What's hard to understand about that?" A storm cloud had replaced the wariness.

She'd never seen that look. What an idiot she was. She felt sick. "Oh, I don't know, nothing I guess, it's just . . ."

"What is it?" His tone had softened, like he was holding the clouds at bay.

"I guess I was wondering if it's okay for me to talk about our relationship with a close friend of mine." She didn't feel comfortable saying that it was Helene.

"In this area?"

"Probably."

"Probably," he repeated testily. "It's really better if you tell no one. Especially around here or on the political scene. Rumors fly fast, and if anything comes out about us it could destroy my reputation, which is really all I have. I'd lose my effectiveness. A lot could go down the drain. I thought you understood that." He was looking at her intently.

"No, I do, I do, I guess I just needed to be sure."

"Well, thanks for asking. I don't want any vigilantes coming after us!" He laughed, and the clouds receded.

She never wanted to see those dark clouds again. She'd try to work things out on her own from now on. She never wanted to add to his problems, only to help smooth them away.

They stood up, and he pulled her tight against him. She could feel her heart pounding like a piston, and knew he must be able to as well. She was scared she had jeopardized the relationship, that he would think her too young and foolish.

He held her face against the crook of his neck. "Jeanna, I worry about hurting you, about all this being too much to handle. Maybe I should step out of your life. Give you a chance to be twenty without all the complications."

Jesus. Now he was voicing her worst fear. She was frantic at the thought of losing him so soon. "Don't talk that way," she said in a fierce, strangled whisper. "I want you, to be with you, more than anything I've ever wanted in my life. Don't worry, I'm older than twenty seems."

He held her tighter yet. "You are, you're an old soul," he said. "I felt it from the start."

She felt his words like a benediction.

"You take care of you," he said.

"I will," she said, realizing she would have to. There would be no one else.

CHAPTER TWENTY-EIGHT

How Many Times Can a Heart Be Sliced to Smithereens?

When Jeanna entered Helene's apartment for dinner on Friday evening, Helene gave her a peck on the cheek, but Jeanna noticed that her eyes seemed troubled.

"You okay?" Jeanna asked, touching Helene's arm.

"I'm not quite myself, but I'm okay."

They sat across from each other at the small round table. Helene worked the cork out of a wine bottle and poured the ruby liquid into both glasses. They touched each other's glass and Jeanna said, "To good food and good times."

"And good friends," Helene added.

Jeanna was touched. "Why aren't you yourself today?"

"I'm just feeling down. I usually do this time of the year."

"Why now?"

"It's not important," Helene said as she buttered a piece of bread, and, absently, buttered it again.

"Yes it is, tell me."

"Well, it was my birthday yesterday."

"I didn't realize—"

"No, of course not. Oh Jeanna, I've been wanting to tell you for so long about this. It's over and done with, so it can't hurt to share it now. But you have to promise to keep absolutely silent about it. I've never told anyone but my sister, and she's three thousand miles away."

"Helene, believe me, I won't tell a soul."

"Well, eleven, twelve years ago, when I first moved out here, I joined the Group almost right away. At that time, it was pretty disorganized."

"Which you helped change." Jeanna smiled.

"Right," Helene said, smiling back. "I built the organizational infrastructure, and Land was totally supportive. It felt great to be valued by someone."

"And?"

"Well, after about a year of us working hand-in-glove, he called me. It was April 5th. I remember, because I had girded myself for another birthday alone. I was always down on that day. He said, 'Happy Birthday, Helene, I have a little something for you. Can I come over?' I was dumbfounded. To me, Land was God. I know that sounds absurd."

"Not at all." To Jeanna, Land still was God.

"He brought over a pecan pie, my favorite, still warm, with vanilla ice cream. I guess he had been paying more attention than I realized." She looked down at the table. "So we sat out there on my old wooden bench on the back porch and ate that pie. Best I'd ever had then or since."

"I'll bet it was," Jeanna said, feeling a touch jealous.

"He thanked me for all the work I was doing and told me how stunning I was. I just laughed because I had met Pearl, and knew I was no match for her golden glow."

"I doubt that," Jeanna said, thinking how similar her own reaction had been to Pearl, and how drab she was compared to both of them.

"He told me that he had struggled for years ever since they were first married to stay true to Pearl, but he couldn't keep going with her absent most of the time. He hoped we could get closer."

Now she understood why Land wasn't involved with Helene—he'd already gone that route. She didn't know what to think. *Of course*, her rational mind said, but her feelings were all over the place.

"It must have been huge for you at the time." Jeanna thought of how floored she'd been at Land's invitation. She was even younger now than Helene had been when she'd gotten involved, and of course Land was a good bit older.

"It was my entire life, but unfortunately not his."

Jeanna knew what she meant. "Was it good?" she asked tentatively, not sure she wanted to know.

"Oh, it was stupendous. But it was tough, you know, having to keep it under wraps. It does a number on you."

"I can imagine," Jeanna said, feeling horribly guilty at the pretense she was being forced to pursue with Helene. "What happened?"

"Pearl returned and stayed this time."

"Really? I thought she was too sick."

"That's what we all thought. But they had developed a new drug, and it worked wonders on her. For several years she was back on the scene, and I fell totally by the wayside. While they were not your most happily married couple, they were together again. Land was very apologetic, said he wished it hadn't turned out that way for us, but he was glad for Pearl and he had to stand by her."

"God." Jeanna blanched, thinking what that would be like. "How did you feel at that point?"

"Well . . . mixed, actually."

"You weren't devastated?"

"Oh, yes, I was devastated. You don't know the meaning of devastated until you've loved and lost Land."

Jeanna felt her own heart seize. "What was the 'mixed' part?"

"Well, the terms of the relationship were chafing me. I wanted more even when I knew it wasn't reasonable to demand it, and I was an emotional wreck with Pearl gone one minute and here the next. And all the while we were killing ourselves with the work we were doing."

"Is that why even though Pearl's not here now, you're not with him?"

"Yes." Helene shrugged. "When it was over for us back then, it was over. It was just too agonizing for me to imagine starting up and having to stop again. I mean, how many times can your heart be sliced to smithereens?"

Jeanna imagined a heart laid out on a cutting board and sliced in crisscross fashion an infinite number of times, oozing blood. "Jesus, Helene."

"I tried to hang on, but I couldn't. After a while, it just wasn't worth it. So I left the area for a few years and tried to forget Land and the Group, but I was a wreck—no meaning, nowhere to go. Then he called me, said he needed me to keep the Group afloat administratively, would understand if I couldn't, but it would mean the world to him. So here I am." Helene flicked the tears out of the corners of her eyes with the tips of her fingers.

Jeanna reached out to give Helene a hug. "I'm glad you're here. I don't know what I'd do without you." But even before their embrace ended, her feeling of gratitude for Helene gave way to a powerful sense of foreboding.

CHAPTER TWENTY-NINE

I'm Famished

A FEW DAYS LATER, JEANNA WAS JARRED OUT OF AN exhausted sleep by her alarm. It was 5 a.m. With a nervous rush she remembered that Land was coming over for dinner, and before that, she had a series of meetings—first with Land, then with Lillian and Phil at the West Side Center. She was excited and nerve-racked, feeling the glow of all the amazing developments with Land and the Group, yet feeling the strain even more. Ever since Helene's confession, the anxious inadequacy that flowed beneath everything she did was back full force.

She managed to get through the day's classes; then she drove over to the community center to meet with Land. She waved at Gideon as she went by his office, but as usual he just looked through her. She went to the adjoining room and sat on the couch to go over her class prep and wait. An hour later Land had still not arrived, and neither had Lillian. The room had gotten suffocatingly hot. She was sweating and uncomfortable.

Gideon's deep voice sounded in the hallway. "Land, we've been trying to find you. Come in a minute. There's trouble on the North Side project. You too, Phil."

Jeanna waited a while longer, then finally got up and walked over to the window of Gideon's office, wanting Land and Phil to at least know she was there. Land looked up and saw her. He raised two fingers and mouthed, "Two minutes." She nodded and returned to her place.

An hour and a half later, hot, sweaty, and upset at being totally ignored, Jeanna slipped out the door and went home.

Land never showed up for the dinner she prepared. She tried to work on her next day's lesson plans, but felt scattered and unable to focus. Finally, she pulled out a stack of student papers and began to correct them. She had better luck with that. By nine she was listless from hunger and waiting. She ate half of her fish and bit into a roll, but had trouble swallowing. Why hadn't he at least called?

She brushed her teeth and lay down in bed, her back stiff and achy. Her throat was sore when she swallowed. She had left the lamp on her oak table turned on. It was a little too bright, making it hard for her to sleep, but she wanted Land to have some light when, or if, he came in. She pulled up the quilt and finally fell into a hot, sweaty sleep, dreaming of sitting stiffly on the couch at the community center, baking in the heat, various people ducking their heads in and out of the room and looking through her each time she waved at them with an odd, robotic arm motion.

She felt someone's hands on her and dreamt they were Lillian's, comforting her, looking at her with concern. The hands got stronger, and she felt lips on her cheek, the side of her throat. She awoke with a start. Land was sitting beside her, brushing back her hair. She was immediately elated, then angry.

"Sorry, Jeanna. We had to go over to the North Side construction project. Some of Abe's men were let go and replaced by union men from outside the city. Abe got into a confrontation with them and it only made matters worse. So we had to meet with the head of the union and the contractor to try to clean the mess up—it took awhile to track him down."

She wanted to ask why he hadn't called, but Land had stopped explaining and was caressing her, moving in close and kissing her. The force of his intensity transformed her thin flame of resentment into an aching cavern of need. They sank into bed and stayed there. She was lost to everything but breath and skin, softness and hardness, her love for Land engulfing her, until Land lay exhausted and they both drifted into sleep.

She awoke from a deep, sensual sleep, Land's hand on her bare shoulder, both of them naked in the moonlight.

"I hate to wake you, Jeanna, but I'm famished."

Jeanna had trouble taking it in, then felt a sharp stab of anger. She looked over at the clock: 1:32 a.m. Land pulled the covers up under his chin and lay on his back.

"Okay, I'll warm up your plate." She got up awkwardly and walked barefoot over the cold floor to the kitchen, feeling his eyes on her naked body, wondering if this was what women did, had always done—trying not to feel submissive or shamed, but unable to feel anything else.

CHAPTER THIRTY

I'm Sick a Hearing That

THE LAST WEDNESDAY IN APRIL, THEY WERE DEEP into Check-In, and Jeanna could see that Olly was working himself into one of his fighting moods.

"Why you keep saying 'just be yourself'?" Olly muttered under his breath. "I'm sick a hearing that. What if you don't know what your self is?"

Jeanna realized that he was right, that probably lots of her students wondered the same thing, and that she wasn't all that sure herself.

"See, there you sit, saying nothing. Sometimes you just piss me off. It's like it's all up to us."

Valle laughed. "Yeah, ain't that a shame. Miss J making us come to terms with our own selves for a change instead of telling us, 'Be this, do that, you ain't good enough, you think you're too good—'"

"Yeah, she lets us find ourselves, who we really are," Karima said. "That's not for her to say, or anybody else."

Silence.

"See? She don't say one damn thing. Sometimes I just hate her," Olly muttered just loud enough to be heard. He averted his eyes from Jeanna. She knew this wasn't a rebellion. This was an urgent question that was driving him nuts.

"I know it's really a drag sometimes, Olly," she said, "but you're not alone. We all have the same struggle. Who am I? Who am I becoming?

Who's in charge here? Me? My parents? My teachers? My friends? Why am I here? Why don't people see the real me? Why am I so confused?"

"But you're not supposed to feel like that. You're supposed to have it all together, teach us who we're supposed to be," Olly responded.

"Is that so?" Jeanna said, knowing that silence would enrage him at this point.

"Yeah, it's so, idiot," he whispered under his breath.

"Excuse me?" Jeanna said.

Silence.

"I hear you saying that you could use some help in finding out who you are."

"Ain't that what I been saying?" He looked ready to jump out of his skin.

"I'll tell you one thing I think is true."

"About me?" He raised his chin to her.

"About everybody."

"Jesus." He flounced in his chair with frustration. "Why can't it be about me?"

"This school," Cassius broke in. "It ain't no psycho-shrink session."

"That's right," Jeanna said, "that's why what I'm going to say is true of everybody. See, I believe that every person has a special gift, a reason for being here on earth—a purpose, a set of qualities that makes them uniquely who they are and not the same as anyone else—which is also why no one is better than anyone else, just different."

Everyone was looking at her intently.

"So let's have about five or six people volunteer to say something about Olly that is his positive gift—a quality, an ability, an aspect of him that's good and that makes him special, makes him who he is. Take some time with it before you say anything, scribble down some ideas." Jeanna knew she was taking a big chance. Olly was tough, a real brat much of the time. Would they come up with positives that were real or just tear him down?

Quite a few students were already scribbling down their comments. Jeanna gave them a few minutes, then asked, "Who'd like to go first?"

Cassius lifted a finger. She nodded to him, holding her breath. Cassius wasn't known for his compassion.

"He tells it like it is. Cuts through the bullshit."

Everyone laughed and the tension was broken. Olly nodded.

"He raises the questions that are pecking in the back of my mind," Big Blue said, "and sometimes I don't even notice the pecking until he says it and then I say, yeah, I've been wondering the same thing."

"He's got the guts to speak up," Alley said, turning crimson. Olly looked at him with surprise.

"Yeah, that's true," Will said. "He puts himself out there."

"He's a mover-shaker," Big Blue said. "He'll make a move when the rest of us is just laying around not going anywhere, he'll have this great idea and we're off and rolling again. He keeps us on our toes."

"Yeah, and he keeps us laughing too," Karima said, "with some stupid joke or other. When we get all wrapped up and super serious about everything, he'll crack right in there and it gets light and airy and we can breathe again. And I like the way he doesn't just fall in line. He's a non, non-con . . ."

"Non-conformist?" Pepper said.

"Exactly," Felice said. "He'll stand up to authority. Just because you have a big position, or a degree, he's not fazed by that—he'll deal with you just like anybody else. He won't give in to get by."

"Right," Valle said, "he tells the truth, his truth, you don't have to guess is he saying this or that just to please somebody or to get over—he means it."

"Yeah, but sometimes all these good things you saying seem wrong and bad," Olly said. "I mean, my family would take all that and see it as bad."

"Yeah, but here it's more on the good side . . . maybe because you have the freedom to let it out that way," Karima said.

"So I'm not just a pain in the ass like they say?" Olly asked, a hopeful look on his face.

"No," Jeanna said. "Didn't you hear what everyone said?"

"So you think it's good to be how you think and feel instead of always pleasing others? I'm just asking because as far as I can tell most of the rest of the world—you know, the guys in charge—just want you to do what they want you to do."

"Yes, I'm saying I think it's good to be true to yourself; don't you?"

"Yeah, maybe, but it gets you into a hell of a lot of trouble!"

Everyone laughed.

"Okay," Jeanna said, "let's take that as our journal question for the week: How can we be ourselves in a world that doesn't always seem to accept us for who we really are?"

"You think you're so smart, but I bet you don't know who you are any more than I do!" Olly said, pointing at Jeanna.

The bell shrieked that class was over just then, but Jeanna felt a thud-like hit to the belly with his words. All the way home, she worked it over in her mind.

Who was she? For a first-year teacher she was damn good, despite all her fears and anxiety and crazy feelings of inadequacy. She could draw out the best in each student and did it every day, and if on a particular day all hell broke loose or the world fell flat, she came back fresh the next day and things came back together again. There was no doubt that the kids were learning and growing, and she was too, no matter how far she still had to go.

She knew, too, that she was committed to social change. It was as vital to her as her own breath and blood, no matter how often she felt ineffective or out of her league. She never questioned whether this was what she should be doing, not even when she was ordered about by Cam, undercut by Frederick, or dismissed by Gideon.

But personally, she was a mess. She had no real friends, if she didn't count Helene—and she couldn't, really, since there was so much she wasn't able to share with her. Jackie, maybe, but she couldn't be real with her either. Her mother was generally unavailable, and would totally oppose her relationship. Her father and brother were long gone. She'd love to open up to Lillian, but that would be a disaster. She'd hate to lose her respect.

She had virtually no experience with love, and here she was, involved with the most compelling man of the century. She was with him 100 percent in mind, body, and spirit on the political action front, but she hadn't a clue where she stood on the sex, love, man-woman front. She wasn't sure what it all meant, except that she loved him with every fiber of her being and wanted somehow to measure up to whatever it was he needed, and knew this was impossible.

CHAPTER THIRTY-ONE

Cat in a Fix

A WEEK LATER, LONNIE POPPED HIS HEAD INTO Jeanna's office.

"Miss J, you got a minute?"

"Sure, come on in." She moved her bag from the chair by her desk to the floor.

"That's okay. I'll set here." Lonnie sat a few feet away on the upside-down crate she had just emptied of books and papers.

"What's up?"

"Well it's been taken care of, so I'm not telling you nothing to take no action on, you know? Fact is, ya say or do something, it could be a problem." He looked at her intently.

She nodded.

"Cat been talking to me before our reading an' writing group start? He been in a heap of trouble."

Jeanna nodded again, looking right into his eyes.

"I just wanna bring you into the loop enough so's you know what's going on, not to do nothin'."

"I understand, Lonnie. I appreciate your telling me."

He brightened and his shoulders relaxed.

"Cat been in a fix—not hardly eatin' nothin', bein' hurt by this lady."

"A lady?"

"Yes'm. See, his father got sent up the hill long time ago now."

Jeanna nodded. Matt had told her that Cat's father had been in prison for quite a few years.

"So Cat been living with his prime ho."

She squinted at him. Did he mean his father's prostitute—that he was a pimp?

"Ho a, uh, prostitute," Lonnie said, as if reading her mind.

"Okay." She swallowed.

"She, 'scuze my language, a prime bitch."

She nodded, thinking he meant she was beautiful, lucrative, top of the heap.

"But she been hurtin' Cat." He paused. "Beating him, wear these big rings." He held up his fingers and rubbed them, as if feeling for rings. "She backslap him hard upside the head till he bleed. That where he gets all them cuts on his head an face and whatnot."

She nodded. No wonder Cat jumped every time she moved a hand near him.

"She make him lick the blood off the table."

Jeanna's stomach turned, and she had to swallow hard to keep from gagging.

"That's not all."

She just looked at Lonnie. What else could there be?

"She grab him by his privates, an' I ain't gonna go into it, but this been goin' on for years."

Jeanna stopped breathing. "Years," she repeated.

"Yes'm. But that ain't all. She don't let him eat at the table, he have to stand and eat, and sometimes she don't let him eat nothin'. She say he ain't doin nothin' to earn his keep. She say go scravenge like she had to do growin' up.

Scravenge—scavenge, like a dog or cat, Jeanna thought, biting her lip. No wonder his hair was falling out. "You said it's been worked out?" She couldn't imagine how.

"Yes'm. I spoke with Mr. Guff coupla weeks ago, the man sit outside on the step, smoke that pipe."

She nodded. Guff. He sure did a hell of a lot more than sit and smoke his pipe.

"He went up to the prison. Met with Cat's father. He done changed in there an' been worrying about his kid. He got others 'side Cat, a course."

"How has he changed?"

"He met up with these Muslims in prison. They done set him on the straight and narrow. Real righteous now."

"I see."

"So him and Guff talked it out an' he already moved his ho out the house an' into a detox/rehab an' moved his youngest sister in. She a daycare teacher with the Sister Sahara Mohammed School. He done converted her awhile ago, all the way from prison."

"He owns the house?"

"Oh yeah, that man rich as a bitch at one time, still is. Off the hos, drugs, and whatnot. Security."

"Security?"

He shrugged. "Street security, y'know. Protection, threatnin', and what have you. So his sister done moved in just a few weeks ago. Biggest problem is all the mens come by looking for their regular service. Ain't there no more. They see her and want her. She cute an' whatnot. She say she not for sale and oh, they gets mad." Lonnie's whole face lit up and he laughed. "Now Cat, he sets up at the table with her and her little girl and eat till he drop."

She smiled with him. "What's Cat doing for money, for lunch, clothes?"

"Oh, his dad and Guff got him all set up now, dressed up in a funny little black suit and tie, them white white shirts, sellin' that Muslim paper."

"Where?" That Guff was something.

"On the street near his home. He doin' fine. I been hearin' change just a-jinglin' in his pocket." Lonnie wiggled with pleasure and smiled.

That explained how Cat's tattered sneakers had been replaced with two black shoes so hard and shiny they stuck out like iron doorstops on his feet, and his dirty-gray T-shirts with starched white ones. She'd been wondering.

"What's Cat's real name?" Her roster actually had "Cat" on it, despite the fact that it must be just a nickname.

"Why, you asked you a good one, Miss J," Lonnie said, smiling. "I don't know. I'm-a gonna find out if I can. I'll let you know."

Jeanna reached out and touched Lonnie's arm. "Thanks for keeping me in the loop. It really helps me understand Cat's whole situation."

"That's why I tol' you. You'll be cool with it, right?"

"Won't breathe a word, not to a soul." She knew he was afraid she'd go to DSS or something and Cat would be institutionalized and eaten alive on the inside, since he certainly was not a good candidate for foster care.

Lonnie nodded. "I got to go get my boys ready, Miss J."

"Okay, you go ahead—and thanks again, Lonnie. I really appreciate it."

He was off, walking in a smooth glide that was faster than most kids' running.

Jeanna sat there at her desk in the quiet late afternoon. It came to her, and not for the first time, that if she were ever in a real bind, a bad scrape of some kind, she'd rather call on Lonnie than anyone else she knew, bar none.

CHAPTER THIRTY-TWO

You Think That's Wise?

SEVERAL WEEKS LATER, AT THE END OF THE DAY, Jeanna's footsteps rang out loudly in the empty hallway. Everyone else had already gone home. She decided to walk the four blocks to the church where she'd seen the Black Panthers Free Breakfast sign on her way to work. Cat's gaunt face and patchy scalp alarmed her more every day, even with the improvements at home. Lonnie, Cassius, Big Blue, and Jam could use a decent breakfast too, and others as well. She'd meant to stop by ages ago.

She slung her bag over her shoulder and set forth, the sun in her eyes. She walked past row houses that were barely more than shacks, windows broken and front steps crumbling away, where several heavy-set and famine-gaunt women sat nursing babies. Decades-old litter and broken glass covered the ground where sidewalks should have been. Some young boys were huddling up, sharing a cigarette, as she walked by. She was the only white person as far as the eye could see. In a few more blocks she found the church, Twelfth Baptist. There was the free breakfast sign, with a gorgeously rendered, semi-abstract Black Panther curling around the print. Somebody had talent. The late-afternoon sun lit up the dark red and gold stained glass windows like goblets of fine wine.

Inside, she walked down a dark hall until she discovered a large set of doors with a kitchen sign that seemed to serve as the Panther office as well. The exact same poster of Huey Newton that was displayed on her own classroom wall (à la Karima) was tacked up on the door. A breakfast menu for the week was beside it, along with announcements for self-defense classes, tutoring, a free health clinic, and political discussion and planning meetings.

She stood on her tiptoes and could see through a small window in the door. A large man was sitting hunched over a table with his back to her. She tapped lightly on the door. He whirled around like he'd been shot. She jerked back and felt an adrenaline rush. The man raised his large bulk out of the chair, moved slowly toward the door, and opened it with a threatening look on his face.

Jeanna forced herself to hold her ground and look him in the eye. As the man looked down at her, his eyes registered surprise, then bewilderment, and, finally what could only be described as fear. Knowing she must look scared herself, Jeanna tried to calm her face down to look natural.

"Hi," she said. "I'm from West Side Alternative High down the street. I'm looking for the free breakfast program?"

"Uh, that's here, but . . ." He was backpedaling away from her and biting his lip. He stumbled as his heel hit the chair he'd been sitting on. "Ah, shit, 'scuze me, ain't no one here but me." Beads of sweat were forming on his forehead.

She was confused by his reaction and hesitated in the doorway, not sure what to do.

He was clenching the top of the chair.

"Could I come in?"

"Yeah, sure, sit down. Lost my manners." He gestured to a seat, then walked around the table and took a seat as far away from her as he could. The distance was awkward, but allowed Jeanna to get a better look at him. His face was puffy. A scar cut his eyebrow in two. His hair was uneven. A few pieces of lint in it kept catching her eye, making her annoyed with herself.

"We run breakfast every morning seven to eight," he said, looking somewhere beyond her left shoulder. "First fifteen minutes is political education with Gorman—he the chairman—then the food. It's hot."

"I'm Jeanna Kendall." She extended her hand across the table.

He plunged his hands into his pockets. "I . . . my hands is dirty, been cleanin' and whatnot." His right knee started jiggling up and down where he sat.

"Where do the kids sign up for breakfast?" she asked as she drew her hand back, feeling she'd been clumsy. "Or should I have them call the chairman . . . Gorman, right?"

"Oh, no. Call Sister Dessina a little after eight. She and Sister Kendra here ever' morning six to eight-thirty. Then they off to work. They handle everything."

The door opened and a man in his late twenties came in and loosely shook his shoulders to slip out of his jacket.

"Hey, Sonny," he said. He looked Jeanna in the eye. "Can I help you?" His tone was polite. He was tallish and limber looking, wore jeans, sneakers, and a white shirt with the sleeves rolled up.

"I'm a teacher at West Side Alternative High. I came to see about the free breakfast program for some of my students."

He looked at her and nodded thoughtfully. "I've been meaning to find out more about that school. I'm Clayton James. I run the health clinic." He stretched out his hand.

She took it. It was dry, smooth.

"I'm Jeanna Kendall. I didn't know you had a health clinic until I saw the sign by the door today."

Sonny got up and left without a word.

"Yeah. We have it every Wednesday evening and Saturday morning. I was a medic in 'Nam, managed to make it out alive and saw even more mayhem after I got home. So we set up a clinic especially for the young guys dealing with gang and street violence, guys back from the war, men out of prison, detention, whatever. Sonny's one of them. Ex-con. In ten years on a totally bogus sexual assault charge."

Jeanna was impressed. "Great work," she said, hating how Sonny had been destroyed.

He laughed. "First time I heard that from . . ." He stopped.

"The likes of me?" She smiled, realizing how out of place she looked with her auburn curls and light skin.

"I guess." He gave an exaggerated wince. She liked him—trusted him already.

"Do you work here full time?"

"Oh, no. Nobody gets paid here. I'm an EMT at City Hospital, and come over here Wednesdays after I'm off."

"An EMT, that's great! It makes me think maybe I could twist your arm to come to one of my classes, maybe even help mentor some of my kids who think they're so very tough." She laughed, hoping she wasn't driving him away with too many demands all at once.

"Sounds interesting. What kind of classes?" He raised his eyebrows.

"I have an Urban Issues and Basic Skills class that meets every Tuesday and Thursday morning at eight-thirty. Would you consider coming in one day to speak about the clinic?"

"Sure, sounds like my dream school."

"Mine too, when it's not a nightmare."

They both laughed.

"Just like here," Clayton said. "How'd you hear about us?"

"I saw the sign on my way into work. Someone here's quite an artist."

"That would be Dessina. Artist extraordinaire, cook, fundraiser, community organizer, tutor, you name it." He looked at his watch.

"How would my students sign up for the health clinic?"

"That would be my wife, Corinda. She does most of the health consults and exams. I, uh, administer it and talk with the guys."

As usual, women did the actual work, while men "ran" things. Maybe she should ask Sister Dessina to come speak—but something told her she wouldn't have a spare minute.

"Listen, thanks for coming," he said, getting up. "I have to say I was kind of surprised when I came in and saw you sitting there. You think that's wise, though, coming into this area by yourself?"

Anger coursed through Jeanna even though she'd asked herself the same thing. The North Side was about as rough as it got.

She shrugged. "Well, no one was free, and I needed the exercise."

"Still, I'm not sure it's a good idea."

Rage overtook her. Virtually everything she'd wanted to do in her life had been for men only: sports, jazz, community organizing, traveling on the cheap, walking down any street alone without being prey . . .

She must have had a dreadful look on her face, because he put his hands up and said, "I didn't mean to offend you—"

"You didn't," she said. "I wondered the same thing. It's just that I wouldn't be able to do anything at all if I only did what a woman's supposed to do." She was amazed she'd actually said that. She'd never been one for bluntness. "I'm sorry," she said, "I don't know what got into me."

"No. That was real," Clayton said. "It just took me by surprise—the anger, I mean."

She hadn't known she'd expressed any anger. That was something she'd always guarded against lest she put herself in an explosive situation.

"Did I say I was angry?"

"No. It's just the 'Nam in me. I can tell a ticking time bomb when I see one." He laughed—to soften the harsh edge of his words, Jeanna thought. She had certainly never thought of herself as a ticking bomb. More like one of Kafka's bugs.

"I never thought much about women and men, women's issues, until I saw how we treated the Vietnamese women over in 'Nam," he said. "And how the men talked about women, period—when they weren't crying themselves to sleep over them, that is." He laughed again, but the laughter didn't reach his eyes. "It was horrifying. What they did one night, torturing a young Vietnamese woman to death, made me so sick I still can't get it out of my mind. It's like I die with her over and over again."

Jeanna loved him for saying that, feeling that. She had always thought that men didn't feel as much in that way. It sometimes enraged her, but she had learned not to expect empathy from them—not on anything women-related, at least. And not on anything race-related, if they were white.

"You just resurrected my faith in . . ." She paused. "Humanity."

"Men, you mean."

"I guess." She laughed. "I don't usually say things straight out."

"Who does?" Clayton said. He looked at his watch again. "Damn, I'm late for the guys. Would next Tuesday work for me to come to your class?"

"Perfect." She watched him move fast out the door, wondering how her emotions could have gone from pure rage to such a feeling of warmth inside of a few seconds.

She was putting her jacket on when someone else came through the kitchen door. Well-built. Big Afro. Sunglasses despite the evening hour. Black leather jacket. Black turtleneck. The uniform.

They eyed each other. He gave her the slow once-over—a full-body scan. She waited, feeling the slow rage she always felt, until he gave her eye contact again.

"Who are you?" he asked.

"I'm just going. Jeanna Kendall. I was signing up some of my students for the free breakfast program."

"You don't sign anybody up. They sign themselves up."

"Okay, I'll have them do that then." She wondered if she dared ask his name. "You are?"

"Robert Gorman."

"The chairman?"

"No, that's my brother, Ron. I'm Minister of Defense."

She felt a sensation of surreal humor overtake her and almost said, 'Nice to meet you. I'm Minister of Education.' Instead she said, "Well, I'll be on my way," and grabbed her bag, her palms sweating.

"Good," he said under his breath as she turned to walk away.

She walked down the hall and passed an open doorway. She saw two women leaning over a table and helping several children. Eight or nine other kids were studiously bent over their books. This must be the tutoring program.

She walked the four blocks to her car, thinking about the three vastly different men she had just met, and if any members of Group Survive might gravitate toward Clayton James's EMT field as a possible future.

CHAPTER THIRTY-THREE

The Excluded

JEANNA HAD BEEN MAKING CALLS ALL AFTERNOON FOR the All-City Congress, but her last call to Elaine Browning—Wesley's aunt—had been her best. Not only had Elaine—who was the head of Parents' Action for Change in Education, PACE—jumped on the idea of the Congress and bringing her organization's membership to it, she'd also expressed an interest in joining the Group itself. Jeanna had promised to set up a meeting with Elaine and representatives of the Group's steering committee.

She was excited about the prospect of someone with Elaine's leadership experience and extensive community connections joining the Group. They could really use another strong black woman, since Lillian was fairly quiet and often deferred to others, and Ma Carrington, as chair, tended not to push her own views. Jeanna suspected that Elaine could give Cam and Helene a run for their money in the leadership department, and that would be a very healthy thing.

They set a meeting for May 25th, and when the day came, Cam, Helene, and Jeanna took their seats around the table, waiting for Land and Elaine. Jeanna had suggested that Lillian participate instead of, or in addition to, Cam since she was involved as a parent on the Education Committee, but Helene had nixed the idea, saying that Cam could give her a better idea of the big picture.

The phone rang just as Elaine arrived. Jeanna took Elaine's coat and introduced her to Helene while Cam answered. He came back nodding to Elaine and said, "That was Land. He got called away on an emergency. A teenager was shot by a police officer and his mother wanted Land there to help her deal with the situation. He said to go ahead with the meeting and he would catch up with us tomorrow."

Jeanna wished that Helene had listened to her. Without Land and Lillian, they were three white folks representing a multi-racial group.

Elaine didn't skip a beat. "I'm intrigued by your idea of an All-City Congress. When we spoke the other day, Land was telling me that not much has been done on getting funds for the project . . . and, well, I was thinking that we've had great luck with the Alcott money. They've funded our parent organizing efforts three years running, and their chief priorities are education, youth, and community development, which I understand are some of your priorities as well?"

Elaine faltered slightly here, and when Jeanna saw the disapproving looks on both Cam and Helene's faces, she understood why. *What the hell?* she wondered.

"It could be a good fit," Elaine said, more tentatively now. "What do you think?"

"That's not a direction we'd want to go in," Cam said. "We've dealt with them before, and they're too conservative."

Elaine gave him a quizzical look. "That's not been my experience."

"Well, it's been ours," Helene said imperiously. "We went after some of their CD money several years ago and it was clear that our philosophies differed."

"Well of course your real philosophies are going to diff—"

"We've made it a principle to only get money from foundations and funds we can trust," Cam said. "Otherwise our agenda gets derailed."

"With some foundations you can pretty much do what you want," Elaine said, "and we've discovered—"

"It's a choice we've had to make to stay on track," Helene cut in.

Elaine folded her hands on the table. "Well, actually—"

"It's not something we'll change our minds on," Cam said, cutting her off again.

Now Jeanna was really angry—and so, she saw, was Elaine. It was clear by the tightness in her face and the blank look in her eyes that she had decided to back off completely.

Jeanna could feel Elaine slipping through their collective fingers as Cam and Helene droned on and on about the congress, no doubt explaining things that Elaine had understood from the beginning. After thirty minutes of this, she felt compelled to reenter the conversation.

"Can't we hear about PACE—"

"Well, of course we want to hear about your parent organizing efforts," Helene said, giving Elaine her most brilliant smile.

Elaine looked at her watch and said, "You know, I'd love to, but it's five-fifteen and I'm running late. I have another appointment before I head home, and I know you folks are just as busy as I am." She gathered up her bag to go. She had ice in her eyes as she extended her arm for a brief handshake with Cam first, and then Helene. To Jeanna she said, "My coat?"

"Yes, of course, it's out here."

Elaine followed Jeanna out into the main room. Jeanna gave her the coat and tried to think of a way to salvage the situation.

"How about I call you when—"

"That's alright," Elaine said. "I'll call Land when I have a moment." She turned and walked briskly out.

Jeanna was furious at her helplessness in the face of Cam and Helene's arrogance. She had to say something to them. Why were they so determined to drive away such a good person?

She turned to go back to the table, and the phone rang again. She picked it up. "Hello."

"Jeanna, that you?" It was Land. "Could you tell Cam and Helene to come over to City Hospital to meet with me? I'm in room 710. We need to get a press release out. The boy just died."

"Jesus, Land, I certainly will."

"Thanks, Jeanna." He hung up.

She sighed. She could forget about doing a post-mortem on the meeting. She walked back to find Cam and Helene. They were getting on their coats to leave, talking low.

"Land wants the two of you to meet him over at City Hospital ASAP. Room 710. The boy died, and Land needs your help to do a press release."

"We'll head right there," Cam said. There was something smugly self-important in his tone.

"Thanks for setting up the meeting with Elaine," Helene said, and flashed a false smile.

What is it with her? Jeanna wondered. Was Elaine Browning too much of a threat to her status in the group? Was she even aware of it?

"Right," Jeanna said under her breath.

Several days later, Jeanna was on her way to the storefront to make calls for the Congress. She still hadn't had a chance to discuss the whole Elaine Browning incident with Cam and Helene, and it had been nagging at her. That, and the way Helene had treated Jackie, too. Jeanna still admired Helene and valued their friendship, but big, ugly doubts kept popping up. Maybe she'd have a chance to talk with her after the calls were done. First, though, she needed to get a start on planning her next day's classes or she'd be an anxious wreck all evening.

She entered the storefront through the side door, and settling into the small alcove off the main room, began to organize her papers and jot down some notes for her class.

"You *what*?" Helene's voice, easy to hear through the thin wall.

"Yeah, that right," a gravelly voice responded, "I tol' him he ain't no better than the racist bastards we fightin' against if he wouldn't sign on to the petition."

He must be talking about the police community review board petition. It was an initiative that had sprung up spontaneously from the neighbors around yet another police shooting of a black teenager the previous week.

"What the hell were you thinking?" Cam's voice.

"What the hell you thinking, big boy?" The voice was familiar.

"Now you wait a min—"

"Not likely. Seem like you two want to pussyfoot around, but these no-account politicians don't do nothin' you don't make 'em do. Lemme tell ya, we ain't goin' for that shit." A chair scraped, and the gravelly voice said, "I'll be on my way. You-all have a real nice day."

Jeanna eased out of the side door, hoping to catch a glimpse of whoever this was. She saw an old man was getting in his black truck—Guff. That was the voice. Of course.

Upset and disgusted, she threw her bag over her shoulder and began to walk away from the storefront, toward a small park nearby. She still had twenty minutes to spare. After Jackie's unexpected visit several months ago, the Elaine Browning fiasco, and now this exchange, she had plenty to think through. The Group she had been so enchanted by was beginning to give off a bad smell. Surely it was one Land couldn't stand either, she mused as she nestled her back into a curved wooden bench protected by a tall pine.

The sun was beginning to set, and the smoky grey clouds above her filled with pink, then a dusty rose as she sat there full of doubts and questions. Could she do anything about these exclusions and manipulations? She had so little power. All her power came by association—originally with Cam, then Helene, and finally Land, who'd supported everything she'd ever brought up, which meant virtually everyone else had as well. Was there something she was missing? Was Jackie untrustworthy in some way? Was Elaine Browning out of sync with the Group's real politics—maybe too conventional? Was Guff too crude and impolitic to be effective? Was she being naïve to think all these kinds of people could and should work together?

She didn't think so. And it made her ill to realize that they were being so contemptuously pushed away from the Group, when they should be embraced.

When she got home, Land was asleep in her bed, his face puffy from the exhaustion of weeks, months, of pushing too hard. She was sure that when he woke he would find a way of handling things, hoped he would see it her way. It felt odd, though, to talk with Land about Helene. One short month ago, Helene had been Jeanna's primary mentor, her best and only friend. It was a friendship she didn't want to lose, but she had to say something.

Land opened one eye and looked at her. "I see those wheels turning. What's on your mind?"

She laughed, surprised he'd noticed. "It's about three different people and the Group, but it's all the same theme."

"Okay."

"You know Jackie O'Keane?"

"Jacqueline, yes. I encouraged her to join the Ed Committee a few months ago. Very bright. Great with teens, like you. Good person."

Jeanna nodded. "She came by here one Sunday afternoon a while back, crying, after she'd been down to the office and talked with Helene."

"Crying? She's so upbeat!"

"Not that day. Shortly after you referred her to me, I encouraged her to tell her youth program connections about the All-City Congress. So she went down to the storefront to get some literature and talk with Helene about the groups she planned to contact, and Helene basically told her that those bases were covered—which they weren't, not at all—and not to bother."

"Not to bother?" He frowned.

"Right. She said she'd call her if they had need of her help."

"Whoa."

"Yeah."

"Any idea why?"

"Jackie said she thought it was because of her family being so racist and caught up in the corrupt politics of the city."

"That's probably it. The O'Keanes do go back, decades, into the muck." He nodded. "Helene probably wants to make sure the Group doesn't get compromised. I know her father—he's a real piece of work. But Jackie's good people." He was musing on it, biting his thumbnail.

Jeanna let the silence develop, not wanting to push it but not wanting to let it go.

"What else? You said there were others?"

"The other situation involved Elaine Browning."

"Really," he said, his brow furrowed.

"Yeah, unfortunately. Remember, you, Cam, Helene, and I were supposed to meet with her last Thursday? But you had to deal with that boy being shot?"

He nodded. "And?"

"Let's just say that after that meeting, I highly doubt she'll be joining the Group."

"What d'you mean?" His tone was quite testy now.

"Well, she was kind enough to share some inside information about a funding source that she thought might help finance our Congress, and they just kind of shut her down."

"So because they think differently about fundraising, you think there's a big problem?"

Obviously he didn't think it was a big deal. She was skating on thin ice.

"They just wouldn't listen to her at all. Kept cutting her off. She was really turned off, is all I can say. I know she won't join the Group now. You needed to've been there to see it, I guess."

"I'll give her a call. I've known her for years. We'll work it out. And the third person?"

"This one is about Leon Guffrey. Apparently Cam and—"

"Ooooh." He held up a hand. "That one I'm not going to touch." He laughed and shook his head. "Good ol' Guff."

She wanted to tell Land what she'd heard through the thin wall at the office. "Why not?" She tried for a pleasant, quizzical tone. "He seems pretty sharp to me."

"Oh, he's sharp alright. So sharp he digs his own graves all over town with that sharp tongue of his, and I stopped digging him out years ago."

"Really?" She didn't see at all. She realized in that moment how much she'd come to love Guff for exactly that—telling it like it was.

"Really," he said with finality. "That about cover it?"

"Yep." She still didn't get his take on Guff, but she sensed pushing the issue would be fruitless.

"Why don't you just keep Jackie involved yourself if she wants to work with us? I'll mention to Helene that I encouraged her to get involved with the Ed Committee and Congress outreach."

"Okay, thanks, I'll do that." *Two out of three ain't bad*, she thought. And maybe someday down the road the mystery of Land's distaste for Guff would be solved.

He drew her close and they kissed. She felt a little giddy from the kiss, the conversation. He got up to go shower and she sank back under the covers. She loved the feeling he exuded, that everything could be handled, nothing was too big, too difficult, if he chose to deal with it. He could make the crooked straight, the way smooth.

But when would she ever feel right taking these issues on herself? And who would listen to her if she did?

Within a week of Jeanna speaking to Land, Jackie became an active part of the Ed Committee. Helene went along with it without comment, although she certainly didn't go out of her way to be nice.

That side of Helene bothered Jeanna. Their Friday night dinners every few weeks at Helene's had become a regular thing and were still one of the highlights of Jeanna's month, but her feelings about her kept shifting. She worried constantly, too, about her duplicity regarding Land. She had wanted to be open with Helene from the start, but so long as Land didn't want it, her hands were tied. She hated it.

Jeanna and Jackie had been meeting frequently at the West Side café, and she loved how she could really let her hair down with Jackie. They'd grab the farthest corner booth, where no one could hear them, and laugh and cry and have it out about every crazy thing in the Group. She loved Jackie's radiant exuberance about life. Jackie continued to be perplexed and troubled by Helene's treatment of her, however.

"I don't know why Helene hates me so much," Jackie said one evening over cheeseburgers, fries, and beer. "What did I ever do to her?"

"I hardly think she hates you," Jeanna said.

"You're right, hate's the wrong word. She treats me as if I don't exist. That's even worse."

Jeanna felt guilty since she'd somehow managed to make it onto Helene's A-list almost from the start, when so many others hadn't. They were practically old friends now. But she knew very well that Helene wasn't perfect. She could be dismissive of people who didn't deserve it, and was often patronizing. More and more, Helene's arrogant side was turning her off.

"I know, Jackie. Helene has her list, and either you're on it or God help you if you're not." It was awkward, her being on and Jackie off. But at least she'd been able to bring Jackie back into the Group through Land.

"Well, you're on her list," Jackie said. "Maybe you could get me on, put in a good word."

Like it would make a difference, Jeanna thought—but she didn't tell Jackie that.

After Jeanna and Jackie had hugged and Jeanna was driving home, she felt uneasy. It would be virtually impossible to be so involved in the Group and not be friends with Helene. Yet she wanted to have it out with her about Jackie, to find some way of cutting through all the power games. Maybe as she and Helene became even better friends, she could find a way to talk with her. Otherwise, she would keep finding herself in this crazy position of being in with the ins, while her real soul mates were on the outs.

CHAPTER THIRTY-FOUR

This Blank Absence of Connection Was a Killer

THE GROUP MET ON JUNE 10TH TO REVIEW THEIR progress on organizing for the All-City Congress. Jeanna arrived early, hoping to touch base with Fred, her supposed co-chair, to plan how they would present their Ed Committee work to the group. Fred had finally returned her calls, but after she'd given him a detailed overview of the progress on all fronts, he'd cut the call short. She thought about the little he'd done in the past weeks, while she'd been stretched to the limit, and fumed.

She was feeling anxious about all the threads in her life that were hanging in the air that had never been worked through, not just her issues with Fred. Like talking with Helene about Jackie.

She flipped open her notebook and absently jotted down a list of items she needed to fix dinner for Land on Friday night. She got up to go to the bathroom and out of the corner of her eye saw Helene come in. She smiled and waved, and Helene smiled back in a radiant way that gave her a lift and immediately settled her nerves.

She hurried to the restroom, still hoping she'd have time to get in a word with Fred. When she came out, she saw Helene standing over her chair, a folded piece of paper in her hand that she was placing on top of Jeanna's notebook. But then Helene stopped and leaned closer to read something in her notebook. Her jaw clenched, she balled up the note in her hand, fast and hard, and she moved at a clip back to her seat. What on earth?

Jeanna walked to her seat as unobtrusively as possible, sat down, and looked at her open notebook. She saw what she had written: *Pick up Ld's faves for Fri—BBQ chick, Black Raz IceCrm, Java Coffee. Wash Nite gwn.*

Jeanna felt Helene's stare and looked up. Helene looked away, lips tight and white at the edges. Helene *knew*. Fuck.

Ma called the meeting to order just as Fred slipped through the door and into his seat. They would have to wing it, but that was the least of her worries now.

"This evening's meeting of the Steering Committee," Ma was explaining, "is to review the progress we have made on outreach for the All-City Congress. We'll start with the Ed Committee." She looked at Jeanna, then Fred, who was already beginning to speak.

Fred spoke for a long time, giving the information verbatim from what Jeanna had told him on the phone as if he'd been on top of it all along, not missing in action. Jeanna was nauseated, but less with Fred than with herself and her stupidity. She'd have to find some way of making it right with Helene. She looked over at Helene, but Helene immediately looked away again. She swallowed hard. This blank absence of connection was a killer.

Jeanna stopped listening to Fred drone on. She felt a sick, sinking sensation. Their friendship was over. There would be no going back. She glimpsed an image from their talk the other evening: a heart cut to smithereens. She no longer knew whose it was, her's or Helene's.

Around her, the meeting was breaking up. Had that much time gone by? Then she heard a voice as if from a great distance . . . "not fair . . . know how much work you did on this . . ."

Jeanna looked at Lillian as her voice faded away. Looking embarrassed at Jeanna's lack of response, she turned to go. Jeanna stared helplessly at her retreating back. She wished she could reach out and stop Lillian and thank her. She wished she could tell her everything. But Lillian was gone.

Jeanna felt the roomful of people crowding her, engulfing her, and Helene's cold, hard face suspended above them as she stood up and looked straight through Jeanna as if she weren't there. Jeanna had to get out. She rose to leave, but Cam put a hand on her arm. She pulled away sharply and headed out the door, feeling ridiculous and utterly lost.

Once Jeanna got home she fussed around her apartment, trying to figure out what to do, how to make amends with Helene. She'd just have to call her and try to talk it through. She dialed Helene's number. There was no answer. She was probably still at the meeting.

At 10 p.m. she called again. Helene answered.

"Hi Helene," Jeanna said in a shaky voice, "I just wanted to—"

Helene hung up on her.

The sinking sensation she'd had all evening hit rock bottom. She wanted to crawl away from the Group and never have to deal with Helene again. She wished there was someone she could talk to, but in this situation, no such person existed. Land had made that perfectly clear. She wished she could take that moment back with Lillian and say, 'Could we talk sometime?'—but of course that would only make matters worse. Lillian might say something to Land, and then she'd be in deep shit with Land *and* Helene, and lose everything.

She pulled out a piece of stationery and stared at the blank page. Finally, she put pen to paper. At 1 a.m. she felt she had something down that at least said how much she valued Helene's friendship and hoped there was some way they could work it out, and how sorry she was that she hadn't been able to be more open with her. She sealed the letter. She would mail it on her way to work tomorrow.

CHAPTER THIRTY-FIVE

Couldn't Pray No More

AFTER THE FIASCO WITH HELENE, JEANNA THREW HER energy into her work at the school and organizing for the Congress. She was overwhelmed with all she had to do and kept hoping that Helene would respond to her letter and forgive her. Every day she came home she looked in her mailbox in the hall to see if she had responded. Every time the phone rang, she was disappointed that it wasn't Helene, willing at least to talk.

One Saturday evening in mid-June, Jeanna put a kettle on the stove and began reading her students' Turning Point interviews with their parents. Lonnie's was on top of the pile:

This here how Ma told it to me - (By the way I been working on my writting. Can you see it looking better?)

This ai'nt easy to speak out loud about. I don't mean you no hurt. But this the day I was goin to take John's rifle, our last five bullets, one for each of us. I was low as low could go an I did'nt have no prayers left. I could'nt stand to see you boys starve no more or hear John cry out in pain without his medcine. I was fainting two, three times a day from honger, the rent 6 months overdo, lost my job takin in wash cause I could'nt get the clothes an sheets and things clean, the water done turn brown from all the digging around been goin on an I could not aford the starch, then the iron would'nt work when they turn the electric off. I tried to get me a job cleanin houses outside the city, but could'nt find no transportion. All the facteries was long gone an I was way too old an run down to hook.

I walk over to Ma's house where she bedriden to kiss her goodbye. It was rainin a steady rain. I was walkin back as hevy in my heart as I ever been, I had stopped prayin for help. I just could'nt pray no more. I was walking with my head down, not like God usually wants, but that's where I was lookin that day, an I saw this green piece of paper floatin in a puddle on the wet street. It said:

Hungry?

Poor and out of work? Welfare check run out?

Kids Sick? Need Help?

Come to the NSWRO, North Side Welfare Rights Organization, at 6th and Broad and fight for your rights.

I pick up that piece of paper and ran, tears streaming down my face, and ran and ran, flyin over the puddles and stones and glass like I'd grown wings, an here I am hevy as a horse, but I ran anyway, about some 8, 9 blocks until I found the place. I broke through that front door and these womens were settin there lookin at me bust in wavin the paper in my hand and me yellin at them: this paper say you can help me, can you help me? Cause me an my family dyin, and I slid down almost to the floor, but they all three, jumped up and catched me up in their arms, like the Angels of Galilee, an helped me to a chair. Put a big glass of juce in front of me, and a piece of butter tost. I ate it in one bite, they just kep tostin one after the other, and then we talked, and talked and

I got a sense of what they was doin an what they beleefs is, an they said they could help me get food and clothes and medcines for my husband. They would help me with my electric an get my welfare chek back from the landlady who stole it outa the mailbox, said it was hers to pay the overdo rent, but they said it was mines.

They ask me to help them fight the system, fight for others like me and I said, yes, I'd do it, that if they can send a man to the moon—these was the things we was talking about—and bild them skyscrapers downtown, throw away good money killin them little brown Vetnamese never hurt a flee, I would fight til my dyin day to see that us poor women tryin to raise our chilrin get a half a shot at life. Justa half a shot, we'll go the rest the way.

An that's what I been doin ever since. It took us a good year a fightin, but we won an increese in our chek by $200, my husband got his pain meds free, I pay my rent ever month on the first, an have a few dollars left over for food, put that together with your seventy a week an we ain starving no more. I put shoes on the kids feet this winter and coats on there backs from the clothes exchange we been runnin with the church peoples out a town. I learnin bout the welfare polisy rules and how to appeel all they wrong desisions, we appeel up the kazoo, so now they sees us comin and they just gives us what we wants to avoid no kinda truble. We got us some truble makers make your hair stand up; even I would'nt want to mess with'em and peoples say they afraid a me. We got our electric back so's the kids can study an I can iron. I get fifteen cent a shirt for that. Make me prowd to be back to work. That pay our water bill. We got nothing for heat yet. That there's our next fight. My newest prayer is I get my GED, maybe go into the hospital field, be a nurses aide or *something like that, lord knows I've done enuf of it with John. I need some edication and trainin for so's I can have a better life, or let me just say I want a life. It was the WRO got me over. I thank God for putting the WRO paper in my path that day.*

Every line in Lonnie's story was etched into Jeanna. The moment she finished, she called his number to invite his mother to come speak to her current issues class. It was a story that everyone needed to hear.

CHAPTER THIRTY-SIX

More Than You Know

On the last Saturday in June, Jeanna got up early, looking forward to going out door-to-door organizing for the All-City Congress with Lillian. She wanted to beat Helene to the storefront so she could to do the flyer on community districting that the Group had asked her to do without the usual surveillance—and the guilt. She'd called Helene twice since that horrible meeting to apologize, try to talk it out, but Helene had hung up on her both times. Jeanna had cried for hours at her own stupidity, and her helplessness in the face of Land's need for the utmost discretion. In fact, besides missing Helene's friendship, she was worried Land was going to be pissed at her for Helene finding out about them. He couldn't have missed Helene's coldness towards her, her utter stoniness where before there had been a rare warmth.

She made it to the office early and used the good typewriter on Helene's desk, anxious as hell that she might come in, and reworked it until the flyer was perfect. By eight she was on her way to the printers, feeling pleased with herself, the flyer, and the sun-drenched, breezy day.

A hand grasped her arm from out of nowhere. Frightened, Jeanna jumped away. It was Helene. So now she couldn't even say her name anymore—she had to grab her from behind?

"What's up?" Jeanna asked, feeling disoriented and guilty.

"Nothing's up. But what are you doing?"

"Going to the printers. I just finished the flyer."

"Without anyone seeing it?"

Her face hot, Jeanna handed it to her. It was a simple flyer, for Christ's sake.

Helene took her time looking it over, then thrust it back at her. Jeanna could taste her former friend's disappointment at not finding a mistake.

"Go on. But things have to be looked over before we lay them all over the city. It could be a recipe for disaster otherwise."

And who looks your shit over, little Miss Precise?

"Do you have money for the print job?" Jeanna asked, realizing Helene hadn't reimbursed her for anything since that awful meeting.

"No."

"See you later then," she said, and walked on.

The printer took her job right away. Thirty minutes later, she'd paid him the last of her monthly spending money and was on her way to West Side Neighborhood Park to meet Lillian.

Lillian was already at the park when Jeanna got there. They hugged hello. Lillian's eyes looked strained as she shifted the big pile of Calls under her arm.

Jeanna took half of them. "Is everything okay?

"Well, my five-year-old just knocked his front teeth out falling off his bike. And his brother got a bloody nose falling off his bike trying to help him. My seventeen-year-old is in jail, as you know, but I cannot for the life of me get used to it, and my husband just got turned down for a promotion out on the construction site." She shook her head in exasperation.

Jeanna had never heard Lillian complain before. "Glad to hear things are going so well," she said, raising an eyebrow and making Lillian laugh. "Well, here are the flyers, fresh off the press."

"You just did this?" Lillian asked.

"Under very close supervision," Jeanna said.

"Say no more," Lillian said, and they laughed.

They came upon a woman wrestling two garbage bins down her drive.

"How you doing this bright day?" Lillian called to her.

The woman looked up with a surprised smile. "Well it Saturday, so I ain't doin' too bad. Who be asking?"

"I'm Lillian Johnson and this is Jeanna Kendall. We're from the community group Landon Waters is with." Lillian stepped into the small yard and Jeanna followed suit.

"Oh yeah, I heard of that. What he got you-all up to now?"

Lillian and Jeanna laughed. "It's not just him. We're all up to it," Lillian said. "We're putting on an All-City Congress July 25th for the community to decide its most important issues and line up some candidates for school committee and city council. Jeanna and I are going around to see if folks like yourself will come out for it."

"You got all kinds involved, then." The woman looked at Jeanna and away.

"We sure do," Lillian said, holding her smile steady.

"Could use a little of that 'stead of all this bein' at each other's throats," the woman said.

Jeanna nodded and smiled. "We're also trying to pass a community districting initiative."

"What might that be?"

"It's a way of getting someone from each community on the school board and city council instead of just the same old group running everything." She handed her a flyer.

"We'd finally get us someone from the West Side and North Side too?"

"That's it—that's what we're fighting for. Why don't you join us?" Lillian said. "Here, sign this and we'll give you a reminder call." She handed her the clipboard and pen.

"I like that Landon Waters. My husband say that man'll get us in a whole heap a trouble, and I say so what? We in a heap anyways. I mean, look at the sorry excuse for a school our kids go to. He say that school ain't never going to change. He's right, too." She gave the clipboard back to Lillian, unsigned.

"I hear you," Lillian said, "but the schools is our number one issue."

"Yeah?"

"We're trying to get more of a parent voice in the schools too," Jeanna said.

"Now, that's something I'd like to see."

"If you come to the Congress, you'll meet the women who are making that happen," Jeanna said.

"Yeah, come on out and let your ideas be known," Lillian said. "We need you."

"Aw shaw, no one wants to hear my ideas, just ask my husband. Besides, I'm not into all that political stuff."

"We want to hear your ideas," Lillian and Jeanna said in unison.

The three of them laughed.

The woman looked at them. "Don't that beat all. I might come after all, just to see what mess I can get myself into. Where's that paper you wanted me to sign?"

They left the yard, waving, and went back up on the sidewalk.

"I think we hit pay dirt. But we better move along a little more quickly," Lillian said.

"Or Miss Efficiency will have our asses?"

"Exactly. Helene thinks it takes me too long to do whatever I do," Lillian said, "and I tend to agree with her."

"Why?"

"Because everything I do always makes me late for the next thing."

"Well, what's more important," Jeanna said, "getting to the next thing, or really communicating with people?"

"That's what I thought too—"

"You out for some candidate?" a voice called. It was an older man a few steps away. He was watering the tiniest vegetable garden Jeanna had ever seen, his goatee clipped to perfection.

"Not exactly," Lillian said. "We're out to get folks to come decide the issues the candidates should support."

"Now there's a concept. Focus on the issues, not the politicians. I like that." He looked up from his task and signed up, and even offered to distribute more Calls at his senior center.

They hit thirty more homes where about half the people signed up and thanked them for coming out. The rest ranged from a polite no thanks to a surly slammed door.

At one house they had to go into the kitchen to talk with the woman because she was feeding her baby in a high chair.

"Well I'd say sign me up, but I don't have no one to take care of the baby if I go. My mama passed and my man left last year, so there's no one to help. He couldn't get no decent work and couldn't stand to see us hungry at the end of the month. I'm ashamed to say I had to go on welfare. It was that or starve. But let me tell you, with the little bit they give you, we still starving."

"I'm sorry to hear that," Lillian said. "Anyway, thanks for hearing us out. Here's our newspaper." She handed her a Call, said good-bye, and they left.

They were on the sidewalk when Jeanna said, "Wait just a sec," and hurried back. She stopped at the door and wrote, "North Side Welfare Rights Organization," along with Lonnie's mother's name and number, on the back of a flyer. She knocked and went in, Lillian right behind her.

"Here's a number you can call if you want to get together with some other mothers who are in the same boat, on welfare and fighting for what they need to live," she said, holding the flyer out. "One of my students' parents, a Mrs. Henderson, is part of the group."

"Thank you," the woman said, a glimmer of hope in her eyes.

When they were back on the street, Lillian asked, "You know a lot about this welfare rights organization?"

"Yeah, I discovered the WRO in college when I was working with a youth group and got to know some of their parents. I joined them for food and clothing sit-ins at places like the governor's mansion. Some really incredible women on welfare lead it."

"Incredible women on welfare," Lillian repeated. "I never heard a professional-type woman talk like that—white or black. And they wouldn't go anywhere near a sit-in, not if you gave them the keys to the kingdom. You know, I hate to say it, but I was on welfare myself way back."

"I didn't know that. And I'm not so sure a lot of professionals are all they're cracked up to be, by the way."

"You right, but the crazy thing is, I want to be one myself, just as soon as possible," Lillian said with a touch of embarrassment.

"No, that's good. You'll be a credit to the professional race. We can use all the help we can get." Jeanna laughed.

"You too funny," Lillian said, "the way you twist words around all the time. You get me to laughing at things used to make my blood curdle."

"It still curdles mine," Jeanna said. "I wonder if there's some way the Group could take up welfare as an issue, or at least support the WRO."

"Oh, honey, I already brought that up a number of years ago, but Helene wouldn't have it. You should've been there. She was just disgusted. Said it would taint the rest of our campaigns."

"You must've wanted to slap her."

"That much too mild a word for it."

"I bet you had a comeback for her that time!"

"I didn't have a chance. The whole group agreed with her before I could say anything, Land too—and to be honest? I was too damn ashamed of my own stuff to really lay it on the line." Lillian exhaled. "You know, you saying that gives me a light kind of feeling, when I used to feel heavy as hash on a winter's day. But getting back to the professional thing—Cam would call that a contradiction. He always giving me little lessons on that."

"Cam?" Jeanna said. "Cam's a full-blown walking contradiction. Look at the way he talks down to people while seeing himself as the great liberator. And he gives you lessons?"

"It's not like you think; I asked him to. He pointed out one of my so-called contradictions once and I said to let me know if he noticed anymore." Lillian laughed. "You know, kill 'em with kindness? So he gave me a little lecture on wanting to climb the professional ladder. Said it was counter . . . counter . . ."

"Counter-revolutionary?"

"That's it. He's raising my revolutionary consciousness." She laughed again.

"Same with me," Jeanna said. "Ever since we met at the U, I confess, I had a crush on him, which I have vastly gotten over, but all he cared about was my so-called revolutionary potential—that is, when he wasn't trying to get me into bed. But just so you know, Cam's almost got his doctorate in political economics and philosophy, so I don't know who he thinks he's kidding."

"Oh I know Cam's a mess," Lillian said, "and I still want me a college degree and all that inside-learning-strength that goes with it, that I feel in Tommie Lee already, and see in Land, and you, and people like Matt. And the money, too. I'm tired of always having to scrimp and scramp."

"I don't know about me on that list. But you sure don't have to apologize for wanting a decent life."

"And you don't have to keep erasing yourself off my list, or any lists," Lillian said, looking her in the eye.

Jeanna started. Lillian was right. Why did she do that? She was sick of feeling so anxious and inadequate.

They had come to a house where the garbage cans were overflowing, raising quite a stink. Lillian had stopped to shake a pebble out of her shoe, so Jeanna was in the lead. A huge rat ran across the path and Jeanna jumped.

"What the fuck's the matter wit you?" The question came from a woman leaning back on an overstuffed chair inside the screened-in porch, a slant of sunlight directly on her. Her Afro was wild above a black eye. Her blouse was torn, revealing a high, rounded belly.

"Nothing," Jeanna said, "we just—"

"We're here from Landon Waters's group to give you some info on a community event, but if it's a bad time . . ." Lillian had caught up with Jeanna and stepped past her.

"Anytime's a fucking bad time, so get the fuck out."

A large man dressed only in jeans came out on the porch.

"Sorry to bother you," Lillian said and turned around, putting her hand at the small of Jeanna's back to move her along more quickly.

"And keep your faggoty white girlfriend outta here for good, or she'll be fucking dead white meat."

Jeanna's legs trembled as she stepped over a large crack in the sidewalk.

The man laughed, and then they heard a sharp slap.

They moved quickly down the block. Jeanna stopped suddenly, her legs still trembling.

"You okay?" Lillian asked, touching her arm.

"I'm fine, but she looked like she'd been worked over pretty good."

"Sure did, hate like hell to see it. I'll be hearin' that slap in my sleep tonight. Are you sure you're okay?"

"I think so. It brings up some old memories is all."

Lillian put a hand on Jeanna's shoulder. "You not alone, girl. We all got them memories. You want to talk about it?"

"No. Not now. You?"

"No. Too much ugliness to drag back up."

"Think it'll ever end?"

"I don't know. I just don't know. It time people did something about it."

"Yeah, past time." But Jeanna knew better than to suggest the Group take this kind of women's issue on. She could hear the lectures now, everyone telling her about how it was black men who'd truly been brutalized. And they had. No arguing with that. But why did it have to be an either/or thing?

They stopped to rest on a stone wall by the park in some shade.

Lillian looked at her watch. "My God! I'm way late to get Giddy and Carl! Would you mind dropping this stuff back at the office? You know, I never lost track of the time before out here. It really flies when we do it together."

"I know. I lost track too. Usually I'm worrying about getting back to the papers I have to write for my master's, but not today," Jeanna said. She was dreading having to deal with Helene again, but she took the Calls from Lillian. "I'll drop this all off, don't worry."

"Isn't that something, you doing your master's and I haven't even made it to college yet," Lillian said. "That's my dream . . . I just can't seem to make it happen."

"Why not?"

"Kids, family. Job. Church. The Group. Me. Mainly me, I guess."

"Meaning?"

"Meaning I doubt myself. You know, can I do it, am I smart enough—"

"You're one of the smartest, most thoughtful, capable people I know," Jeanna said. "I'm positive you can do it."

"Oh, you trained to say that kinda thing," Lillian said, giving a little laugh, but she reached over for a hug. Jeanna thought of how many times she'd felt Lillian was her one true mentor—more than Helene, Cam, and Matt combined, and even Land.

"I do mean it, more than you know," Jeanna called out to Lillian as she hurried away.

~

Back at the storefront, Jeanna went in and put the clipboard on Helene's desk, relieved to see that she was busy in the back office. She piled the Calls and flyers along the wall, and was almost at the door when she heard Helene's voice.

"You only got as far as 4th Avenue?"

Jeanna turned around. "That's right. But we covered most of the area, and we got a lot of positive responses." She struggled to keep her tone even.

"Who's going to do 5th and the streets off it? That's the heart of the community. Were you and Lillian making small talk with every Tom, Dick, and Harry?"

Jeanna turned and walked out of the office without a word. She was so angry she didn't trust herself to speak. But she was also sad, knowing she had hurt Helene in a way that she would never get over. She walked toward her car, head down, trying to bring her blood back to a simmer, trying to recapture the good feeling she'd had with Lillian.

As she drove home, she thought about all the things she'd needed to talk through with Land over the many months. So many she'd lost track of them all. And he'd never had the time, or the energy, to really get into any of it. She was often reminded of the two sentences he'd uttered when she'd finally managed to get up the nerve to bring up the issue of how little time they had to even talk, much less do anything together. He'd said, "Lord, Jeanna, I've had enough relationship issues with Pearl to last a lifetime. I really can't handle any more."

Of course he couldn't handle any more relationship issues. She'd known that all along. She'd resolved then to deal with all such problems by herself, and she had ever since.

When she entered the hallway to her apartment, she looked in her mailbox and found a lone envelope. It was the letter she'd sent to Helene, unopened, with RETURN TO SENDER scrawled on the front in angry red ink. Utterly deflated, she picked it up, walked into her kitchen, and threw it in the trash, realizing for the first time that some things in life were irrevocable.

CHAPTER THIRTY-SEVEN

It's Like I Fell into This Dark Abyss

It was July, the start of summer term, and Jeanna was looking forward to the half-day schedule. At 10 p.m., just as she was falling asleep, Land called to say that he and Matt had gotten Tommie Lee out of jail.

"Lillian and Carl drove him home a few hours ago. He's out for good."

Jeanna gasped. "That's incredible. How did you manage it? I thought he had another two years."

"That was last week. We went over the warden's head to the Director of Youth Services for the whole state. Matt and I gave him the full scoop on Tommie Lee's record, how exceptional he's been in every way. How Carl's layoff and the kids' needs threw him for a loop." He cleared his throat.

"I'm so glad . . . it hasn't been the same without him."

"I know, none of us has been the same." Land cleared his throat again. "So he'll be back in class tomorrow morning."

How does he always manage the impossible?

The next morning, Jeanna was searching for the attendance form when she heard Valle cry out, "Well I'll be! If it ain't Tommie Lee!"

Tommie Lee came through the door, his forehead creased and jaw tight, forcing a smile.

Everyone jumped up at once and circled him. Big Blue hugged him, long and hard, setting the tone, and nearly everyone else did the same; even shy Alley took his turn. Everyone, except Jam, had surrounded Tommie Lee and was crying and laughing.

Jam got up from his seat—something he had never done before during class. A hush descended. He walked over and extended his hand. Tommie Lee took it and they looked at each other. Tommie Lee put his arm around Jam in a half hug that Jam allowed and said, "Thanks, man. Now I know I'm back."

As they all went to take their seats, Tommie Lee hesitated.

"Here," Olly said, motioning to Tommie Lee's former seat, "we kept it empty for you all this time."

"Thanks guys." Tommie Lee smiled as he took his seat, wiping his face with the back of his sleeve.

Jeanna was about to open Check-In when Valle spoke.

"Tommie Lee, if'n you want to talk about it, and only if you do, tell us about how things were for you up at Chisolm's, and how you come to go there."

Tommie Lee turned a shade paler and stayed quiet for a long moment.

Jeanna hadn't prepared for this. She'd had no idea how it would go upon his return, and hadn't felt it was her place to control it anyway.

Tommie Lee took a breath and looked around the room. Jeanna noticed that his face was gaunt, harder now, making him look older than his seventeen years.

"I've got to say what I did was wrong, stupid. I don't quite know what took me over, but I wasn't myself. It's true, my stepdad lost his job, and we were on the edge, but there was more that happened, things I can't talk about, and I'd appreciate it if no one asks me about it, or I won't be able to stay here at the school. But it was something I couldn't deal with."

He cleared his throat and went on, "I got a part-time job at a store after school, and I stole money from the cash register a couple times to help my mother pay the rent. But we could have managed in other ways. I knew I was headed for a fall and I didn't care." He gave a hacking cough and Abby handed him a paper napkin. He coughed into it, apologizing, saying everyone at Chisolm's had it, whatever "it" was.

What the hell was going on in his life? Jeanna wondered. It was as if he'd been lashing out to get back at someone or something, but who . . . and why?

"Then I walked into a situation," Tommie Lee said. "Two men I'd seen around the store parking lot asked me to drive a car over to Springfield one night, leave it at a Shell station, walk to the bus depot a few blocks away, and take the bus home. Said they'd give me a couple thousand dollars."

A few students gasped.

"I found out later that they had automatics, and heroin, in the trunk. I had just got out of the car and was walking down the street to the depot when the police caught up with me. They told me right on the spot I'd be sent away. You know, like it was a done deal."

There was a stir around the room.

"It's like I fell into this dark abyss, like this huge dark hole to nowhere was swallowing me up. And it happened just like the cops said."

"Shit, man, that's hard," Big Blue said.

"Anyway, Chisolm's wasn't much fun. I was beaten up every day my first week by these same five guys." He hesitated, looking down at the table. "Actually, they did a lot more than just beat me up."

The group gasped. Karima moaned and hugged herself. Abby was crying. Felice's mouth was twisted. All the boys were silent, immobile, staring at Tommie Lee.

"No lasting damage though, I'm told." He laughed without humor. "We dug ditches to nowhere every day I was there. It was crazy. They never did tell us what for. But see, I have a whole new set of muscles." He put his fists together close to his chest with his elbows straight out and tightened, and his arm muscles bulged. He smiled slightly as the others whistled.

He was all hard bone and muscle now. He had lost the youthful softness of most of the other kids, Jam and Lonnie excepted.

"We had classes, but they were a joke. I almost lost it with the teacher in there. He was off or something. Once he backhanded me across the face, knocked me to the floor."

Everyone started jabbering at once.

"The main thing I wanted to say"—he raised his voice and they quieted down immediately—"is that you-all were the ones who kept me alive in there. By letting me be part of your projects. Every time Jeanna sent or brought me a project package to read and respond to, it was like Christmas. I'd open the package and read it real slow and write down everything I loved about it and all my questions. I'm telling you, you-all kept me alive."

"We really loved your comments. They kept us going too," Abby said.

"Yeah, all those questions!" Karima joined in. "They made us think, like it was real life, not school."

"Us too," Pepper said. "We would've drifted all over the place if you hadn't kept on us."

"You know, while I was in there," Tommie Lee said, "I thought so much about this school, about all of you, and Jeanna and Matt, how amazing it is here. This may be a lot to ask, but I'd appreciate it if we could just go on from here and not talk about any of this anymore, just let me make a fresh start." He paused. "Can we do that?"

Loud "yeahs" and "of courses" came from the group.

The group work was dynamic all morning, and charged with electricity. Everyone was operating on all cylinders. Jeanna went from group to group, not saying a word, just soaking up the energy. After class she even saw Jam actually talking with Tommie Lee and showing him a hefty booklet of some kind. She saw them touch knuckles in agreement and wondered what was up.

Later, as she drove home, she ruminated over what could have driven Tommie Lee to do things that were so unlike him. She knew everyone was wondering the same thing, and was almost certain no one would be asking. Maybe Tommie Lee would always remain a mystery. A beautiful, unerringly sensitive young man, but an impenetrable mystery.

Over the next few weeks Tommie Lee seemed to be re-adjusting well to school again, and excelling in his work. Occasionally, however, Jeanna noticed that he got a terribly dark look on his face when he thought no one was looking.

He was excited about one thing, though, that brought the old light back into his face: he had confided in Jeanna that every Saturday at noon, he and Jam were meeting at his house to go over the auto mechanics test review workbook that Nate Smith said Jam needed to learn. If Jam didn't pass the test, Nate was threatening to let him go. If he passed, he was going to hire him on full time.

That had lit a fire under Jam, and as a result he had initiated his first conversation with another member of the class: he'd asked Tommie Lee if he would help him. They'd spent hours together poring over the explanations and pictures of engine parts and mathematical equations and plowing through the tons of food that Lillian always left them before taking her young sons for their Saturday afternoon outings. Tommie Lee said how amazed he was at Jam's grasp of all the mechanical stuff, and that he was learning new vocabulary by leaps and bounds.

Jeanna was thrilled that the two of them were working together, and said, "You know, you may be the first friend Jam's ever had."

"I never thought of that," Tommie Lee said, "but I'm learning a heck of a lot more than he is!"

A few weeks later Matt called Jeanna on Thursday evening with the stark news that Jam was dead.

"He can't be," she cried. "He's just begun to live!"

"I know, Jeanna—"

"What happened?" Jeanna demanded.

"He was coming out of a laundromat on the North Side earlier tonight, and someone shot him . . . in the face. I'm so sorry. I know how much you cared about him."

"God." She was in tears, seeing Jam stand there, not knowing the next second would be his last. "Will there be a service?"

"I'm sure there will be," Matt said. "But I'd advise against going. It's not safe."

"Not safe?"

"It's a gang-related funeral, and lately at such services, opposing gang members have come in and torn the body out of the casket. When people have tried to stop them, there've been more shootings and killings."

Jeanna was quiet, taking it in. But she knew she would be at the service. Of course she'd go. Most of the school would probably show up. There would be safety in numbers.

~

The morning of the service Jeanna dressed in black velvet pants and a sweater, with no other adornment. She drove alone through the grey mist to the church, which was in the most impoverished part of the community—a place she'd never ventured to before. As she entered, she walked past a gauntlet of men wearing gold chains and black berets.

It was dark inside except for a garish light directly above the casket, which was on top of a table at the front of the room. Fake plastic flowers flanked both sides of the table. She looked around, uncertain where to sit, and then she heard a familiar voice in the back.

Lonnie was speaking. "Look like they patched Jam up good. Can't hardly tell he was shot in the face."

"Glad a *that,*" Big Blue responded. "Where's Chefman?"

"I told Chef not to come. He listened for once. Guess he like to keep that fat ass a while longer." Lonnie laughed and turned away from Big Blue to see who he was looking at. "'Scuze me, Miss J. I din't know you was here." He gave her a wide-open, approving look.

"Hey, Lonnie. Blue."

"You sit here with Valle, Miss J," Lonnie said. "An Blue? C'mere, man. You stay right by Miss J on the other side."

"I got it," Blue said. "Thanks for coming, Miss J."

Jeanna walked down the pew and sat by Valle. Tears streaming down her face, Valle reached over and squeezed Jeanna's hand. Jeanna squeezed back, wishing she could be reassuring, or wise, in some way. Her presence would have to do. She had no idea what to say. Big Blue had moved in beside her, and she felt well sheltered by her students.

She saw Will slip in and sit by Valle's other side, next to the aisle. Jeanna smiled at him and he smiled back. She could see he was nervous too, not his usual laid-back self. His shoulders were tense, his eyes a little wild. He wore a black suit that was too big for his wiry frame. Besides her, he was the only white person in the room.

Valle whispered something to Will, and his eyebrows darted up in surprise. He pointed to himself and looked around the room doubtfully. Valle just smiled and nodded vigorously, smiling encouragement . . . but for what?

Most of the pews had filled. Jeanna saw Cassius slide in next to Blue, and they shook hands in the elaborate way young men did. He nodded to Jeanna. She raised her hand in greeting.

Where were Matt and the other teachers? She looked around the hall and twisted to look behind her. She saw Guff standing by a column in the shadows, talking low with Nate Smith. Guff looked very distinguished in a handsome vest and tie. He'd made it there, yet none of the school staff had. If it had been a white kid killed, the whole world would have shown up.

She thought of Land, and realized it hadn't even occurred to her to try to reach him. She thought about how little she counted on him for anything, especially if it might look like they were together. She felt how alone she was in this relationship that meant everything to her.

Out of the corner of her eye, she saw Tommie Lee and Lillian come in. They took a seat in the back near Lonnie and Guff. Lillian reached over and gave Guff a kiss. Jeanna was surprised; she hadn't realized they knew each other.

The pews began to empty of people as they walked to the front to look down into the casket where the body lay. She blanched, not ready for this. Big Blue and Cassius had already started out, and Valle stood up. "You want to go up, Miss J, or stay here?"

"I'll go up," Jeanna said, although that was the last thing she wanted to do.

"That's real good," Valle said.

Jeanna was carried forward by the stream of bodies moving to the casket. Who were all these people, and how did they know Jam . . . or did they? He'd seemed so friendless, family-less at school, so stolid and alone. Maybe he was. Maybe this was a congregation taking in one of its own, not in life but in death, to make sure he passed over to the other side whole, even if they'd been unable to keep him whole on this side.

She found herself brushing up against the table that held Jam's body. She looked down at him and saw that he looked very much like he'd always looked. Like a wall of grey stone. But in death he held more power to move people than he had in life. Except for that time in her car, she hadn't been able to connect with him. But Nate Smith had, and Tommie Lee, and in all those months since, Jam had seemed almost content, not because he'd smiled or spoken or walked free and easy, nothing like that, but just because . . . he had.

She looked up then and saw Nate Smith standing directly across the casket, looking at her. Their eyes met. Hers were wet; his were not. He looked tired and remote, and she wondered if this were something he'd done over and over again. How many other young men had he seen cut down and buried? He nodded to her and turned to walk back to his seat.

Out of nowhere, a heart-wrenching wail pierced the air. Everyone froze; Nate Smith stopped walking, one arm extended in front of him. A woman held a hand in the air over the casket. An elder held on to a pew and stopped there as if braced for all time. A small child sat bolt upright. Then music cascaded down like a waterfall, cleansing them all. As the music softened and strains of the blues floated over the roomful of people, Jeanna realized it sounded tantalizingly familiar. She looked around for the source and saw Will, his brown hair hanging over his eyes, playing his mouth harp in the shadows.

As the last note quivered in the air, people began to move again, slowly, out of the church. Blind with tears, Jeanna walked to her car, only half aware of Big Blue and Lonnie escorting her and taking their leave without a word of good-bye. Everyone was in slow motion, floating through the air, not of this earth and not yet of the other side, trembling in that space between life and death.

CHAPTER THIRTY-EIGHT

All-City Congress

JEANNA AND OTHERS IN THE GROUP HAD BEEN CANVASSING every weekend and many evenings throughout May, June, and July for the All-City Congress. Now today, July 25th, was the big day.

There was a surprisingly fresh breeze in the air as Jeanna parked her car and entered the First Baptist Church. She had never worked so hard for anything in her life.

Helene was dispensing orders to everyone else, but ignored her. Jeanna shrugged it off and jumped in to help Ma and Matt put out refreshments, then gave Cam and Abe a hand in setting up hundreds of chairs in the shape of a horseshoe, facing the stage. She put the radio on to the local jazz/blues program. Ray Charles's "Georgia" filled the air, and Matt gave her a big thumbs up.

She wondered where Lillian was. She always felt so much better when she was around. Through the wide-open doorway, she saw Land outside greeting the men with a handshake, while every woman gave him a big hug and kiss as they went by.

By nine-thirty almost 400 people had flooded the room, and more were coming in. Jeanna helped Matt and Gideon bring in more chairs. She was ecstatic about the turnout and had begun to feel more comfortable reaching out to people she barely knew, smiling, introducing herself, and asking what organization they were from.

Jackie rushed in, radiant, set down her bags, and gave Jeanna a big hug. "What a crowd! You must be so proud!"

"And you too!" Jeanna responded. Jackie had been an incredible help.

"I am!" She hurried to the ladies' room, her arms full of extra rolls of toilet paper and paper towels.

Jeanna looked out the open doorway and saw Lillian hurrying down the walk, leaning forward with her hands on her two younger boys. Tommie Lee was right behind her, balancing a huge tray of walnut dream bars, Lillian's specialty. When they entered, he made a beeline for Ma Carrington.

Jeanna went over and gave Lillian a hug.

"Sorry I'm so late," Lillian said. "I wanted to get here to help set up, but Giddy here decided to flush the car keys down the toilet."

Jeanna laughed. "Where's Carl?"

"He had to work. Everyone's on overtime, working nights and weekends now."

"That's too bad, but I'm glad you made it. I was beginning to worry. I know you're scheduled to speak fairly early, right?"

"Yes! But where are the agendas? I still don't know exactly when. I'm so full of nerves, I've been jumping out of my skin. I practiced all last night and got more screwed up each time."

"But you always speak so well," Jeanna protested. "It was what you said at the very first meeting I came to that made me want to join the group!"

"Oh, I love you, Jeanna. But that's when I don't prepare so hard. It's having everything down in print that screws me up. I'm at my wit's end. I know I'm being stupid."

"Forget the print," Jeanna said. "Speak from your heart. You know what you want to say."

"That's what Carl said! At the stroke of midnight he grabbed that paper out of my hands and said the exact same thing." She laughed and imitated Carl grabbing the papers from her.

Jeanna loved how excited and animated Lillian was. Usually she was so reserved, almost as if she didn't feel entitled to speak.

Lillian pulled several pages out of her purse and waved them. "See, I go back and forth between the papers and talking and it just messes me up. I can't find my place. Helene thought having it down in print would help me, and I know she's right, but . . ."

Jeanna reached out, gently took hold of the papers, and looked Lillian in the eye. "How 'bout I hold them for you and you go back to your own style, Lil."

Lillian let go of the papers and looked right back at her. "Thank you." She gave a little sigh of relief. "That feels better." She leaned down and wiped young Carl's nose with a Kleenex, and pulled up little Gideon's pants. "You have any ideas where those agendas are? I still need to know when I'm speaking."

"I'll get them. Why don't you and the kids grab some seats up near the stage and I'll be right back."

Jeanna walked to the back of the huge hall where the literature and refreshments were, picked up some programs, and looked back through the crowd for Lillian and the kids. They were in the third row. Helene was standing over Lillian, saying something to her. Jeanna decided to wait until Helene left and opened the program.

She looked down the speaker list. Helene was the MC. Land was speaking first, of course, then Letona from Jackie's youth group, the City's Finest, then Frederick from the Black Administrators Association, Elaine Browning representing City Wide Parents Action for Change, and Phil from the progressive caucus of the Teachers Union—all speaking on education issues. Then on jobs and community development, it was Cam, Gideon, then Land again. No Lillian on the agenda. There must be some mistake, a typo probably—or maybe not. She looked up. Helene had gone and Lillian's face had lost its nervous excitement and looked strangely flat.

Jeanna went over and sat next to Lillian. "What's up?"

"Helene just told me I'm not speaking after all."

"Why not?"

Lillian said nothing for a minute, regaining her composure. "I don't really know. She said something about Elaine Browning was speaking instead, that they'd run out of time."

"But Elaine was always going to speak."

"That's what I thought." Lillian shrugged, but Jeanna saw her blinking a tear away.

"What the fuck is going on?" Jeanna whispered fiercely into her ear. Hopefully saying what Lillian would've wanted to say if she hadn't been Lillian.

Lillian gave her a flicker of a smile. "Don't worry about it. It don't matter. I should be relieved."

Jeanna wondered on what basis they had cut Lillian out, and whose decision it had been. And what, they couldn't have two black women speaking?

"What's the matter, Mommie?" Little Gideon looked up at her with a frown.

"It's okay, sweetie. Mommie just got a surprise, that's all."

"What kind of surprise?" young Carl asked.

"The lady just told me I'm not going to have to get up and speak after all."

"But I want to see you up on the stage with Daddy's scarf on!" Gideon wailed.

Lillian touched her new scarf, a lovely blue and green. "It's okay. I'll do it another time."

Jeanna wanted to shoot Helene.

"Jeanna, would you mind getting some juice and muffins or something for my boys?" Lil asked, giving her a pleading look. "We didn't have time for breakfast this morning."

"Of course. I'll be right back." She was glad to be able to do something under the circumstances, however small. She hurried to the back table and filled a tray with fruit and muffins. She didn't want to miss Land's opening. She couldn't believe Helene's gall. If time was short, cut Frederick, for one. He'd done virtually nothing. Or Phil, who always got nervous and had to tell a stupid sexual joke.

Suddenly, Land was by her side, his hand on her arm. She froze at the unexpected closeness of it and looked up at him.

"Good work, Jeanna," he said. "Look at this crowd. I know how much you put into this."

He didn't. He couldn't. But that was okay. Now she had been anointed too. She wanted to ask him about Lillian, but just as quickly he left to go up on the stage, leaving Jeanna sailing on his touch. She looked around her. There had to be more than 500 people in the room, and folks were still trickling in. She hurried to her seat next to Lillian and handed the kids their plates of food.

As Land walked up to the microphone, the entire crowd hushed as one. The speakers for the morning sat behind a table to his left. Land seemed to be looking right at her. Could he be? He must be. He was. Now maybe her and Lillian. Yes. Good.

"We're about something different today," Land said with a quiet power. "We're about the people, all the people, saying what we need and what we need to change. It's not about any one person or any one group. It's about all of us here, and all those who couldn't come but wanted to, and about those who don't yet know they have a right to come and be heard, or a right to even want to. It's about every single one of you being the most important person in this room, in this city, in this universe—because every single person has something important to contribute. We're going to listen to what that is and we're going to carry that forward into the fall and beyond until those who sit in positions of power hear us—and until we sit in those positions of power to do the will of the people. So let's listen to each other today. And when the day is over, let's not stop. Let's keep moving together in the coming year, and the next and the next, until we bring our ideas into being."

He stepped away to a standing ovation. The day had begun.

Letona, a girl from Jackie's youth group, was one of the first to speak. Dressed in chic blue jeans, sandals with heels, and a sleeveless cream-colored top, she looked stunning. Perspiration beaded her forehead. "What I'm here to say is that education is supposed to be about us, the youth, but somehow that gets lost. It's supposed to be about us learning, challenging, inspiring us, but instead it's usually about putting us down, ordering us around, making us feel less-than, like we have to be constantly remediated instead of simply taught, helped to learn. We're not dumb. You don't have to go to Raleigh Academy or the rich 'burbs to find talent. We've got the best and the brightest, the city's finest," she smiled and gestured toward her youth group, "right here."

Two rows of students raised their fists and shouted "Power!" with big smiles on their faces.

"We need teachers and principals and parents to believe in us, to respect us rather than try to control us. We need counselors who are like us and where we come from. We want school staff to relate to us like we're human beings. We want to say what we think in class, ask the why questions no one ever wants us to ask, and do things that are real—things that will make a difference in the community, in life, like finding a way to end the war, or helping to rehab housing for people who need it, not just sit at a desk and take tests.

"We want to learn about our own history, race, and culture, and not have to make a big to-do about it, but just have it be the normal, natural thing to do. All the different cultures. And we want to deal with the big issues in school, like hunger and hate, and what have you. We want to have fun too, now and then, laugh and dance without being yelled at, do a play that we write, you know?"

Jeanna looked around. Everyone in the room was nodding.

"One more thing. We don't need tracks. That's wrong. We all have something special to offer, like Land said here today—well, that's the way a school is, too. We need to all stay together to learn from each other and not be stuck in the slow track or the fast track, because that's just another way they have of letting some people know they're no good and other people that they're too good. Oh, yeah, I almost forgot, we want students to be part of the leadership in the schools. That's about it!"

The room thundered their approval, and the kids went wild. Jackie poked Jeanna from behind and Jeanna turned around and gave her a big hug. Without Jackie, half the kids in the room wouldn't be here.

Of all the speakers that day, Elaine Browning was the most eloquent, persuasive, and surprisingly humble in speaking about the importance of parent voice and leadership. Jeanna still couldn't believe that Lillian had been cut from the program, but she was smiling by the time Land wrapped things up.

After the speakers finished, they had everyone in attendance break off into groups to develop stands on the issues that the candidates would be held to when endorsement time rolled around. A cacophony filled the hall, and when Helene rang the bell for all to return, no one wanted to stop talking.

When they'd finally gotten everyone to return to their seats, Helene and Cam pulled all the issue positions together on stage, and Land MC'd the final discussion—and then the entire body voted on the most progressive platform the city had ever seen. It was an amazing feat.

Jeanna was reeling by the time it was all over. As she was helping clean up, Land brushed up beside her and whispered, "See you tonight?"

She nodded, a smile overtaking her. Life couldn't get much better than this.

CHAPTER THIRTY-NINE

Queen of the Universe

JEANNA FLEW HOME STILL HIGH ON THE ENERGY FROM the Congress, but Lillian's face kept coming up with that look of humiliation and deflation, and it brought her down, like a bird swept up then dashed down by the wind. Her excitement flared up again, though, at the thought of Land coming over to celebrate their success. Coming to her, of all people. She still couldn't get used to being the special woman in Land's life, couldn't quite take it in as truth. She didn't want to spoil the occasion by bringing up Lillian, but she'd try to mention it tomorrow morning before he had to go.

She took a leisurely bath, dressed in her creamy gold nightgown, dimmed the lights, and was in bed by ten, electric with anticipation. At ten-twenty she heard his key in the lock. He came into the bedroom, into her arms, and they spent half the night making love and talking about high points of the Congress. Land was enjoying the moment to the fullest, saying that this could clinch the elections. Jeanna was flying high. But after Land fell asleep, her anger about Lillian being knocked off the speakers' panel returned to haunt her.

She awoke early—Land had told her he had to be somewhere by nine—to make his breakfast. She needed to talk with him before the whole Lillian thing became a non-issue, like so many issues had, only to create a worse problem when least expected—a pattern she was only just beginning to grasp. She wished she could just luxuriate in the happiness of this moment with Land, but she knew she couldn't let it go.

When the bacon and home fries were sizzling on the stove, she made a pot of coffee. Land moaned happily and looked at her from bed. He smiled at her. "Something smells good."

She went over to him and lay down gently on top of him, kissing him and letting her robe fall open around him. "I gotta talk with you about something that came up yesterday, okay?"

"Okay. Shoot."

She slid down and lay on her back beside him.

"You know how Lillian was supposed to speak at the Congress?"

"Yeah."

"Well, yesterday she told me she'd been up half the night practicing her talk. She was nervous, but it was really important to her, you know?"

He nodded.

"Well, she didn't find out until two seconds before the Congress started that she wasn't going to speak after all. I could tell she was—"

"Really? Helene said she would phone her."

Jeanna looked at Land, confused. So he had known, then. This wasn't just a high-handed Helene thing.

"So you knew."

"Well, of course. Helene told me Lillian didn't want to speak. That she was going nuts about it. And that we had too many speakers anyhow. I suggested she cut Phil or Frederick or something, but she had good reasons why that wouldn't work. She didn't call her?"

"No. Like I said, she told her two seconds before the thing started."

"Lillian got her feelings hurt."

"Well, wouldn't you?"

He laughed. "Babe, I'd love not to have to talk at one of these things."

Jeanna looked away, angry.

"Hey. I understand what you're saying. It shouldn't have happened that way."

It shouldn't have happened at all. "What were her reasons?" Jeanna knew she was pushing it now, and felt a kind of helplessness.

"Oh, it's too much to go into. C'mon, babe. The thing was a success. It went way beyond our expectations. Let's not always go to the sour note."

Now she was furious and didn't dare show it. How many sour notes had she avoided? Just to avert this precise reaction.

"Is that what I do?"

"No. That's why I like you."

Jeanna felt like he'd stabbed her—because of course it was true. He liked her because she was his sweet, cheery little girl who caused him no trouble and admired his every move.

"I love that you're positive, not full of negative huff and puff all the time," Land said, seeming to sense her anger. "Is that bad?"

Was Helene the one full of negative huff and puff all the time? Was that who he meant?

"Who do you mean?" she asked.

"Oh nobody, nothing." He'd had it now. "I gotta go." He reached for his clothes on the chair and began to put them on. "But thanks for mentioning it. I don't want Lillian feeling bad any more than you do. I'll talk with her."

Pacifying Lillian wasn't the point. Getting straight with Helene on her high-handedness was. But what could she say now with him halfway out the door, and the smell of burnt bacon and home fries in the air?

"Bye," she said, kissing him before waving him out.

She was feeling just like Lillian had looked yesterday, dismissed and deflated. Why couldn't they ever talk anything out? Finally she picked up her flute and played her heart out, trying to find answers to questions that weren't there.

Jeanna called Lillian several times to commiserate with her about the speaking gig fiasco, but had never reached her. The Group was meeting that night and now it was feeling like old news, and hard to bring up.

"The business of the meeting," Ma began, "is to process the Congress, take stock of where we are, and talk about where we want to go from here. Group?"

Nearly everyone took turns chiming in with ringing endorsements of the Congress and possible ways to move forward.

Karima raised her hand. "I felt good about all that too," she said, "but I do have a question that's been bothering me a lot."

Silence descended.

"Yes? Go on." Ma prodded.

"I thought we agreed that Lillian was going to be on the speakers' panel, but somehow she wasn't. What happened?"

There was a long, loaded silence.

"Well," Helene finally responded, "what happened was that as we looked over the list of speakers, we realized we had too many for the time allotted and had to make a last-minute and difficult decision. Since Elaine was already covering that base and Lillian had expressed some doubts about speaking anyway, we made the adjustment there."

"Yeah, and who made you queen of the universe?" Karima looked straight at Helene.

Jeanna was silently cheering Karima, and she wondered how many others were as well. Maybe nobody. Maybe everybody. Lillian was looking down, but everyone else was looking intently at Helene, who had chosen to ignore the remark and was staring at Land. How unusual. Helene's typical reaction to any such challenger was to tear the poor soul to shreds with cool precision.

"Look," Cam said, "we did have to figure something out. You lose an audience if you have speaker after speaker."

"You spoke," Karima said, giving him a level look.

"Well, that was on co-ops, which no one else—"

"Look, I approved it," Land said in a weary voice, and Jeanna realized that Helene had been staring at him to make him speak. "It's as Helene already explained. There was no intent to hurt or disrespect Lil—"

"Listen everyone," Lillian interrupted. "I don't want this to become a big issue. What's important is that the Congress was a great success, and that's due to the hard work of everyone here. People like Jeanna and Karima, Helene and C—"

"Alright, alright already," Frederick cut in. "We get the point. Let's get on with the agenda."

Lillian looked stricken, then immediately impassive. Jeanna could have killed him, and Helene, with one long thrust of a sword.

"Last time I looked, I was chairing this meeting," Ma said, cutting Fred off. "I realize that the spotlight has been off you for several moments, Frederick, but please have the good grace to let Lillian finish her sentence."

Lillian flipped her hand up off the desk as if it were of no importance.

Jeanna felt a rush of rage overtake her. "This is important." She was surprised to hear her own voice, loud and clear for a change. "Karima's right. We make a decision as a group, and then somehow it gets changed."

"You and your ridiculous obsession with process." Helene spat out the words. "If you had an even slightly responsible position in the group, you'd know why some tough decisions need to be made from time to time."

I sure have a hell of a lot of responsibilities for someone without a responsible position, Jeanna thought as muttering began all over the room. Jeanna couldn't tell if they were agreeing with Helene and Land, or her and Karima, or both, or no one.

"All right, let's end it right here," Ma said. "I will not have this meeting turn into a dumping ground. Reverend Barrows, Matt, and I will meet with Land, Lillian, and Helene on this issue. If we have anything useful to report at the next meeting we will do so. We are adjourned."

"But—" Frederick began.

"Adjourned," Ma repeated with emphasis, peering at him over her glasses.

Jeanna looked at Land. He was avoiding her eyes. She guessed he wouldn't be over tonight after all. Helene was still looking at him—and

Karima was looking at her, she realized. She would have to be more careful about keying in on Land with Karima around.

She looked around for Lillian, but she was already at the door and walking out. Shit, that's who she should have tried to connect with immediately. What had she been thinking? Lillian must be embarrassed as hell. Insult added on to injury.

Land was following Helene, slowly, like he was on an invisible string, into his inner sanctum. As Helene closed the door, Jeanna caught her look of triumph. So she and Land were back into their long-ago affair. Jeanna was so sure she could taste it.

But why wasn't she shot through with jealousy? She wasn't. She felt terrible, but she didn't feel jealous.

That night Jeanna played *In a Silent Way* all evening, trying to transcend Helene's power and control games, and find a way to deal with Land's obliviousness to her needs. She wondered, too, why Land didn't try to deal with any of this childish conflict in the Group, why he chose to stay above it all. Why he rarely checked Cam and Helene's arbitrary power—power they wielded in his name. Why he didn't even seem to notice it.

Jeanna thought back to her initial image of Land and the Group. She had been transfixed by this movement love-power that had its source in him and that he sent out in so many directions, making so many feel like they were the specially chosen ones. She thought of how his leadership contrasted with her own, slight as it was, in her classes at West Side. Land was so much to so many, but he was the source upon which they depended for their worth, their everything, rather than depending on themselves and each other. She was virtually nothing to anyone, yet her students grew by leaps and bounds, dependent more on each other and themselves than upon her.

A few days later, Land called to say he needed to deal with some other "matters" and wouldn't be around for the next few weeks.

"Matters," indeed.

CHAPTER FORTY

A Slippery Slope

THE SECOND WEEK OF AUGUST LAND HAD STARTED coming by again, and as far as Jeanna could tell, he and Helene had decided to cool it after all. She suspected that Helene had been playing one of her power and control games—had reeled Land in for a little while, then let him slide out again. She was beginning to realize that as invincible as Land seemed, he needed Helene to manage things. He couldn't take her completely for granted—might even stoop to having sex with her in order to pacify her and keep his ship afloat. Maybe that's why Jeanna hadn't been more jealous of their renewed affair.

Now that Land was free again, he had been coming over every night. She was still getting used to him—mostly to being his political muse, and trying to detect whatever else he might need or want from her. She tried not to think about what she wanted or needed from him—tried to tell herself that his presence alone was enough.

The phone rang just as she walked in the door from school. "Hey Jeanna."

"Hi!" She couldn't keep the excitement from her voice if she'd wanted to.

"I've got some bad news, I'm afraid."

"What happened?"

"Well it's actually good in a sense, but not for us."

Jeanna felt her insides constrict.

"Pearl's on her way home by the end of the week. She's been doing much better, so they say."

Jeanna felt like a heavy magnetic hand had reached inside her and changed everything with one perfunctory motion. She was silent.

"Remember I told you she returns from her rehab center occasionally? When she begins to feel better?"

Jeanna did not respond. A large stone rolled between them.

"Well, she's feeling better, and this could mean she'll be here anywhere from two weeks to three months. I never know, and neither does she." He sounded like an old man who'd been through this a hundred times.

She was still quiet, trying to absorb a reality that she'd been only dimly aware of until now.

"Jeanna, you okay?"

"Sure, yes, I'm sorry. I just wasn't expecting it."

"How could you? You haven't lived with it."

Her heart went out to him and closed to Pearl, even as she knew that Pearl was the one in real need. She saw that she had started down a slippery slope that she had no business being on with Land, but she was way too far down to clamber back up and out.

"Of course you have to be with her." She tried to rally, to be what he needed her to be, but she felt an odd seeping sensation, eating away at her insides like acid. She gritted her teeth.

"I'm sorry, Jeanna. We'll need to stop all personal contact until she leaves. Except for at meetings, of course. I'll call you when she's gone back." His tone had become stolid, firm, almost businesslike.

"Okay. It's just . . ." her voice broke.

"What, baby?"

"I love you so much."

"I know," he said softly. "I'll call you when she's gone, I will. You take care till then."

"You too."

Jeanna just lay there after she hung up, not crying, not cursing, not moving, not thinking, knowing it was what it was—and it wasn't good. For anyone.

Jeanna wandered through the next weeks in a daze, lost and troubled. What was it about Pearl? Why was she mentally ill? Why was she back? What did she hope for with Land? If she was well enough to come home, what made her go out of control and have to leave again, over and over? Was it how Land responded to her? Was it that she somehow knew about Land's affairs? Or did it have nothing to do with them and everything to do with her own inner illness, which would persist no matter what Land or anyone else did? Everyone seemed to believe Pearl was incurable. That it was chemical. Jeanna wished that were the case, but she was full of doubts, and feeling kind of crazy herself.

It was mid-August, and summer school was winding down. Jeanna had been struggling with a particularly challenging group of students in one of her classes. That morning she'd lost her cool with a student who'd made a nasty sexual remark about her. Later that day she'd dimly recognized that she was checking out at the staff meeting, but didn't care. She was immersed in doubts about her relationship with Land.

The "mistress" role was not feeling at all good these days. She despised the very word. But how else could you describe it? What was the counterpart name for the man? She felt passive, impotent, and then suddenly drenched in shame for trespassing into a sacred place where she didn't belong. She'd told herself all kinds of things to justify her relationship with Land, but it wasn't okay, and it never would be until Land gave Pearl up, or vice versa. Neither seemed likely to happen.

Jeanna looked up. Matt was standing over her and speaking. The rest of the staff had left. He was looking at her with grave concern.

"What?" Jeanna said sharply, not wanting his scrutiny or his concern.

"What's the matter, Jeanna? I've been worried about you."

"Why?" she asked, silently berating herself for not hiding her feelings better.

"Forget I'm your boss—you know I hate that whole notion anyway—and let me be your friend. Please, tell me what's going on."

"Nothing, really, I just have a lot on my mind lately. I shouldn't have allowed it to get in the way of staff meeting."

"I'm not criticizing. I'd like to help. I . . ." he stopped.

"What?"

"I've been really concerned about you. I worry that you're taking on too much, in the Group especially, and that you're in too deep. I feel kind of responsib—"

"What are you talking about?" Jeanna was mortified. Did Matt know about Land and her?

Matt drew back, but kept looking steadily into her eyes. She hadn't meant to sound so aggressive, but what business was it of his?

"You tell me, Jeanna. I hope you know you can talk with me about anything. I won't betray your confidence."

"Has my performance here become a problem?"

"No, not at all. You're one of the most committed teachers here. It's none of my business, I know, but . . ." Matt's face begged her to talk, to tell him what she was struggling with, but she couldn't; she needed to deal with it on her own.

"Matt, I'm fine. I was just lost in thought there for a few moments. You needn't concern yourself, really. But . . . thanks." For one desperate moment she wanted to grab on to him and pour out her confusion of fears and desires, but she turned and walked away, struggling to keep her composure until she was out of sight.

That night, she reran the scene with Matt in her mind and was glad she hadn't opened up. He would never approve of what they were doing, though she knew he would blame Land as much as her. He was nothing if not fair. No, she had to figure this thing out—alone.

CHAPTER FORTY-ONE

A Force to Contend With

JEANNA STILL MADE SURE SHE KEPT UP WITH THE original four from Group Survive, attending their after-school reading and writing tutorial every week.

"How's it going at home, Cat?" she asked after their session one day when he seemed especially relaxed.

"Good. It different now."

"How so?"

"My aunt, she teachin' me not to jump away. At first I din't know why she say that. So I tol' Lon an Chef an' all what she say, 'cause I knew I never did that, but they say I do. We went in the men's room so's I could see it in the mirrors, and I was like, wow, there it was. I felt bad; I'd always been so cool, I thought, like a cool cat, but they say it isn't me should feel bad but the ones that hit me. They say it a habit. My aunt helpin' me with it. It nice now."

"That's wonderful, Cat. I'm glad it's feeling better at home now." They had Guff to thank for that; he was the one who'd gone up to the prison to meet with Cat's father. "Are you still having breakfast at the Panthers?"

"Yeah. And the men's group ever other Wednesday night with Clay. He let me sit there. They somethin'."

"How so?"

"All they seen an' done. In ''Nam, on the streets being knifed, gettin' shot at, bein' hassled by the cops, gettin' down with girls but it don't ever work out, tryin' to stop doin' smack an' stuff. Then they be talkin' big about protecting the womens and the community from the man, the system, but I don't know." He shook his head.

"What?"

"How they gonna do all that protectin' when they be havin' all they problems? I mean I like to be a big man too, but I'd like to fly to the moon too, you know what I mean?"

"I do. Being a real man, like being a real woman, takes a good while." Jeanna wondered how long it would take her to feel like a woman, and if her relationship with Land was increasing or decreasing her chances. Both at once, probably.

"Yeah."

"Anything else going on?"

"Clay an' his wife, Miss Corinda, havin' me over to they place one Saturday a month. I stays over." He beamed.

"Wow!" Jeanna said.

"Miss Corinda treat me like a full-grown man, call me by my real name. She teachin' me stuff—'manly habits,' she call 'em."

"What's your real name?" Jeanna said, upset she hadn't learned it before they had.

"Calvin—Cal. It not far off from Cat, but I like it better."

"Cal. That's very cool," Jeanna said.

"Miss Corinda been showing me how to rub oil into my skin and hair." He held his arm to his face. "It smell funny, but it so smooth. I gave Lonnie some, 'cause a his ashy skin? He ate it up an' wanted more. It feel good givin' to Lon 'cause he all the time doin' for everone else."

"He sure does. And I know what you mean about the giving."

"It make me high," he said, and somehow propelled himself out of the chair into the air and landed right at the doorway to her office. He waved before walking off.

Jeanna shook her head and smiled. Cat—Cal—had finally found his voice, and his style.

September had arrived, along with a whole new crew of students. What surprised her was how quickly she'd fallen in love with almost all of them. But underneath all of that, Jeanna had fallen back into a deep sadness over Land's absence and all the dilemmas she couldn't see past, wanting desperately to talk it all out with him. Then, one day, the phone rang.

"Hey Jeanna." It was Land, his voice soft and husky.

Her heart stopped. The wind fell silent. The clock stopped ticking.

"Pearl left a few days ago. It got very difficult. She had to go back."

Jeanna didn't know what to say. Her happiness was his wife's misery.

"I'm, I'm sorry. I mean glad . . ."

"Me too, babe. I was thinking about stopping by, unless . . ."

Electric sparks shot through her. She was still confused and angry at their whole situation, but the prospect of seeing Land . . . She was as nervous a wreck as she'd been the first time. She raced around cleaning up her apartment, hurried into the bathroom to wash up and change into his favorite terry slacks and the shirt he'd given her their very first time together, and lit the candle that had been waiting there gathering dust in front of her bedroom mirror. Just as she was turning down the light, he knocked.

Sometime very early in the morning Jeanna extricated herself to go to the bathroom, her whole body full of contradictory feelings—elation underlaid by deep doubt. She wondered how it had been with Pearl. Had they slept together? But of course they had. How could he go from one to another like that? How did he feel; whom did he really love? His wife for certain. Jeanna, on the other hand, he "cared about"—or so he said from time to time. That was a far cry from love. She went back into the bedroom, slipped in behind him, and stretched her arm around his chest.

As she lay there, Jeanna realized how odd it was that they hadn't talked about Pearl's leaving, her stay with Land, anything. He turned to lie on his back, and she finally got up the nerve to raise the question.

"You haven't said anything about Pearl."

"What should I say?"

He got that look she hated to see, like a gathering storm. Couldn't they ever talk about anything real, personal? Or was she just supposed to navigate all these treacherous waters totally alone? That didn't seem like an especially good idea, but then neither did bringing anything up, ever.

"Oh, I don't know. What brought her back again? What made her go? How do you feel, how does she?" She was sure that she herself wasn't supposed to have any feelings in the matter, according to the implicit rules of their game. How absurd was that? "How did you get involved with such a fragile woman in the first place?"

"Pearl? Fragile? Pearl's the most powerful force I've ever encountered." He laughed without humor.

"What kind of power?"

"Well, it started out as sheer, outright intensity. In everything. She was a force unto herself. A constant electric charge. Pure gold. I couldn't deal with it—and neither could she, I guess.."

Pure gold. That had been Jeanna's impression the one and only time she had seen her—and felt her electricity—at the West Side Center.

"Sounds hard to handle," she said.

"Yeah. After we got married I was trying to do all this community work and she was into her art. I needed some support in those spare moments when we were together. I'd come home and she was this, this thunderous light coming at me full force, full of all this intense creativity she was in the midst of, and when I'd back off to get my bearings, she'd get so dark and violent. She scared me, she scared herself. She'd tell me how scared she was."

"Of what?"

"Of her own power. I'd hold her. We'd be shaking and not know why."

"Did you get help?"

"We did. We went for counseling. My parents insisted. But I think the counselor, we all, missed the point. It was like a force of nature, and no amount of talk would tame it."

"Was that the goal . . . to tame it?" Jeanna wanted to taste a tiny bit of that power, just to know what it felt like. She was suddenly aware of constantly smothering hers.

Land looked at her sharply, and she saw rage come into his eyes and go out again just as quickly, like he'd learned to hold his anger in check eons ago. It was obvious he'd expected complete support from her, not questions.

"If you'd seen the mayhem it caused, you wouldn't ask; it could get pretty ugly. I mean, totally out of control."

Jeanna wanted to know how Pearl went out of control, and what would precipitate it. Maybe there was something that set her off, or something missing, some reason for it. Jeanna imagined mirrors shattering, sharp objects flying through the air, a letter opener held tightly in a slender hand.

"Did she hurt you physically?"

"Never. She would hurt herself, wreak havoc in the house, but never me. She loved me." He gave a helpless laugh. He put his arm across her body and held her tight. "No, she was a force to contend with and still is, but this is the last thing I wanted to lay on you."

"It's okay, it helps me to understand a little bit." She squeezed his hand where it curled around her waist.

"I'm glad, babe, but let's let it be, okay?"

"Okay."

He snuggled close and drifted off to sleep.

Jeanna felt privileged that he'd shared his innermost struggles—but where did she fit in the scheme of things? Loving mistress to a great man married to, and in love with, an impossibly ill woman? Lover of a man in a highly charged marital mismatch that he couldn't end? Or lover of a man who couldn't meet an intense, creative wife halfway, and didn't want to?

Despite all the affirming things he said to her in their late-night talks, she was sure Land wouldn't choose to be with her out in the open, even if Pearl was out of the picture. She was too young, too white, a threat to his mighty rep.

But in private they seemed to be kindred spirits in every way. She was always lifted up in his presence. He had often said how good he felt with her, that she was a kind of healing balm for him. Lately though, she'd felt restricted by the "healing balm" role. Maybe there were some wounds that needed opening. And what if their harmony was built on her self-diminishment? How else could she explain him—that he never said he loved her, or asked how she felt? That he never wanted to talk about their relationship? And what was worse, she never expected him to do any of that.

That night Jeanna dreamt about a boulder in a river. The rock was partially submerged in the rushing water, but standing strong against the current. Then she saw that underneath the water's surface a gaping bite had been taken out of one side of the rock, right near its base. The rock seemed strong, but it was wearing away relentlessly, and would soon give way.

The shock of the image woke her. She couldn't wear away. She had to be strong, to hold things up. People were counting on her. Land was counting on her. Until this moment, she'd always thought he was the strong one, the rock. But he was the river, rushing ever onward, not giving a thought to anything but the movement.

CHAPTER FORTY-TWO

It's Like You Don't Think Nothing of Yourself

"HOW ARE THINGS GOING AT THE CENTER, META?" Jeanna had set up an apprenticeship for her at the new Women's Health Center.

"Oh I love it, Miss J," she said. "I've walked into a whole new world of real live strong beautiful women. At first I was so embarrassed at the way they talked; they joke a lot and say whatever they want to about the female body, about men . . . Here, look at all the stuff they keep giving me. I don't dare take it home." She laughed and waved a stack of papers in front of her. "About women, birth control, and a lot on abuse in the home. See, here's one about women and depression in a man's world. I saw my mother in that one. And one on women's poverty and job discrimination." She spread the papers out on the table. "My father would have a stroke if he saw me reading any of this."

Jeanna laughed. "What have you been doing there lately?" she asked, loving this new, more confident version of Meta.

"I'm setting up their library," Meta said, "and when my training is done, they are going to try me out as a part-time paid receptionist in the health clinic."

"Wonderful," Jeanna said as they walked out the door together. "What do you tell your dad?"

"That I'm working at a health center as part of my school program, just not a women's health center."

"I see," Jeanna said.

Meta looked at her watch. "I have to get home and cook dinner before my dad gets there. See you later, Miss J." She took off down the sidewalk.

Jeanna waved good-bye. She watched fondly as Meta ran to catch her bus, her sandy braids askew, her heavy body moving with such energy and animation. Only last year she'd walked like a sack of old potatoes—head down, shoulders hunched, a worried frown on her face. Noticing her own slumped posture, Jeanna felt almost as if they'd traded places.

Over the next week, all the teachers at West Side were supposed to be evaluated by a sampling of their previous year's students, orally and in writing.

"What we supposed to be doing again?" Cassius asked, folding his muscled arms across his chest. He had chosen to stay in her Group Inquiry class for a second year, one of the few Matt had permitted to do so.

"It's your chance to evaluate me as a teacher," Jeanna said. "My strengths and weaknesses—where I could improve, what I do well."

"That there's a switch," he said. "What you want me to talk about?"

"Whatever you think is important."

He stretched his legs out, crossed them at the ankles, and stared at his sneakers. "Well, I always wonder why you is the way you is, you know?"

"I'm not sure," she said. "Spell it out for me."

"I mean, why you so meek and mild and shit."

Jeanna blushed.

"I mean, once you calm down and get in your group groove, you're cool. If I had to tell the truth, which is not my usual style, you'd be about the best teacher I ever had. But half the time, you don't seem like a teacher at all. It's like you're a hidden conductor or something, way below the bandstand, and we're the players. I mean I never know what you think. I'm guessing you're gonna react one way and then you don't, but it's like you don't react at all. And I'm saying, why the hell is that; she's the teacher, after all." He stopped and studied her.

She stayed quiet, feeling there was more to come.

"It's like you don't think nothing of yourself. Like everyone else is more important. Like kids say these really weird things to you, and you don't do nothin', when I'd jump up and slap them upside the head or call them out at least . . ." He stopped midstream. "See, even now you just sittin' there, saying nothing."

"Okay, let's take it from the top," Jeanna said, her head spinning. "I seem meek and mild. You may be right. I probably am, even if I wish I weren't. I didn't grow up in the city and have to hang tough. Where I come from, women take a backseat; we don't put ourselves into the limelight, you know—look at me, listen to me, I'm so great. We kind of do the best we can in a low-key way. We might be doing a lot but nobody notices."

"Huh." Cassius grunted. "Some-a that's like they do us blacks, always wantin' us to keep a low profile, blend in, not stick out any more than we have to since we already stick out bein' black, and not make no demands or nothin'. 'Course, I never took to it myself." He laughed harshly.

"Yeah, maybe so," Jeanna said, "there are some similarities, and I guess part of it is bad when we go along, because we're playing into our own suppression-oppression or whatever. But part of it is good, I think, because we don't dominate everything."

"Yeah, don't get me wrong," Cassius said, "I like it that you don't always take over, like do this, do that, say 'shut your mouth' every time somebody says a swear word, because then it would cut off the main thing the person was tryin' to say, like in the regular schools where no one's allowed to say anything real. It's one reason I stopped going. But Christ, you practically don't say nothin'."

"How about the other teachers?"

"They're all the same damn way. They're all a big puzzle. But at least they all have an angle, a definite kick to them. I mean Shanna's a total mystery outta the deep dark underworld. You don't never know what she'll say or do next. But you know it'll be interesting."

Jeanna blushed again, not happy to be seen as the nothing he'd just implied.

"Take Matt: he's like this big ol' woolly bear, got everything under control. You know you safe and sound, can do anything in his class and he'll go with it and help make it happen. He got it all. But with you, it's like, who are you? I can't get a hold of you like I can the others." He held his hands up as if to let something slip through his fingers.

Jeanna was hurt to the core. He was saying something she felt about herself, too. Not that she didn't feel strong things on the inside—just that she didn't know how to bring them out to be seen and felt by others. But was that necessary? Most of the time there were enough feelings swirling around the classroom to sink a ship. Wasn't a quiet, steady presence needed? She thought so. But she also knew he was on to something she should pay attention to.

"How about this class? Is it nothing too?"

"No, it kicks ass," he said "This my favorite class to come to. You're doin' something right, I guess, but damned if I know what it is."

"That's a relief." Her self-esteem zoomed upwards. "But getting back to what you said before . . . I guess I do think my students are more important than I am, when it comes down to it." She knew she felt that way in the Group too, and with Land. Certainly her issues paled in comparison to everyone else's.

"Hum."

"What?"

"I guess I just don't think that's very good—you know, survival-wise."

Cassius slid his chair back and got up to go. He stood there patting down his pockets, searching for his pack of cigarettes, while his final comment sank in.

Was her survival in danger?

She pointed to his almost-flat pack of Marlboros, rolled up in his sleeve, right at his bicep.

He smiled—a tough, cool smile—reached for it, and sauntered off.

A week later, Jeanna found herself in bed, crying, choking on her fury. Her heart was racing, and she could barely breathe. This was the third time Land had stood her up, and tonight it was to celebrate her birthday and see the great jazz flute player, James Moody, play at a club two towns over. The previous two times when he'd called to cancel, his reasons had been impeccable—some community crisis he needed to intervene in. But this time there had been no call. He had been due to pick her up at six and it was eleven now.

She knew that some real crisis must have occurred, and that her issues were petty in comparison. Still, she was sick of always being last on his list. Everyone and everything else came before her, yet she was supposed to continue to function as the all-loving Rock of Gibraltar no matter what.

She cried herself to sleep, and when she awoke early the next morning, her body ached and her throat was raw. She needed to sort out what had become of her life. How had her ecstatic embrace of the great Landon Waters turned to this? She knew he would call soon with a reasonable explanation, but she knew just as surely that they would never make it out into the world together to enjoy life.

She was losing her self-respect in the hiddenness of their relationship, and she was beginning to show signs of wear and tear—in thoughtless remarks to students, and missed calls to members of the Group. Her feelings hadn't changed, her but capacities had, and without prior notice or consultation.

She had always thought that Land might ultimately reject her, let her go. That she might let *him* go was barely imaginable. To give up Land, she thought, would be to give up her life and everything that mattered to her. Yet now she felt that's what might also save it.

If only she could talk with someone about all this.

She wondered what Lillian would do. She wished she knew. But she had given up trying to connect with the older woman on a friendship level. Lillian was completely swamped by others' demands—and besides, Jeanna was afraid that if she knew about Land, she would condemn her. She wouldn't be cruel like Helene, but that would be even worse. Jeanna couldn't risk that.

If she couldn't talk with Lillian, she could at least imagine how Lillian might handle this. She might talk honestly and openly with Land—but Jeanna knew there was no real point in that. The constraints were what they were, and no amount of conversation was going to change that. Land's reputation was his life, and he wasn't going to give that up for her or anybody else.

As she drifted back to sleep, something slipped away from her. It was almost invisible, and quite far away. She tried to reach down and grab it by the tips of her fingers, but it was like liquid light, and she couldn't hold on to it. She reached and reached, twisted and contorted in bed, until a loud ringing woke her up.

"Hello," she whispered, still in her dream.

"Hi, Jeanna. I'm sorry about last night."

Her heart leapt and turned over at the sound of his husky voice.

"It was Justine," he said. "She arrived on my doorstep at five-thirty just as I was dressing to come pick you up. She signed herself out of the psychiatric ward at Seattle General and used my sister's credit card to get a flight here. She's suicidal. It feels like Pearl all over again. She's asleep now. I couldn't leave her alone last night. She was out of control. Crying hysterically, lashing out. I'm about to call my sister to see if I should bring her back or keep her here for a while or what, but I wanted to let you know what's going on." He sounded exhausted.

"I'm so sorry," Jeanna said, and meant it. It was a relief to mean it. "Do whatever you need to, and I'll be pulling for her—and you."

"Thanks, Jeanna. I'll call you when I can. I'm not sure when."

"That's fine. You take care. I love you, Land," she added in a breathy rush.

Once again, he didn't respond in kind. It made her feel sad, and impotent. *But I never expected him to actually love me*, she realized. What did that say about her? If only she could finally get up the nerve to talk with Lillian one of these days. She might have the answers.

CHAPTER FORTY-THREE

The Sound of Nothingness

It was Friday, October 30th—only a few days remained till the November City Council and School Committee elections. Jeanna had been making dozens of calls ever since dinner, focusing on Land leading the city council slate and Elaine Browning the school committee slate. She was dripping with sweat from some ghastly problem with the heating system, the phone slippery in her grasp where she sat at the old oak table.

At nine-thirty she stopped, not daring to call anyone else at such a late hour. The sweat had dripped into her eyes. She took some ice and touched the edges of her eyes to ease the smarting. Lost in thought about whether or not Land and Elaine would win, she began to doze off.

The phone rang, and she jumped.

"Hello?"

"Jeanna? It's Garner. Your mother's been trying to reach you all night, and she's at her wits' end. She asked me to call."

"Gee, I'm sorry. I've been on the phone all night for a political thing."

"Of course, we thought it was something like that, but . . ."

She waited. She loved Garner, but why didn't he get to the point? A bad feeling was crawling across her skin.

"I'm so sorry to have to say this Jeanna, but your grandmother passed away this evening at her home. She was having dinner with her friend, Loretta. She had a heart attack."

Jeanna couldn't take it in. She was swallowed up by a deafening roar of nothingness. She heard a sharp, loud rapping noise, on and on. Why didn't they stop? She thought she might scream. She looked around her. She was on the floor by her chair, half under the oak table, her leg bent awkwardly under her, her arm over a foot of the pedestal, her body twisted.

She looked up at the door as it lifted up and off its hinges. She must be going mad. A man was holding it up and setting it aside. He was familiar. It was Garner. She saw another figure wavering behind him. Her grandmother. She wasn't dead! The figure reached down to her. No, it was her mother. She heard a terrible, gurgling animal sound. Her mother drew back, alarm mixing with disgust in her eyes. Garner reached down, slipped his arms under Jeanna, carried her into the bedroom, and laid her on the bed. Her mother sat beside her, leaned over her, and put her hand on her cheek, her eyes now flooded with love.

Jeanna reached for her mother. "Oh, Mom. I can't believe . . . What am I going to do?"

"I know, I know," her mother murmured. "She'll always be with us darling, she'll always be with us . . ." She had slipped her arms around Jeanna and was rocking her, whispering the same words over and over, a lullaby of grief.

Jeanna slipped into unconsciousness. When she awoke, her mother was stretched out beside her on her bed, asleep, holding her hand. Garner sat, his legs outstretched, in her stark wooden chair, nodding in and out of sleep.

Jeanna felt like she'd been in an accident. Every bone, muscle, and joint ached. She was fatigued in an insurmountable way she'd never felt before. She closed her eyes, and fell back into unconsciousness.

Jeanna returned to work on Wednesday. Her students assumed she had been sick, and she didn't explain. Her loss was nothing compared to what most of them had already dealt with in their short lives. Still, this was the greatest loss of her life, and one she couldn't accept. It made her bone-weary, and filled her with a sea of sadness.

Thursday evening, November 5th, she called Land at home, at nine and again at ten, but he didn't answer. She called the office on Friday, after her apprenticeship meetings around town, before she headed over to her mother's for the memorial service. Cam answered and said he hadn't seen Land. He was in such a hurry to get off the phone that she didn't even have a chance to tell him what had happened. And why would she, anyway? She was bitter at there being no one to call. All her so-called friends in the Group were not really friends at all. Except for Matt, no one at school would much care either. And Jackie was out of town, caring for her sick grandfather.

There was Lillian! She suddenly, desperately, needed to call Lillian. She dialed her number.

"Hi, Lillian. It's Jeanna. I'm sorry to bother you on a Friday evening." She could hear the kids screaming about whose baseball glove it was.

"It's no bother. What's up?" She shushed the kids.

Jeanna wasn't able to speak. Tears were running down her cheeks.

"Oh, Jeanna, something's wrong. What is it?"

"I'm sorry, Lil. I know you never met her, but my grandmother died, about a week ago, and I can't seem to deal with it."

"I'm so sorry, Jeanna. You must have been very close."

"We were. She was everything to me. She was the only one who understood what mattered to me. She was what I always wanted to be. She started me on music and social change and on being myself, on wearing blue-green . . ." She laughed weakly through her tears. "I'm sorry, I've stopped making sense."

"Yes, you look so good in that color. That's not silly; it's touching. I wish I'd known your grandmother. She sounds like a wonderful woman."

"I wish you had too. You would've liked each other."

"Well, I have the pleasure of knowing her granddaughter."

She couldn't respond. The silence was awkward.

"Are you with your parents? Your family?" Lillian's tone was a little cooler now.

"Not now. I was with my mom and my stepfather until Tuesday night, but then I had to get back to work. My dad works for the Peace Corps in Africa. I haven't seen him in years."

"I'm sorry. This must be so terribly difficult for you. I wondered where you were at the party after the elections on Tuesday. Nobody expected Land to be voted in by such a landslide. And Elaine Browning, too. Oh, it was a time! I'm sorry you've been caught up in so much sadness instead. I wish I'd known."

"Ma!" one of the kids called. "It's time to go! Dad says we're gonna be late!"

"I didn't want to bother you," Jeanna said hastily, "but thanks, you know, for listening."

Lillian clucked. "It's not a both—"

But Jeanna had already hung up. She hadn't meant to cut Lillian off, but she was amazed. She hadn't even thought about the election after hearing of her grandmother's death. Still, she was relieved she'd missed the party. Except for Lillian and Jackie, she realized there was no one in the Group she felt comfortable with anymore. The main thing was that Land and Elaine had been elected by a landslide. She wondered if he had called her to come over to celebrate when she'd been at her mom's on election night.

Mom. She was late. She packed quickly. At the last second, she went over to the closet and reached up for her flute and took it down. She didn't have the strength to try Land again, couldn't chance calling the office and getting Helene. That would snap her in two. It was just as well that he didn't know until it was all over. What could he do? Come to the memorial service out of the blue and introduce himself to everyone? "Hi, I'm Land, the new at-large city councillor and your daughter's illicit lover"?

On Saturday, Jeanna played Debussy's "Prelude to the Afternoon of a Fawn" to begin the memorial service, her grandmother's one and only request. She closed her eyes and played to the spirit of her grandmother, improvising around her memories of her, and then the song was playing her—simple, sublime and joyous. When she finished and returned to her seat, she sat in the silence, feeling a kind of cleansing peace she'd never experienced before.

For two hours, dozens of people of all ages and backgrounds spoke, weaving the web of her grandmother's life in all its rich hues. They told similar stories of her positive and tenacious spirit, and how she was one of the few people in their lives that they could really talk to. Several noted that she had probably never been written up in the news, nor quoted as a speaker or touted as a leader, but she'd always given what every movement group needed, the wisdom and glue that made all the difference. Most spoke of what a good friend she was and what she had taught them about friendship.

As Jeanna drove home from her mother's, she began to wonder: Where were all her friends? While at twenty-one she couldn't expect to have as many as her grandmother had at eighty-four, the fact that she couldn't name one frightened her. Even Jackie didn't count, since Jeanna had to withhold so much that mattered from her.

Now that was sad. She was clearly doing something very, very wrong.

CHAPTER FORTY-FOUR

Sometimes You Can Give Too Much

On Sunday, the day after the memorial service, Jeanna had forced herself to catch up on student journals and papers, and her class prep for the week ahead. She was feeling restless and couldn't do another dutiful thing if it bit her. All day she had been wanting to get back to her flute, to see if she could recapture that cleansing, peaceful feeling. She got it out and polished it until it shone, and then she put the mouthpiece to the curve of her chin and played—and nothing entered her mind for hours, nothing but the music. She played on and on into the silence.

Land came to her bed that night after she had fallen into a deep sleep. She felt his body slip in behind hers and the warm pleasure of his arms wrapping around her, and she half awoke, but in a moment he fell into a deep sleep himself. She drifted away, dreaming that she was playing her flute by a stream and Lillian had come to sit in the lush grass nearby and listen. Land was looking at them from a distant hilltop but was too far away to hear her play.

Early in the morning she joined Land at the table where he was sipping coffee and eyeing his appointment calendar. She wanted to talk with him about her music—how the old feeling had come over her last evening, how she wanted to make it a much bigger part of her life somehow. This wasn't a good time to talk with him, but when was? She was always deferring things she wanted to talk with him about until later, but later never seemed to come.

He was already tuning into his first commitment. She could tell that he was boring into the heart of whatever he was going to say or do.

"Zoning in on your first gig?" she asked.

"You know me too well." He reached up and touched her hair, letting the drops shower over the table. He eyed his appointment booklet again. Her cue that he needed to think something through.

"I had a feeling last night, a really good feeling."

"So did I." His hand tightened on her thigh. He assumed she meant their closeness.

"That too," Jeanna said. "But I'm talking about another kind of feeling. I used to get it all the time, but I've been so busy with teaching, the Group . . ."

He shifted in annoyance, not looking up. She had never interrupted his concentration before. She stopped, trying to hold down her anger at his inattention. She moved abruptly to get up.

"What kind of feeling?" His focus broken, he looked her in the face.

She settled back in her chair. "Music, my flute. I've wanted to get back into it in a bigger way. I played last night and I got that same old amazing feeling I used to get."

"Hmm," he said. "It sounds nice, but do you have the time? Realistically, I mean."

She swallowed, a metallic taste in her mouth. He was right, of course.

He pulled her to him, gave her a kiss, and got up to go. "What do you think, babe?"

"You're right. As it is, I barely have time to eat."

She felt empty. All of the intense feelings she'd wanted to share with him were gone, evaporated into thin air.

He grabbed his jacket on the way out. "I'll call you."

"Okay," she said to the closed door.

~

The next day at work, Jeanna was demoralized and restless, feeling Land's discouragement about her music like an underwater hum. When she slipped into a daydream over lunch at her desk, his actual words came back to her—*"But do you really have the time?"*

She knew in her head he was absolutely right but felt in her gut he was dead wrong. Then like a fool, she had barged into Matt's office, trying to get his permission to bring more music into her role at the school, but he said she had too much to do as it was, and that Shanna had the music piece pretty well covered. She knew she had hit him out of the blue, but her anger at his puzzled, negative response, along with Land's, was turning to acid inside her.

~

The next day, Lonnie came into her office.

"Hey, Miss J."

"What's up, Lonnie?"

"I just wanted to update ya on some student council things. We got a big fundraiser talent show type thing planned for Tuesday night, December 1st, to make money for school supplies, clothes, food, eye glasses, and stuff, an' we want to know if you got any talents?"

"Me?"

"Yeah, you and all the teachers. Matt gonna juggle. Roy gonna contortion, he say. Jakim gonna do his black belt bit. Shanna a solo dance. Sandra gonna imitate some ol' historical woman. So how 'bout you?"

She thought about playing her flute, but Matt and Land had really doused her fire. She'd have to see if she could fan the flame again.

"What you say, Miss J? The guys takin' bets you don't got no talents, but I said sure you do, everbody's got a talent." He jumped forward and stood on his hands right there in the cramped space of her office. "See?" he said, still hanging there upside down.

Jeanna turned doubly resentful that all "the guys" assumed she was a blank slate in the talent department. Screw them. If that's what they thought, that's exactly what she'd be.

"I'd rather not, I guess."

Lonnie's feet were wavering. "Oh, shit, now I'm-a gonna have to pay up. 'Scuze me, Miss J. Okay, thanks anyway." He flipped back up onto his feet and was gone.

She was furious. Taking bets. What a joke.

Lonnie reappeared. "I forgot one more thing about the council."

She looked at him.

"We startin' to provide protection for people."

"Protection?"

"Yeah. Everbody need protection sometime or other, even you, Miss J . . . especially you, matter fact."

"Especially me?" She didn't have any talent; now she needed protection. What was she, three years old?

"Yeah. I knows you works late sometime, and be making your rounds here an' there. Fact is, I asked Mr. Guff to keep an eye out when you be floating 'round here after dark."

"Really." That explained her glimpses of the elderly gentleman's black truck these past few months.

"I mean, most folks don't mean you no harm. Matter a fact, they keep an eye out for you white teachers. But there's always those few gotta have their fix, knock someone off."

"I suppose you're right. I guess I always hope those few will be having their dinner or otherwise occupied when I'm out and about."

"Yeah." He smiled. "That's what we all hope, but hopin' don't always make it so. No one want you hurt, Miss J."

Jeanna was touched by his tone. "I appreciate it," she said, "though I'm not sure how an old guy in his seventies will help me against a gang of young toughs."

"Are you kiddin'? Guff? Ain't nobody want to mess with ol' Guff."

On the second Wednesday in November, Jeanna got up from her desk in her classroom office, frustrated that she'd only gotten halfway through her student papers. It was time to go meet Clayton James at the Panthers to talk about how his mentoring was going.

Her legs felt sluggish from sitting most of the day as she walked outside, feeling the cool breezes. The sun was setting, sending streaks of rose across the smoky sky. A few blocks into her walk, a gust of wind came up, throwing grit into her eyes and blinding her. She stopped and bent over in pain, the grit feeling like little pieces of glass. She kept blinking until the tears washed some of it away, still leaving her eyes quite sore.

A truck pulled up and stopped next to her. She looked up in alarm.

"You okay?" a voice asked from the darkness of the cab.

It was Mr. Guff, her security man on patrol.

"I'm fine, just got a street full of grit in my eyes," she said, smiling.

He lifted an old army canteen out the window. "You want some water, wash it out?"

"No thanks. It's better now." She cocked her head. "Lonnie tells me you've been keeping an eye on me, making sure I don't get into any trouble."

"Makin' sure trouble don't find you," he said. "That boy oughta keep his mouth shut."

"It's okay. I appreciate it. And I want to thank you for helping Cat—Cal, I mean."

"Lonnie boy's been runnin his mouth some more, I see."

"Afraid so. I've been sick about Cal, though. Not that I've known the details until recently. When I found out how you handled it, going up to the prison to meet with his father and everything, I felt this huge weight come off me."

"Nothin' to it. You can't do it all, you know."

"I know," she said. "I'm the least of it."

"I wouldn't go that far. You're a giver, that's not hard to see, not a taker like so many out there."

She didn't say anything, but savored the compliment.

"Sometime you can give too much." He looked straight at her.

Shit, here we go again. Damned if she did, damned if she didn't. "I guess I can't do anything right," she said.

"Now don't go getting all itsy-bitsy victim on me," he said, chuckling.

That made her furious. "See?" she said with greater vehemence than she'd intended.

He laughed. "Take it easy, now. All I'm sayin' is, a young girl like yourself can give, give, give, till you give it all away 'fore you even get started."

That last part sounded sexual. He had a nerve. But Land immediately came to mind—how much she gave and gave and how easily he took without a second thought. And her students, too, not to mention the Group. Maybe he was right, people did take her for granted. But what the hell was she supposed to do? If she gave up the giving part, what would be left?

She was afraid she was going to cry, but managed to get out a "Yeah, maybe."

"Yeah, maybe," he mimicked her. He was infuriating. And worse, right on target.

She bit her lip to keep it still. Why was he attacking what he'd complimented seconds ago?

"Sometimes you gotta stand up for yourself."

She wanted in the worst way to ask him: Stand up when, where, how, why? But he'd come way too close for comfort to say anything at all. *Fuck this. Who the hell is he, anyway?*

"I've gotta go," she said. "I'm late for an appointment."

"Where you headed?"

"Twelfth Baptist. The Panthers."

"Want a lift?"

"No thanks. I need the exercise," she said, feeling her voice quaver and hating it.

~

That night, Land had come over around nine. Jeanna was stewing under the covers, her mind a crazy quilt of doubts and questions. She had a ton of things she'd been wanting to talk over with him, but been too afraid to bring them up. She didn't want to be seen as a problem, but was tired of being taken for granted.

He stirred out of his drowsiness. They'd just made love—his way, of course. That was another thing that was driving her nuts; his unwillingness to try to satisfy her even after one night she'd finally gotten up the nerve to show him what she needed. When he'd dismissed it as "kid's stuff," she'd been too mortified to pursue it.

"Hey," he said, "how're your kids?"

"They're kids." She wanted desperately for him to ask how she was doing.

"What's the matter? You and your students on the outs?"

"No, I just . . ."

"What?"

"Could you ask about me, how *I'm* doing?" She hated having to say that.

"I thought I was, in a way." He wrinkled his brow.

"Yeah, I know, I'm the one always bringing them up, but sometimes I can't tell how you feel, about me."

"Really?" She saw those shadows in his eyes that came out of nowhere whenever anything personal came up. "I do care about you, Jeanna, a great deal. Don't you know that?" He reached over and held her tight around her waist.

How nice. She cared about her kids too, but she wasn't sleeping with them.

"I just . . ."

"What?"

"We don't talk about us, ever." She paused.

"What should we talk about? We're together. We're close. We're on the same wavelength, which is rare. I trust you. We fit. It's about as good as it gets, if you ask me."

"And we don't go anywhere, or do anything together," she said.

"I don't think I misled you. I said we'd have to be discreet." He rubbed his forehead.

"Yeah, but . . ."

"What?"

"I didn't realize that being discreet meant never going anywhere together, and you acting like we have no connection at all when we're in public." She hated being so hidden away, like something he was ashamed of. "I don't know," she said, "you were a lot friendlier and more open with me in the Group before we got involved."

Land was subdued. "You're right. Since we've gotten involved, I can't let my feelings show in public. I'm sorry. But you've got to know how much I care for you."

Would it kill him to use the word 'love'? Jeanna thought. He certainly seemed happy enough soaking up hers. If anything, she knew, he felt put-upon to even have to be having this conversation. But since she'd started, she'd better keep going. She might never get up the nerve again.

"Even in the Group, I feel illegitimate, like what are you doing here, and it's been over a year."

"But you're central, babe, don't you know that? A real anchor."

"Maybe. But I feel like you don't think that much of me—if you did, you'd show it, at least a little bit, in public." Her voice sounded thin and childish, even to her own ears. No wonder he didn't respect her.

"What? I think the world of you, you know that."

That might be true, but the world certainly didn't know it. She thought about Lillian and Carl. The world certainly knew that they thought the world of each other. What did she expect?

Maybe she was like the woman who had captured her father away from her mother, only a much younger version. She'd always felt so innocent in comparison, but who was she kidding? She didn't have a leg to stand on; she was having an affair with a married man. And here she was, putting Land through the wringer.

"Listen," Land was saying, "How 'bout we go hear some jazz together, over in Wallisville? They have a hell of a club. Truth and I were there awhile ago. I think Dexter Gordon is coming up. We'll go for your birthday—very belated, I know. Let's go Saturday night."

So he hadn't forgotten. Her spirits made a comeback. Them finally going to hear jazz together was a dream come true. Maybe speaking up had been worth it after all.

"Great," she said with a big smile.

"And from now on I'll ask how you're doing first, rather than those sloppy old kids of yours."

He tickled her ribs, and she felt patronized. But he was trying. It was a step.

She forced a laugh. "It's a deal."

Over the next few days, the Group held emergency meetings at Land and Ma's request. Progress on fulfilling their summer's All-City Congress goals had stalled, and Land was not about to take that lying down. They couldn't afford for the Group's, and his, efforts to be construed as a failure—not after having been voted in by a landslide. An all-membership meeting of the Group had voted to demonstrate, to try to take over the Mayor's chambers at city hall and sit in until their demands were met. People were prepared to go to jail. They had chosen Thursday and Friday, November 19th and 20th. Jeanna and everyone else had been busy every free hour of the day, calling all the progressive groups and organizations to sign on to the protest.

Saturday morning of their planned jazz outing, Jeanna was awakened early by a phone call from Land.

"I'm sorry, babe, but I got a call from Pearl last night. It's unusual she's back so soon, but she's coming in late tonight."

"Oh, no. I never know what to say." She felt that wave of acid fill her stomach and eat away. "It's good for her, I guess it means she's doing better. I'll miss you." She felt very tired. Very stranded.

"Me too, babe. I'll call you when she's gone. I know it's not easy—for either of us."

"Yeah, it's rough on everybody." She felt the futility of their situation, their relationship. She felt strangely old, worn out.

"Talk to you soon, babe," Land whispered, and hung up.

Jeanna groaned aloud. It was still dark outside. The leaves dancing on the wall looked ominous, and the moonlight was too much to bear. What brought Pearl back over and over again—and why so soon? What did Pearl hope for with Land after all this time? For that matter, what did she, herself, hope for? What could she?

CHAPTER FORTY-FIVE

Last Demonstration

JEANNA AWOKE WITH A FEELING OF FEARFUL ANTICIPAtion verging on dread that she kept trying to fight off. This was the morning of the demonstration. Matt had arranged for subs to take his and Jeanna's classes.

She got ready. Loose pants, sneakers, her old U sweatshirt, a winter vest, and a denim jacket. A backpack to keep her hands free. She slipped contact info for her mother into her back pocket in case all hell broke loose. She broke out in a cold sweat and goose bumps covered her entire body as she tied her laces in a double knot.

She grabbed the signs that she, Karima, Tommie Lee, and Jackie had worked on the night before, her wrist aching with their weight. They'd each taken a bunch home, in case the office got raided or firebombed. They had been receiving phone threats all week. It had all been a hazy, crazy blur.

They expected a big turnout, but you never knew. She and Karima would be carrying the banner up front. It was kind of an honor. In the last meeting Jeanna had suggested Karima, and Karima had surprised her by suggesting her. Ma had warned them that the cops were "hot as grease on a griddle" and told the young people to stand up and be strong, but not to provoke trouble, and not to get into any fights with police or bystanders. If anyone fell when the march was in full swing, to make sure those behind picked them up. No one should be trampled. No one should be left behind.

Jeanna felt the dampness of her palms on the steering wheel. How they would get into the mayor's inner sanctum, she had no idea. Cam was on logistics. She struggled to carry her pile of signs into the church basement, surprised and glad at how sunny it was. Only six or seven people were there. Where the hell was everyone? Jeanna was bitterly disappointed—and embarrassed. One of her chief contributions had always been getting people to come out.

Tommie Lee came out of the men's room, looking as together as ever. She went over to him.

"Where the heck is everyone?" she asked sharply.

He shrugged. "Guess they're still on their way."

"Your mom?" Jeanna wondered why she was being so curt.

"She's getting the kids off to Carl's sister's. Nana's sick. She told me to go ahead." Tommie Lee was looking at her, his tone even, but she knew he could sense something was off. "I need to find the med armbands. Catch you later, Jeanna."

She looked out the wide doorway and now saw small groups of people walking across the grass, sober, no joking around. No one she really knew. She wished Lillian were here, or Jackie, who'd had to go to her grandfather's funeral in Pittsburgh.

The tension was wearing on her. She escaped into the restroom. Her heart was pounding—not from the demonstration so much, but from inside, like her system was giving her odd warning signals. She'd been a wreck for weeks, trying to make sense of her situation with Land, her life. She ran some water over a paper towel and pressed it to her forehead. She sat on the toilet and pressed her hand to her heart, trying to squeeze it shut, quiet it down, but it only began to hurt more instead. She had to get with it.

By the time she forced herself out of the restroom, the basement was filling up. Ma and Mary Ranier were putting out donuts. She went over to help. Ma looked at her over her glasses, lips pursed tight, but

Jeanna ignored her. She was tired of doing everyone else's jobs as well as her own.

Karima came in, dark circles under her eyes, and walked by Jeanna, giving her an absent wave and a muttered "Hey" as she passed.

"Hey," Jeanna muttered back and imitated the girl's dismissive wave, angry that Karima couldn't give her a decent greeting. Karima looked at her sharply. Jeanna ignored her and began handing out signs to other young people as they came in. Karima followed suit, the tension sparking between them.

"What's the matter?" Karima said.

"Nothing," Jeanna said.

"Whatever you say." Karima shrugged.

Jeanna wished she could magically return to her normal self for Karima, Tommie Lee, Ma, whoever. She went to get the banner from Cam, who was holding it over his arm while he argued with Gideon. Both men ignored her as she eased the banner off Cam's arm.

"It's time!" Ma called out. "We'll convene out on the sidewalk in front of the church. Follow the banner."

"You still want to do this?" Karima asked.

"Of course," Jeanna said. She felt low and alone. She wanted to do nothing.

She took hold of the left end of the banner and Karima the right, and they went out the wide doorway. Ma was motioning to them impatiently. They began moving quickly down the sidewalk, out of step. Jeanna was looking straight ahead, but could feel Karima looking at her out of the corner of her eye.

A hand grasped Jeanna's left arm from behind, catching her by surprise. She yanked away sharply, furious to see it was Helene, once again unwilling to use her name. She stared at her zombie-like, still moving forward.

Helene stepped back with an incredulous look. "Slow it down," she said. "You're running ahead of the group."

"Fine," Jeanna snapped, and saw Karima smile at her.

"Yes, ma'am!" Karima saluted Helene smartly, but Helene had already turned her back.

They slowed their pace and fell into step. Karima looked at Jeanna and Jeanna looked back and winked. Now they were in sync.

She and Karima were the only two out front. She looked over her shoulder a few times. Land, Gideon, Ma, Lillian, Carl, Abe, Cam, Matt, and Reverend Barrows were in the second line, with Helene moving in and out as required by her coordinating role. There were only about sixty to seventy people. Jeanna was worried. They had expected to begin the march with closer to 200 people and pick up the rest along the way. Not a good sign. She glanced back again, acutely aware that not once had Land greeted her or given her any eye contact. True, Pearl was back, but did that mean they couldn't say a word to each other? Her head and body felt like cement.

Guff's truck was following at some distance behind the group. This had to be on his own initiative, since he certainly wasn't a member of the Group, but she was glad to see him there.

They collected protesters all along the route: dozens of tenants from the housing development the Group had saved from university expansion joined the march as they went. They slowed at Jefferson High, where Jackie's youth group, the City's Finest, gave a shout, chanted, and danced their way into the crowd. At the North Star Baptist Church, over a hundred members, with Valle front and center, moved in a fast rhythm to join the protestors, singing "Ain't Gonna Let Nobody Turn Me Around" loud and strong. Everyone joined in.

At the mosque, sixty or so joined the crowd, the men serious in their sunglasses, posting themselves as security at every row, while the women mingled in among the other bodies, eyes smiling behind their scarves and robes, greeting those around them with their familiar words of peace. At the U, more than a hundred students came out behind a Black Student Union banner, marching in time to a powerful drumbeat, all dressed in African liberation colors. A straggly left-wing white student group of twenty or so came out as well, followed by a small group of faculty.

They had entered downtown now, and the crowd of protestors had begun to take over most of the street, allowing only a narrow line of cars to crawl forward. Jeanna felt the fender of a car brush her left leg and jumped to the right, alarmed, causing Karima to stumble and look over at her.

"A car almost hit me," Jeanna called to her.

"Be careful!" Karima yelled back.

People were coming out of office buildings, shops, and businesses, lining the sidewalk and staring at them. A few gave them a thumbs-up, peace sign, or raised fist, but most just stared in disbelief. Jeanna looked behind her. They were more than 700 of them now, and the protest was still growing. Now people on the sidewalk began to spontaneously step in line, eyes shining.

Jeanna felt proud now to be in the front row, holding the banner with Karima, and humbled by the strength and spirit of the people behind her. She must have been more anxious about the march than she had realized earlier. But she could feel Land's silent presence behind her, too, and knew her off-keyness also had everything to do with him, with them, and the bind they were in. She was alarmed that she had so much less control over her emotions than she used to, and wondered if she were becoming Pearl—or worse, Helene. Yet giving in to some of her nasty feelings had an upside. Yanking her arm away from Helene's grasp had felt really good, as had Karima's smile when she did it. Maybe there was such a thing as being too nice. Isn't that what her students had been trying to tell her? And Guff, too.

Jeanna was only semi-conscious of these revelations as she walked along, her wrist and forearms now aching from the weight of the banner. She was surprised that they were being allowed to take over the entire street. They were now approaching the bridge to City Hall, about two blocks away from their destination. Where were the cops? Something was wrong. She was feeling uneasy at their absence, even though she knew they were the marchers' greatest danger. She looked at Karima and Karima looked at her as they marched toward the bridge in step.

Suddenly a terrifying sea of blue uniforms appeared, coming up and over the bridge toward them, fast. They were running in step in riot gear, ready for armed combat.

Now everything was happening in slow motion. The sea of cops was almost upon them. A whistle blew and they stopped as one, inches from Jeanna and Karima. Another whistle shrieked and the cops lifted their nightsticks above their heads and leaned forward. Jeanna felt the shadow of death fall over her. She felt someone slip in to her left and lock arms with her. *Carl. Thank God!*

Two more shrieks of the whistle, and arm-in-arm, she and Carl surged forward, sure they would be assaulted or killed. Instead, the cops rapidly faded back, like a vast blue fan folding up, lining the side of the bridge.

Amazed, Jeanna hung on to Carl with one arm, held the banner high with her other hand, and flew into the void, the mass of protesters surging behind them into free space, sailing over the bridge, feet barely touching ground.

"Malcolm lives! Malcolm lives! Malcolm lives!" the youth shouted. Jeanna's entire body shook with the pounding vibrations of the bridge.

She and Karima brought the banner down to make it easier to carry as they approached the entrance of City Hall. The front doors were all chained closed, guarded by two lines of police in full riot gear. Land drew up alongside Carl, still in full stride, and yelled in his ear, "Wait until the last second, then turn to your left, fast, and enter the side door. Cam will be waiting."

Jeanna gave Karima a nod, and she nodded back. Jeanna noticed that Gideon was now locked arm in arm with the younger girl, and wondered when that had happened.

They moved forward fast. When they were just a few yards away from the riot police guarding the front door, Carl and Jeanna turned sharply to the left, pulling Karima and Gideon with them. They picked up speed to stay ahead of the surprised cops. As they turned the corner, the door opened and Carl moved fast ahead, pulling Jeanna through the door with Karima behind so the banner could fit in, with everyone on their heels. Cam grabbed the banner from their hands, held it high, and leapt up the stairs. They followed him, taking two steps at a time, up one flight to the mayor's suite. The crowd streamed in and sailed up the stairs in waves.

As they approached the doors to the mayor's enormous suite, two security guards grabbed Cam and wrestled him to the floor. Carl released his iron grip on Jeanna's arm as he and Gideon barreled forward toward the guards. Seeing the two huge men hurtling toward them, the guards released Cam and stepped aside. Carl and Gideon grabbed Cam under the arms, lifted him off the floor, and got him back into the crowd. Karima had already squeezed through a door into the mayor's lobby area. She opened all the doors into his conference room, and more people surged through. Jeanna moved past her and opened the next doors, and the next, into the still quite large inner sanctum. There she moved to the far wall under the window and staked out a spot with her knapsack and jacket.

Karima joined her. "You okay?"

Jeanna nodded vigorously. "You?"

"Yeah, I'm alive," Karima said. "We're alive."

They hugged tightly, and Karima took off toward the next room, saying, "I'm gonna try to find my guys."

Within seconds all the rooms were packed with protestors. They had taken over the second floor, the power floor of City Hall. The mayor and his staff were nowhere to be seen. The guards had fled. Jeanna saw Ma walk unsteadily to a low chair and sit down, not looking at all well. Lillian came through the door, gingerly picked her way over to Ma, knelt at her feet, and asked her something. Ma nodded and pushed her purse at her with trembling hands, working her lips in and out a mile a minute. Lillian took the purse and pulled out pills and a bottle of orange juice. She gave Ma the pills and held the bottle to Ma's lips, then sat there, her arm around the elderly woman's shoulders. A late-middle-aged woman came up to Ma and bent over her. Lillian got up to give the woman her seat, and looked around for a place to settle. Jeanna waved to her and pointed to the free space next to her. Lillian made her way over and sat down.

"Thank God," Lillian said as she leaned back against the wall and stretched her feet out, kicking off her shoes.

"That's exactly what I thought when Carl came up alongside me," Jeanna said.

"I sent him up there," Lillian said, "him and Gideon both. Tommie Lee was worried you and Karima were going to get the worst of it if the cops attacked. I'm glad you're still in one piece. How did it go? I was in the back, Ma had fallen back and I was trying to stay close by her."

"How is she? Is she sick?"

"She's a diabetic. She needed her meds and juice. She's okay now. Exhausted, though. That's her eldest daughter who's looking after her. She has to go to work, though, so we'll have to keep an eye out for Ma when she goes. What happened up there on the front line?"

"It was touch and go at the bridge," Jeanna said. "I started thinking, *This is it, it's all over*, when the riot cops raised their night sticks like they were going to slam them down on our heads. Then a whistle blew, the cops gave way, and we plunged straight into all this open space. I felt like I was flying free."

"You must've been scared to death!"

"I was terrified. But when Carl came along I lost my fear."

"Yeah, Carl can do that. Does it for me every day."

Jeanna wondered what that was like. If anything, Land added to her fear. She suddenly realized that she lived in a state of chronic anxiety about Land.

Lillian's eyes closed. That was good. She wanted Lillian there, beside her, just resting. She questioned herself now all the time—what was wrong with her, how could she become more than she was for Land, for his love. But she'd come to the same conclusion over and over—that she was who she was, and she wasn't enough for him. Not for him to actually care. Maybe that's what Pearl wanted too, for him to actually care for her, love her as she was. Be there for her. Maybe that's what drove her crazy. Maybe that's why Helene was so damn hard.

She looked up. Matt caught her eye and smiled. He was crouching next to Ma, making sure she was all right. Jeanna smiled back. Now there was a man and a half. He wasn't at all handsome like Land was, and no one would paint him as a great grassroots leader, though he was committed as hell. But you knew he truly cared about you. Carl, too, had real integrity. He was rock solid in the Group and rock solid for Lillian. She'd thought Land had real integrity too. And he did—just not in his personal life, not with women. Then, again, who was she to speak?

There was a lull in the room, a low murmuring as people settled down to rest. Lillian had already gone fast asleep, her back supported by the wall and her head slumped to the side.

Her adrenaline spent, drained of all emotion, Jeanna dozed off as well.

She must have awakened to Land's voice. He was standing at the doorway to the mayor's office. She jostled Lillian's arm and looked back up at Land. She saw him looking at her and Lillian with that bittersweet look on his face that she knew so well.

"I want to thank everyone for your courage and persistence in getting here in the face of some pretty ugly odds. It looks like we're in for a siege, at least overnight, because the mayor chose to go out of town when he heard we were coming. We are the source of power and change in this city. Without our taking action, no change will occur. You should know we're already on the national news—in fact, the world knows we're here. We just received a telegram from the ANC in South Africa supporting this action."

A huge roar arose from all present.

"Remember, no matter what spin they put on it, what we are doing is right, honorable, and positive. Thank you for being here and putting your body and spirit on the line." He glanced again toward where Lillian and Jeanna were sitting, raised his hand, and left to the roar of everyone present. All of Jeanna's original feelings of love and admiration welled up again, driving her doubts underground.

She had to get to a restroom. She told Lillian she'd be right back and threaded her way through the bodies to the adjoining conference room. She walked by Karima, who was with an all-black youth group sprawled out on the floor. They made eye contact. Jeanna let her hand open as she walked by and Karima smoothly palmed it.

"Who's that?" Jeanna heard a teen say, a sneer in his voice.

"That's my teacher at West Side."

"A white chick teacher here?"

"Yeah, she's cool."

"No way," he said.

Jeanna smiled to herself.

On her way back from the restroom, Jeanna noticed quite a few "white chicks" scattered among the various youth clusters, and among the adults as well, many more than white men of any age.

She passed Matt standing in the hall, laughing at something Lonnie had just said, and Wesley and Abby were laughing too, shoving Lonnie up against the wall. He must have insulted them in his own inimitable way. Ever since Lonnie had fixed on becoming an electrician, Jeanna had encouraged him to join Carl and Gideon's committee to help work to break open the construction trade unions to black men. He had brought his uncle and a few of his uncle's friends who worked under the table into the Group as well.

Jeanna walked over and gave Matt a big hug, and Lonnie, Wes, Valle, and Abby too. Everyone was emotional, holding on tight before letting go.

When she got back, Lillian was awake.

"How you doing?" Jeanna asked her.

"You know, I'm going up and down from one minute to the next.

Proud of what we're doing, wondering if its crazy or futile, worrying about my kids. It'll be my first night away from them ever . . . and yet this is where I want to be, right here." She patted the floor an inch from Jeanna's leg.

"Me too," Jeanna said, wanting to say how glad she was that Lillian was sitting next to her. "But I just have me to worry about."

"That's hard, too, in its own way."

Yeah, Jeanna thought, realizing how alone she felt most of the time.

"Where's Carl?"

"He had to go to work or lose his job, but he'll be back in the morning if he can get in. He's on the three to midnight shift now. Land got him on the U construction site last week, overseeing the night crew. He's also going to be taking Abe's place leading the black construction workers union. Abe finally admitted he never wanted that kind of responsibility. It's a big step up, money-wise, so he's feeling better, but doesn't dare screw it up."

"Of course not," Jeanna said, "Carl will be great in that leadership role." Even as she said it, she wondered how Land could do all that yet remain so paralyzed in his personal life.

"You okay?" Lillian asked her, a look in her eye that invited a real response.

She wanted to say, "No, I'm not." She wanted to tell Lillian everything, ask her what to do about Land, ask her to love and respect her even if she was an utter fool and had screwed things up beyond belief. "I guess I just have a few things on my mind."

Lillian started to say, "What things . . ." but Tommie Lee, Cam, and Gideon came in just then, loaded down with food and blankets, and she and Jeanna jumped up to help distribute the food. They attended to Ma, giving her some more juice, then settled back in their spot. Jeanna took a blue and black handkerchief out of her backpack and laid it out like a small tablecloth.

"Look at you," Lillian said, "thinking of everything."

"It was supposed to be for tear gas," Jeanna said, "but this is better."

"Much better." Lillian smiled.

They set their sandwiches and chips out on the blue square and shared the meal in a peaceful silence, the chaos of voices around them receding to a low hum. Now Jeanna was afraid if she really tried to talk with Lillian, someone nearby might hear. She'd be the fool of the century if a rumor about Land and her spread like wildfire through this crowd.

When they were done eating, she helped with clean-up and handing out blankets, then got settled in for the night, bundling up in her sweatshirt and using her knapsack as a pillow, while Lillian pulled her thin sweater around her and lay her head on her soft purse. A thunderstorm raged outside, and the room had gotten chilly despite all the bodies. Jeanna pulled a blanket up around them, and at some point during the night, Lillian rested her head on Jeanna's upper arm. Jeanna slept easier after that.

In the morning she woke up stiff and cold. She saw Lillian helping Ma to the bathroom. Ma was walking with great difficulty. *The march yesterday must have done her in*, she thought. Everyone waiting for the restroom was encouraging the elders and children to go to the head of the line.

When Lillian settled Ma back in her seat, Jeanna got a bottle of juice out of her knapsack, unscrewed the top and gave it to Ma. Ma took a drink, then enclosed Jeanna's hand with both of hers and closed her eyes. It felt like a blessing.

It wasn't until the next morning that the mayor finally agreed to meet with "a small representative group"—but the protesters weren't buying it. They were down to only about sixty people now, and they could almost all jam into the larger of the two conference rooms. So they did.

The mayor agreed to most of their demands, but everyone knew the real fight would be to get him to act, so they gave him timelines and step-by-step progress demands. He became agitated by this process and lost his cool with Land, Ma, and especially Gideon a couple of times. When Tommie Lee and Abby stepped in to mediate, the Mayor was incensed at their presumption, but calmed down after seeing how respectful they were of him, and how effective they were at facilitating.

After a head-to-head debate with Land on the plank to create jobs by using local black labor to build vastly more low-income co-op housing, the mayor suggested that perhaps Land would like to take on his job as mayor since he thought he knew so much. The room literally roared and shook at that. Didn't this bumbling idiot know that Land was seriously considering a run for mayor at the next election? Did he think he would stop at City Council?

Finally, the mayor agreed to most of the demands and the implementation schedule, and left, supposedly for another meeting across town.

Land thanked everyone and they broke up to go home. He left with Gideon, Cam, and Helene, promising reporters that they would answer all their questions back at the storefront. Reverend Barrows was giving Ma and some other elders a ride home. Karima and Tommie Lee had gone with their friends. Matt was dropping Abby off on his way home. Lillian had left the night before to take care of her boys.

Jeanna wandered out the door alone, feeling let down. They'd won, and she was glad . . . but where was the group feeling? Then she was suddenly relieved there would be no more people to deal with and no more for her to do. She was ravenous, and exhausted. She wanted to go home and hit the sack.

She didn't know the way back to the church by bus, so she decided to walk. Kind of relive the experience in reverse. She bought an Italian hoagie on the way and wolfed it down as she walked, not caring about the onion smell, or the little bits of lettuce and tomato that fell to the ground. She'd never tasted anything so good in her life.

She had no particular feelings as she walked along until she got to the bridge. As she stepped on to it her stomach roiled, remembering her fear, and then how her spirit had lifted as Carl locked his huge arm with hers and they took the bridge by storm.

Soon she was at the church, her legs rubbery. A few people she didn't know were getting into their cars. She waved and they waved back as she got into her car and drove away. She took a back way home, avoiding traffic, through the West Side Park neighborhood where she and Lillian had gone door to door. An old truck was stopped up ahead, pulled over by the park entrance near some trees and bushes. It looked familiar. It was Guff's.

She turned in and pulled up behind it. She saw Guff's arm hanging out the window, clutching a rifle pointed toward some men. Cops. Her heart stopped. She rolled her window down and put her head out to get a better look. The cops were holding a teenager down. They had him on the ground on his stomach; one cop had a foot on his neck, the other had a gun jammed into his buttock.

"You pull that trigger, you dead," Guff growled.

The cop looked up at Guff and the rifle and slowly removed his own gun, straightened up, and let the gun hang down at his side.

Guff moved his head at the other cop, who eased his foot off the boy's neck. They stood looking uneasily at Guff, and at Jeanna as well.

"We was just playing with the kid," the one with the gun said.

"I know. You drive off now and we'll keep it a game," Guff said.

"No need to get flustered, old man," the other said.

Guff just looked at them. They backed off toward their car, not taking their eyes off Guff's rifle, and drove off.

"Get in, son," Guff said. "I'll take you home."

The boy didn't move.

Jeanna started to get out of her car. Guff put up his hand. "Stay in your car, Miss J." Somehow he'd already figured out who she was.

She settled back into her seat, her exhausted body re-flooded with adrenaline, her skin tingling with static.

Guff got out of his truck, bent down, and said something to the boy. The boy rolled over partway. Jeanna could see that he'd been crying. His face was streaked with tears and mud. He wiped his face with his shirtsleeve and Jeanna saw that it was the boy who'd been talking to Karima about her—the one who'd made the "white chick teacher" comment. The whole front of his pants was wet.

Guff gathered him up and helped him to his feet. He guided him to the truck with an arm around his shoulders. ". . . no dishonor in that," she heard him saying, "in the war, the men on the front lines always messed themselves. It natural, just the way it is." Guff got him up into the passenger's seat, then walked over to Jeanna's car.

"You been sitting in all this time at the mayor's office?"

"Yeah, it's over. We got almost everything we wanted. Can I do anything?" She gestured towards the young man. "He was there too."

"No, you done enough, child. You go home now and get some rest."

He walked back to his truck, got in and pulled out onto the road again. He put his arm out of the window and motioned for her to go around him. She drove past and he followed her. After a turn or two, she realized he was escorting her home and felt a deep sense of relief and peace. As she turned into her cul-de-sac, he lifted a hand and drove on.

The next morning, Sunday, Jeanna woke up with the image of Guff holding a rifle on the cops, and again his words to her: "You done enough, child. You go home now and get some rest." Maybe enough was enough.

She drove out to the lake, as she had been doing now that Pearl had returned again. There was no one to be with, and she had so much to mull over. She walked, slow and deliberate, casting her questions out over the water and watching them ripple endlessly. The late-afternoon sun gilded the tree trunks, limbs, and leaves in gold. If only she and Land could walk around the lake together, arm-in-arm, she'd be happy.

What a treadmill they were on. Why didn't he step off? Couldn't he say, "Enough, I want to live again"? Get a divorce, or at least agree with Pearl to freely go their separate ways? But if that happened, he'd have to come to terms with her. It was one thing to have her as his resting place in the night; another entirely for her to get up, take a stand and say: I love you, I want you, let's be together in the light of day. Especially now that he was a city councilor; it would be impossible. She sat down heavily on the nearest rock, feeling numb. It was time to make a decision.

After a while, she pulled out her flute and played the blues that kept coming to her, a call to the universe, a prayer for answers, her "Blues Prayer." She sat in the silence as the rock grew cold and dusk descended, letting her dilemmas go round and round in their eternal whirlpool until she felt that still point of clarity. Not of mind, but of soul.

She knew, finally, that she had to leave Land, and since he was involved in everything that mattered to her, all that as well. She couldn't imagine how she would get through the next month. If only she could talk with Lillian before she left. But that was impossible.

CHAPTER FORTY-SIX

Guff and the Race Man

THE NEXT DAY, JEANNA STAYED AFTER SCHOOL TO TRY to work through the pile of student papers that had been mounting up on her desk. It was unseasonably warm; she raised the window in her office that overlooked the parking lot to get some air. She heard voices below. She looked out at Lonnie and Guff sitting and chatting on the back of Guff's truck. Lonnie was smoking a cigarette and Guff was lighting his pipe. She drank in the aroma of the pipe smoke, feeling a little peace from that, as always. She thought about all the things Guff had done to help her students, like Jam and Cal, and how Guff had protected that boy from the cops after the demo.

Lonnie asked Guff a question that she couldn't quite catch.

"I tell ya son, I don know why you have so many white women in what they calls today the civil rights fight."

Jeanna's skin prickled.

"Now over to the group they got goin', Land an' all, most-a them young girl helpers is white. Now how'd that happen? Sex, I guess. See, when I was comin' up, that was a time when the black man—I don' care how respected and revered, how sucked up with black pride and latched onto them marchin' man's blues he was—he had to have his sweet white gal."

Jeanna felt the blood rush into her face.

"The younger the better, cuz with that nice soft white clay you can do what you want and they thank you for it, downright get to beggin' for it. Not like your black women. They got no time at all for your black dick posturing and activatin'. If'n her man couldn't put a good wad of money in her hand every Friday night, and another, slicker one where it belong every Saturday night, she kiss his black ass good-bye."

"Uhm," Lonnie grunted, "I hear that."

"Now a race man—a 'movement man,' they call 'em now—they don't provide that kind of regularity. Never did. They workin' they tails off for black rights and things ever' day an messin' with white as right ass ever' night."

"Why not hang with a sister?" Lonnie asked.

"They just couldn't see the black woman. She like to be invisible. Can't explain it, 'cept to say they was bline' in one eye and couldn't see outta the other when it come to your black woman. She the rock, the heart, the toughest, lovinest thing God put on this here earth, an' he can't see it. No, the race man hangin' out the freedom sign for us blacks by day, got a whites-only sign by night on the other side, no signature. He ain't wantin' people to know he doin' it, what with his big black reputation an' all, havin to be JC updated, but he do it all the same."

"But not alla them," Lonnie said.

"I don't know a one of 'em ain't gone that road," Guff said. "Not even ol' Fred Douglass hisself. My gramma's folks come up from Rochester, New York way, useta tell me stories about him. Had a runnin' affair with an uptight Dutch, German, something-or-other woman for most his life once he escaped slavery. Slavery, mind you, a *black* woman pulled him out of, saved his goddamn skin, bore his five children, kept his house, then suffered this here white woman on an' on. Why, she even moved in next to his bedroom for awhile."

"No sir!"

"Oh yeah, I ain't lyin'. I can't quite picture it neither, but there they was, flittin' back an' forth like big ol' black an white butterflies under big Mama's nose, who probably like to kill the two of 'em. Yeah, this white gal worshipped his every word, rode on his hip, made a life outta bein' his assistant to the struggle."

Jeanna swallowed hard. Frederick Douglass was among her greatest heroes.

"Who was she again?" Lonnie asked.

"Well now, she a journalist, you see. Backin' up a little bit, that's how he an' she met up. She come all the way across the ocean, all the way to Rochester, New York, walk up the great big hill to his house, knock, and say she here to interview him. You have to understand, back then this was most unusual. Here he a 'scaped slave, an she a white woman able to spread the good word with her pen about ending slavery all over the worl'. Wasn't ever' day a just ex-slave had this to happen. You can see the attraction."

"Oh yeah."

"An' she did that, she did. She spread the word for ten, twenty, thirty year, working hand in glove with Douglass. Ol' Fred, he try to get his wife to learn to read an' write, an' talk about what be goin' on, but she din' have no interest. You ask me, she probably din' have time, keepin' up with the brood, the house an' all. It wasn't easy back then. Ain't now, either."

"You right, leastways to hear Ma tell it," Lonnie said, laughing.

"But you see, this German woman he could talk to. They talked politics, anti-slavery, world affairs—she a anti-capitalist way ahead of her time. Europe always been a step ahead a us. But I think Fred mainly like her for her mine', an' for what she could do for him with her connections and what not. Saved his ass from the slave catchers more'n once, and that's a fact."

"Well that's something, ain't it?" Jeanna heard Lonnie draw sharply on his cigarette and exhale long and slow.

"It is. Anyways, after his real wife dies, he ditches this long-sufferin' white gal who had gone an' got some bad kinda cancer, an' he goes an gets hisself a pretty little rich white girl an kicks this other one to the curb. She kill herself."

"No shit."

"No shit. I'm not lyin. No, Fred Douglass was sumpin' else. When he finally come outta the closet, it's as a granddaddy. He married this white girl his first-born daughter's age. Now you tell me the sense of that, with the likes of Sojourner Truth and who knows who else runnin' round unclaimed. No, the race man a fool where women are concerned."

"But why?" Lonnie asked.

"Well now, the race man, he don' wanna feel. He do all his feelin' about the cause. Then he want sweet honey on soft new white bread, untoasted. That bread can't stand. Most race men have next to no feelings for that white girl. When she cryin', like as not he don' even know, because he don' feel what she feel. He maybe could, but he don't. He gots too many things occupyin' his mine."

"Guff, how come you act like you know so much about the race man?"

"I know cuz I was a race man."

"Oh."

Oh, indeed.

Driving home, Jeanna felt unveiled by Guff's "race man" story. She hadn't known her situation with Land was so common, and even ran through history. How could she have been so blind?

CHAPTER FORTY-SEVEN

You Been Hidin' Your Light

JEANNA HAD TO STRUGGLE OUT OF BED AND FORCE herself to dress and go to work the next day, Tuesday, November 24th. She went through the motions all day, perplexing her students and disappointing herself. Somehow, she made it through the day's teaching.

At home, she pulled her flute out of its case and slowly pieced it together as she reflected on what Guff had said to her when she was walking to the Panthers church about standing up for herself, and about his "race man" story. She thought about Lonnie standing upside down on his hands in her office, saying the guys were taking bets that she had no talents, and she felt her anger rise. Maybe it was time to change that tune. Maybe she would play in the talent show after all. She knew exactly which piece she would play—the one she'd been playing for weeks now, her own composition. "Blues Prayer." To make it whole, though, she needed a singer. Valle.

She looked up her number, dialed it, and Valle answered.

"Hi, Valle. It's Jeanna."

"Miss J! This a surprise. What's up?"

"I've got an idea I'm hoping you might help me with. You know the talent show coming up?"

"Oh, yeah. I just can't decide what to sing. All my stuff so church, you know?"

"Really?" Jeanna felt excitement swell in her chest. "Well, I'm not sure you're aware of it, but I play the flute, and I've been working on a piece for some time now that's spiritual, but not quite church. I call it 'Blues Prayer.' Anyway," she rushed on, afraid she might lose her nerve, "I was wondering if I could play it for you right now on the phone. It needs a vocal part, a very simple refrain. I was thinking it could be, 'Can you hear me calling, Lord? Can you hear me calling?' Can I play it for you now, over the phone, and if you like it maybe we could do it together?"

"Yeah, I'm dyin' to hear it," Valle said. "Just let me grab a seat here on the couch. You go ahead."

Jeanna put the phone on the kitchen counter, sat on her stool, and played. She started low, like she always did, and played her song as she'd played it for the past couple of weeks—meditative, lonely, searching. It gathered intensity as she plunged as low as she could go then rose up in a powerful series of rippling echoes, ending as she took the flute away and sang, with Valle joining in with her deep contralto, "Can you hear me calling, Lord? Can you hear me calling?"

They were silent for a moment.

"Oh, Miss J, you been hidin' your light," Valle finally said. "That's some beautiful piece of music. That's what I been lookin' for. You serious about the two of us doin' that at the talent show?"

"Gospel serious," Jeanna said.

Valle let out a long, joyous, musical laugh that filled up all the emptiness in Jeanna. "You want to meet Monday after school to work on it?" she asked. "That's my only time off."

"Perfect, and I'll tell Lonnie we're in then, okay?"

"You got it, Miss J, and thank you."

"You're the one I need to thank," Jeanna said. She hung up with a huge smile on her face.

That Monday, Valle added a few more lines to the song early on—"I'm calling, Lord, I'm calling, deep down in my soul"—plunging way down deep so the refrain echoed and echoed some more. Jeanna hadn't realized what an incredible range Valle had, and it pushed her to her own lowest note. She tried and tried on her own that night and finally got there, first a thin and breathy, then a full and mellow low C, as low as the flute can go.

Upon arriving at the auditorium the next evening, Jeanna was surprised to discover that Lonnie had asked Guff to MC. He handled it with a natural grace, and knew many more of the students personally than she realized, as well as their parents.

The best part of the night, by far, was Cal. When Chef, Lonnie, and Alley had first awakened him to his habit of ducking away whenever a hand came near him, he'd been mortified. But when they discovered his love for street dancing, they'd suggested he try to dance it out of his system. And so he had—and tonight he put on the performance of the night with "The Dodge," as he called it, his wiry body leaping and pivoting this way and that, his head, eyes, and hand motions jerkily, convincingly, showing his reactive fear, a parody of himself that bloomed into a dance of full self-possession and freedom. He brought the house down.

For some reason, Lonnie had decided to put Jeanna and Valle on last. And for some reason, once they began, Jeanna lost her fear and played like she'd never played before, improvising freely, drawing Valle in then taking over again, deepening the power and intensity of the sound each time around, while Valle matched her, measure for measure, until they plunged down to the depths, rippled up to the heights, and ended by calling out their blues prayer in the echoing silence. When they were done they hugged each other, Guff put his arms around both of them, and they got a standing ovation.

CHAPTER FORTY-EIGHT

I Shoulda Known

AFTER THE HIGH OF HER AND VALLE'S PERFORMANCE, Jeanna crashed, struggling on all levels to come to terms with her life. She had wanted so badly to be of use in the movement and with Land, and had ended up just feeling used. Still, she didn't regret a single moment trying to love Land, nor a single thing she'd done in the Group—she just wished she had it more together. She wanted to be more like Lillian, who kept plugging away no matter what and managed to keep her dignity intact. Or Jackie, who had kept her buoyant spirit alive despite Helene's ongoing rejection. So why couldn't she?

Was she just like all the other white people who ran away from the struggle when the going got rough? But how could she go on after having gotten in so deep with Land? All of her relationships had become compromised because of their involvement. It would be futile to go on in this way. If she left, though, she'd lose everything—Land, the Group, her teaching—that mattered to her.

Jeanna had missed the Group's last meeting, and didn't want to go to the steering committee that night. The very thought of it sent a burst of anxiety through her. But she made it over to the storefront and up to the second floor, her legs heavy, her chest tight.

She was later than usual, and most people had already settled into their seats. Lillian smiled and waved at her across the circle. Jeanna raised her hand and tried to smile back, hating the fact that they'd never get any closer than a smile and a wave.

She listened without hearing most of what was being said throughout the evening. Ten minutes before the meeting was to end, she made her way toward the back stairwell to leave, but needed to stop at the restroom first. When she came out, Land was standing there, waiting for her. He took her by the upper arm and pulled her into the small upstairs office, partially closing the door behind him.

"You okay, Jeanna? You were so quiet tonight."

She looked up at him, not knowing what to say. What was there to say anyway? "I'm fine. Just a little tired." A tear came to her eye, but she blinked and absorbed it.

"Hey, babe." He brushed his lips up against the side of her throat and pulled her close.

She heard the floor creak and realized someone was going by to the bathroom. She looked up—and right into Karima's surprised eyes. Land's face was still nuzzled into her neck and his arms were around her. Karima moved quickly into the restroom. Land hadn't seen her.

Shit. Karima would be pissed as hell. Jeanna felt sick.

"I have to go, I'm not feeling all that well."

"Okay, babe, I'll call you."

"Okay." Jeanna hurried down the stairs and out to her car. She turned the key to start the car and rolled down the window to get some air. A figure loomed up beside the window. Thinking it was Land, she brightened and looked up. It was Karima, a look of cold fury on her face.

"What the hell is this? You and Land fucking now?"

Jeanna just looked at her, unable to speak.

"You fucking white bitch. I shoulda known I couldn't trust the likes of you." Karima moved toward her and Jeanna pulled away, thinking she was going to hit her.

Karima's spit hit her left cheek. As it dripped down, Jeanna felt herself hit bottom. Karima stalked away. Jeanna wiped off the spit with her upper arm and drove home, Karima's words echoing over and over again in her head.

Jeanna struggled through the next day as if in a dense cloud. She stopped eating lunch up on the second floor, and was barely able to facilitate her classes. She was forgetting things, too—this time a notebook for one of her classes that she'd left in her car. She walked out to the parking lot to get it.

"Hi, Jeanna. Do you have a minute?"

It was like Alley was addressing her through a great mist, though he was only a few feet away. He was taller, his chest and neck and arms had filled out, and his skin was a healthy, rosy tan. Only the soft brown eyes remained of the shy, scared little boy she'd taught what felt like so long ago.

"Yes . . . what is it?" She could hear her voice—flat, annoyed. It sounded like someone else's. She had a vague memory that he and Cal would be taking their EMT practice admission test soon with Clayton James. She should encourage him. She tried to rally.

"Oh, nothing." He shoved his hands deep into his pockets, his shoulders bunched up with tension, and quickly stepped away.

Jeanna's eyes moistened and burned at the rift she had created and could do nothing to stop. She felt the crunch of finely ground glass under her shoes as she stepped into the parking lot.

At three she knocked on Matt's door.

"Hey, Jeanna," Matt said. "Did you hear about Guff?"

"No! What happened?" Her focus returned.

"His house was burned to the ground last night. He got out just in time to see it go up in flames. They burned his truck too. He's fine, though."

Jeanna's mind immediately flashed on the cops he'd challenged over the boy, and knew who had done it, or had it done. "Christ," she said. "That's outrageous."

"Yeah, Guff told me about the kid and holding his rifle on the cops after the sit-in. Said you were there."

"I wondered if he was in for some kind of retaliation," she said. "What's he going to do?"

"Oh, ol' Guff, he was crowing about it. Said being homeless moved him to the top of the list for subsidized senior housing. He has to wait three months or so. We're taking up a collection to tide him over. He's staying with Jazzmine in the meantime."

She reached into her bag and pulled out her checkbook. She wrote a check for a hundred dollars and gave it to Matt.

"That's too much, J—"

"Matt," she said without emotion, "I'm sorry to do this to you mid-year, but I'm resigning at the end of the term." That was in less than three weeks, December 23rd.

Matt got up, took her in his arms, and hugged her close. She felt her ribs crunch against his wide, padded girth, and was suddenly aware that she had lost a lot of weight.

"I'm so sorry, Jeanna. I've been really worried about you. I should have done someth—"

"There's nothing you could have done. I've done it to myself." She turned and walked down the dark hall and out the door.

~

That evening Land came over earlier than usual. They made love and he fell asleep. She pulled the gauze curtain aside as she lay beside him. A deep indigo darkness had descended. She felt the dark blue smokiness fill her being and knew it was time. She sat up a little higher against the pillows, feeling centered and clear and deeply sad. She waited for him to awaken.

He finally stirred and looked up at her. "Hey," he said.

"Hey." She reached for his hand and held it tight. "I need to talk with you."

"Okay." He sat up, fluffing the pillows behind him.

"Remember when you said way back that you didn't want to talk out a lot of relationship problems, that you'd had enough of that with Pearl?"

He nodded slowly. "I guess I said something like that."

"Well, I've tried not to do that too much."

He nodded. "You haven't."

"And I haven't partly because I knew it wouldn't change anything. But for a long time I've wanted us to be more open in our relationship. It's been eating away at me, at my self-respect. I know you have your reputation to protect, and I don't want to undermine that, I never wanted to be a problem to you . . . but I can't live with it anymore. I need to leave. I've resigned from my job at school. I'm moving out."

He swallowed. His eyes were moist.

"I never, ever wanted to hurt you," she continued, "never thought I could. But I need to leave and when I do, I won't be able to have any more contact with you. I can't be 'just friends.'" She gave a harsh laugh. "I've never loved anyone as much as I love you, and I doubt I ever will, but I've got to do this."

He was quiet, his eyes wet, his face ruddy. He looked at her for a long moment. "Can't we talk about this?" he asked.

"No." She felt like a cold, hard rock with a molten mass of lava at the center.

He sat there, saying nothing, staring at the far wall. Finally he reached for her and held her close, his face full of pain. Maybe he cared more than she'd realized. She knew he would want to make love again, knew it would be for the last time.

"Let me love you one more time, babe," he whispered.

They made love. It felt like a last-ditch attempt to heal all that was broken. Afterwards, he got up and dressed. He leaned down and kissed her.

"I love you, Land. I always will," she whispered, enveloped in pain.

He took her hand in both of his, kissed it, and walked out the door.

She lay there in the silence for hours. Around midnight she lifted the curtain and looked out. Utter blackness met her gaze.

CHAPTER FORTY-NINE

I Was Hoping You Could Help Me Sort It Out

The next week, Jeanna was sitting at her desk at work, buried in students' final papers, wanting to be gone, wanting to crawl away into the darkness somewhere. The phone rang. Exasperated, she picked up.

"Hi, Jeanna. It's Jackie. Do you have a few minutes if I stopped by?"

She sighed. "Sure Jackie, come on over. Though I should warn you, I have a parent coming in at four-thirty."

It was three-fifteen. Jeanna looked at her stack of papers and resigned herself to a long night. She'd been avoiding Jackie the last several months, for fear she would unload on her, tell her about Land, about Pearl, Helene, everything, and ruin the past few years of discretion that had meant everything to Land but had ended up strangling her. She loved Jackie, but she couldn't deal with another thing. She needed to survive the next few days and get out for good.

Jackie knocked on her office door. Jeanna got up to open it and gave her a hug.

"Thanks for taking the time, Jeanna. I know how busy you are." Jackie's face was radiant, her eyes dancing with light.

"No problem. What's up?"

"I feel really weird talking about this, but you're the only one I trust."

She nodded and wondered if Helene had been on the warpath again.

"It's about Land."

She stopped breathing.

"It's just the oddest, most amazing thing. You know I've been working night and day on helping to plan the long-term strategy for his mayoral campaign?"

"Yes." Except for that one meeting she had forced herself to go to, she had withdrawn from the Group without explanation to anyone, including Jackie. What could she say? And to whom would she say it? No one had asked about her absence, anyway.

"Well, I'd never thought about him in a personal way."

Oh, shit, here it comes. Jeanna felt herself closing down.

"He gave me a ride home a few days ago because my car was in the shop?" A smile overtook Jackie's face. "And he kissed me—not like a friend but really deep and long, like I'd never experienced before. I didn't know what to think. I was excited from here to eternity, scared, upset. I mean, I was thinking, *He's over twice my age—and isn't he married, or sort of married?* I was, I am, just so confused. Nothing like this has ever happened to me." She stopped and looked at Jeanna. "You know, I really respect your judgment. I was hoping you could help me sort it out."

Jeanna laughed, short and harsh. She looked at Jackie and saw herself. *Hi Jackie, meet the new Jeanna.* This was hilarious.

"Did you and he talk about it at all?"

"A little. I guess I looked so surprised, he said, 'I'm sorry Jackie, I thought you knew I was interested in you, and I thought I was getting the same feeling from you.' I hadn't meant to, but I guess I had been giving off those vibes. I mean, how could you not love Land?"

How indeed. "Yeah, everybody loves Land," Jeanna said flatly.

"You're probably judging me . . . I mean, *I'm* judging me." Jackie looked scared.

"No, I'm not judging you, Jackie, not at all." Her voice was cool and aloof. "What're you going to do?"

"That's why I came to you."

This was ludicrous.

"It's for you to decide, Jackie, not me." It was all she could do to keep from shoving Jackie out the door and slamming it.

"I'm sorry, Jeanna. I thought you might get excited with me, celebrate, then talk some sense into me." Jackie looked lost, confused. "You think I'm an idiot. It would only mess things up, I know. It's just that . . ." Jackie paused, and the radiance came back into her face.

She saw that Jackie was caught up in the Landon Waters tidal wave and nothing she could say would stop that. She wanted to warn her, tell Jackie her own story, but she had maintained her silence for so long, she wasn't about to break it now, not at the very end.

Jackie's exuberant smile had returned. She was literally vibrating with excitement.

Jeanna couldn't stand it anymore. She stood abruptly, and Jackie did as well, suddenly looking mortified.

"I'm so sorry, Jeanna."

"Don't be," she said. "It's just that I have this parent coming in."

Jackie walked through the doorway and down the empty hall, her body rigid. Jeanna felt a stab of shame as she watched her walk away.

"Jackie?"

Jackie swung around immediately. "Yes?"

"Just . . . don't lose yourself." Jeanna went back into her office and closed the door behind her. She felt like an empty cardboard box, thrown out in the trash.

CHAPTER FIFTY

I Thought It Was Just the Way of the World

FOR THE REMAINDER OF HER FINAL THREE WEEKS at work, Jeanna struggled through, trying to be present for her students but feeling loss on all levels and like a fraud in everything she'd tried to do.

Her second to last day at school, Matt stopped by her office and surprised her with the gift of a beautiful Parker pen, with *Thank you, Jeanna* inscribed on it.

"I knew you weren't up for a big party or anything like that, but I want to thank you for all you've done here at the school," he said. "You've done amazing things with students who'd been thrown away by their previous schools. You've been able to connect with kids a lot of us couldn't get anywhere near, and now they're thriving. I can't thank you enough. I wish . . . I wish I could've made things easier on you on other fronts. You've been a tremendous lift to the Group, too. I know the countless hours you've put in, and how tough it's been. I—"

"Thanks so much, Matt. I feel like I'm letting you, everyone, down," Jeanna said, feeling like an utter failure.

"You're doing what you have to do. I know that. I respect what you're doing."

Jeanna's breath caught in her throat. He must have known for some time what was going on but hadn't wanted to interfere. She reached for him and they hugged, hard. She was silently crying, and his eyes were moist. "I'll never forget you, Matt, and this incredible school, these kids, all of it. It's been the greatest experience of my life."

"You be good to you for a change. Take care of yourself. Okay?"

She nodded, unable to speak as he left, raising his hand a final time in the doorway.

Shortly after he left, while she was still taking in his words, trying to remember the good things he had said that had already slipped away, her phone rang.

"Jeanna, its Ma here."

Ma, of all people? She had never called her before.

"I know you haven't been coming to many Group meetings lately, but I wondered if, as a favor to me, you'd be willing to come this evening? I'd appreciate it a great deal if you would. I can explain at the meeting."

Jeanna had not planned to go to the meeting that night or any other night, not after saying goodbye to Land, and not after Karima spat in her face. But how could she say no to Ma?

"Jeanna?"

"Yes, I'll be there."

"Thank you, Jeanna." She hung up.

~

It took every bit of courage Jeanna had to go to the meeting. She timed it so she got there at exactly when the meeting was supposed to begin to avoid any awkward moments with anyone she didn't want to see, which was virtually everyone but Lillian. She came in when everyone was already seated, and was immensely relieved that the nearest seat next to Lillian was empty. She slid into it, and Lillian squeezed her arm. She scanned the room quickly, noting that Helene, Cam, Karima, Matt, Land, Gideon, Mary Ranier, Abe, Carl, Elaine Browning, Phil, Reverend Bellows, Lillian, and Frederick were all there. No one was looking her way, thankfully; all eyes were on Ma.

"Thank you, everyone, for arriving so promptly," Ma said. "I won't waste any time. I received a call this afternoon at 3 p.m. from city hospital. It was Jacqueline O'Keane, saying she would not be returning to the Group. She tried to commit suicide yesterday."

Gasps from the group. Jeanna was astounded, and a horrible feeling of guilt and shame washed over her. She looked quickly over at Land, who had that awful, bleached out, remote look.

"She was not successful only because her mother had suspected something was very wrong when she never showed up for their monthly dinner out with her last night as expected, nor did she answer her phone. She had a key to her daughter's apartment, so she went over and let herself in. Jacqueline appeared dead, but her mother called 911, and the EMTs were able to revive her, and induce vomiting. She took over one hundred pills."

More gasps.

"Now I'm not going to soft-pedal this, nor am I going to go into detail. Apparently she had gotten into a relationship with our leader here, Landon Waters, at his initiative, who shortly thereafter decided he was through with her in favor of another woman, and was unwilling to talk with her about it."

Ma turned to directly address Land. "Now, I am sick and tired of watching you take young white girls as mistresses to you and the movement, and then destroying them, along with a string of other women as well. It's about time you stopped thinking you're God's gift to the female sex and get some priorities. I am not going to stand by and watch you undermine the Group and hurt these young women one more minute. We've had enough. Now, perhaps you menfolk can stay here tonight and get yourselves straight. The women also need to set themselves straight as well. But I have to say, we should be expecting more from a forty-seven-year-old, respected community leader than from an impressionable twenty-year-old girl who worships the ground you walk on. Land isn't alone in this; some of the other men need to take a look at themselves as well."

Land sat in stony silence, not meeting Ma's eyes.

"But before we leave . . . I want to apologize to all of you," Ma said. "I have been chairing this group for well over a decade, and have been part of the movement for fifty years, and this kind of thing has been going on all that time—long before Landon here came on the scene. I always understood the racial struggle and the economic struggle, but I thought the sexual struggle was off-limits—I thought it was just the way of the world, no matter how angry and uncomfortable it made me. I've been blind to what's been staring me in the face since I was a young girl myself, going through the same things all women in the movement go through, but I just never had the foresight or guts to face it and deal with it."

There were supportive murmurs from some of the women.

"So I've let you down, all of you; none of us is untouched by this thing. I should have spoken up sooner, but I was too set in my ways. Now I'm ready to change, and I invite the rest of you to join me. I believe we need to call a halt to business as usual in the Group for the next several months and meet, separately, as women in one group and men in another, to ask ourselves some hard questions about our relationships with one another, how we treat each other and work together—as men and women, and, while I'm at it, as blacks and whites too. We have some long-standing racial issues to deal with as well."

Ma took a breath. "On that score, no matter how hard certain white individuals have worked in the Group, no matter how committed they are, this still isn't an excuse for taking more than their fair share of power and control over the things. I've seen this for decades, too, and it never fails to amaze me—this sense of entitlement in white activists who are certain they know better than anyone else about what should be done, how to do it, and by whom. It needs to end. Again, my apologies for not having asked that we deal with these issues earlier. I am as much at fault as anyone."

Jeanna looked over at Helene and saw a glacial coldness hardening her face. Cam was looking down at his outstretched feet, his throat flushing red.

"But let me be clear," Ma said. "This is not a time to dump all over each other, to destroy one another. It's a time to be real and honest with each other. It's a time to balance things out between men and women, blacks and whites, in the group. How can we fight injustice out in the world if we can't keep our own house clean?"

Many of the men and women present were nodding now.

"I suggest that the men and women's groups meet bi-weekly until we reconvene back here on March 17th," Ma said. "Hopefully, we can come back together as a whole with a greater capacity for mutual respect and renewed commitment to the Group and the movement. We can all bring our suggestions about how to positively rebuild the Group at that time. I am stepping aside until then and have asked Elaine Browning to facilitate our women's meetings. I suggest that Land step aside as well, and I've asked Carl and Matt to co-facilitate the men's group, if that meets with the men's approval."

She stopped and looked around the room in the deadly silence. "Do I have your support in this matter? Hands?"

Slowly, one after the other, all hands went up except Frederick's and Helene's. Land looked stunned, and he stared blindly at the far wall beyond Ma, still holding his hand partway in the air after everyone else had brought theirs down. Carl reached out and touched Land's arm and he brought it down slowly to his lap.

"I see we have not reached a consensus. All opposed?" No hands went up. "Let the record show that Frederick and Helene have abstained. Thank you both. I appreciate your honesty."

Ma got up and walked out. Lillian got up to follow her, with Jeanna right behind, stunned to the core. Mary Ranier and Elaine Browning came along, and then Karima got up as well and walked out, with only Helene remaining. They stopped for a second at the doorway and Jeanna heard Carl say, "Maybe we men should meet on our own, like Ma said." Helene got up to leave, and the rest of the women walked out to the sidewalk. Helene walked to her car, got in, and drove away.

"If any of you want to still build together as a group in the coming year, you're welcome to meet in my home, 36 Glendale, next Wednesday at seven," Ma said. "I certainly don't have the answers, but together, maybe we can make some sense of what's been going on, and what needs to change." She turned, got into her car and drove away.

"I plan to meet with Ma," Mary said.

"Me too," Lillian and Elaine both said.

Mary drove off and Elaine walked toward the subway.

"I'm leavin this bullshit and checking out the Panthers," Karima said, and she walked away.

That left Lillian and Jeanna staring at each other in dazed wonder.

"How 'bout a cup of coffee, Jeanna?"

"Sure," Jeanna said. "Belle's?"

Lillian nodded, and Jeanna led the way to her car. They drove to Belle's diner in silence and took a seat in the booth in the far corner.

"Jeanna, there's so much I've wanted to tell you," Lillian said in a gentle voice.

"Me too, but I've been afraid if I did, you'd hate me," Jeanna said, almost in a whisper.

"It's way past time we talked." Lillian reached out and held Jeanna's wrist gently. "You're not alone, you know."

Jeanna looked up into Lillian's eyes, full of a kind of compassion she'd never felt before. She couldn't imagine that anything Lillian had ever done could come anywhere near her own stupidity. "Let me go first," Lillian said. "That might make it easier. So many times I've wanted to reach out to you and tell you my story, but I just couldn't face it, and I didn't want to impose. And I'm so much older than you, I was afraid you wouldn't want an old fogey messing in your business!"

"And here all this time I was dying to talk with you, and I kept asking myself, 'What would Lillian do?' but was too afraid to ask *you* that."

"Good lord, you were in trouble!" Lillian said, and they laughed together, breaking the tension. "Jeanna, when I was coming up and still just a kid, I was in love with Land. But he was with Pearl, she was always the one. Still, all those years, growing up, we had a special bond. He always looked out for me like a kid sister. As we got older, though, our feelings got stronger." She looked down into her coffee cup. "When I was still in high school, he went off to one college and Pearl to another in the arts, but it was understood that they would marry after graduation. Their parents—and they—had decided that early on. Pearl was amazing: stunning, artistically gifted, a straight-A student . . . not so political as Land, but extremely kind and sensitive to all us riff-raff. How could he not fall for her?"

Jeanna nodded, riveted by this new picture of Pearl—and Land, too.

"Anyway, after he left for college, he was all I thought about. I wrote him silly, embarrassing letters." She laughed self-deprecatingly. "I mean, I knew I didn't stand a chance because of Pearl—but I just knew I'd be better with him. And he wrote me back. Beautiful, encouraging letters. We understood each other. He'd tell me he could be himself around me in a way he couldn't with Pearl. It gave me hope even when I knew it was hopeless."

I know the feeling, Jeanna thought.

"Then October of his senior year, out of the blue, Land called me and invited me up to campus for the long weekend. He said he'd been waiting for me to grow up. We agreed to keep it quiet."

"Here we go," Jeanna said softly.

"Right. He was living in a little studio off campus. We spent that weekend in bed and we had exactly nine others like it, once a month until he graduated. I fell hard—and I mean *hard*. He said he loved me. And I began to think we could actually be together. But then right after he graduated, he married Pearl."

"Just like that? No talking it through?"

"No, nothing. After I went off the deep end and finally called him, he said he did love me, but thought he'd been clear about what he had to do, thought I understood."

"Jesus, that's hard. Cold. All this so he wouldn't let his parents and Pearl down, even though it wasn't what he wanted?" Jeanna was having trouble making sense of it.

"Partly. There was something fragile and scary about Pearl even back then, and Land felt he had committed himself and couldn't go back on it. Plus, he wasn't one to deal with any real emotional crisis, especially one he helped cause. But the other thing was that his father was a prominent doctor and wanted him to shape up into a man of prominence too. He wanted Land at the top of the ladder, not running around stirring up trouble with folks like me, I suppose."

"That's awful," Jeanna said, feeling teenage Lillian's pain.

Lillian shrugged. "It was. I went into a tailspin for years: didn't graduate high school, couldn't connect with any men—"

"You were really left stranded," Jeanna said. "And for reasons that didn't really hang together."

"Exactly. That's what kept eating at me. He loved me—I could feel it. And I loved him. We were good together, so why couldn't we be together? I just couldn't accept it, and I couldn't do a damn thing about it. But there's more to the story.

"When Pearl went away for the third time to the treatment center, after a long, crazy bout with her illness, maybe eight or nine years into their marriage, Land called me wanting to reconnect. I'd tried like hell, but I still wasn't over him, and I couldn't make a go of it with anyone else. He was etched into me. I'd had a terrible time, and so had he. He said he couldn't give up on Pearl because of her illness, but did I want to spend some time together, once again on the QT. He'd missed me. He'd understand if I didn't want to."

"His better self would advise against it," Jeanna said.

Lillian grunted. They looked at each other, feeling their mutual struggle.

"We got re-involved. I was twenty-five and he was thirty. We were together for two years straight, undercover, and I loved him like only a woman who knows it won't last forever can." She laughed harshly. "And it didn't. Pearl came home again, and I stepped aside."

Jeanna, nodded, knowing the cycle only too well.

"Only it was different this time."

"How so?"

"I discovered I was pregnant, even though we'd been very careful. Land is Tommie Lee's father."

"God, Lillian," Jeanna said, all the pieces suddenly clicking into place. Now she could see Land in the set of Tommie Lee's jaw, his dark eyebrows against bronze skin a shade darker than Land's, his quiet power and way with people. And there was his raging hurt right before he was incarcerated. "Was finding out about Land being his father why he ended up at Chisolm's Farm?"

"Yes. We were completely out of money after Carl lost his job, and Land came over late one night to give us some to pay the rent. Tommie Lee found out, and I had to tell him everything . . . and he went off the deep end. It was horrible. But it was also a relief, finally having the truth out in the open, not having to keep on lying to protect myself, to protect Land. Of course, I told Carl before we married. At least I did one thing right."

Lillian wiped tears away with her fingers as Jeanna placed a tissue in her hand and held on tight. They sat together in the silence.

"I wanted desperately to talk with you about my situation," Jeanna said, "but I thought you'd . . ."

"What?"

"Well, most black women—"

"Wouldn't like it?"

"Right."

"Well, most black women wouldn't, but I was certainly in no position to judge. And you were so . . ."

Jeanna knew she was searching for a way not to say "naive."

". . . so young. It was obvious you were in for a world of hurt. I knew you were going through a lot of what I went through so many years ago. I wanted to help you, badly, but I didn't know how. I was so hardheaded myself back when. I knew I wouldn't want anyone telling me what was good for me. And I'm ashamed to say, I didn't want my own story to come out, and I guess protecting Land and the movement is still a big block for me in saying anything to anyone."

"Yeah, that's the really rough part," Jeanna said. "The crazy thing is, what I wanted most in the beginning was just to be part of the movement, to make a difference somehow—that was my real hope, and later maybe being friends with Land, despite our age and race difference. But he made it clear that wouldn't be possible, he had plenty of friends and allies in his life. It was going to be a sexual relationship or it wasn't going to be anything. And then once it happened, it was like I was swept up in this tidal wave and it took me forever to find my way back to shore. Most of the time I was just swimming hard, trying not to drown." She hesitated, looking to see how Lillian was taking it. "But still, aren't you angry with me?"

"No," Lillian said firmly. "Believe me, Jeanna, I've had years to come to terms with Land. And don't forget, I have Carl. As much as I thought I loved Land, I love Carl a thousand times more. He's my rock. Land was never there for me."

Jeanna nodded. "He made it clear from the first that he didn't want to talk through any relationship issues. He said he'd had enough of that with Pearl, not to mention all the other weight on him." She paused. "Funny thing was, at the end he asked me if we could talk it through."

"What did you say?"

"I said no."

"Whew. Good for you." Tender strands of tears were running down Lillian's face.

Jeanna reached up and touched her own tears. She hadn't even been aware that she was crying.

"You know, Jeanna, one of the worst things was seeing how badly

Helene was treating you. Like lint on her sleeve while she dispensed orders a mile a minute. It just made me cringe."

Jeanna laughed, feeling embarrassed yet validated as well. "She was pretty heavy-handed with you, too. Remember the newsletter, way back? And when she dropped you as a speaker at the Congress, I wanted to kill her."

"I know. I'm the lint on her other sleeve," Lillian said with a laugh. "But you really took the sting out of it for me. And then Karima put on the finishing touch. I'll never forget her, 'Who made you the queen of the universe?'"

They doubled over their coffee and laughed till tears came.

"Getting back to Pearl," Lillian said, "I could be wrong, but I always felt the crux of her illness was Land's inability to love her and truly support her, despite his constant reassurances. She simply couldn't accept it. It destroyed her. That is, until she finally met someone who could love her for who she is."

"What did you say?" Jeanna wasn't sure she'd heard right. Pearl had found someone else?

"I just found out too. From a friend of mine who's kept track of Pearl all these years. Apparently Pearl got into a relationship with a creativity coach who came to the rehab center to do a workshop—a woman from the Islands, a healer of some kind. They're living together in New York, and Pearl just landed an exhibit at a big museum in New York—"

"Pearl is in a relationship . . . with a woman?" This was a whole new thing for Jeanna.

"Yes, and they couldn't be happier."

Jeanna suddenly felt all the suffocating bonds that had held her and so many others closely tied to Land float free and silvery out into the night air. She looked out the diner window, feeling lighter. "I'm glad for her."

"Me too." Lillian looked out the window. "Look how dark it is! Carl's going to wonder what's happened to me. Can you drop me back at the Center?"

On the drive back, Jeanna told Lillian of her plans to leave the school and the Group.

"I totally understand," Lillian said. "It took me years before I could return to the Group and stand to be in Land's presence. We'll miss you, though."

"I'll miss you too," Jeanna said. "But I'm not planning on going to Ma's, either. A big part of me wants to, but I know I need to take a break from the Group and kind of rebuild myself, my life, before I can be part of rebuilding anything else. I do wonder what the women's meetings will be like, though. And wasn't Ma amazing tonight? I respect her so much."

"And she respects you. She told me she did. She said she was amazed at how much BS you've taken from Helene, Land, and Frederick, and so forth and still hung in there—she said it's obvious how committed you are."

"Really?" That meant the world to Jeanna, but it was embarrassing too. Had they both known about her and Land?

"I don't want you to think we were always talking about you, Jeanna," Lillian said, as if reading her mind. "It just came up yesterday. Ma called and told me about Jackie and what she was planning to do this evening, and how it was similar with my situation, Helene's, and yours, and she'd had enough. I guess she knew about all of us . . . and we didn't even have a clue! I think she was feeling me out to see if I could handle her bringing all this up tonight. Said she'd coined a phrase for it: 'sexploitation in the movement.' I've been turning that over in my mind ever since."

"Sexploitation," Jeanna repeated, nodding. "That sounds about right. I guess we're all like Ma said, not wanting to interfere in each other's lives or ask for help, even when our silence is killing us. Speaking of which . . . did you see that cold, hard look on Helene's face the whole time Ma was talking?"

"Yes," Lillian said hesitantly, "but Helene lost her humanity a long time ago. You see, one reason I never spoke with you is that many years ago I got up the courage to try to talk with Helene when I could see she was getting in over her head with Land, and she just sliced me up—you know what it's like when she wants to make mincemeat of someone." She sighed. "I guess I never recovered from that. I went into it with this feeling of compassion for her and ended up just shredded."

"I'm so sorry, Lillian," Jeanna said. "She never stopped twisting the knife in me either. But, you know, I wouldn't give up our lives for hers, not for one second. When Ma said that these relationships with young girls in the movement destroys them, Helene may be the prime example. Look at how alone she is."

"That's true. You just took away my anger toward her." Lillian shook her head. "I can't believe it, I've felt that bitterness for so long, and now it's gone," she said in a tone of wonder.

As they approached Lillian and Carl's parked car, it was clear that the men were still meeting—all the cars were still there, and the lights were on.

"You know the one thing that's still making me crazy," Lillian said softly, like she might break in two, "is Tommie Lee. He's trying to get things back with me like it used to be, we both are, but I can feel him still smoldering away at me inside, way down deep. There's a distance I can't bridge. All because I lied to him."

"Or because Land needed you to lie to him," Jeanna said. "You can't take all that burden on yourself."

"That too," Lillian said, but the sadness was still there.

"Well, maybe his bitterness will change too. He's got time to heal."

"I hope so, impossible as it seems. Now, enough of all that," Lillian smiled at her. "What are you going to do? Your last day is tomorrow. What then?"

"I'm not sure. I might . . ." Jeanna hesitated, not being able to say it aloud. She had denied it for so long, it didn't seem any longer within the realm of possibility.

"What? Tell me," Lillian urged.

"Oh, it's just a crazy dream I've had forever. But it's way too self-indulgent."

"What is it? I'm not getting out of this car till you tell me—that is, if we're going to be friends."

Jeanna saw that look of vulnerable dignity come over Lillian's face.

"Now that would be a dream come true," she said, the words coming out on their own.

"Thank you, Jeanna. I'm going to hold you to it, and don't you let me get too busy on you. But I want to know if you want to tell me. What's your crazy dream?"

"Music. To play flute—jazz, blues, movement music, you name it."

"Ah, I didn't know you were into music. That's a wonderful dream. Music brings the soul alive. What's more important than that?"

They hugged long and hard. Just then Carl came along, and Lillian opened her door. As she got out of the car, she said, "Call me soon, and let me know how that dream goes."

CHAPTER FIFTY-ONE

Sometimes There Ain't No Right Way

THE NEXT AFTERNOON, JEANNA PACKED UP HER office. The only thing holding her together and getting her through her last day was Lillian's offer of friendship—a gift beyond her wildest hopes. She'd told Lonnie that morning that she was leaving, and he had been mad that she hadn't given the students enough time to pull together a party for her. He'd given her a spontaneous kiss on the cheek that embarrassed him and touched her to the core.

As she packed, she made a mental note to go and see Jackie as soon as she worked up the courage to apologize for her gross insensitivity. There was no point in utter secrecy now. Not that she would go into gory detail, but Jackie needed to know she wasn't alone.

And she needed to contact Cardienne School of Music to find out about their admissions requirements. When Jeanna called to ask her mother if she could come home for a while, she'd reminded Jeanna of her grandmother's trust fund and sent her a brochure that emphasized a new program Cardienne was initiating in the coming year: the music of liberation. She said that her grandmother had given it to her the week before she passed, but she had forgotten to pass it along. That sealed it for Jeanna. Maybe she would finally find a way to bring together the things that mattered most to her instead of having to choose between them. She even had a song of her own she could play for her audition, "Blues Prayer." She needed to tell Valle about the program, too. They offered several scholarships every year. It would be perfect for her.

Her office was almost bare now, and she was on her last box, filling it with all her notes on students' crises and growth over the years, and her own questions and revelations. She could hear Lonnie, Chefman, Alley, and Cal back in the lounge area, arguing over a book of Langston Hughes poetry that Jeanna had given them to read and write about. They had kept up their little group all this time. It was their lifeline.

Tommie Lee passed her office, looking anguished. He stopped when he saw her. He had given her a good-bye hug yesterday, so heartfelt it nearly killed her. "Let me know if you need any help with those boxes, Jeanna," he said.

"I'm all set, thanks. Remember to let me know what college you decide on." She turned to give him a smile, but he had walked on.

"I will!" he called back.

She could see him through her open doorway, walking over to what had once been Group Survive. He knocked on the column next to the lounge area, a look of desperation on his face. "Can I come in?"

"Hey, Tommie Lee," Lonnie responded. "Whatchu doin' here, man? 'Course you can." He motioned to the empty easy chair. "Set yourself down."

Tommie Lee touched knuckles with Cal and clapped Alley on the shoulder and got a warm smile back. Jeanna could see Tommie Lee clearly from her half-open doorway as he settled into the chair.

"Hey, what's goin' on?" Chefman asked. "You look really burnt."

"Yeah." Tommie Lee's voice broke. He was fighting back tears, looking down at his lap, his face strained and contorted.

"Hey, man, take your time, ain't no rush," Lonnie said.

Still looking down, Tommie Lee said in a strangled voice, "I'm dyin', man." The late-afternoon sun bathed him in amber light.

"Why, man?" Lonnie asked. "You the most together dude we know."

"No, you guys are," Tommie Lee said. "You lay your stuff out there and deal with it. I been keepin my stuff jammed up inside me for so long I think I'm gonna explode." He broke out in strangled sobs, trying to smother them.

"Let it out, man," Lonnie said gently.

But Tommie Lee was quiet again, still looking down.

"What, Tommie Lee, what stuff?" Lonnie urged him on.

"I hate to even bring my shit up, when you guys have it tougher."

"Cut it right there, man," Chefman said, "and tell us what's goin' on."

Tommie Lee gulped down another sob. "Before I did all that crazy shit and got arrested, I found out who my real father is—found out my mom's been lying to me my whole life. He wasn't some one-night mistake and long gone. He's been right here in plain sight all along, the fucking bastard."

"Whose your real father, man?" asked Cal in his hoarse voice.

"Landon Waters."

"Holy Shit!" Lonnie exclaimed.

Sharp intakes of breath all around.

"If that don't beat shit," Chefman said. "Yeah, I guess you do look like him—but man, that's low, not to know."

"Yeah, why your ma never tol' you?" Cal asked.

"Oh, you know, it wouldn't do for the great Landon Waters to own up to a bastard kid with a no-account woman on welfare. They had to keep me under wraps back then so as not to upset Land's apple cart. And it could, you know, still mess up a lot of good stuff."

"Fuck that!" Chefman practically yelled. "That why you went off and got arrested? I mean, I never could figure that one out."

"Yeah, I guess. I just went crazy." Tommie Lee shrugged.

"What made your mom tell you the truth after all these years?" asked Alley.

"After my stepdad lost his job, Land came over one night, late, and

I saw him give my mom an envelope out on the front step. I went downstairs and picked the envelope up off the table. There were five one hundred dollar bills in it. I asked why was Land giving her all this money, and she said because we needed it. I said does Land walk around at midnight handing out envelopes of money to everyone who needs it? I was like half getting it and half not getting it and yelled something really off, like, 'What, are you fucking Landon Waters?' And she got real deathly quiet and sat me down and laid it all out, what happened all those years ago, apologizing every five seconds to me, but I just kept repeating over and over again, but you lied to me, you lied to me . . ."

"But when you got out of Chisolm's and came back to class," Alley said, "you seemed so together—almost like the old you."

"I was trying to get back to normal," Tommie Lee said. "But I can't. I hate my mom now. I hate Land. I hate myself. It's eating me alive. I want to blow him away like he's blown me off all these years, like I was this nice little boy he could help out from time to time from a safe distance. I always knew something was off about me and him and Mom and Carl, like there was this weird tension, but I didn't know why. And shit, I admired the man. I fucking tried to model myself after him, for Christ's sake, even though I barely knew him." Silent tears were running down his face.

"You ain't the only one," Lonnie said. "He might be the only man 'sides Guff I ever looked up to."

"Yeah, that's part of the problem. The whole fucking community loves him, and I hate his guts. I swear I'm going crazy." Tommie Lee pounded the arm of the chair with his fist.

Jeanna felt like pounding the desk with him on that. How often had she not said what she really felt for these same reasons, discounting how she was being treated since he was the great, beloved leader? But of course Tommie Lee was the truly innocent one. She had agreed to her own diminishment, and to Pearl's as well.

"You ain't gonna go crazy, man. We not gonna let you," Lonnie said in a quiet tone. "What you need, man? Tell us what you need."

There was a long silence.

"I don't know what the hell I need," Tommie Lee said. "Maybe I just need to talk with him. Ask what he's been thinking all these years with me just a few blocks away. And my mom with her big shame thing going on."

"What about your mom?" Alley asked.

Tommie Lee was shaking his head again. "I always wondered why she was always putting herself down, acting like she was ashamed of herself, saying stupid stuff I never understood, like she didn't deserve me. Meanwhile, I'm thinking she's the truest, finest thing in the world, and it was all a big, fucking lie . . . But in my head I know it's more Land. He did her just like he did me, so I don't know why I'm so mad at her—but it's like he's untouchable, like he's some fucking god or something."

"But he ain't," Lonnie said.

Tommie Lee nodded. "You know, just talking this out, I already feel that stone of hate at my mom rolling away," he said in an amazed tone. "Maybe it's because I can't touch him, he's so far away, that I lash out at her."

Jeanna was sitting at her desk, open-mouthed, taking this all in, seeing so much of her own experience in Tommie Lee's.

"Sounds like you really do have to have it out with him," Lonnie said.

The other boys nodded their agreement.

"Yeah, I've tossed it around in my crazy mind at least a thousand times, but I can't figure out how to approach it, you know, how to do it the right way."

"Now see here," Chefman interrupted, "that's your big problem, Tommie Lee. Always havin' to do things the right way. Sometimes there ain't no right way. Ya just have to fucking do it. Face the motherfucker and send him to hell."

"Yeah, why don't you call him right now?" Lonnie said. "Tell him there's a big problem over at the school you need his help with. Ain't that his thing?"

"Right—'cause if I told him I needed to talk with him, something tells me he'd be real busy," Tommie Lee said.

They all laughed, a harsh laughter.

Jeanna eased the door shut to her office so they wouldn't know she'd heard every word.

"Let's go use the outside pay phone," she heard Tommie Lee say.

As they walked by her office, she heard the other boys saying, "You can do this man, you always be speakin' up for us, it's time you did it for you. You're the man, don't you know that? Don't pull no punches . . ." until they were out of earshot.

Thrilled at how Lonnie and the group were supporting Tommie Lee, Jeanna pulled her boxes together and carried them out to her car. As she was struggling to get the trunk to shut, she saw Guff's truck pull up. She felt an ache back in her throat that they'd never really connected, and swallowed it down as yet another loss.

He got out and came over as she made one more effort to slam the trunk. "Whoa there," he said, "let me take a look at that." He opened the trunk and shoved the boxes around, then brought the roof of the trunk down with a solid thump and smiled at her. "I want to thank you for that check. It was mighty generous of you. I heard tell this your last day? Lonnie boy was pretty surprised. You mind my askin' why?"

"Yeah, this is it." She tried to smile back at him through her sadness, but was taken aback at his question—how to say something that would make any sense? Then it came to her. "I guess I thought it was about time I stood up for myself," she said, giving him a real smile back.

"That's real good, then," he said softly. "Listen, since we won't probably keep bumpin' into each other no more helpin' these scrambly-brained kids, any chance you'd like to have some barbecue at my new place from time to time so's we can settle the world's problems? I been enjoyin' listenin' to you teach out there on the step by your windows when I be takin' my rest—now I'm gonna lose out."

"I'd love to, just tell me when and where," Jeanna said, feeling lifted up, and beginning to think maybe dreams could come true after all. First Lillian and now Guff. They shook on it.

As she drove home, she thought about how far Lonnie and his buddies had come since that first day of class when he felt he "couldn't touch" the likes of Tommie Lee. She thought of Lillian's grief and had a feeling that she and Tommie Lee would make it through after all, that they all would. Even Land. If anyone could penetrate his shell, Tommie Lee was the one.

Most of all, she looked forward to her new world of music, and to finally fully connecting with Guff and Lillian. She could feel a song coming on, "A New Dawn," and felt the urge to get it down as soon as she got home. The setting sun sent streaks of red and gold across the sky; Jeanna drank in the colors and breathed in deeply. It would be a long and good night.

ACKNOWLEDGMENTS

I would like to thank the following people, whom I have listed in alphabetical order, for their invaluable friendship, example, support and/or assistance in helping me bring this novel to fruition and share with the world:

Sam E. Anderson, Maureen Andrew, Nancy Aronie & Chilmark fellow creative writers, Lisa Borders, Elaina Brin, Gail Burton, Kevin Castle-Grytting, Maralyn & Carin Chase, Nathaniel Clark, CEQE friends, Hannah Davis, V. Paul Deare, Kenneth Dolbeare, Georgina Duffy-Hetzel, Lee Duffy-Hetzel, April Eberhardt, Editors at She Writes Press: Krissa Lagos, Cait Levin, & Chris Dumas, Jennifer Ellwood, Paula & Donald Flemming, Susan Freedman, Eugenia Friedman, Isabelle Lisa Glasner, Tanya Gold, Cheryl Gooding, Grub Street, Lisa Guisbond, Jesse Hagopian, Bobbi Harro, Hedgebrook, Mike Heichman, Cerci & Salaam Imani Hernandez, Millie, Willard, & Charles Hetzel, Ellen Hewett, Andrea Hurst, Yamila Hussein, Iowa Writers workshop, Kayhan Irani, Christine James, Gina Joseph-Collins, Robin Joyce, Jonathan Kale, Jacqueline King, Martha Kolmar, Jonathan Kozol, Kate Layte, Paul Levy, Betty Mandell, Deborah Malone, Louisa McCall, Sandra McIntosh, Myia X, Najma Nazy'at, Monty Neill, Shaari Neretin, Karla Nicholson, Jeanne & Aidan Nixon, Gil Ontai, Philadelphia Parkway Program 1969-1971 students & colleagues, Sayra Pinto & Circle friends, Neil Rizos, Rochester School Without Walls 1974-1975 students and colleagues, Ruth Rodriguez, Theresa Perry, Carmi Soifer's creative writing group, Springfield College School of Human Services 1989-2013 students and colleagues, Nancy Stephens, my original editor Pam Summa, Chris Summerhill, Beverly Anne Sypek, Dora Taylor, Giema Tsakuginow, Becky Tuch, Chuck Turner, Sherri VandenAkker, Bridget Wack, Brooke Warner, Harold Washington, Marian Sway Washington, Anna & Joe Wexler, Robert Willey, Malikka Williams, Lauren Wise, Jean Wyld, Junia Yearwood, and my publicist, Eva Zimmerman.

BIBLIOGRAPHY

Diedrich, Maria. *Love Across Color Lines: Otttilie Assing & Frederick Douglass.* New York: Hill & Wang, a division of Farrar, Straus and Giroux. 1999.

Giddings, Paula. *When and Where I Enter: The Impact of Black Women on Race and Sex in America.* New York: William Morrow and Company, Inc. 1984

Moses, Robert P. and Charles E. Cobb, Jr.. *Radical Equations: Math Literacy and Civil Rights.* Boston: Beacon Press. 2001 by the Algebra Project.

Payne, Charles M. *I've Got the Light of Freedom: The Organizing Tradition and the Mississippi Freedom Struggle.* Berkeley, Los Angeles, London: University of California Press. 1995.

Ransby, Barbara. *Ella Baker and the Black Freedom Movement: A Radical Democratic Vision.* Chapel Hill & London: The University of North Carolina Press. 2003.

ABOUT THE AUTHOR

photo credit: Beverly Anne Sypek

In a Silent Way: A Novel is about a young teacher activist in urban America that emerged out of Mary Jo Hetzel's experience teaching in one of the first alternative high schools in the late 1960s, and from her lifelong involvement in grassroots social movements for racial, economic, and sexual justice. She was the founding director of the Boston Campus of Springfield College, School of Human Services and faculty member of the college for 24 years. She is currently active in the struggle for justice and quality in urban public education, and in co-hosting Circle processes, rooted in indigenous principles, in an effort to break down hierarchies of power and oppression in order to co-create the conditions for community self-empowerment and institutional transformation. She enjoys jazz, creative writing, film, drama, athletics, nature, spirit, and friendship. Mary Jo lives in Jamaica Plain, a community of Boston, Massachusetts.

SELECTED TITLES FROM SHE WRITES PRESS

She Writes Press is an independent publishing company founded to serve women writers everywhere.
Visit us at www.shewritespress.com.

Class Letters: Instilling Intangible Lessons through Letters by Claire Chilton Lopez. $16.95, 978-1-938314-28-5. A high school English teacher discovers surprising truths about her students when she exchanges letters with them over the course of a school year.

Again and Again by Ellen Bravo. $16.95, 978-1-63152-939-9. When the man who raped her roommate in college becomes a Senate candidate, women's rights leader Deborah Borenstein must make a choice—one that could determine control of the Senate, the course of a friendship, and the fate of a marriage.

Cleans Up Nicely by Linda Dahl. $16.95, 978-1-938314-38-4. The story of one gifted young woman's path from self-destruction to self-knowledge, set in mid-1970s Manhattan.

Just the Facts by Ellen Sherman. $16.95, 978-1-63152-993-1. The seventies come alive in this poignant and humorous story of a fearful rookie reporter at a small-town newspaper who uncovers a big-time scandal.

The Rooms Are Filled by Jessica Null Vealitzek. $16.95, 978-1-938314-58-2. The coming-of-age story of two outcasts—a nine-year-old boy who just lost his father, and a closeted young woman—brought together by circumstance.

Vote for Remi by Leanna Lehman. $16.95, 978-1-63152-978-8. History is changed forever when an ambitious classroom of high school seniors pull the ultimate prank on their favorite teacher—and end up getting her in the running to become president of the United States.